BULLETS THROUGH THE MIST

Contents

CHAPTER 1. OVER THE TOP 5
CHAPTER 2. THE CALL TO ARMS. 8
CHAPTER 3. ALL JOINED UP 16
CHAPTER 4. ROWS OF TENTS 19
CHAPTER 5. ONE LAST JOB – Frankie Baker 23
CHAPTER 6. FIONA CAMERON 28
CHAPTER 7. A STRANGE DAY OF ESPIONAGE 31
CHAPTER 8. NURSE! - Frankie 35
CHAPTER 9. JENNIFER FRANCES – Charlie Turner 38
CHAPTER 10. DECODING 43
CHAPTER 11. GREY MEN 49
CHAPTER 12. MOBILISATION - Charlie 58
CHAPTER 13. STEAM A LITTLE FASTER – Charlie 62
CHAPTER 14. ENTRENCHED - Charlie 68
CHAPTER 15. WITHOUT ORDERS - Charlie 73
CHAPTER 16. GERMANS ARE ALWAYS ON TIME – Jack MacGregor 78
CHAPTER 17. SURGEONS IN KHAKI – Doctor Robert Jones M.D. 84
CHAPTER 18. WARRIORS FROM WHERE? 86
CHAPTER 19. THE PRIVILEGE OF RANK – Lt. Montague Shipley 91
CHAPTER 20. SABOTAGE 103
CHAPTER 21. A MAN WITHOUT HONOUR 110
CHAPTER 22. A PROBLEM SHARED. 119
CHAPTER 23. ITS ALL IN HIS MIND 127
CHAPTER 24. SUB CRUCE CANDIDA 139
CHAPTER 25. A BACHELOR FOR LIFE 145

CHAPTER 26. A CONSULTATION	159
CHAPTER 27. SURGICAL INTERVENTION	165
CHAPTER 28. BAD NEWS TRAVELS FAST	171
CHAPTER 29. A TANGLED WEBB	178
CHAPTER 30. STOP PRESS	184
CHAPTER 31. BACK TO FRONT	190
CHAPTER 32. CONFESSIONS OF AN OFFICE CLEANER	197
CHAPTER 33. ECHOES OF WEDDING BELLS – Rhianydd MacGregor	205
CHAPTER 34. DECLARATION OF WAR – Sibyl	212
CHAPTER 35. AN AWKWARD CALL - Rhianydd	218
CHAPTER 36. THE PRIODIGAL'S RETURN – Sibyl	220
CHAPTER 37. TOMORROW – Sibyl	229
CHAPTER 38. PETRICHOR – Gwyn ap Meredith	234
CHAPTER 39. EXILE – Gwyn	245
CHAPTER 40. A VOICE IN THE DARK- Sibyl	252
CHAPTER 41. BOY TO MAN- Gwyn	257
CHAPTER 42. MATER QUERCUS – Gwyn	260
CHAPTER 43. THE LIGHTS ARE ON – Gwyn	265
CHAPTER 44. TIMES ARE CHANGING	269
CHAPTER 45. A CHANCE MEETING	274
CHAPTER 46. BOYS NEED A FATHER	281
CHAPTER 47. LONDON CALLING - Rhianydd	290
CHAPTER 48. FLIGHT INTO WAR - Sybil	296
CHAPTER 49. OUR COVER IS BLOWN	303
CHAPTER 50. JUST LIKE THE O.K. CORRALL – Red	308
CHAPTER 51. I MUST GO HOME - Rhianydd	317

CHAPTER 52. A MEETING OF MINDS – Rhianydd 321

CHAPTER 53. THE ART OF DISAPPEARANCE – Red.........................327

CHAPTER 54. INVASION 332

CHAPTER 55. MODERN WEAPONS - Ralph 337

CHAPTER 56. THE MARCH NORTH - Eryr..348

CHAPTER 57. A KING IS MADE – Gwyn 358

CHAPTER 58. A SLEEPLESS NIGHT - Red 363

CHAPTER 59. REDEMORE 367

CHAPTER 60. CHECK MATE - Gwyn 372

CHAPTER 61. DIRTY WORK - Gwyn 379

CHAPTER 62. SOWING THE SEEDS – Gerald Shipley 385

CHAPTER 63. TURN AGAIN – Arthur Cole 394

CHAPTER 64. HEADLINE NEWS..396

CHAPTER 65. CROSSING THE VEIL – Rhianydd & Red....................402

CHAPTER 66. RESURGAM - Red 411

CHAPTER 67. THE HUNTED - Margaret 416

CHAPTER 68. THE CLOCK STRIKES THIRTEEN - Red 429

CHAPTER 69. SEEING THE LIGHT – Jack MacGregor 439

CHAPTER 70. BACK-TO-BACK..447

CHAPTER 71. FINAL RESOLUTION - Sibyl......................................457

EPILOGUE. VIVE LA FRANCE 463

APPENDICES AND USEFUL TRANSLATIONS 472

ACKNOWLEDGEMENTS..475

COPYRIGHT 476

OTHER BOOKS BY THE AUTHOR..477

CHAPTER 1. OVER THE TOP

1st July 1916,
Valley of the Somme.
France.

    Lieutenant Montague Shipley leant on the slightly rickety ladder, whistle in his mouth and his service revolver in his unsteady right hand. It was uncannily quiet. He waited. He clenched his teeth on the whistle to stop them from chattering, not from the cold. How could he be cold, for God's sake, it was July in France, it was summer. He swallowed hard to stop himself from throwing up.
    Beside him a private whose name he did not know, threw up his breakfast of half-digested, terror coagulated porridge. The smell of fear was everywhere, cold male sweat, loose bowels, and vomit. Lieutenant Shipley was not the sort of officer to dispel it, he had no calming words, no last minute ribald throwaway line for his men.
    The heavy artillery launched another salvo at the enemy trenches, shells falling short of the mark. Exploding in volcanoes of wasted earth, another crater to fill with the bodies of the fallen, could they never get it right? He prayed to God from habit, for no forgiving, caring, peaceful god would surely let his people come to this.
    He stared around him at the lines of men waiting to climb the ladders to their death, ordered and ready to give their lives, and for what? Ten yards down the trench to his left floated the sound of Welshmen singing, damn them, bloody Welsh, they had a song for everything. This morning it was, '**Nearer my god, to thee**.' Like so many of the infantry, they'd grown up together, they ate together, sang together, did everything together, and now they would all in all probability die together.
    He should not even be standing with one foot on this particular ladder. Where in God's name was MacGregor? This was MacGregor's post with those bloody rifles of his. If he came through this morning alive, then he would see the bastards shot. MacGregor, those two London lads and that bloody huge Welshman he had acquired, the whole bloody unit, he would see them all shot.
    Then, the singing stopped and there was silence, an eerie patch of silence, the shelling had stopped, a signal in itself, the bastards would

know they were coming! Down the line a whistle screeched, and the shout came to advance.

*'**Over the top**!'*

His unwilling feet propelled him like an automaton up the ladder and into the maelstrom of bullets and barbed wire above. As his head emerged over the parapet a 7.92 calibre round embedded itself into the earth beside him, splattering mud, and grit over his freshly shaven face. A fucking sniper - that's all they bloody needed, as beside him the young private's head exploded, covering his right shoulder with blood, brains, and snot. The crack of the Gewehr 98 rifle echoed in his ears, then it stopped. There was nothing. Then, a muffled cheer from the men and then the whole unit started to move, up the ladders to their fate, but at least those bloody Bosch marksmen were gone. Where the fuck was MacGregor?

Shipley's legs carried him all of ten strides into the thick mud, his smartly polished officer's boots finding no grip in the quagmire. He was sinking. The crash of the explosion rang in his ears. Then he felt the blood-soaked earth hit him hard in the shoulder. The grenade shrapnel caught Shipley in the neck, his world went red and black around him, spiralling out into the distance and then there was nothing. The nothingness continued for what seemed like hours. Eventually he grew cold, but not cold, and heavy, but weightless, and in the still nothingness the light was failing, as was everything else which mattered to him. The screaming of men subsided to the occasional plaintive cry of 'Mam' and in the eerie silence that followed the chime of his pocket watch marking the hour. It was four o'clock, tea-time. On the lawn, Earl Grey, Assam, a splash of milk, fruit cake. How strange.

The next voices he heard were speaking in what to his confused ears sounded like German but in dialect he was not familiar with. Then he felt the canvas of a stretcher under his back, but he could not see, his eyes seemed sealed shut, he could not talk, he could barely breathe, his only working organs seemed to him to be his ears, and even they seemed to be deceiving him.

The canvas moved and he was lifted clear of the mud, something strangely soporific in the movement, pulling him towards sleep, but he must not sleep. Sleep meant the end. Sleep meant death, and a long time dead. He started to count numbers in his head, just to keep himself from falling back into to pit of blackness, but eventually that darkness embraced him. He listened to the voices of his rescuers, not bloody Germans, they were Scots, that thick highland accent was now unmistakeable In his recognition he must have groaned for in his cocoon of darkness he was sure he heard,

'Hey Jock, we've got a live one here! And a bloody officer.' That comment from the end where he thought his feet must be, and the reply from where his ears were.

'Abbéville it is then Jock, hospital for him, lucky bastard, his war is over.'

Montague Shipley's fighting days were done, but there was one thing he would do before his war was over. He would find MacGregor and his unit. There would be no place for them to hide.

CHAPTER 2. THE CALL TO ARMS.

2nd April 1915,
London.

    Charlie Turner and Frankie Baker were best friends. They grew up on the same dirt-poor street in north London, played in the same gutters, threw stones at the same milkman's worn-out horse, hid down the same dark alleys, they did everything together. As boys growing up, they'd both had equally snotty noses and particularly light fingers.
    Home for them was adjoining terraced houses in Agar Grove just off the Wrotham Road in Agar Town. Houses which had once housed the gentry who had now migrated to the green spaces around the fashionable parks of north London. Houses which had, with the influx of industry, been reduced to rooms crammed with workers from the newly built factories living alongside the cockroaches and the rats and fighting for an existence. Home.
    Charlie was one of six children and the only surviving boy. His father worked on the railway and his mother Ethel was in service as a housekeeper in one of the large and swanky houses on the well to do side of Primrose Hill.
    His elder brother Herbert Charles, older by two years, had died of a fever before young Charlie's birth, leaving Charlie as the eldest of the Turner brood.
    At fourteen Charlie was a bright boy but, tired and bored of lessons, he left school as soon as he could and found himself a job in the Vickers factory making gramophones, those new-fangled machines the wealthy liked to play their dance music on. The factory also made the shiny black shellack discs which had the music engraved into their tiny spiralling groove. No more school for Charlie Turner, oh, no.
    At fourteen his job was simply to tend one of the pressing machines that made them. It was pay and that put money in his pocket. What more could a boy want?
    Everything he earned vanished swiftly into his mother's housekeeping pot which lived on the mantle shelf above the kitchen fireplace - his Mam deserved that at least, and she made sure he always had some of it back to

spend on himself even if his father managed to take the remainder and spend it in the pub or gamble it away across a cribbage table.

His father, Jesse Turner, was a hard man, a short, bulldog of a being, as broad as he was tall. Arms bulging with muscle across a barrel chest, he was as bald headed as a newborn baby and had a back more fitting to a zoo exhibit. Nonetheless, he worked hard all day and sometimes all night, laying the railway lines into the new St Pancras, station. When payday finally arrived, he and his gang of labourers would adjourn to the Duke of Clarence Pub where he would shove most of his hard-earned coin over the bar, rolling home drunk well after closing time. He ruled his house with an iron fist, used liberally on anyone close enough when the fancy or the effects of strong ale and raw spirits took him. His wife and children were servants to be chastised and beaten, but always careful not to leave a mark. A wife in service could not confront her employer with the blemishes of an unhappy home and expect to keep her job. He would never countenance an accusing finger pointing at him.

When sober, which was most of the time to be fair, he was a raconteur, a bit of a wag, liked a joke and could be kindness itself. Jesse Turner would give you the shirt off his back if he were sober or maim you with one punch if he were fighting drunk.

Charlie's mother, Ethel, worked six days a week, her only respite being a Sunday. She was up and gone before dawn. Before she left she poked up the fire and added more small coal to the night's embers. The Turners had plenty of coal, at least. One of the few perks of Jesse's job, the freight trains had coal aplenty in their tenders, the occasional sack-full being liberated silently and by stealth on the graveyard shift while the world, and the foreman, dozed on. Charlie saw to his sisters, making sure that they were at least dressed before he too ran off to work. Too ground to the bone by a drunken husband and six children, Ethel had little time for her eldest child, leaving Charlie to his own devices. He acquired the essential life-skills quickly. By the time he was fourteen he was an accomplished pickpocket with a menial job in a factory and no prospects apart from a hard life and a cheap funeral. He was a handsome lad in his own way, with a cheeky grin and, like his father, he had a way with words. He was above average height but by no means tall, with a wiry frame and floppy hair of a peppery sort of brown. Charlie Turner had one big talent. He made people laugh.

Frankie Baker was Charlie's best friend. They were a team. Charlie had a job and earned his money, apart from the odd fat wallet lifted from a wealthy gent enjoying the sunshine on a park bench. Frankie had no job.

Frankie was a thief and a burglar, and, under cover of darkness, he broke into houses, he broke into shops, fencing his ill-gotten gains through a character called Black Eric who inhabited a dusty, brown room at back of The Duke of Clarence in the early evening. There, Black Eric could be found sitting, quietly cradling his pint pot in the tranquillity of a dark corner by the fireplace.

Eric was black, his hair was black, his clothes were black, the dirt under his fingernails and engrained into his skin was black. Eric had moved to London, the 'big smoke,' from the even grimier South Wales valleys, where he had laboured in coal mines since he was a small boy. Now, he coughed with 'the dust,' was bent with arthritis and walked with a limp, a legacy, he said, of a roof fall which had left him lucky to escape with his life, let alone his sanity. For him, the streets of London were paved with gold, other people's gold, and he would give you a good price for it. No one knew quite where he lived. That was a well-kept secret. He seemed to disappear imperceptibly into nowhere as if into a coal black niche in a mine tunnel as soon as he left his seat. No-one was sure of his age but anyone hazarding a guess would say between thirty and forty years, but he seemed to have been sitting in his corner for at least fifty, if you listened to the old men talking. In the valleys back home, they'd have said he was buggered.

Frankie, in complete contrast to the dark, malevolent Eric, was blonde headed, pale skinned with piercing light blue eyes, thin beyond belief, built more like a snake than a human being, but he was strong from climbing, and agile, and had the reflexes of a cat together with an inbuilt sense of when he was in danger. He could also run like the wind and cover the ground over hazardous walls and rooftops at some speed. There was not a constable north of the Thames who could catch the Will o'the Wisp that was Frankie Baker.

Frankie had been shooting a rifle ever since he'd traded one with Eric for a consignment of jewellery skilfully liberated via a barely open sash window and conveniently situated drainpipe at the rear of one of the great houses on Regents Park. Frankie could never sell the jewels himself, they were far too identifiable, but with the gold melted and the stones removed, Eric would make a handsome profit. The rifle was as old as the hills, an old army issue Martini Henry. It had seen service against the Hottentots and the Boers in Africa, but it was still accurate, and Frankie had a natural flare for hitting a target. He practiced on the mud flats along the Thames, shooting old cans and bottles using ammunition he made himself, recovering the spent cases and re-filling them. He knew a local gunsmith who had showed him the ropes and honed the skills, and let him use his loading equipment, rather than have his premises relieved of half its stock overnight, or worse, finding a corpse on his workshop floor.

Frankie was a foundling. He lodged with Mr and Mrs Baker in the house next door to Charlie. He never knew his parents and had taken the name Baker as he had no other to use. The Bakers had no children of their own, and had informally adopted young Frankie, loving him as a son. Despite his errant ways, they fed him, clothed him, gave him a bed, and made sure he washed and went to school, all done through a haze of cheap gin, coal smoke and the reek of boiling cabbage. Frankie, like Charlie, was a clever boy, smart, quick on the uptake, clever with his hands and even cleverer with his wits.

He and Charlie had been inseparable since Charlie had taken refuge from his father's belt and fists in the Bakers' outdoor privy. Crashing through the door to find Frankie installed on the seat, Frankie had slammed the door shut and provided cover for Charlie then as he always would. Charlie would reciprocate. They had each other's backs.

It was 1915. Both boys were sixteen years old, eager for adventure and seeking a way, any way at all, to get out of their spartan circumstances.

The enlistment posters filled every available space on the billboards of the city. The pointing finger followed them everywhere crying out its message – **YOUR COUNTRY NEEDS YOU!**

It was April. The country had been at war for nine months, the army needed soldiers, St Pancras was raising its own company of riflemen, Frankie was up for enlisting, he was good with a rifle. Charlie was not quite so sure, but swept along on his friend's enthusiasm he agreed, after all it was the right thing to do. Didn't the posters say so?

After a short discussion, they'd scrubbed themselves clean, acquired two smart-ish suits from the local pawn shop, on loan of course, slicked back their hair with beeswax, and, in an attempt to look older than their sixteen years, smoked several cigarettes to roughen up their voices and taken themselves off to the recruiting office. Charlie, visibly green and coughing as though his lungs would burst and Frankie laughing like a drain, Charlie decided he'd not smoke another cigarette as long as he lived.

The queue outside the working men's college on Crowdale Road filled the pavement and stretched around the corner for several hundred yards, it was formed mainly of young unmarried men who Charlie and Frankie knew from the streets and older men hoping to re-enlist and resume service in the regiments they had been in for the Boer War. Many, from any observant bystander's perspective, quite clearly did not fall into the category of:

BETWEEN 19YRS AND 38YRS and OVER FIVE FEET THREE.

Clearly painted in bold, black letters on the recruitment office wall. At the required height from the floor of course.

Frankie and Charlie jostled their way into the queue behind a group of lads who they knew were only twelve or thirteen, hoping that the comparison in fresh faced boyishness, age and height would go in their favour. Charlie at least had some evidence of stubble on his chin, even if he were not yet shaving, and Frankie could fire a rifle. couldn't he. How could they fail?

Charlie had picked the lock on his mother's special box where she kept all the family papers. He'd pulled out his brother's birth certificate and had memorised all the details He was now Herbert Charles, but everyone calls me Charlie!

Frankie had no birth certificate that he knew about, but Black Eric had acquired one, suitably adjusted, from a Registrar of Births, Marriages and Deaths looking for a more lucrative lifestyle. Money had changed hands and Frankie became, at a price, Albert Frederick Baker, as if by magic, aged nineteen years, born in Scotland, of all places, Inverness.

'But I've lived in London all my life!' protested Frankie, frantically rehearsing his patter. 'Sir, my parents are dead, and everyone calls me Frankie.' He hoped this would do the trick.

The real Albert Frederick Baker was buried under a slab of Scottish Granite in the graveyard at Grantown on Spey along with his mother and father, victims of a house fire, Albert had been six months old at the time. As Black Eric had mused, grinning at the certificate with its copper-plate script and official stamp, and with a voice straight out of the Rhondda, 'He prob'ly won't be needin' it where he's gone.'

The recruiting officer took one look at them, with their too-big suits, and their waxed fringes and smiled.

'Come on then laddie!' His accent was broad and Scottish,

'Convince me!' huge hands like boiled hams spread across the table, in anticipation of the next implausible story.

Charlie was first to the wide table full of forms behind which sat a huge man with twinkly brown eyes, black eyebrows, short cropped black hair, a big bushy moustache, just like the man on the poster, a barrel of a chest bursting out of a khaki tunic and over a Sam Brown belt.

The recruiting sergeant was having a bad morning, he had just turned away half a class of children, six men well into their fifties and too old to fight, and one girl dressed in her brothers' clothes. He was not in the mood for nonsense.

Sensing the moment, Charlie stood to attention in the best way he knew how, drew himself to his full height of five feet eight and threw out his chest. Placing the birth certificate on the table in front of the sergeant, he announced himself:

'Herbert Charles Turner, sir! Age eighteen sir! And nineteen in a few weeks, sir.'

'And I'm the Queen of Sheba, if you're eighteen I'm a monkeys uncle, ye wee gobshite.'

'I am eighteen, sir! Ask my dad if you like.'

'Ye expect me tae believe ye actually have a father as well then!'

Charlie's dad had lost count of children many years ago.

'See it says so here.' Charlie pointed at the birth certificate.

'I din'nae care what it says there, sonny, ye din'nae look the age.'

He picked up the birth certificate and read it, then humph'd to himself several times, then cleared his throat and spoke.

'And ye were born in good old blighty? '

'Aye Sir!' Charlie's natural talent as a mimic picked up the officer's accent. The officer raised an eyebrow at him, and half smiled.

'Are ye fit and well lad?'

'I am so, sir, and I can fire a rifle!' He lied bravely, hoping that Frankie would back him up or at least teach him the rudiments before they were sent to training camp.

'Get yersel through there then, and I'm sarge, not sir, got it?'

'Yes sir, sarge!,' blustered Charlie.

He was ushered through to the next room where he was told to undress to the waist, his chest was listened to and found to be sound, his eyes tested, and his feet checked. A bit like a horse being put through its paces for the vet, he thought. Sound in limb, eye, and wind.

The army doctor ran through a long list of diseases which Charlie swore he had never had,

'Tuberculosis? Do ye cough up blood?'

'No, Sir!'

'Good. Syphilis? Are ye poxed?'

'No Sir!'

'Haemorrhoids, lad? That's piles! does yer arse bleed when ye shit?'

'Never Sir!'

'Any heart disease in yer family, flat feet?' The list went on and on, he was then instructed to drop his trousers and underpants so that the doctor could examine his privates for some form of incriminating evidence. Of what, who knew? He was asked several more questions about his personal habits and then he was sent to another desk and another more senior officer, where he swore an oath to his country.

'I... Herbert Charles Turner swear by Almighty God that I will be faithful and bear true allegiance to His Majesty George V His Heirs and Successors, and that I will, as in duty bound, honestly and faithfully defend His Majesty, His Heirs, and Successors, in Person, Crown and Dignity against all enemies, and will observe and obey all orders of His Majesty, His Heirs and Successors, and of the Generals and officers set over me. So, help me God.'

Parents names: Ethel and Jesse Turner
Next of kin: Ethel Turner
Home address: 4 Agar Grove, St Pancras
Then he signed the proffered form.

'I'll put ye down for the brigade of rifles then, shall I?'

'Yes sir!'

Private thirty-one, Herbert Charles Turner of the St Pancras (Prince Consort's Own) rifles was born. He was given papers with instructions on how to join the basic training camp in Regents Park and a date to be there, told to bid his family good-bye. You're in the army now son.

Ten minutes later Private 32 Alfred Frederick Baker joined him on the pavement.

'I'd better show you which end the bullets come out of then Charlie.' Frankie was always practical about these things.

They ran back to Frankie's house at 3 Agar Grove full of excitement and not a little trepidation.

CHAPTER 3. ALL JOINED UP

April 1915,
St Pancras. London.

Charlie and Frankie walked back through Camden heading for Frankie's house. They had done it. They had enlisted as soldiers. Both of them in the St Pancras Rifles, even though one had never fired a gun in his life.

Frankie let themselves in through the unlocked front door, the paint peeling and the door handle hanging askew. The Bakers never locked the door, that way you never forgot your key and, besides, there was nothing worth stealing at 3 Agar Grove.

The dark hallway led to a set of darker stairs which climbed to the first floor where Frankie's room was at the back of the house facing the overgrown patch of garden and the railway tracks.

Frankie pushed open his bedroom door to reveal his neatly made bed and reached beneath it to pull out the old Martini rifle. It was wrapped in an old grain sack

'Here she is, beautiful, isn't she?' He whispered to Charlie.

Frankie ran a practiced hand over the polished wooden stock of the four-foot weapon, the barrel polished, and the firing mechanism oiled and kept in pristine order.

'Charles Turner, meet Tina – Tina, this is Charles.'
Formal introduction over, Frankie placed Charlie's hand on the wooden stock of the rifle.

'This is the friendly end.'

'Hmm,' replied Charlie.

'This is the breech.' Frankie pulled down the underlever of the weapon exposing the empty chamber.

'She's empty, always check she's empty before you do anything with her.'

Another 'Hmm,'

'The bullet goes in that slot there, then you push the lever forward and back and the bullet is pushed into the chamber. Now she's loaded.'

'Ah' grunted Charlie, his eyes wide, engrossed in his first lesson in guns.

'Don't worry, I haven't any bullets so you can't fire her, and there is no bullet in the chamber now, but if there is,' He pointed to the end of Tina's highly polished barrel, 'when you pull the trigger it comes out there. That's the nasty end.'

In the dim light of Frankie's bedroom, Charlie was shown how to strip down Tina and clean her. Frankie could do this in the dark, punch out the pin, take out the falling block, drop the weighted rag down the barrel and pull through, or run water down the barrel to wash out the powder residue.

'Always keep her clean, if the barrel gets pitted then just like a dirty whore, she might just kill you.'

Charlie was certain that his friend had never been with any form of whore, clean or dirty, that must be a phrase he had picked up off Black Eric.

Then he made Charlie hold the rifle to his shoulder,

'Hold it well into yer neck, and tight, the recoil will push you back, and it will put your arm out of joint if you let it, now line up the sights, those pips there.' He pointed to two small metal lumps just in front of Charlie's eye, 'Close your other eye stupid! Now line up with the one on the end of the barrel, and line up to the target. Now pull the trigger.'

The trigger mechanism clicked, harmlessly, the weapon was not loaded.

'That's the basics, for long distance you need to allow for wind, and the bullets arc - the bullet falls over distance.' he said with the air of a practised rifleman.

Frankie pulled out paper and pencil and started to draw,

'This is how the bullet flies, not straight see! It goes in an arc, with practice your mind will work out how far to aim above, to hit the target. Strong wind will blow it off course, with practice you can account for that too. That's all I can show you without bullets, and I have none, but at least you can talk your way around a gun now! It might keep you and I together until we get to the ranges.'

Frankie pushed his best friend off the bed, come on mate, let's celebrate, we are in the army now.

Out through the Bakers' front door, a quick dive into Charlie's house for his wages from the housekeeping tin above the fireplace in the kitchen, then down the road to the 'The Duke.' If they were old enough to join up then surely, they were old enough for a beer or two.

The following day Charlie told his bosses at the factory that he was now enlisted, they wished him well, telling him that the factory would be there when he came back. 'When', they stressed, not 'if' he came back, and when and if the factory had not been converted for the war effort. He collected his outstanding pay and the kisses of several of the young girls who worked with him.

'Rifles ay?' said his foreman 'Have you ever fired one Charlie?'

'Not yet,' he replied, 'but I'm a quick learner.'

Then he went home and told his sisters, and his father, knowing that his mother would be straight to the recruiting sergeant with his real birth certificate, his sisters would believe what he had told them and his father, well his father would be happy with one less mouth to feed, and some pay sent home no doubt.

Frankie had no job at which to give notice, but he told the Bakers, who poured them all a gin and drank a toast to the brave boys, may they come home safe.

On the upside, the crime rate in Primrose Hill was about to fall dramatically.

CHAPTER 4. ROWS OF TENTS

12th April 1915,
Richmond Park.

Monday 12th April 1915 dawned clear and crisp. At 6am sharp Frankie was banging on the Turner's door, his kitbag with all his belongings hoisted over his shoulder,
'Come on Charlie boy, we are going to be late!'
Charlie came down the stairs two at a time. His sisters were still in bed asleep, his father had gone to his shift, his mother was at work, his oldest sister Sophie would have to do for her siblings this morning, at fourteen she should be able to get them all off to school. Breakfast was little more than bread and scrape – scrape being the fat scraped from the cooking pan, not tasty enough to be called dripping, but enough to moisten the bread which was on the stale side of life. Sophie was better at plaiting hair than he and far better at dressing girls for school.
Charlie's kit bag was smaller than his friend's. He had packed only what he needed, he did not want his mother to twig that he was gone, any sooner than necessary. They caught the bus to travel the eight miles to the training camp at Richmond Park and prepared to say goodbye to civilian life.
When they arrived at the park, they were greeted by line after line of fellow recruits, and row upon row of tents. Signing in tents, stores tents, barber's tents, hospital tents, cookhouse tents, and tents to sleep in. A whole city constructed mainly of canvas, populated by men dressed either in khaki or their civilian clothing, taking orders from officers, many of whom were little older than Frankie and Charlie were themselves. So, this was three months basic training.
They stood in line to sign themselves in, then went through the induction process, haircut, shower, uniform. Not much in the way of uniform, just the basics, the army it seemed was short of uniform. Charlie came away with a pair of heavy serge khaki trousers a pair of regulation boots, and a leather 'webbing,' the rest he was assured would be issued as and when they were available. Frankie fared slightly better. He at least had a tunic to go with the trousers.

As Riflemen they would move on from the basic training camp to the Brigade of Rifles camp for more specialised training at Paddock Hurst, a country estate south of London in Sussex. There they would be taught to shoot and be issued with rifles.

Until then, the next three months would be a round of drill, learning to march, cleaning and polishing, bulling boots to an unreasonable shine, and fitness, PT every day, assault courses, cross country running as a unit. Yes, and taking orders without question, even when it seemed they were pointless. As the very loud sergeant major with the big moustache and the barrel chest was fond of telling them,

'I'm your mother now, boy.' This, it seemed, applied to every recruit from the youngest to the oldest.

Frankie and Charlie were both good runners. Frankie was exceptional. He could run for miles, he found the assault course easy, a life of climbing the drainpipes of the wealthy and occasionally legging it from the old bill had set him up well for this part of army life. Charlie was not so fast but could run just as far. With a bit more practice and some fine tuning he would soon keep up with his friend.

After the second month they met their commanding officer of the Rifles, and their section Sergeant, Jack MacGregor.

Jack MacGregor was a quiet man. Small and wiry in stature, his dark brown hair was cropped short at the back and sides with a floppy fringe hanging over dark eyebrows and eyes which were so dark a brown as to be nearly black. He had a wide mouth and a top lip adorned by a clipped moustache. He seemed to always have six o'clock shadow on his chin though he professed to shave twice a day when he had time, which was seldom. His uniform was pressed with razor creases, his leather webbing polished to a gleam, He wore his stripes with immense pride and a quiet authority. He commanded respect before he ever opened his mouth.

When he did speak, his words were few. He did not shout, well, rarely, but he would make himself heard. When he did speak, his voice was moderately pitched, and with the soft burr of a well-educated Scotsman.

Frankie and Charlie were amongst some thirty young men recruited so far to the Rifles. They sat together on long benches in one of the tents waiting to be given the 'once over' by their officers.

'Welcome to the Brigade men,' Sergeant MacGregor began. From the first he called them men.

'St Pancras Rifles is the 16th Company of the Rifle Brigade. We are a new company, recruited from the borough of St Pancras. Many of you men will know each other. You may work together. You may be neighbours, or school chums. Some of you may be related. During your training you will become brothers, brothers in arms.'

'This Company has no time for petty jealousies. We will all work together to become a fighting unit. There will be those amongst you who will excel at somethings and not at others. We will help each other along. The able will help the less able. There will be no slacking. Our great country is at war. This is not a picnic. Lives will be lost. Many of us will not come home. If we work together, we can lessen that number. '

'You all have a week's leave, then you report back here for transport to Paddock Hurst, where you will get an introduction to weapons. Have a good leave, see your families, and I will see you in a week. Is there a Private Baker amongst you?'

Frankie slowly raised his hand, 'Yes, sir.'

'A word later, Baker, and I'm sarge not sir, nothing to worry about. Oh, and Turner'

'Yes, sarge,' piped up Charlie,

'You as well, I have been told that you both have experience of shooting, what manner of weapon have you used?'

'Martini Henry rifle sarge!' chirped up Frankie 'Only an old one mind you, and I've never shot more than a tin can in anger.'

'Tin can or man's head, as long as you can hit it lad, when you come back you can help me show the rest. Turner, how about you?'

'I've handled a rifle sarge, but I've never fired one.'

'Ah, I see, mates, are you? Not to worry, Baker here can teach you the ropes. Thats all for now, I shall see you after your leave, din'nae get up tae too much mischief aye.'

Frankie and Charlie made a quick dash to their tent and then ran like greyhounds for the bus back to London and Agar Grove.

It was early evening, and they were sitting in the snug of The Duke, drinking small pots of ale when Eric tapped Frankie on the shoulder and gestured to him to come outside. He motioned to Charlie to stay where he was. Charlie was used to this. He did not want to be part of Frankie's more nefarious dealings. He sat tight, keeping their table in the busy bar, a room full of railway men finishing work, he half expected his own father to put in an appearance. He and Frankie had such an assortment of uniform between them that they were still wearing civvies, at least until they had both tunic and trousers to their name. The only thing which marked them as soldiers was the brutal haircut. The army barber took no prisoners. The fortunate were allowed to leave his chair with their ears intact.

When Frankie returned, he was quiet, very quiet, he drank his beer and excused himself.

'I need to go home,' he apologised, 'I've a job, one I cannot afford to pass up on.'

CHAPTER 5. ONE LAST JOB – Frankie Baker

Fernleigh House,
Primrose Hill,
London.

April 1915

Frankie left Charlie in The Duke. He made his way home having drunk only half a pint of beer. He let himself into the house and climbed the stairs silently to his bedroom. He changed into his 'working' clothes which were all essentially black or dark in colour and pulled his poacher's bag from under the bed. There was a job to be done.

He had thought that this way of life was behind him, but he owed Black Eric a favour, this was payment for a debt. He had been given strict instructions and an address. The information was good, he was told. The important item was only valuable to certain people, and should he get caught then the consequences could be dire. It was important that he left no evidence behind him, no one should suspect that anything was out of place. He pulled on his old jacket and made his way to the park gates and into the park, a brisk walk to the fine houses on the other side warmed up his limbs.

The house was a large, villa style property, facing out onto the rolling green space where, in the daytime, cavalry officers exercised their horses and elegant courting couples sat beneath the huge horse chestnut trees. The villa, 'Fernleigh' had a walled garden at the rear with stables and a coach house which led out to the road behind. These were the houses of the gentry, he knew the layout well, he had broken into enough of them before, but not this one.

The night wrapped around him like a blanket. The moon lit the sky from just behind a solitary cumulus cloud, casting a glow across the patterns of the stars. Frankie stood motionless in the long shadows of the corner made by the walls and looked upwards past the cream painted stonework at the window, barely open, above him.

An easy job this, he thought. The long French windows of the balcony of this imposing house were on the first floor, a simple climb. He could see the net of the curtains blowing in the slight breeze. Yes, the window was open. He pictured the scene, a humped figure sound asleep under warm blankets, the cloying heat of the summer lifted from sleeping skin by the cool night air. His finely tuned ears listened and heard the reassuring rasp of a man snoring.

He took off his shoes and socks, preferring to climb barefoot, and hung them around his neck, pushed his hands into the soft leather gloves and without further ado reached up the iron drainpipe to begin his climb from the shadows of the rose scented, leafy garden. Within a minute he had boosted himself over the ornate stone parapet which bordered the balcony and was inside.

Creeping catlike across the wooden floorboards, keeping to the edge of the room to avoid a loose one and careful to avoid tripping on the thick Aubusson rug, peering at the sleeping occupant, he noticed the uniform neatly hung out on its mannequin. The polished supple leather of a Sam Brown belt and brown gloves laid inside the khaki cap all gave notice of a decorated and high-ranking officer.

The sepia photograph in the frame alongside the bed was of a family, formally posed, mother, father, and daughter. The second frame contained a miniature, the daughter, he thought.

A beauty, oh, yes. A fine boned face with an aquiline nose, broad forehead, high cheekbones and blue eyes, the hair was a mass of dark red curls, barely contained under a small and slightly ridiculous straw hat. The dress high collared and prim in Edwardian style. The facial expression mocked him from its frame, his heart skipped. He reached out one long stealthy arm and removed the miniature from its place and dropped it into his bag.

'Careful Frankie,' he chided himself, 'too personal, it will be missed.'

The figure in the huge luxurious bed grunted, turned over to face away from him, broke wind, and continued to snore. Frankie could just see the pyjama clad shoulder hunch as the eiderdown was pulled over it in an unconscious movement. He padded to the bedroom door, pushing it against the frame while turning the Delft porcelain doorknob gently to the right, fearful of the click of the latch, and silently let himself out onto the landing, then, down the sweeping staircase and across the marble tiled hallway, into the study. He knew the layout of these houses well. His contact had told him that the safe was in the usual place, concealed in a cupboard disguised as a plant stand, in the corner by the fireplace. The two keys to its locks were in the small central drawer of the huge leather topped desk. What was in the safe would, he'd been assured, be well worth the taking. A leather roll and a wash leather bag, the contents of which he could fence easily, and most important, the canvas document folder and its contents. Do not open it, do not read it, pass it unopened to the contact who will be waiting on the far side of the park. For this he would be paid handsomely, enough to ensure his future if he survived the war. It had been a job he could not turn down.

All was as described. He turned the keys in the well-oiled locks and emptied the contents of the safe onto the rug. He dropped the contents of the wash leather bag and the small leather roll into his pocket, replaced the roll and the bag into the safe. Then he picked out the khaki bound document folder. The gold and red embossed writing on the front declared, TOP SECRET. Frankie hurriedly but carefully replaced the remaining contents of the safe as he had found them, locked it back up and replaced the keys in the drawer.

Curiosity getting the better of him, he sat down in the over padded leather desk chair on its spider leg castors, laid the folder on the desk, undid the red ribbon which tied it shut and started to read. He did not get very far. The thin sheets of copy paper contained in the folder were typed in a language foreign to Frankie. He could see that there were lists and there were numbers, but the rest might as well have been Greek. Even in this foreign language the words did not read like words should. Code, that was it, it was in code. He closed the folder and slid it down his shirt. None of his business he told himself, he was just here to do a job.

He felt the eyes on his back. He had not heard the door open. Instinct told him that it was not just eyes that were trained on the rear of his newly cropped army short back and sides. Hands on the edge of the desk, he pushed his right leg against the drawers, rotating the chair slowly on its swivel base, to find a figure standing in the open doorway, half-lit by the moonlight which shone in through the study window to bathe the room.

She was dressed in a lawn nightgown. It should have been decorously buttoned to the throat, but the buttons were open showing a hint of pale skin. Red hair draped untidily over her shoulder, very successfully trying to escape from its plait. The rest of her was covered right down to her bare feet. She was balanced and ready for action, and, holding in both hands a double-barrelled shotgun, breech closed, Purdy, twelve bore if he wasn't mistaken. No stranger to the hunt, it would be folly to consider that it might not be loaded.

The round mouths of the barrels stared at him like a pair of too close together eyes rimmed with silver spectacles gleaming in the dim light.

She spoke. The voice, when it came, was deeper and more husky than he had expected, cultured but with a lilt, a hint of something not quite what it pretended to be. She fixed him with a blue-green gaze which seemed to penetrate to somewhere just behind his head and which held more power than the shotgun that reinforced it.

He stared back, transfixed as a rabbit in a lamp, unable to move.

'You may put all of that back when you want. Leave now and I will tell no one.'

'Be careful with that gun miss, you might damage yourself.'

What was he saying, the business end was pointed at him, and she looked entirely capable of using it. Only one result there.

He emptied his pockets onto the desk,

'That is all I have taken.' he lied, 'Let me out and you won't see me again.' He raised his hands in submission.

She walked softly round the desk, examined the pile of jewellery which was in a small but valuable heap on the green leather surface. Seemingly satisfied with her examination she spoke again.

'Follow me.' She gestured with the barrel end of the gun- pointing to the door. 'Through the kitchen!' she hissed, pointing towards a door beneath the stairs.

Frankie knew his way to the world of below stairs.
He walked before her and allowed himself to be let out into the kitchen garden.

'Before I go,' he asked, a wry smile forming across his mouth, 'I'm Frankie, would it be cheeky to ask your name, just for the sake of politeness?' He held her gaze with his, suddenly unafraid.

She smiled back. Breaking the gun as she did so, he saw at a glance that it was indeed loaded!

'Fiona, Fiona Cameron.' she told him, 'You are lucky. Papa is drunk and sleeping or you would not get by him. Now go or I shall call the law.'

Needing no prompting, he took the offered exit, the folder still pressed to his chest inside his shirt and the miniature portrait of General Sir Archibald Cameron's daughter in the black cloth poachers' bag beneath his coat. She was shorter than he expected and curvier, and in all the right places.

Once outside the garden wall, he broke into the long striding ground devouring run which had saved him from arrest many times before and put as much distance between him and the beautiful Fiona as possible. He had been told where to leave the folder, but instinct or something more warned him not to. He let himself in to the house on Agar Grove and softly climbed the stairs to his bedroom careful not to wake his parents. Charlie would be able to read the documents. He would ask Charlie. Then he would decide.

Back at the house on the park, Fiona Cameron replaced her mother's jewellery in the safe, locked it, replaced the shotgun in its rack in the gun room and retired to bed, haunted by a pair of piercing blue eyes in the thin faced but undoubtedly handsome countenance of the most accomplished burglar in St Pancras. Sleep was a stranger for the rest of the night, and she watched the sun rise over the park and heard the servants stirring in the small bedrooms at the top of the house. Then the latch opening on the back door as Mrs Turner the housekeeper let herself in and started about her business.

Tidying her hair, fastening the neck buttons of her night dress, and donning a pair of silk slippers and a dressing robe, she crossed the landing and tapped on her father's door. Hearing no gruff voice waking up, she let herself in. The hunched figure of her father was lying in his bed asleep, dead to the world, or, simply, dead.

She shook his shoulder 'Papa, wake up its late.'

Then the shoulder rolled towards her, and the household was alerted by her screams.

CHAPTER 6. FIONA CAMERON

The General was dead. His face was peaceful as though asleep, but his mouth was set rigidly open, frozen in mid snore and his skin was already the colour of badly cooked liver. A thin congealed rivulet of spittle was dripping from the corner of his mouth and his tongue now turning slightly black was wedged between his teeth.

Nineteen-year-old Fiona Cameron was now alone in the world.

The doctors would declare that her father had died of a massive stroke, brought on by his continued heavy drinking. He would be replaced at his desk at the war office without undue fuss, no one was irreplaceable after all, another desk-wallah would avoid being posted to the trenches with the men. Great shame for his daughter mind you, lovely girl. Wonder how she will cope rattling around in that big house on her own.

His funeral would be conducted with appropriate military pomp, a funeral befitting a knight of the realm and a General of his majesty's army.

Born in 1857, at the age of 22yrs Archibald Cameron had fought with distinction in the Zulu War as a lieutenant, his forte had been tactics, he had had a natural ability to read the geography of a place, pick the best sites for a camp or a battle and how best to use the landscape to his advantage. Now aged fifty-eight, he had hated his desk job, he missed the thrill of active service, but on inheriting his title, and taking his seat in the Lords, this together with his age this had sealed his fate.

His only daughter was born in 1896 when he was thirty-nine years old, a product of his brief and tempestuous marriage to Philomena Morgan the daughter of a Welsh Coal owner. Philomena was spoiled, flighty and demanding, passionate and downright irresistible. She had been twenty years of age and living in London to gain an education and be introduced into society, when she met the tall distinguished looking lieutenant with the soulful brown eyes, dark rakish looks and endless humour and patience. After a whirlwind courtship and an ostentatious wedding at St Martin's Church in Central London they had set up home in style in their villa on Primrose Hill.

Philomena had left him on New Years Eve 1900. She had left along with the old century. She hated London life, yearned for Wales, and had started to associate with a group of women who wanted more. Women who wanted to vote, for goodness's sake, but a woman's place was in the home was it not, entertaining guests, running the house, and producing and looking after the children. She had left their daughter aged four with him, to be brought up by a succession of nannies and governesses, making sure that his military career was confined to a desk.

That was when the drinking had started. Archibald Cameron had always liked a 'snifter' of an evening when the sun was 'over the yard arm,' but after Philomena had left, this had turned into visits to his club, more than an occasional hand of cards, and drinking to forget. He had still managed to leave little Fiona well provided for, but he did not spend much time with her, she reminded him too much of her mother. Fiona had never seen her mother again, though she did dream of her, and sometimes she sensed that her mother was still there, somewhere. If she wanted to see her, she only had to look in the mirror, after all she was the image of her, right down to the chaotic hair. Fiona, however, had inherited her father's organised brain and cool head under pressure, she was unflappable, capable, and totally in control, or so she thought.

Fiona was resourceful, she had been her father's mainstay since her mother had walked out on them all those years ago. She had overheard enough of her father's conversations with his colleagues over the Port of an evening to know that The War as they called it, would not be over anytime soon, that it would suck in every available man, leaving a country where women would have to play their part. She intended to join the nursing corps, behind her father's back of course. He would never countenance such a thing.

The running of the house would have to change. Soon, James her father's new valet and Thomas the young footman would be called up, Tilly the young chambermaid would be drafted into one of the munitions factories, leaving just Osborne her father's elderly butler, Dorothy the cook and Mrs Turner who came in once a week to clean. All of whom were too old to serve.

The house was big, far too big for her alone. The seed of an idea came into her mind as she tied up her hair and slung her cloak over her shoulders and set off to where she was enrolled as a trainee nurse. She had been working with the Red Cross for several years and was now eligible to enlist as a registered nurse.

She knew she would likely be posted to the frontline once she had completed her training unless another option was found, not that she did not relish the thought of treating the wounded amongst the fighting.

It was 1915 – there were wounded already coming back and few facilities to treat them. The house with its lovely views across the park, large rooms and plentiful spaces would make a great rest home, a place for wounded soldiers to recuperate after treatment. How should she go about this – who should she write to? How long would it take? Returning home exhausted after her day of bed pans, bottles, and bed sores she coaxed the rickety plumbing and gas water heater into running her a bath and climbed in for a soak. With a towel behind head as a pillow, she closed her eyes and relaxed.

The first image to enter her head was the blonde St Pancras burglar, he of the piercing blue eyes and cheeky smile. She could not get him out of her head, how dare he! She had caught him red handed, but for some reason had not called the police. Why?

His image faded and as she added more hot water to her tub, the voice of her mother came into her head,

'Fiona my dear girl, that boy is trouble, trouble in spades.'

As she closed her eyes, and settled down to soak in the hot water she was sure she saw her mother's fetch, sitting on the seat of the loo, shrouded in steam, a distant memory from her past, or was she? When she opened her eyes again there was no one there. Just her overtired brain playing tricks on her again.

CHAPTER 7. A STRANGE DAY OF ESPIONAGE

Frankie hid the folder under the loose floorboard in his bedroom, the same floorboard he hid all his treasured possessions under. With it, he placed the miniature of Fiona Cameron. He felt bad about taking it, but he knew he could not take it back. He also knew that Black Eric had a contact waiting for the folder. Who that contact was, he did not know, but sooner rather than later Eric would want answers. This job was important, but to who? Whoever he was supposed to hand the folder to would be pretty pissed-off. Frankie felt uneasy, a worried feeling sat in his stomach, he must see Eric, but first he would ask Charlie to look at the papers.

Top Secret papers from the safe in the home of a General, what was that all about? Early the following morning, Frankie knocked on the Turners' front door. Jesse Turner answered it, dressed in his working clothes, his leather braces hanging down around his backside, his trousers held up only by his belt, his immense chest covered only by a dirty coal and sweat encrusted vest. He was unshaven and stank of beer.

'He's not here.' Jesse Turner growled at Frankie, his lips parting in a grimace which showed his missing top teeth, as he stretched the knots from his back.

'Is he in bed?' queried Frankie

'No, he didn't come home last night, he's a man now, what of it, I am not his bloody keeper.'

'Where is he then?'

'How the bloody hell should I know, he left the pub with a girl.'

'What girl, he doesn't know any girls.'

'Well, he does now.' The door slammed in Frankie's face.

As the door finished vibrating, an upper window opened, and a tousled head looked out. Little Mabel, Charlie's sister, leant out. She had heard the discourse below. She was only twelve, but she rather liked Frankie.

'Frankie, Frankie, if I see him, I'll say you're looking, where can he find you?'

'Tell him I'll be in the Duke later, but now I'm going to Nob Mansions.' Mabel knew where he meant, he was going across the park to the street where her mother worked,

Frankie made his way through the daytime streets, busy with traffic of workers trams and buses, shoppers, and bicycles - not the deserted streets he liked to roam under cover of darkness.

He let himself into the Primrose Hill park through the great iron gate and walked purposefully towards Fernleigh House, the house he had burgled the night before. What he thought he was going to do when he got there, he really did not know. Before he got within one hundred yards of the building, he saw Mrs Ethel Turner striding towards him, she was in tears.

'Frankie Baker, what are you doing here?'

'Just walking Mrs T, just taking the air. Early finish, is it?'

'He's dead, the General is dead, died last night, they don't need me today. Miss Fiona is in a terrible state poor lass and her left all on her own.'

Mrs Turner pulled her coat tighter around her shoulders and shuffled off back towards Agar Grove and home.

Frankie found a large chestnut tree and sat under its leafy shade, staring into the distance not focusing on anything in particular. He breathed in deeply and collected his thoughts. He wanted to see Fiona, perhaps talk to her, but what would he say, her father was dead, did she have family to care for her? Mrs T. had said she was all alone. What would she do now? He was still in the middle of his reverie when he heard the grass move beside him. He did not open his eyes, he expected it was Charlie, come looking for him. Frankie felt the metal against his head and heard the click of the pistol's action.

'Don't open your eyes lad.' The voice had a pronounced Irish accent. 'Stand up, slow, hands behind yer back, don't look at me.'

He stood, slowly. As he rose, whoever it was placed a hood over his head, then with great dexterity cracked Frankie on the back of his head and everything went black. He felt himself being lifted by his arms and carried between two men, then nothing.

On the balcony of her father's bedroom some distance away, Fiona Cameron saw this tableau acted out in front of her. She recognised the hair, the same blond, young man. She also recognised his assailant, Patrick O'Malley, her father's former valet. The one he had 'let go' a few months earlier. The other man she did not know, but he was dark haired and dressed like a vagrant.

'I'm going for some fresh air.' She called out to Osborne who had taken charge of formalities with the doctor and the coroner and the undertaker. There was nothing now for her to do but wait. She could not see the family lawyers until Monday. Then there would be an inquest. Her father's department would come to take away any paperwork he had left in the safe, nothing important, anything of importance never left the War Office, that much the Ministry had told her.

That boy, Frankie, he had been in the safe, he would know what it had held. And what was O'Malley about, bashing him on the head and bundling him away like that? She'd seen where they went, and with her nurse's cape pulled around her, she followed them into the depths of the slums of Agar Town and towards the railway tracks.

When Frankie came to, he was tied hand and foot, trussed like a chicken, and lying in some form of cave. The walls were damp, and he could hear the rumble of trains above. He was gagged with a foul-tasting length of cloth. He opened one eye, and on cautious inspection saw the back of a familiar dark head. It was Eric. Eric was in conversation with the Irishman.

'He's a good lad, reliable, best safe cracker in the whole of the smoke if he knew it.' muttered Eric.

'Well, he brought me nothing. My contact will be very disappointed, you assured me he was up for the job.'

'We'll ask him, man, he may have had a reason.'

'Or taken it himself.'

'He wouldn't do that. He'd have no use for it. I'm not sure he can even read.'

They both turned to Frankie, the Irishman spoke first.

'The safe, man, did ye get into the safe?'

He pulled the gag from Frankie's mouth, so that his captive could answer, at the same time squeezing his face between thumb and fingers so that his words came out in a stifled squeak.

'I found the study, as you said. I found the keys, as you said, then I was disturbed. The daughter had a shotgun and told me to get out, rather took my mind off the safe. Then she must have found her father dead. I could hear the screaming as I legged it into the garden. I had to run before I was caught.'

The plausible lie flowed from Frankie's lips like silk.

'So ye have na been in the safe at all?'

'No, I have not!'

'Why were you back in the park watching the house?'

'I was casing the place, to have another go, tonight, it's a lot of money hanging on this job!'

'What do you say, Eric, is he good for it, or should I dispatch the evidence? If he is lying, what he knows would hang us all.'

The Irishman pulled the pistol from his belt and cocked the action speculatively.

'Give him one more chance, O'Malley. He wasn't to know the old buffer would croak. Untie him, let him go!'

O'Malley did not untie him, instead he punched him several times in the gut just as a warning and with the bag over his head walked him back through the maze of old derelict carriages and freight wagons. Removing the hood just before the gates, he pushed him from the railway yard and into the street. Frankie staggered into the gutter, stumbled, and fell, knocking himself unconscious on the cobbles, his hands still tied, unable to break his fall. As his eyes blurred for the second time in a day, he thought he saw the Red Cross of a nurse's uniform bending over him. This day could not get any stranger if it tried.

CHAPTER 8. NURSE! - Frankie

Frankie awoke staring upwards at an ornate plaster ceiling. This ceiling was more than a few feet above him. There was no familiar damp patch above the bed. It was not his ceiling. He lay still and got his head around the situation. He seemed to be in bed. He did feel a bit sick. Everything ached when he tried to move it. The bed beneath him was soft and smelled clean and fresh, the sheets crisp and pulled up to his chin. The whole of his face hurt, and he could hardly see out of his left eye. His left ear had a humming noise in it, as though a bee was trapped in his ear hole searching there for nectar, when all it was likely to find was wax. He slid a hand beneath the neat blue counterpane. He suspected that he was not wearing his trousers. His right hand confirmed that this was the case, he was wearing only his shirt and his underpants. As he was taking this subtle inventory of his body parts, and their function, he heard the door open, and his ministering angel entered the room. Fiona, how on earth had she found him, and where was he? Surely not in her house. How had she managed to get him here.

A firm but gentle hand lifted his head from the soft pillow and a glass of cool water was held to his bruised lips. That soft melodious voice with its slight accent spoke:

'Rest a while Mr Baker. When you are more recovered, we really do need to talk.'

Through the tall window, with its elegant glazing bars and net curtains he could see the sun and, by its position in the sky and the shadow across a tree, he deduced that it was about three o'clock. The chiming of a clock on a distant mantelpiece confirmed this. He needed to get a message to Charlie, tell him where he was at least. He swung one leg out of the bed, and tried to stand, holding on to the bed frame for support. His rebellious body refused to assist him in this endeavour. He felt as if he were about to throw up and despite his best efforts, his usually strong but very skinny legs refused to bare his weight and he crashed to the floor onto the finely woven Turkish rug, knocking the glass of water from the bedside table. There was a thud and a crack as the fine shards scattered over the varnished floorboards. The noise brought Nurse Cameron back into the room.

'We are determined, aren't we!' she patronised in a rather delicate Cambrian lilt he was beginning to enjoy. 'They made a right old mess of your face, your nose is broken, and you have a tooth missing. Your ribs are bruised, and you definitely have concussion. Moving is not an option at least not for twenty-four hours.'

'I need to see Charlie. Oh, Jesus!' He muttered through bruised cracked lips.

'Who is Charlie?' she asked.

'My best friend, he lives next door at number four. He'll be in The Clarence by now, waiting for me.'

'Shall I fetch him then?' said the lilt.

'Find him, tell him: bring what is hidden under my bed, bring him here.'

'You must promise me you will stay here. O'Malley did a fine job on you, damn him.'

'You know him then?'

'He was papa's valet until last month when he was caught rummaging in the study. He was sacked on the spot and turned from his lodgings. He is a thief. Father also found out that he has some friends in very low places. Lower places than even you inhabit if that is even possible.'

She handed him a small hand bell saying, 'If you need the necessary, ring for Osbourne, he will help you, don't try and make it on your own.'

'Where are you going then?'

'Me? I'm going to The Clarence, and number four, number four where?'

Frankie told her the name of the street and she left the room in a whirl of skirts and determination. He sank back into the soft pillows and surrendered himself to the warmth of the bed and the incessant cooing of the pigeons perched on……., the balcony, oh, yes, that balcony. It suddenly dawned on him that General Cameron had died in this very bed only last night. The bed was hardly cold for goodness's sake! He hoped she really had changed the sheets.

On this cheerful thought, he reached for the hand bell and summoned Osbourne. He could not put the call of nature off for a minute longer.

Nurse Cameron descended the sweeping staircase of her home in twos and let herself out through the front door and on through the wrought iron gates into the park at Primrose Hill. It was mid-afternoon and it was

Saturday. The park was full of people going about their business. Mothers pushed babies in perambulators under the wide shady trees, nannies in uniform did the same with their charges, young couples lounged on the grass, many of the men now in uniform and preparing to march off to war. The grass was green and dry under foot, the sky was blue with only the occasional white rabbit of a cloud skipping across its face. The sun was out and the scene before her was one of deceptive pastoral peace.

Fiona drew in a breath, shook her head to clear the strands of hair from her face, asked herself the rhetorical question, 'Why am I doing this?' and set off down the well-trodden path through the avenue of trees which led to the St Pancras gate. She would call at Charlies house first. Whatever was hidden in Frankie's could stay there, she wasn't of a mind to carry anything suspect across town to her own home.

CHAPTER 9. JENNIFER FRANCES – Charlie Turner

The Duke of Clarence,
St Pancras, London.

Charlie Turner watched his friend and drinking companion disappear from the smoke hazed bar of the Duke of Clarence. The drinkers, shoulder to shoulder in small groups, closed around his disappearing back, and the door to the street, with its frosted pane and polished brass handle, closed with a gentle thud.

Charlie nodded quietly and ordered himself another beer, thinking quietly, 'This could be a long night.' Three small beers later and he had surrendered his table to another a group of soldiers who were in company with their current sweethearts. He half envied them their lively chatter, light-hearted and unconcerned with anything but themselves - simply enjoying their own company.

The girl, the one he found himself trying not to gawp at, was one of their party, but an odd number, someone's sister perhaps, or just along for the ride. The conversation seemed to by-pass her. She was an outsider, like himself, in company but alone.

Her hair was light brown and wavy and curled around a pretty heart shaped face with a snub nose and a wide mouth with full lips which didn't seem to smile very often.

Charlie caught her eye as he went to the bar to replenish his beer. She was nursing a glass of Dubonnet and ice, the fashionable drink of the time, he thought, though she looked more like a cider girl to him. She seemed lost amongst the sea of faces and bodies crammed in amongst the stout but worn, brown wood furniture and jovial atmosphere that was Friday night at the Duke of Clarence.

He nodded towards her tentatively, and to his amazement her face broke into the most heartbreaking smile.

'May I buy you a drink?' he ventured optimistically.

She wrinkled her nose and regarded critically the dark red of the Dubonnet in her hand and shook her head.

'Something different perhaps? A glass of cider might suit the atmosphere a little better?'

Her right eyebrow raised in a question, and she nodded, then rose from her seat, excused herself from the table and disappeared to the rear of the pub to the necessaries.

He ordered her a glass of cider, pulled up two bar stools and waited. Within a few minutes she returned, twisting, and turning her way through the crowd, graceful as a dancer. Without a word she slid onto the stool beside him and took a sip of her drink. Her face lighting up with relief at the fresh taste of the apples.

'Jennifer Frances Munro.' She offered him a delicately boned but deceptively strong hand.

He took the hand and in a thoroughly impulsive gesture raised it to his lips and kissed it. 'Charles Herbert Turner at your service, but call me Charlie, please.'

'In which case, call me Frances, everyone else does. My mother is Jennifer, it saves confusion.'

Her absence had not been particularly noticed by her friends, who, she explained, were her twin brothers, Neville and Jeffrey and their girlfriends. Her eyebrow raised at Charlie again. 'They tolerate me,' she said, 'but don't overstep the mark! You may think they don't watch me, but Neville has already marked your card.'

Charlie noted that both brothers wore uniform. Unlike Charlie and Frankie, they were fortunate to have been issued with full uniform and wore their khaki dress with some pride. As Frances spoke, Neville rose from his seat and approached him. He was huge, well over six feet tall and a mountain of man.

'Have ye no' joined up then?' He addressed Charlie with mild derision.

Looking up, Charlie replied. 'St Pancras Rifles, but we have no kit yet, still in civvies mate – and you?'

That seemed to impress the huge man before him. Then Charlie noticed that Neville was wearing a kilt!

'Black Watch,' growled the Scot, 'me and ma' brother! You mess with our sister, and ye'll be first amongst the fallen, man.'

'I have sisters of my own, mate.' replied Charlie. 'We are only chatting, she is safe with me.'

'Ay well then, as long as it's only chattin' ye'd best join us. After all, it was your table, make a night of it, aye?'

They did make a night of it, too. Neville was bear of a man, but his bark was worse than his bite. He had a dry and very bawdy sense of humour and was a keen watcher of people. He soon had the whole table in fits of laughter with his barrack room repartee and his impressions of the officers, and, in particular, their Sergeant, one Malcolm Ferris.

Jeffrey was the quieter twin, he was a different kettle of fish altogether, imagining insult in everything. Their girlfriends were sisters, both nurses in training and living at the nurses' residence near to St Thomas' Hospital, as was Frances. The twins were on leave from the camp in Regents Park. They were due to be posted to France within the next few weeks.

Charlie walked Frances back to her lodgings near St Thomas' and the Nightingale School of Nursing. They walked slowly, talking continually, and sitting on every available bench to make the most of the time remaining until she closed the heavy oak door to her accommodation behind her and surrendered herself to the mercies of matron, who would reprimand her roundly for her lateness and infer that she had been up to all manner of ungodly things.

At the railings on the corner of the street, Charlie gathered her to him and clumsily kissed her goodnight. Their lips met with a clash of noses and foreheads followed by a gentle meeting of lips which sent a tingle down more than his spine.

It occurred to him, as he walked homeward across Westminster Bridge, that he had never kissed a young lady that way before and hoped that it might happen again before too long.

'See you again then?' he had called after her as she disappeared indoors.

'Call for me!' she had whispered almost too loudly.

He would. Oh, yes, he would.

It was gone eight o'clock in the morning by the time Charlie let himself in to 4 Agar Grove where he was greeted by his sister Mabel, who gave him some garbled message about Frankie and the park. Charlie brushed her off, assuring her he would catch up with Frankie later. He went to bed and slept until late that afternoon, his restless slumbers punctuated with mildly lewd thoughts about Frances, his left hand resting on his cock as he turned and drove his hips into his creaky mattress prompting cries from downstairs.

His sisters taunting him in unison.
'You'll go blind Charlie Turner!'
'It will rot and drop off brother!'
'Give it a rest Charlie, the springs won't stand it!'
'Mother will never get the stains out!'

He pulled the blankets over his head and with his hand clenched tight around his balls tried to catch another hour's sleep.

He was woken by a pounding on the front door. He turned over in his bed, waiting impatiently for someone else to attend to the front door. Whoever was there was determined to get an answer.

Realising that his lie in had come unceremoniously to an end he fell out of bed wrapped the sheet around his waist, opened his bedroom curtains with an impatient rattle of the rail and its brass rings, and pulled up the sash window.

'Alright, alright, is there a fire! What the devil do you want?'
'Charlie Turner?'
'Who wants him?'
'I've a message from Frankie!'
'And you are?'
'Fiona, Fiona Cameron, you need to let me in!'

Charlie descended the stairs two at a time, opened the door discreetly hiding his half naked body behind it, gestured to the front parlour,' Go in! Sit down while I get dressed.'

He rubbed a hand through his rumpled hair and stubbly chin and stumped back up the stairs to make himself decent. Whoever she was, this girl was quality, so what on earth could she have to do with Frankie Baker?

Fiona Cameron cast her eyes around the Turners' front parlour. It was clean and tidy and lived in. All the furniture was old but well-polished, the chairs well sat in, the upholstery slightly saggy and worn and there was a crucifix adorning one wall, maybe a sign of Mrs Turner's faith. A faded picture of the King hung neatly on another wall and a China statue of Queen Victoria, its pottery glaze cracked and worn with polishing, stood on a lace doily, front and centre of the sideboard.

The wallpaper was peeling slightly with the inherent damp, and the ceiling was yellow above the armchair by the fire. Pipe smoke, or cigarettes, she wondered. Turner, the name was familiar but there must be many Turners in St Pancras. She stood up and walked to the sideboard where she saw a small silver pincushion, its navy-blue velvet pad stuck with pins in the style of a hedgehog. She recognised it immediately as an item she had loved to play with as a small child.

She smiled to herself and called up the stairs 'Your mother is Ethel Turner, then?'

'Yes,' replied Charlie from halfway down the stairs, 'why?'

'That hedgehog pincushion, it belonged to my mother. Father said he gave it away. I didn't believe him. Your mother must be our housekeeper.'

Pennies dropped in Charlie's sleep fuddled mind. This must be the General's daughter. What in god's name had Frankie been up to? Walking into the kitchen at the rear of the house to collect his thoughts, he put the kettle on the range.

'Do you want tea? I'm making it anyway then you can tell me what all this fuss is about.'

CHAPTER 10. DECODING

London
April 1916

Twenty-four hours later. Three heads bowed over the almost transparent sheets of type written paper. Line after line of letters, broken neatly into pairs and totally unintelligible to the uninitiated.

Frankie, Charlie, and Fiona had taken refuge in Frankie's small bedroom poring over the documents in the folder which Frankie had stolen from the safe.

The only safe and sensible thing to do with them would be to put them back. If the General was not supposed to have them then at least it showed that they had not gone anywhere else.

'No,' said Fiona, 'I heard him talking about what he does, what he did, I mean, at work. He hated being stuck in an office, he wanted to go with the men, with his regiment, but they made him organise supplies, because he was good at it! He organised supplies, and troop movements! If this is to do with his work, then we destroy it, or my dear father's reputation is ruined.'

'Well,' said Charlie, 'we can't be sure about that. Firstly, we need to see what it says, and it's not designed to be read so it's not going to be simple. This is not like we used to do in school, just changing a few letters around.'

A shout came up the stairs. 'Frankie, do you and your friends want a cuppa?'

Letty Baker was at home. She was a homely looking woman, tall and impossibly thin. She wore wire framed spectacles to improve her vision. Years of clerking in an office and keeping the books for Mr Baker in better times had dimmed her eyesight. Arthur Baker had run a small but busy printing shop before alcohol took over his life and now he worked for the man who had bought his shop as a typesetter, and lived in reduced circumstances with his wife and Frankie their adopted lodger. Letty clerked for the local bookmaker, Mr Jack Brown. Letty had a fine head for figures.

'Yes, please, Ma!' He shouted back, momentarily lifting his head from the cyphered pages.

A few minutes later, the comforting rattle of teacups was heard on its journey up the stairs. Fiona opened the door to the crowded room and Letty placed the tray on the small bedside table.

'What's that you have there?' Her spectacles had descended to the tip of her nose as her head bent forward. 'Frankie, what have you gotten into lad? That can only be trouble.'

'It's………., well, we don't know wha….' He started to say.

'Don't, *'it's'* me, I can see what that folder says, Top Secret, and that's a cypher, not a code, here let me see!'

Curiosity got the better of Letty Baker. She picked up the top sheet of the documents and examined it.

'Is there a word?' she asked, 'There should be a longish word, one that you can read, it might not be with the papers, but whoever wants to read this will need it.'

Between them they checked everywhere among all the papers and the front and back of the folder. There was nothing.

'What now then?' Fiona asked. 'Do we just destroy it or put it back? If we are to put it back, then it must be by Monday. The bods from the War Office are coming for papa's stuff on Monday. They will take the safe away with them.'

She threw her arms up in a gesture of frustration, bouncing the mattress of the single bed where the three of them sat, and tipping her tea all over the bedclothes and the inside of the leather-bound document folder.

All three of them leapt out of the way in consternation, pulling the small jug of milk and the rest of the tea away from the papers.

'That's buggered it, then!' Letty exclaimed, pulling the folder out of harm's way. 'It will all have to be dried out, now, and slowly!'

'Hold on, what's that?' Charlie pointed at one of the leather corner pieces placed to hold the documents flat. It was worn, the one which was at the top right-hand corner, away from the spine. It had been soaked by the deluge of tea and was curling away from its mountings. On the back Charlie could see the faint marks of writing on the rear of the cardboard mount. The words ***Travel Obscured*** were written in pencil.

'Could that be what we are after, Ma?'

Letty pushed her spectacles up to the bridge of her long nose.

'It might be, you can only try it! Do any if you have a pen and paper?'

Heads shook in the negative, and Letty collected up the spilled tea things, leaving the plain homemade shortbread biscuits, and clomped down the stairs. A couple of minutes later she could be heard returning rather more quickly with several sheets of writing paper and a pencil and a ruler. With a deft hand she started to draw on the paper what looked like a crossword grid with no blank squares.

Letty Baker busied herself with her pencil, with a practiced hand working through the sheets of thin typing paper, reproducing the lines of typing using the arrangement of letters from the grid. She wrote in a clear and careful hand, periodically pushing her spectacles up her nose, and reading back to herself that she had written. Then she sat up straight, ran a hand through her hair and spoke.

'Frankie, get and put the kettle on, then you can tell me where on earth you got this from.'

Fiona put her hand on Letty's arm. 'Maybe I can help with that.'

'This is Top Secret war correspondence!' Letty spat out the words. 'It must go back, and soon!'

'It cannot go back!' replied Fiona 'My father's superiors cannot know he took it! It should have been returned with the rest of the safe.'

Letty was staring in disbelief at the first of the decoded documents, her spectacles falling from her nose and dangling dangerously on the skimpy string which kept them safe from loss.

General Headquarters
British Army in the Field

Memo to Adjutant General
Lieutenant General Sir Nevil MacCready.
From General Haig

SECRET
To AG
I have meeting on Friday re best date for general offensive with Joffre. Please let me have your estimate of troop numbers and reinforcements for four dates:
Viz (a) 1st July
*   (b) 15th July*

(c) 1ˢᵗ August
(d) After middle August
And state from your point of view when we will be in the most favourable position for action.

     Yours
      DH
       22ⁿᵈ May 1916

23ʳᵈ May 1916
British Army Headquarters

SECRET

To GH

Have several Battalions of enlisted men awaiting deployment. Can arrange deployment of same by mid-June if needed.

Could take the field 1ˢᵗ July in my opinion. Avoiding poor weather and maintaining pressure on Bosch. Will also relieve Joffre and the French at Verdun.
I await confirmation of your order to move these troops into embarkation to travel Southampton to Le Havre.

6ᵗʰ Battalion West Surrey Regt
7ᵗʰ Battalion West Surrey Regt
16ᵗʰ Rifle Brigade St Pancras Rifles
2ⁿᵈ Battalion The Black Watch.

All leave cancelled. All enlisted men to return to Barracks.
Proceed via rail link to assembly point Morn Hill, Winchester
For onward transport to Cherbourg.

Yours
AG MacCready.

'We are at war girl! Those ships have not yet left port! They could be sunk, men will die, if these plans don't change.'

'But no one else knows!'

'What else has been stolen before? That is the thing girl, pound to a pinch, this is only part of the leak!'

The door creaked open, it's latch dropping with a click as it closed behind Frankie and the tea tray.

'Now Frankie,' Letty began, after a deep breath in, 'explain!'

Frankie told her all about his last 'job.' Being kidnapped by O'Malley and Eric, being beaten by them, and threatened. The money he had been offered to do the job. He left nothing out. Letty sat on the bed her face ashen and shocked. Then steeling herself she poked Frankie hard in the shoulder with the pencil she had been turning over in her hands.

'You must tell someone of this O'Malley character. He is only a link in the chain, but it is probably him who passes the information on.' Frankie was silent, his eyes fixed on one of the sheets of paper. Charlie spoke first.

'Frankie, we must do something with it, read it and read it well. Our Battalion is mentioned, it is our mobilisation order. We are being posted. If this is in the hands of the enemy then we will all be dead, even before we get there!'

There was silence suddenly in the little bedroom, a shaft of sunlight sparkling on the dust particles floating in the air. Reality had begun to sink in. Eventually, Frankie replied, slowly turning the paper over in his hands.

'What do you suggest Ma?'

'Is there anyone you could hand it to, an officer, perhaps? What about your sergeant, you know, Sergeant MacGregor? You say you trust him, could he not help?'

Then Fiona piped up. 'Say that you found the folder in the park, and that you do not know what the contents are, but it says Top Secret on the front. Just hand it to MacGregor, no one is likely to say anything different. O'Malley can only implicate himself if he does!'

'But what about your father, his reputation and all that?' interrupted Charlie.

Fiona took a deep breath in and held it for what seemed an age then she sighed the let her breath out and spoke in a measured, firm voice. 'My father is one man in a war. I do not know his motives, but I can assure you he was no traitor. If they choose to blacken his character, then so be it. He is dead and those that matter know the truth. If you do not act, then thousands of lives may be lost. We all have a duty to our country and those who knew father will see to it that the truth is found out.'

'Best if we must burn all this.' muttered Letty, picking up her work and crumpling it into a ball. 'The fire is lit in the kitchen.'

They all watched as the ball of papers burned and agreed. They would tell no-one anything of what they knew.

But, and for better or worse, Charlie and Frankie now knew the date of their mobilisation for France and their eventual destination. Once seen it could not be unseen, and they were due back with their Battalion in two days' time. Just time, thought Charlie, to see Frances one more time.

CHAPTER 11. GREY MEN

London, 1916.

They spent the final night of their leave drinking beer in the Duke of Clarence, all of them together, an evening in a moment, facing an uncertain future at home or across that grey, cold strip of sea the French called La Manche - the English Channel. Frankie, Charlie, Frances and Fiona, and Frances's brothers who had been called back to their regiment early but knew nothing of the mobilisation.

'Damned inconvenience,' muttered Neville over his pint of stout. 'I had plans tae travel north tae Glasgow and see the folks, aye. I hav'nae seen them fer over a year an' I may never see them again if we are posted.'

'It's bound tae be more bloody square bashing.' put in Jeffrey 'It's about bloody time we saw some action, brother, I did 'nae join up tae spend ma' time polishin' ma' boots, man.'

'Whatever,' replied Charlie, 'let's make the most of it - it's our last night an' all.'

Frankie and Fiona were deep in a conversation of their own. Charlie could see the two heads drawing closer together. Frankie looked worried, and Fiona looked determined.

'I've been followed.' He heard Frankie whisper.

'I know that. They beat you up - I rescued you remember?' replied Fiona.

'No, not that lot, by a woman!' he muttered almost under his breath. 'She's been hanging around at the bottom of our street all week, looking at our house, watching us.'

'We burned all that stuff well, didn't we?' Fiona's voice was tense.

'Yes, it's all ashes! Ma tipped it all on the back path with the rest of the cinders from the fire, then she tamped it all well in. It's been well trodden in by now.' said Frankie. 'That's not the point though. I think I've seen her before, but I've never met her!'

'So, what does she look like, Frankie? I haven't seen anyone hanging around. Maybe you're imagining things, you had a nasty bang on the head!'

'I've seen her picture!'

'Good god, where?'

'In your father's study, on the desk, in a silver frame.'

'No, that's not......, well that's not possible!' Fiona's voice was raised now. 'That is just not possible. She's long gone! She went years ago!'

But, deep in her soul, Fiona knew that she was wrong. She had sensed that her mother was near with that animal sense of impending doom, a feeling that arrived imperceptibly when everything was about to go horribly wrong. She had felt that knot tight in her stomach for weeks now, and a sense that something or someone was watching her. She realised now, that she had chosen just to ignore it.

'Who is it, Fi?' Frankie used the shortened form of her name.

'If it truly is the woman in the photo, then that is my mother, Philomena, and nothing good can come of it. When did you last see her?'

'She was walking towards the park gates as I was coming to meet you, but you came straight from the hospital, didn't you? You wouldn't have crossed paths.'

Fiona dragged Frankie by the arm. 'If she's going to the house, I must stop her! We must go now. She has no business there, not anymore.'

They got up from their seats, offered a quick, 'See you in bit!' to their comrades and left, his arm resting gently on her shoulder. Something was definitely in the air with these two.

'Get a room, you two!' called Jeffrey Munro after them with a grin, as they made their exit.

'I have plenty of those!' called back Fiona. She and Frankie stepped out into a moonlit street, glistening with raindrops.

They walked casually up the park towards the General's house. Fiona pulled her key from her small, blue handbag and walked, as she would usually, up to the front door. She let herself in with the key. The hall, the staircase, the clock, the elegant hall stand and the portrait of that ancient ancestor astride his horse with his favourite hound running alongside -

nothing out of place so far. She stood in silence while the shafts of moonlight picked out the familiar features of home.

Frankie, meanwhile, had made his way round to the scullery window which was habitually left open for the cat. He slid in an arm and then his shoulders and before you could say 'knife' was seated on the stone slab below the window, inside the house.

He felt his way around the furniture until his eyes became accustomed to the dark, found the baize covered kitchen door, pushed it gently ajar and made his way out and upward by the stairs and into the hall. There was Fiona, standing stock still.

As her senses made a more detailed enquiry, she noticed that the door to the general's study was closed, but a sliver of light fanned out from below it, casting a gentle glow on the polished red and amber tiles leading to the front door. She could hear voices. She motioned silently to Frankie and took three light steps forward. With her right shoulder against the door, she grasped the white porcelain doorknob with her right hand and pushed without making a sound.

Hunched over the desk were the backs of Philomena Cameron and Patrick O'Malley. Alongside the desk, the safe door hung open. Was Philomena Cameron really O'Malley's contact?

'Where are the papers, the coded stuff? They should be here!' grunted O'Malley. 'The boy swore they were still here - said he'd not touched the safe! They should be here!'

'Well, he lied, didn't he!' The aristocratic tone of the woman cut through the shadowy atmosphere of book-lined shelves and leather.

'Archie swore he could get them! Then I would have had him over a barrel, and he'd agree to a divorce. He's already betrayed his blessed country to get free of me. Herr Tirpitz is paying well for this stuff.'

Frankie cleared his throat loudly. He did not know why he said it, but the words came falling out of his mouth as quickly as he pushed Fiona against an adjacent door.

'I believe I have what you want,' he continued, calmly.

The two safe crackers spun around almost knocking each other senseless as their heads collided and they grabbed the edge of the desk to steady themselves, feet spinning from under them.

O'Malley yelled, his wide eyes resembling organ stops, 'Ferchrissake, what the feck're ye doin' here, an' what is it that I'd be wantin' then, ye wee gobshite?'

'I have the folder and its contents.'

'Ye do, do yer?' It was O'Malley who spoke, marginally regaining his composure.

'It's well-hidden. It can be yours for a price - I can get it to you, but it'll cost you one hundred guineas.'

The woman spoke. 'Cheap at half the price! You have a deal, young man and you will be well rewarded. There may be other work for you in this line. You must be the housebreaker they all talk of.'

'Former housebreaker.' said Frankie. 'My friend will meet you at the park gates at five on Tuesday evening. You will leave the money with him.'

With this he regarded them warily, then backed his way out of the General's leather-bound sanctuary. Feeling sufficiently safe, he spun on his heel and walked towards the imposing front door which Fiona had failed to close, and which now hung open, letting in a draft of summer night air and a spatter of light rain. But where was Fiona? They were all about to find out!

The gun room door, which should have been locked, was open. The first shotgun in the rack was kept loaded. It was the same one she had pointed at Frankie on the night they had first met.

Frankie heard the word 'Mother!' spat at the woman with a venom he hardly imagined his delightful and well-educated accomplice could command, followed by a tirade of abuse more suited to a lower deck sailor than a General's daughter. As he turned, he saw the shotgun being raised, and tucked securely between a firm upper right arm and the curve of a pert breast. With a practiced hand which befitted her upbringing, she delivered contents of one barrel square into her mother's chest, leaving a gaping hole in her silk wrap from which blood sprayed in coarse, red droplets, skywards towards the delicate glass of the chandelier as her mother reeled backwards against a bookshelf. Then, uttering a shriek of unimaginable anguish, Philomena Cameron slumped forward onto the rug, just as the contents of the second barrel hit O'Malley in the face, widening its glib Irish grin to a hole twice its size, leaving his eyeballs almost suspended in space and spewing the contents of his skull onto the General's desk.

Cool as a cucumber, Fiona broke the shotgun over her arm, located the telephone and dialled the police.

'Good evening.' Frankie heard her say, her voice trembling only slightly, 'I have just disturbed two burglars in my late father's study. They have broken into his safe.'

There was a short pause. 'Yes, they are still here, officer, no I won't let them go.'

Another short pause. 'They are both dead, I shot them.'

Then, turning to Frankie, she hissed at him, 'Make yourself scarce, I need to be on my own for this.'

He did not need telling twice. Frankie sprinted across the park and back to the Duke of Clarence as fast as his legs could carry him, pausing to inspect himself in a shop window before entering, just in time for last orders.

Fiona removed her father's wedding photo from its frame and threw the sepia tinted image of the happy couple onto the fire in the kitchen, Then, having searched her mother's body for any sign of identification and finding none, only the spare set of house keys usually kept by Mrs Turner, she went and sat on the front porch and waited for the police to arrive. It was going to be another long night.

In short order a Detective Inspector arrived accompanied by another man in military uniform, one of her father's colleagues, she presumed.

Captain Jeremy Shipley introduced himself. 'I worked under your father, my dear.' he told her. 'Blackmail! Nasty business! We feared he had been compromised several months ago, though he has managed to be the worst provider of information to the enemy they have probably ever had. In fact, he's more of an asset in counterintelligence to us than anything else. We knew that he was being held to ransom over something. Now we know what the lever was. I can tell you no more than that. Your father was a good and honourable man. There is no stain on his character, rest assured.'

Fiona looked at her hands and saw that they were shaking. The shotgun was still hanging, the breech broken over her arm. She looked at Captain Shipley and with tears in her eyes asked, 'What now?'

'You make yourself scarce, my dear and we will do the rest. O'Malley is well known to us. The lady is your mother I presume?'

'Captain you are correct, but she was no lady, and I haven't seen her for years. In fact, I'm surprised I can remember her at all!'

'Go then.' smiled the Captain. 'Oh, and give our regards to young Frankie Baker. Tell him he is in the clear. His blonde hair is very distinctive on these moonlit nights - he was seen leaving you know - tell him he needs to buy a hat.'

Fiona wrapped her cloak around her and left her home, turning briefly to lock the front door. With nowhere else to go, she too headed for the Duke, and then to Agar Grove, where Letty made up a bed for Frankie on the sofa and asked no awkward questions about what had happened in the preceding hours.

It was Monday morning, and all leave was cancelled. Frankie awoke early, still slightly in shock after the events of the previous evening.

He was alone in bed. His was a single bed, so it didn't take much effort to check for the presence of another human being. Then he felt the lumpy cushions of the Bakers' ancient sofa under his back and remembered exactly where he was, and who was in his bedroom upstairs. The lounge door pushed slowly open, and his mother appeared with a mug of tea and a slice of fresh toast.

'Well, good morning, Frank.' This was bad, she only called him Frank if she was annoyed. 'I don't know quite what went on last night, but the whole place is buzzing with it, even at this early hour.'

'What time is it, Ma?' He rubbed his hand over his eyes and pushed his fingers back through his hair.

'Half past six.' she replied. 'Your kit is in the hallway, remember? You've to be back at your depot by ten, you and Charles, wherever he is.'

'Fiona?' He queried.

'Is upstairs and still asleep, I will wake her in a minute poor girl. I'm still trying to get the stains out of her dress, what in the world went on last night?'

'Mother, you really do not want to know.'

Soft footsteps crept along the passage and the lounge door opened again. Fiona stood in the doorway, wearing Frankie's brown woollen dressing gown, her feet swamped in his worn-out carpet slippers.

'Mrs Baker, good morning.' she yawned. 'You really can't know everything, just know that everything is okay.'

Letty opened her mouth to speak.

'Yes, a mug of tea would be wonderful, with one sugar please.' Fiona cut in, before Letty could ask the question which was hanging unspoken on her lips.

Letty Baker took the hint and disappeared into the kitchen.

Frankie took Fiona's hand in his.

'You know we leave tomorrow for the coast, and soon after for France?'

'Yes, and I will miss you, Frankie Baker.'

'Then marry me, Fiona Cameron. We can get a special licence - we could do it this morning, couldn't we?'

'No, we couldn't Frankie, there isn't enough time, and besides….,' she trailed off

'You will say yes, won't you?'

'Frankie, I will marry you, but not yet, let me deal with all of 'that' first. I have no one now, I need to find myself first, who I am, what she was, who she was, my mother, I mean, and father,'

'But Fi,' he started, 'I……,'

Fiona cut in. 'I will wait for you. I will marry you. You are the thief that broke into my house. You stole my heart - you must keep it safe for me, please!'

Then she lowered herself onto the lumpy sofa and kissed him full on the lips, softly, lingering perhaps a second too long,

HMMM – the clearing of a throat came from the passageway. Tea with one sugar had arrived.

Frankie wrapped the beige striped blanket around him and, rising from his makeshift bed, crossed the threadbare carpet to the sideboard. Its top was decorated with an array of what Letty called 'dust collectors,' small porcelain ornaments, presents from her husband and Frankie over the years or left to her by her mother, cleaned on an ad hoc basis when visitors were expected. He opened the top drawer of the three which sat between the two end cupboards and reached into to back of the drawer to pull out a brown leather box containing another smaller bag.

Letty inhaled sharply. The bag contained the only possessions the boy had had when she found him in. She remembered how, when he was ten, he had sat and handed the box to her 'in lieu of rent,' he had said. He did not need to pay rent, he was part of their family, and part of their community. For Agar Town and Agar Grove in particular was a community and they knew how to stick together in a crisis.

Inside the bag amongst a jumble of bits and pieces of broken jewellery was a ring fashioned of silver chased and engraved with leaves and flowers, no gemstones, but beautiful in its simplicity.

'Wear it for me Fiona, it is not stolen. I do not remember who wore it last, but it was honestly come by.'

He placed it on the third finger of her left hand. It fitted a little loosely but would not fall off. Then he kissed it.

'It is beautiful!' she gasped. 'I will never take it off.' she promised him. 'Now hurry, or you will miss the bus. And you need a bath. You won't get another in camp for days.'

In the kitchen she heard Letty dragging the tin bath in from the yard and the slosh of jugs of water being poured in from the boiler on the fire.

Frankie shuffled meekly to his date with hot water and soap. 'Nag, nag, nag, we ain't even married yet young lady!'

Half an hour later he emerged, dressed in what passed for his best kit, though he still had no matching tunic and trousers, boots polished and cap at a jaunty angle. They left Agar Grove together and headed for the tram stop, joined before the end of the road by Charlie, his uniform unpressed and hurriedly put on, but at least not late.

On the tram stop to wave him off, Jennifer Francis Munro stood twisting a ring made of copper fuse wire on her engagement finger.

'He's promised me a better one, on his next leave,' she whispered to Fiona, 'and I'd best not let the brothers see it until he does. Jeffrey would rip him limb from limb if he thought I was even engaged, though I think Neville knows it's coming, and I've written to Ma and Da to tell them.'

Later that morning, Letty was intrigued to see Ethel Turner leaving her house and getting into a large black car. The car was driven by a military type, and she got into it willingly. No one else saw her go. Jesse Turner was already at work and the girls had gone to school hours since. And, young Charlie, well he had shot down the street with his kitbag just moments before it arrived, hot on the heels of Frankie and Fiona, all heading for the tram, and then to who knows where.

CHAPTER 12. MOBILISATION - Charlie

May 1916

When we reached barracks after our eventful leave in London, we each found a pile of kit waiting for us on our cots. At last there was a full set of uniform. This was an indication that something was happening, some of the other lads just saw it as a pile of uniform, essential clothing for a soldier, but why now, we had been making do for months, always last in line when it came to kitting us out.

Frankie and I knew – we knew that we would be mobilised soon. In fact, we knew the date.

The station was packed with departing soldiers boarding for the assembly camp on Morn Hill, near Winchester. Men hung out of carriage windows in last minute embraces with their wives and sweethearts, children waved fathers goodbye and fathers promised to return, promises that some were destined not to keep, promises that some would choose not to keep.

I had said my farewells in London, so too had Frankie. Frances and Fiona both had jobs to do. They had promised to wait for us until we returned, if we returned, no need for hasty weddings, though Frances and I were engaged with a ring of sorts. We made our way along the platform until we located Sergeant Jack, he too had said his goodbyes. Frankie and I had never met his wife, Rhianydd, sometimes shortened to Anni, but never to Rhian, but Sergeant Jack spoke of her often, how she was tall and red haired, fiery, opinionated, clever, and mother of a daughter Agnes May, born only a few weeks ago, who he had never met. Estranged, he said, from her mother after some family falling out over her father, Rhianydd never spoke of her father, ever, it was a closed subject.

From what Jack said, and the little he knew was through her sister Helena who spoke of her father as a slightly flamboyant apothecary and chemist from Mid Wales. A kind man who had believed that daughters should be educated, he grew exotic flowers in his glass house and made exquisite scents which he sold to the ladies, and the gentlemen alike. Father, she said, was dead, the shop lost to them along with their life in the Mid Wales town they had loved. Helena never spoke of her mother, only that she was called Sibyl and that she was in both their words 'away with the fairies.' From this I had conjured up a certain picture of Sergeant Jack's mother-in-law. I wondered if he would ever meet her, for the truth was often very different from family propaganda.

A carriage door opened. There he was. I dropped my pack from my back and turned to see if Frankie was still behind me in the crowd. Frankie did not much like big crowds, and I could see his white blonde head a few yards behind me, cap on the back of his head, rifle over his shoulder, but right hand firmly on its strap, fighting his way through, twisting through the log jam of people like an albino eel, one foot on the carriage step. I leant out towards him

'Frankie! Over here mate!'

He heard me and within seconds had climbed to refuge in the compartment alongside myself and Sergeant Jack. We were his unit, but he also had other duties and excused himself, ducking out through the door to take a head count of the rest of the riflemen who were supposed to be on the train. There would be those who had gone Absent Without Leave or just plain deserted, their fear of possible death outweighing their fear of being branded a coward and imprisoned and possibly shot at dawn.

Outside on the platform, the mass of khaki was gradually disappearing through slamming carriage doors, the steam from the engine and the smoke from the boiler as it rolled back along the length of the train and the platform. When it cleared, the platform was empty, or was it? I was sure I could see the shadowy figures of four women cloaked in steam, one was tall and red headed, and holding a bundle in her arms. I blinked, and started to wave to them, surely they would bid us goodbye, but when I opened my eyes, they were gone, all that was there was the swinging sign which marked the platforms end. The last door slammed and the guard blew his whistle. With a scream of metal on metal and a hiss of steam, the driver sounded the whistle twice in reply and we were on the move.

As the last carriage cleared the end of the station canopy, I could hear the troops at the far end of the train, conscripted infantrymen begin to sing, 'It's a long way to Tipperary.'

Singing is infectious, especially in times of great uncertainty and soon the whole bloody train was singing, including me and Frankie. To hell with Tipperary, we still had a long way to go.

London streets gave way to open green countryside, trees and fields flashed past at ever increasing speeds, 'Tipperary' gave way to other more bawdy songs, mainly featuring the Kaisers manhood or other parts of his anatomy.

'I don't want to join the army! I don't want to go to war!' piped up a voice from several compartments further back in the train. Well, it was a bit too bloody late for that now. I sat back in my seat, my pack wedged between my feet, my rifle propped with Frankie's in the corner by the door.

'Well Frankie, I'm getting some kip, it was a long night.'

I pulled my cap over my eyes and was just picturing the curvaceous form of Jennifer Frances Munro in all her glory in my imagination when the compartment door crashed open and two huge Scotsmen in the uniform of the Black Watch fell in through the door.

'Room for two little 'uns is there, shift up yous two, ye can'nae be havin' a whole seat to yersel', yer no' an officer yet.' The Munro brothers had arrived. No chance of peace and contemplation this side of the channel then. Neville and Jeffrey took up occupation, equipped with a large flask of good whisky, Frankie's face perked up, he took a long swig from the offered receptacle and smiled at me, that totally disarming smile of his, his demeanour changed, he seemed to steel himself against the world.

'Right then Charlie, are we up for this then?'

Were we? I really didn't know. Another crash as the train jolted around a bend in the tracks, the door opened again, and Sergeant Jack appeared accompanied by another sergeant of the Black Watch

'Lads, this is Malcolm Ferris, Sergeant Malcolm Ferris to you! Make room for his hairy one.'

Neville and Jeffrey muttered a deferential, 'sarge.' And moved away to allow their comrade to sit by the window. Neville handed me the flask, wiping the neck in the hem of his kilt as he did so,

'So, wee Charlie, ye'll be after makin' an honest woman of our sister then.' It was a statement and not a question.

'If she'll wait for me, Neville,'

'Well, she's no' a flighty wee thing, and me and Jeffrey there will be on yer case if she gets hurt mind.'

'I've told you before, I've sisters of my own, Neville, I hear what you are saying, loud and clear.'

'Aye, well I don't want tae be huntin' fer you to put things to rights when this strammash is over. Does anyone know where we are going anyway, apart from France?'

Frankie stirred in his seat. 'Ours to find out when we get there, but if I hear Tipperary again, I'll be off and swimming to Ireland.'

Something was up with Frankie, he was quiet, too quiet. I watched him pull himself further into his uniform, trying to fade into the seats, all the bravado of enlisting was gone, the reality was setting in. Frankie was afraid. In the space of half an hour he had gone from brave and bold to withdrawn, terrified even.

The train continued its jolting, shuddering, clanking journey through the green Hampshire countryside, the strains of singing speeding it on its way until finally we arrived at Winchester. A march then to the holding camp at Morn Hill, these downs and the nearby plains of Salisbury plain had always been a collecting point of some sort since time began. How many ancient warriors had congregated on this soil in times before ours? It was a random thought which crossed my mind while I was waiting for Frankie.

'How long will we be here sarge?' I heard Frankie ask Jack.

'Not been told yet, but not long, there's a rumour of some big offensive planned, soon, I don't think it will be more than a few days.'

Those memos were right then. I saw Frankie take a breath in and gave him my sternest look and shook my head, the look that said, 'Say nothing.'

He said nothing, but I could see he was recalling the memo.

Then he shouldered his rifle and his pack. 'Let's find our bloody cots then, before some other bastard gets there, I'm not sharing with either of those bloody Scotsmen.'

'Ye will na have to Frankie, they've shipped out already, their whole regiment is away to Southampton to board ship,'

It was nearly June 1916.

CHAPTER 13. STEAM A LITTLE FASTER – Charlie

June 1916

It was two days later that we finally boarded the train to Southampton and the ship which would take us across the grey churning expanse of the English Channel to Le Havre, not Cherbourg. The SS Rochelle was a small, converted passenger ferry. She had seen better days. Her paint was peeling and the stains of green, rusting water ran down her camouflage painted sides from her gunwales to the waterline. Below decks all the plush furnishings of her glory days had been stripped out, leaving wooden deck benches and some of the larger more permanent banquette seating, but the tastefully art-deco ceiling lights were gone as was the waiter service and the cocktail bar. The lower decks were crammed with servicemen jostling for a comfy seat for the seven-hour crossing or bagging a position on the open sided promenade deck to get away from the constant fug of cigarette smoke, bilge water and oil, and the heaving of those with no sea-legs.

Frankie and I leant on the stern rail as we left harbour, eyes peeled for danger, not that we could do anything about it if we saw any. The stink of seasickness was added to the smell of unwashed bodies, fear, and fags. The currents of the English Channel can conjure up a nauseating pitch and roll and many a seasoned sailor has lost their breakfast to the heavy, churning swells just outside the channel ports, Southampton included. Another good reason to stay above decks in the fresh, salty air.

As we watched England disappear behind us, Frankie lit another cigarette and pulled his cheeks in, inhaling the smoke deep into his lungs. The lit end glowed red, and a wisp of smoke rose, curling upwards and floating off into the breeze. He exhaled and leaning his elbows on the rail pointed his cigarette towards the shore.

'Will we see her again, do you think?' His voice was a whisper.

'You cannot think like that, Frankie, we'll be home before you know it. The Bosch won't know what's hit them when we get there.'

I knew I sounded far too cheerful for reality, but there was really little point in dwelling on the future when we might have none.

From below deck a faint chorus of Tipperary drifted through the companion ways, echoing on the steel walls of the majestic, but wallowing old tub, which was our transport, her hastily painted camouflage poor protection from the Germans' ever-expanding fleet of U-Boats.

'Charlie, old man,' Frankie put on his best toff's accent, 'which way is fucking Tipperary, can't we go there instead?'

I pointed in the direction I though was west – down the channel towards the Irish Sea and replied in a suitably supercilious tone,

'Sorry, Frankie, old son, we seem to have boarded the wrong bloody ship. Tipperary is that way!'

We leant on that rail for the whole of the seven-hour crossing. We both knew what we were looking for in the churning grey water of what the French call La Manche. We counted seagulls as they flew low alongside the rusty hull beneath us and watched for the telltale sign of a disturbance in the white caps of the wake churned up by the propellers.

> *'Could you steam a little faster,*
> *while we lean here on this rail,*
> *There's a U-boat close behind us,*
> *A torpedo on our tail.'*

Frankie misquoted Lewis Carroll's poem making up his own words to fit.

'Very witty, Baker, but ye din'nae be wantin' tae tempt providence, now do you?' Sergeant Jack MacGregor's soft Scottish burr heralded his arrival.

'At ease, you two, I'm just doing the rounds. Was that just a random thought, Baker, or are ye psychic? The captain informed me, just now, that he's had a U-boat warning in the last half hour.'

In the distance on the Starboard side of the Rochelle I could just see the majestic sight of the SS France steaming behind us, the Versailles of troopships, a real live French registered luxury transatlantic liner, the lucky buggers aboard her would be travelling in better style than us. And, out to Port, just on the horizon, the comforting sight of the funnel smoke of a British Destroyer.

'That's the Eden. Captain says she's shadowing us all the way to Le Havre.' Sergeant Jack pointed to our left. 'And hopefully, the beauty of the floating gin palace behind us will blind the Germans enough for them to lose interest in a rust-bucket like us.'

'That's not a very nice thought, sarge.' commented Frankie.

'No, Baker, but I can read both of yer wee minds.'

I saw the shake of his shoulders as he chuckled to himself, turned and, pulling his cap down more firmly over his newly cropped hair, paced slowly towards the front of the ship in search of more of his men.

As it happened, no U-Boat was spotted in our vicinity, maybe deterred by the presence of HMS Eden patrolling nearby. We docked safely under a darkening Normandy sky and after some chaos while the various companies of men sorted their gear and formed into some sort of order, we were marched off to the nearby railhead and onto another train, destination Abbéville, a small French town near the mouth of the river Somme. We waited for what seemed like hours, passing the time with two privates from the South Wales Borderers, Arthur Cole, and Nesbit Evans, both married men from a small mining town in the Welsh Valleys called Maesteg.

They were good company, especially Private Cole who fancied himself as a bit of a poet. We were still sitting waiting for our transport when we heard the sounding of fog horns and ships' sirens from the port, and a commotion as though something terrible had happened. There had been no explosion - we would have heard that, and there had been no exchange of fire from HMS Eden. Word came down the lines from the port faster than General Haig could post a telegram to his staff. The Eden had been sunk.

Frankie went ashen. 'Could have been us, Charlie-boy! We should have said something.'

I called to one of the Welsh boys who had carried the news up the line.

'How did she sink? Don't say she was torpedoed!'

Without stopping to discuss matters at any great length, he replied. 'No butty, she collided with the floating gin palace, only the bloody SS France! Rammed her straight in the bows as she turned to go into the harbour! Cut her whole front end off, it did, terrible mess!'

'There we are.' I said to Frankie who didn't seem comforted by the news. 'Accidents happen!'

'It's a bad start, Charlie, a bad start. Wait here. I'm going to see if I can scrounge a smoke.'

He did not have to go far. Nesbit Evans produced a half-used pack of Wills Cigarettes from his tunic pocket. 'You can pay me back when you get some.'

'Hey, thanks, Taff.' Frankie's hands shook as he applied a match to the business end of his smoke, the thanks drowned out by the arrival of our allocated transport.

Rail transport, we found, was a bit hit and miss, the rolling stock already showing the effects of its existence in a war zone. We found ourselves in open cattle trucks sheltered only by a canvas roof. An old box for a seat was a luxury. The officers, of course, were directed to the few proper carriages situated just behind the engine where there was rudimentary heat. The ancient steam locomotive commissioned to pull this ramshackle assortment of cattle wagons, now containing cavalry horses, flat freight trailers loaded with heavy artillery covered with camouflaged tarpaulin, open wagons containing fighting men and the, once first class, leather upholstered carriages allocated to the officers, took on its unprecedented load. Metal spun on metal as steam blasted against pistons and delivered power to the spoked steel drive wheels, eventually achieving the necessary traction, and slowly we drew away from the rather drab port of Le Havre.

The French countryside to the south of the Somme Valley was lush and green and as yet unaffected by the strafing of gunfire, not yet pockmarked with the acne like scars caused by artillery shells. Carcasses of animals killed in action did not yet litter the roadsides and the farms and their outbuildings still had their roofs. Without break, our transport travelled on with only brief stops for men to relieve themselves alongside the track. We stopped at the supply depot in Rouen where more wagons were hitched on to the rear of our train. The coal tenders were replenished, and the engine took on water. The locomotive hissed and ticked almost contentedly. The driver and fireman exchanged banter with the trackmen in incomprehensible French, liberally seasoned with the local 'argo,' on breath heavily laced with garlic and just a hint of Calvados. All the while the unique aroma of a Gaulloise cigarette clamped into faces blackened by soot and cinders contributed to the atmosphere that was France. Then, moving once again, on through more unspoiled French countryside, finally stopping at Abbéville.

Abbéville, population just over twenty thousand, not including the influx of troops. The over-long snake of assorted wagons and carriages which formed our transport was shunted into the impromptu goods yard just outside the town's railway station. We alighted and formed up into neat ranks, our section under Jack MacGregor finally herded together in one place and united as a unit.

We marched proudly from the freight yard where we had climbed down from the train, onto the cobbled forecourt in front of the long low gothic style railway station with its clock, gothic bell tower and huge arched windows that allowed light into the public areas of the passenger station. The town itself was almost totally given over to the large military hospital, stationed in corrugated iron Nissen huts and tents, on its outskirts. A few of the neat stone-built houses with long sloped slate roofs showed signs of damage inflicted by bombs, but this was a town which was behind the lines, at least for the present time.

We would make camp just outside the hospital confines for the night, before boarding another train to Amiens and from there we would receive our orders. So explained Lieutenant Shipley, who was the officer in charge of our troop of thirty men. We found ourselves a billet for the night in one of the empty Nissen huts destined to become a hospital ward, already lined with cot beds. The thought crossed my mind that we might end up back here as patients sooner rather than later. I did not dare share this image with Frankie. For once, he curled up under his blanket and slept like a baby. I curled up under mine and, fending off disturbed dreams of Frances, I tossed and turned all that night, resisting the temptations of the flesh, but treated to the exertions of those around me who had not.

The morning brought the usual round of cold water washing at the line of standpipes and troughs which served our ablutions, a visit to the very professionally dug latrines, breakfast in the canteen tent, porridge prepared in large quantities by the ladies of the Queen Mary Auxiliary.

Frankie went looking to scrounge another cigarette and was told in no uncertain terms by his victim to, bugger off!' No ration of cigarettes had been issued and everyone was running short. I don't smoke and Frankie had already puffed his way through my allocated two ounces of tobacco. He would just have to suffer until today's ration arrived. By lunchtime we had received our supplies and were marching back through the town to board the transport to Amiens. It didn't seem to be as far to Amiens as it was reported to be to Tipperary.

The countryside leading to Amiens showed the scars of war. Buildings reduced to lone chimneys, some pointing skyward and some at gravity defying angles their walls blasted to rubble by Bosch shelling. The town itself was in friendly hands, but constantly at risk of attack. Our train stopped outside the town where Lieutenant Shipley was met by an orderly with our instructions, and we formed up to march to the front.

In ranks of three we marched along the long straight roads, flanked by trees and with farmland on either side. As we drew closer to our destination, we could hear the thud of the artillery and see the clouds of smoke rising from the battleground. The landscape changed from picturesque and pretty rural France to a desolate wasteland devoid of human life, punctured by the spikes of ruined trees and tainted by the sweet smell of rotting flesh.

CHAPTER 14. ENTRENCHED - Charlie

Shipley's Mire,
June 1916.

Was human life expected to exist in this? It was a bloody, literally bloody, living grave. Didn't all life end like this, rotting in a ten-foot-deep trench in the waterlogged, rat-infested ground? Men slept on narrow ledges which they fashioned themselves, dug into the chalky soil of the trench walls in an effort to keep themselves from sleeping in the filth they walked in daily. Soldiers were not fussy where they relieved themselves. Few used the latrines preferring to piss against the wall where they stood. The thought of running into the face of machine gun fire was enough to loosen any man's bowels. It was not unusual to find the result amongst the other detritus on the floor.

Some of the junior officers tried their best to instil some modicum of hygiene into the enlisted men, but some of them had come from a home life little better than what they found on this battlefield and paid scant regard to the requests of the company sergeants to, 'keep this fucking trench clean, you herd of pigs, yer mothers taught you better than this, didn't they!'

Would we die here? Men had. Men did. Their blood stained the walls and the floor and sometimes their bodies were not moved for days. If anyone tried to tell me now that hell was an inferno, I'd tell them they were wrong. Hell was a hole in the ground, it's floor and walls of runny, sticky cloying mud, permeated with the waste of all humankind, rife with sickness and misery, and cold, that bone chilling, never get warm cold that comes when the shadow of death awaits you every dawn and every hour in between.

To chance a look over the top of the ladder to the surface was to risk a bullet from one of the German snipers who occupied the trees some two hundred yards away and to the left, or the ones in the rocky scree to the right. But the view was nothing to look at anyway, more mud, punctuated with coils of barbed wire and mantraps, peppered with the carcasses of dead horses and mules rotting where they lay, and the bodies of our fallen comrades, those who we had not been able to drag back to safety, as if they needed safety.

Several times a day that kraut bastard hidden on the left flank would practice on us, taking pot shots which pinged off the tin helmets left to air on the lip of the trench. Prompting the cry of, '**Heads down boys!**' from the sergeant in charge, and another wave of shitting, pissing, and vomiting from the terrified young soldiers, boys, barely men, trying to make sense of a world of death. Then there was the artillery fire, launched from either direction, our own gunners firing over our heads out into the quagmire of no man's land, destroying all that remained of any recognisable structure, aiming for the German trenches. The object, being to destroy as many as possible before we were sent over the top. God bless the artillery, but they needed to improve on their range finding.

Much of what they fired over our heads fell short, and much of what found its target failed to explode. At least when the artillery was active the snipers were kept quiet. The German artillery returned fire, of course, their range finders not as accurate as ours, thank God, but they pounded away just the same. Every shell which fell yards short of its mark was cheered. The gun batteries taunted with a waving of helmets held up on long sticks. Heads were kept well down below the parapet.

Frankie was taken bad with it, he sat in the corner of the trench on an upturned slops bucket nursing his rifle or endlessly cleaning it, rocking back and fore, reciting prayers he had learned at school. Some wag had heard him and joked,

'When he gets to the one that starts *'for what we are about to receive,'* we ain't going to be truly fucking thankful, are we, my ol' mate.'

Teasing and the friendly banter of the men made him worse. He sank into his shell, staring into space. He hadn't eaten for days and had hardly drunk. He counted the days by making a mark on the trench wall, scratching five bar gates into the mud. Already thin, he was now skeletal, his uniform hanging off him as a pair of farmer's old trousers hung from a scarecrow.

I tried to jolly him along with news from the other lads, of home - we all shared our letters. Sergeant Jack read out his letters from his wife Rhianydd, Anni, who, we discovered, was a proper doctor and wanted to be useful to the troops. We had both received letters, he from Fiona, me from Frances, but for some reason this had upset Frankie. He was in love with Fiona, but she would not commit herself. I knew she loved him too, but she was driven, focussed on turning her family home into a hospital, focussed on her nursing, focussed on dragging herself through the horrors of this war. She did not have time for romance, she had said. So, he existed in a state of unabated misery as did all of us. Peppered with sniper fire at least twice daily and salted with enemy shelling in between meals.

Our officers took their orders from General Haig, strategy being dictated from the top, and it was our job just to obey orders. Jack MacGregor had pleaded to be allowed to lead a detachment to sort out the German snipers. He knew where they were. He knew that we could find them. We could do to them what they did to us. Pin them down, kill them, stay hidden and do the same to the next ones they sent. It was what we were trained for. Jack would have gone himself with Ralph, a lad who had been posted with another regiment and was very handy with a rifle. He would have sent Frankie and I as well - better we met our end doing something constructive than just sitting in our own shit, waiting for fuck knows what.

Some of the lads kept diaries, writing down how they felt, what they saw, what they experienced. It seemed to help them, but Frankie was not a diarist. He needed action. He needed to be out of this confined place, or his mind would break, if it hadn't already broken.

There was no fresh drinking water. Rum was added to what we had. It made the water taste better and it took the edge off the crippling fear which made all but the seasoned soldiers freeze when the shout came to go over the top. For my part I tried to keep myself healthy. I ate what rations were provided. I kept my feet dry. I slept as close to Frankie as I could, making my scrape out bed near to where he sat. I listened to what Jack MacGregor said of the strategy of the Officers. We had no orders as yet. It was seemingly endless sitting and waiting like ducks on the edge of a very muddy, fetid, and unpleasant pond, wing feathers clipped so we could not fly away.

It was Thursday. There had been a mail delivery and the lads of the Black Watch had come under cover of darkness with supplies for us, such as they had. They would stay with us until darkness fell again and then leave, back to the supply depot, swiftly through the blackness, on foot and silently. They were sitting, taking what ease they could, giving us news from other trenches, most were suffering as we did, when there was a sickening thud and Private Ingram who was taller than the rest of the Scotsmen by at least six inches slumped forward. Dead within seconds, the bullet had entered through his eye leaving a large hole in the back of his skull as it left. We scattered like mice before the cat into hidey holes. This sniper had been good, very good. We had heard that the German snipers had new sights for their rifles, optical sights. They could see right into our trenches, even see what we were eating for breakfast. Here was proof, one accurate shot, one dead man, job done, the first of many.

Jack MacGregor put on his tunic over his filthy shirt, tied his tie and pulled on his cap, then strode up the trench towards the officers' bunker. I followed discreetly at a distance. Jack was a quietly spoken man, but I could hear the barely controlled anger in his voice, hear the tremor in his tone. In my mind's eye I could see Lieutenant Montague Shipley, the weak chinned ferret of a man, physically wincing before Jack's words, delivered calmly, assuredly, respectfully but with menace!

'Sir,' Jack started, 'Black Watch have lost another man to that bloody sniper.'

'Sergeant MacGregor,' came the reply, 'the men have been told before to stay under cover. Make sure they do.'

'Sir, they cannot live out of sight the whole day, we must tackle the sniper problem. I will lead a detachment. We will find their nest and dispose of them. That is what my men are trained to do. We cannot fail to act. We must act now or many more will be lost. Would you have your men shot like rats in a barrel?'

'Sergeant, we await Haig's orders, we stay put, we keep our heads down, and we do as we are told. Is that clear?'

'Clear as fucking mud, sir. A few hours is all we need, sir!'

'MacGregor, you have your orders, we stay put.'

'On your head be it, Sir!'

Jack MacGregor spun on his heel and marched out, incandescent with rage, for probably the first time in his well-ordered military life. He did not reply to the parting shot from Shipley.

'Sergeant, disobey me and I will have you shot, and whatever men you take with you!'

Jack MacGregor sat at his small portable writing slope of a desk and wrote the orders. He placed them in a sealed envelope and handed them to his counterpart of the Black Watch, Malcolm Ferris.

'Take this back with you to supply. It is fer Haig's eyes only.' Jack's mild Scottish brogue became thicker 'If he will na take it, man, give it tae yer own Colonel and tell him tae keep it safe, ye ken!'

Malcolm Ferris shook his head, 'I will na give it tae Haig. My officers are sound men, I shall make sure this is safe. I din'nae know exactly what it is, but I suspect it may save lives, aye, such things have been known to vanish for lack of air, if they are sent too high up, like an officer's brains eh!'

Jack laughed, his first laugh for months.

'Turner!' he shouted, 'I know yer out there listening! Fetch Owen, and Baker! Carry Baker if you must! We have work to do! Now!'

CHAPTER 15. WITHOUT ORDERS - Charlie

30th June 1916.

    I grabbed Frankie by the collar of his shirt and frog marched him to the small bunker at the junction of the trenches, the small shelter where the sergeants had made their nest. It was empty of men except for Private Ralph Owen, a tall, athletic Welshman with jet black curly hair and disturbingly green eyes. He carried his rifle like a twig, holding it in long fingered, sensitive looking hands which looked like he probably played the piano quite well. His face broke into a very white smile.
    'Charlie Turner, is it? I've heard of you, and your friend Baker. I'm Ralph, Ralph Owen.'
    'Good to meet you, Ralph.' I offered my right hand.
    He shook my proffered hand. His was stronger than it looked, leaving a strange feeling running through my sinews and up my bones, almost a crunch.
    'How long have you been in this hell hole then?' I asked,
    'About two weeks longer than you - my section was wiped out just before you arrived. I'm the only survivor of that last push forward, criminal it was. I was lucky, I fell under one of the poor dead bastards, I stayed there 'til dark, waited here alone until you lot arrived.'
    I nodded towards the frail and jittery looking Frankie.
    'This is Frankie Baker. He may not look much just now, but he is the best shot in the regiment.'
    'So, I've been told.' replied Owen, raising a doubtful eyebrow.
    A squelch of boots on the muddy floor heralded the arrival of Sergeant Jack McGregor.
    'Sit down!' he ordered quietly, 'Listen well and make your decision when I have finished talking. We will not be disturbed.'
    We sat, as ordered, on a motley array of upturned packing cases and broken chairs which had started life as some French farmer's furniture, inherited from the last incumbents of the bunker and marked, 'Not Firewood,' as if that was going to make a difference.
    'This is a mission for volunteers,' he started. 'volunteers who are accurate with a rifle and can move with some stealth, and from my own pool of potential volunteers, which leaves you three and myself.'

He paused. 'The mission is not sanctioned by HQ. In fact, they do not know of its existence. Lieutenant Shipley does not know what I'm about and may take reprisals on us all. If we leave this trench without orders from above, we risk being shot as deserters. Do you understand?' We nodded.

Another pause. 'But if we stay inactive against the sniper fire, we will all face death without going over the top, every hour that we are here. The snipers have become more accurate. Intelligence says they have new improved optical sights, and they can pick off a man with a head shot with ease, as proven by the death of Ingram earlier today. Our mission will be to find and kill the snipers. Do you understand?'

'Yes, sir!' we replied, in unison, as if already primed.

Jack reached into a crate alongside the table and produced a bottle of Rum. Reflex made each of us produce a tin mug.

'So, who is with me? Do we act on initiative, or die in our own filth?' Frankie was the first to speak, as if shaken from a dream.

'At last, common sense! I am with you. I'd rather die fighting than sit here like a fairground coconut.'

'I'm in, sarge!' echoed Owen.

'And me, sarge' I heard my voice answer, but my mind was still digesting the enormity of what we were about to do. Jack spread out a map on the packing case. He had circled two areas, one to the right and in front of us in the woodland about five hundred yards away, the other to the left, a similar distance and in a rocky outcrop, hidden by gorse and light scrub.

'From the direction of fire, I have worked out that our German friends are dug in here and here.' He stabbed the map with his finger in the appropriate places.

'They are armed with standard issue Mauser rifles. They would usually have a range of about five hundred yards, but our intelligence and recent experience suggests their new sights increase their accuracy over distance, and their effective range by three hundred yards. Hence, they can now pick us off at will from a long way out.'

He stopped for a drink from his mug, grimaced and continued.

'They dig in and are relieved after three days when a fresh man with three days supplies takes over. That day, gentlemen, is tomorrow, by my reckoning at around 6am - they like to run by the clock. We will catch them as they change over. They have only one optical sight per position so there is a window of opportunity while the incoming man is setting up and calibrating his rifle. But remember – the left-hand position is in firing range from the right and vice versa. If we are seen by either side during our approach, we are all viable targets. Your thoughts, gentlemen?'

Frankie suddenly came to life. 'Charlie and I will take the scree - we're smaller than Taff, here. He'll be better concealed by the trees.'

'Suits me,' replied Owen, 'and less of the Taff, butty bach, at least until you've bought me a pint!'

'Right!' said Jack, finally, rounding up proceedings. 'We leave at dusk. No one must know we are gone. Clean your rifles in here and don't attract attention to it. We'll black up in the next trench just before we get going. I will have ammunition for all of us. Oh, and if it all goes to smash, there is a copy of my orders housed with the commander of the Black Watch. It may save you if Shipley comes for us, he is a vindictive little snake, don't trust him, whatever he says!'

Frankie went and sat on his perch, cleaned his rifle, and resumed his normal rocking and praying routine, but there was a light in those pale blue eyes of his that had not been switched on for weeks.

I sought out Ralph Owen and tried to get the truth from him about his former regiment. What he said, well it didn't ring true. Was he a hero, a coward, or something else completely? I found him at the far end of our trench where a narrow passage only as wide as a man's shoulders led the fifty yards to the next series of earthworks. Here there was a small area where the mud was not churned to slurry. The next trench was deserted, or so it had appeared. It was true that a whole battalion had been lost in there and the bodies of those that had made it back to die still lay unburied. No one went in there. But, what joy, it was a way out, a way out into the woods and onto the flanks. It was a blind spot, a safe corner, and these were few and far between in this little part of France

Ralph Owen sat on his heels. A groundsheet was spread out on the floor before him where his rifle was lying in pieces for cleaning. Those long fingers worked swiftly over the mechanics of each piece, swabbing them with oil, passing the long-weighted cloth down the barrel, then reassembling it all with amazing speed. He could do this in the dark. He did not look up until he had finished. He began to speak as I sat alongside, mesmerised by his dexterity.

'Monmouth regiment, if you must know. My section got isolated. No way forward and no way back. Poor bastards. Those who could crawl back died where they fell into the trench. I expect it'll be their grave. You'll see when we go through it tonight, but it's the only safe way out and into the wood.'

His green eyes looked directly at me, holding me with a gaze which went straight to my soul. He went on.

'There's no room for doubt, Charlie, we are all dead men anyway. Orders must have come. I heard Shipley throwing up with fear in his officer's private bucket!'

He held out a hip flask to me. 'Have a nip of some good stuff, none of that Scottish crap. This is Welsh. We don't make much of it, but it will put hairs on your chest and give you balls like a bull!'

'May I use your kit, mate?'

'Feel free, if this goes wrong I may not need it again!' He laughed.

Genuine enough then, on the surface, but somehow I still had my doubts. He would not be drawn into conversation on any subject which involved family, or home. I knew from experience that most Welshmen loved to talk, and their favourite subject was their homeland.

I stripped down my faithful Enfield .303 rifle and started my well-practiced cleaning routine, then sharpened my bayonet, and my smaller fighting knife until both would cut a falling sheet of paper. Owen nodded approvingly.

As dusk fell, the four of us met again at the entrance to the narrow passage between the trenches. Ralph knew the way. None of us had ever been into the next-door trench. He replaced the boards which closed off the passage behind us, then, squeezing past us, he led us into a ready-made grave and already filled. Bodies, disfigured bodies lay in positions adopted by circus contortionists, twisted limbs, faces purple and pale, frozen in pain, bellies bloating through battle dress and the smell of rotting flesh, sweet and sticky, hanging in our nostrils and on our clothing. I wretched and put a hand out to support myself as I threw up.

'Breath through your mouth, Turner, we'll be through this bit soon enough.' whispered Jack MacGregor, as I heaved the contents of my stomach into the fetid soup of rotting detritus we were walking through. Eventually we got to the end of it and arrived at our destination. Trees overhung the earthworks, their roots reaching out through the soil walls. A wooden ladder was already propped against the parapet.

'Black up!' Jack gave the order. Then he handed me the map, 'Follow the stream, Charlie. That will take you behind our lines, then follow the scree line along, keep low, our target is in the scree at the start of no man's land.'

Each of us was armed with a rifle and bayonet and all except Ralph carried the fighting knife issued to our battalion as standard. We'd been taught to fight with one. Kept sharp, many of our comrades shaved with them, instead of a razor. Ralph also carried a knife, his own, a thin balanced blade designed for throwing, but he said he preferred to use his hands, if things got as he said, 'up close and personal.' Hands not, perhaps, as delicate as they, at first, had appeared.

Frankie and I headed off like a pair of sheepdogs, noses to the ground, away to the left, through the woods and out onto the scree, crouched low, sniffing for sheep, feeling our way over the ground, our eyes gradually becoming accustomed to the darkness. Carrying only our weapons and enough ammunition for three days in a light pack, our usual rig had been left behind, conveniently conspicuous, to give the impression we were still in the trench, somewhere. But we were not.

A few hours later dawn broke over the Somme valley, it was July.

CHAPTER 16. GERMANS ARE ALWAYS ON TIME – Jack MacGregor

1st July 1916.

    Rain dripped through the foliage. The rain had stopped, but the leaves were still busy emptying themselves onto the ground. The moss and leaf mould beneath him was still dry, but this would soon change if he moved. For a few stolen moments Jack was lost in the scent of a French summer morning, the weather undecided, the rain laden clouds bobbing at anchor in a sky which was trying its best to smile with a few rays of sunshine. In these moments he could banish the sights and smells of death from his mind and be at peace with a world which could not make peace with itself.
    He thought about Rhianydd, how did she fare with a new baby, a child he had never met. He could feel the carefully folded lump of her letter in his breast pocket, with his paybook. He would have loved to read it over again, but the movement involved in its retrieval would risk his life. He could visualise the words anyway and that would have to do.
    He was dug in in a hollow under a large oak tree, nestled between its roots with a fine and unobstructed view of the German snipers' den. It was a long shot, nearly maximum range for the Enfield even with the optical sights, and he would only get one chance. Time spent in reconnaissance is rarely wasted and it had paid off. Ralph was a short distance away in a similar scraped out nest to his own and with a clear view of the path the enemy snipers took when they relieved each other of duty. Always the same time, always the same rotation, a schoolboy error, he considered, or a show of extreme over confidence. Jack wriggled his hips flatter into the scraped-out earth releasing the rain drop which had been perched between his shoulder blades. He felt it run down his spine, under his belt and down the cleft of his buttocks, one of many that would make the same journey before he could move to any great extent. He clenched his bum-cheeks together, arresting its progress so that it soaked into his regulation army underwear.
    Ralph would be suffering the same privations, of that he was sure. He checked the view down the sight again and looked sideways through the trees. He could only just make out Ralph's khaki clad form, about fifteen yards away, so still he could be part of the moss-covered ground he lay on.

Jack had known the Welshman only a few weeks and already marvelled at his ability to disappear into his surroundings. One minute he would be there, large as life, and he was large, the next he would have faded into nothingness, almost ghostlike. He had an uncanny knack of being in the right place at the right time, and, though he handled his rifle like a cow with a toothpick, he was a crack shot with it, and he could throw a knife accurately enough to kill a man over the length of a cricket pitch. The man had all the required skills and Jack wasn't about to ask too many questions about him. It was enough that he was on their side. He waited. Timing was crucial. He knew that the German marksmen relieved their comrades at the same time and the dug out on the other flank did the same.

Frankie and Charlie were, he hoped, plotted up similarly to himself and Ralph. The fresh sniper would take up position. The relieved man and he would share a cigarette and exchange a few words and a nip from a metal flask. Then, he'd crawl the short distance out of cover to the narrow path which would take him back to the German lines and relative safety. There was a window of only a few seconds when both snipers were vulnerable, and Jack's little expedition had to hit them all together or be sitting ducks themselves. Then they could retrace their own route back to that muddy hellhole they called home, safe from bullets at least for the time being. It was a plan fraught with danger, probably a recipe for disaster, but all four of them would rather be killed doing something, than sit like mice waiting for the cat to come out to play.

Jack picked a blade of rain-soaked grass from just in front of his nose wedged it in the small gap in his front teeth and savoured its freshness. It was nearly time; he could sense it. The hair on his neck had started to bristle like a dog and the air around him was becoming charged with expectation and impatience. He checked his line of sight one more time, mentally making the calculation to allow for the fall of the bullet over distance, and the light, warm French breeze.

Jack heard the crunch of boots before he saw the soldier, a scruffy Corporal wearing the grey uniform of an infantryman, with red piping, his collarless shirt open at the neck, tunic buttons undone to his chest, hair slightly longer than was acceptable from what Jack had seen of the enemy army. Jack would put him in his early twenties, unshaven and showing signs of the light scruffy stubble of one who did not grow a substantial beard. The Mauser rifle however, shone in the sunlight, another mistake, thought Jack, and the hands that cradled it as he weaved through the bushes to the hide were long fingered and artistic, the nails short trimmed and manicured clean, even allowing for the ingrained dirt which permeated the rest of him.

Jack's mental picture of his target saw him as a student, an educated boy, still living at home, intelligent and artistic. He probably played the piano and played it well. His mind drifted to a quieter night in the trench they called Shipley's Mire. A night when there had been a break in the shelling, and through the occasional distant crack of gunfire from a faraway ridge they had heard the Germans celebrating something, and through the still night air he had heard the sound of a fiddle being played. A pound to a pinch this boy was the fiddler. He probably played piano as well.

As Jack watched, his target emerged from the hide. He did not smoke, but chatted with his newly arrived comrade, lazily passing the time of day while they handed over. Getting ready to leave, his mate, an older sweat, buttoned up his tunic, adjusted his cap to face forwards and lit a cigarette. The sounds of muted German carried on the light breeze. The flask passed between them, was it Brandy or Schnaps, Jack wondered? The older man picked up his rifle, tapped his relief on the shoulder, and then lay back down. In horror, Jack saw both snipers take up firing position, Ralph's shot would not be possible.

The shrill blast of an officer's whistle from their own trenches shattered his thoughts. SHIT!

Then the distant cry of, 'Over the top men, get at them!'

He saw both snipers squeeze their triggers, heard the crack of the rifles firing.

Jack squeezed the trigger of the Enfield, the older man's temple large in the optic sight. He flinched for a moment with the recoil, but the shot was good. The man slumped forward, the remains of his head resting on his gun stock.

From his left, Jack heard more shots fired, then silence, then the cheers from the British soldiers relieved from the unseen threat from the sidelines. The fiddler was also dead. As Jack watched, he saw Ralph removing the long, perfectly balanced, razor-sharp throwing knife from the lad's neck. He would not be playing the fiddle anymore. Sad that - Jack had rather enjoyed listening to him.

Placing two fingers in his mouth, Jack whistled a signal to Ralph and pointed out the direction they should run. Along the forest track, they picked up Frankie and Charlie at the fork by the big oak tree. In front of them a battle was raging, and men were dying in their hundreds. The British troops were struggling through the wire and the traps laid in darkness while the British officers had waited, doing nothing, laying no plans. The Germans had been busy. The heavy artillery pounded the earth to shreds, reinforced by rifle-fire from dugouts and placements all across the wasted patch of earth called no-man's land.

Jack cast his eye across what was unfolding before him. His mentor Archie Cameron had taught him well. He guided the four of them to a small patch of high ground to the left of the action. The cover was good, light scrub trees, with thick tufts of grass beneath. From this concealed point they could see the German dug outs clearly.

'So, we pick them off, one by one! We don't have much in the way of ammunition, so make every one count!'

Silently, the crack unit of the St. Pancras rifles made themselves invisible and began to do what they did best. It did not go unnoticed.

One by one, German riflemen began to fall. Jack became aware that field glasses were being trained on their position. They would need to move, and soon. They were also nearly out of bullets. Before he could give the order to move, he heard movement behind him and felt the prod of something metallic behind his ear, just above the collar of his shirt.

'Put down your weapons and then none of you move.'

The command came in heavily accented English. The voice was cultured, home counties English but with a definite German accent. Jack sensed that they were all in the same unenviable position. Prisoners.

They were searched, thoroughly, while they lay prostrate on the floor, hands behind their heads, in the efficient manner they had come to expect of the German army. Then, pulled roughly to their feet and with their hands raised, marched not towards the German lines, but further up the hill.

Three of them captured, Ralph had melted away into the forest, invisible as only he knew how to be. Jack knew he would be following them, unseen and unheard. Wherever he had got to, he had had the presence of mind to take his rifle so that there was nothing to mark the presence of a fourth man. He may not be looked for. Jack shot a sideways glance at Frankie and Charlie, a slight shake of his head and a look that clearly indicated they should say nothing to suggest that there had been four of them. Frankie was looking mutinous. One sniff of an opportunity and he was likely to bolt, getting them all killed. They must bide their time. They seemed to be heading south, towards Abbéville. Jack knew that the British held Abbéville, but now that the ground Shipley was supposed to hold had been lost, there was nothing between Abbéville and German occupation.

They reached the top of the rise at the highest point of the forest. From this vantage point, all three men could see the heavy artillery of the enemy ranged on the lower slopes, all trained on Abbéville, and nothing to prevent their advance save about eight miles of French farmland. They were herded into a small corral erected near a large tree, tied hand and foot and to the tree. Nothing to do for the present except wait, darkness may present an opportunity, or Ralph might make an appearance. As the sun descended into the trees and their German captors began to settle for the night, a guard was posted at the entrance to their makeshift prison.

The smell of some form of stew emerging from a cooking pot hung over a campfire, reminded them that they had not eaten since breakfast, and that had been the singularly unappetising porridge served up every morning by the mess cook.

Charlie's belly grumbled as his nose took in the smell of some form of sausage cooked in gravy. Frankie looked as if he would collapse if he were not fed soon, Jack swallowed the saliva which was watering in his mouth and looked for a blade of grass to chew, at least that would give his teeth something to do.

They sat close together for warmth, the French evenings were chilly, and contemplated their fate. Eventually the guard was changed and the officer who had taken them returned. His name was Albert Schulz. He was a Captain of artillery. He came bearing three mess tins with a small ration of stew, a flask of schnaps and three blankets.
In his thickly accented English, he spoke to Jack.

'You are their sergeant, yes?'

'I am.' replied Jack.

'You were not acting on orders, were you.'

'I used my initiative.'

'You realise initiative could get you a court martial. Sergeant MacGregor, isn't it?'

'We have had a spy in your trench for weeks, Sergeant MacGregor - long enough to know that your officer, Shipley, is a fool!'

'Lieutenant Shipley has much on his mind.' Jack was defensive of the officer even though he knew the German spoke the truth.

'Lieutenant Shipley has lost your army its advantage. Tomorrow, we march on Abbéville. Your trenches are empty. There is nothing now to stop us. Capture Abbéville and we have a route to the coast.'

'Why do you tell me this?'

'You caused my friends a lot of trouble. They have lost many good men. Shipley should have deployed you from the start as you begged him to do.'

'All this is immaterial, Herr Capitan Schulz. We are captured, what will you do with us?'

'Once we take Abbéville, you will be taken to a detention camp. Do not try and escape. My marksmen are as good if not better than yours and they hunt in pairs. Is it not usual for your men to hunt in pairs, sergeant?'

'Uh, huh.' Jack muttered through a spoonful of gravy.

'I assumed one of your men was dead, until I received the report from my General on his losses. He has found no British sniper's body amongst his dead. Where is your number four Sergeant MacGregor?'

'If I knew, I would kill him myself, cowardly Welshman. He has deserted - he had no stomach for killing.'

'Tut-tut, MacGregor, you will have to do better than that! He is the man with the knife. I have seen his handiwork, and you, sergeant, will never make a good liar. He will turn up, and we will be waiting.' Schulz turned and strode from the stockade.

'Good night, Capitan Schulz.'

'Gute Nacht, Sergeant MacGregor.' came the reply.

CHAPTER 17. SURGEONS IN KHAKI – Doctor Robert Jones M.D.

July 1st, 1916
Field Hospital Abbéville. France

Field Diary of Captain Surgeon Robert Jones RAMC

It's eleven o'clock here and the night is pitch-black with threatening rain. It has been raining all day. Shelling has been heavy over the trenches and the scream of artillery shells and the crack of rifle fire has been assaulting our ears for most of the day. It continued into early evening.

We have had a hellish busy night. Every stretcher party we could muster from the various ambulances was out in the field collecting the wounded. The operating tent is pretty well prepared and gets brilliantly lit up with the huge acetylene lamp we somehow managed to acquire from stores. The operating table is centre stage in the middle of the tent and along each side are the instruments, basins, and dressings lying on the lids of the panniers which have made excellent side-tables. Sam O'Connor was ready to deliver any surgical help he could. Sister Delaney acted as anaesthetist. We've had no third medic to act as such and Sister Delaney is remarkably proficient in the role, really getting the hang of it. She's been taught the basics by a Dr Boyle who's constructed some kit he can carry around on his back. Ether and Chloroform. Hope there's not an explosion!

Very soon after we were on stand-by and it all kicked off, the ambulances lumbered up with the men picked up from the fields closer at hand. The stretchers, each holding a wounded man, get taken out of the wagons and laid on a heap of straw near the door of the operating tent, ready to be carried in. Straw seems to be the best way to ensure a mud free arrival at our table. It's good for blood, too!

Sixteen men were taken out and laid side by side waiting for our attention with more following. New stretchers were put in the wagons, which again set out to bring in more wounded. Quietly and quickly, one wounded man after another was lifted on to the table, wounds speedily dressed, and carried out again and laid on the straw with a blanket below and another above him. Those with painful wounds were given hypodermics of morphia. All who were fit to take nourishment had hot soup, tea, bread, and jam. Stimulants were given freely to those requiring them. The wounds were mostly from shrapnel, and only one case required an anaesthetic. He had a bad compound fracture of his left femur and was in terrible pain.

One of the recovering men from earlier had been put to work fashioning effective splints from the slats of wood salvaged from supply cases, pretty effective, too. The limb was fixed up comfortably and in good position. One poor devil had a bad abdominal wound for which we could do nothing. He was given a good dose of morphia and slept quietly till five this morning, when he ceased to breathe.

One of the officers retrieved from the battlefield carried no identification at all. He was hit both by shrapnel to his neck and face, and also by rifle fire through his lumbar spine. If he recovers, he'll certainly never walk again. I managed to remove the Mauser bullet lodged above his iliac crest, but his first lumbar vertebra is totally shattered.

The shrapnel wound to his neck severely damaged his larynx, he'll likely never talk again. By some miracle it had missed his carotid arteries, but maybe it would have been a blessing if it had not.
Sam and I sewed him up after an hour of probing and stitching. Sister D dosed him thoroughly with morphia and bandaged his neck and face to give the stitches some support. His life hangs in the balance.

At one o'clock in the morning, wounded were still coming in. With coat off, bare arms and wearing just an operating apron, Sam and I have continued our spell of surgical duty all night in this small town on the banks of the Somme.

Our stretcher parties at last were finished. It was reported that all the wounded that could be reached had been brought in. We have made them as comfortable as possible and wait for news of transport. The railhead at Abbéville is destroyed and no rail transport is available to Dieppe. We'll have to sit tight and wait for horse drawn wagons, though horses are in short supply. Those not worn out from overwork are pulling artillery to the front. Those still with flesh have likely been butchered. Having made a last round of our patients, I fell exhausted into my cot. I am not a religious man, but I do have faith in something and before I slept, I prayed for some sort of miracle. This war is closing in around us so if there is a god who is listening, please don't let us get surrounded.

CHAPTER 18. WARRIORS FROM WHERE?

July 3rd, 1916
Abbéville. France.

The Germans treated us fairly. They had little food or supplies, but they kept us fed, even if we were confined and tied to a bloody tree.

'Fuck this for a game of soldiers!' Frankie grumbled. 'I need to stretch my legs. I need my freedom. Jack says to play the game, do as they say and wait. He has endless faith in that Welsh bastard Ralph, wherever he is. I say we break out.' Frankie was muttering to himself into his blanket, but just loud enough for Charlie to hear him.

'We'd be dead before we got a hundred yards, you idiot. Haven't you been listening? The krauts are waiting for the rest of their force to cross our trenches. All our men are gone, Frankie! Killed, Frankie - D.E.A.D dead. Comprendi? If we go back the way we came, they will find us and kill us, too. If we go forwards, it's into open country and there's no cover and this lot are about to take the town. So, do as Jack says - and wait, and no fucking heroics. Got it?'

'But it has been three fucking days and there's no sign of him. What if he's dead?'

'No fucking heroics Frankie! We wait.'

And so, we waited, another two days. We heard the sounds of men and equipment arriving for the attack on the town. We could not wait much longer - I was beginning to see Frankie's point of view.

The guard did not see him, or hear him, and did not feel his head being partly severed from his body, which was lowered to the floor soundlessly, an arm like a steel hawser supporting its weight all the while. The blade had traversed his neck just below his larynx making a hole in his trachea that rendered speech impossible. As he gasped for air, the nick in his internal jugular vein let in a sizeable quantity of air that, with luck, would be sufficient to end this final and alarming chapter of his life. Then, on the subject of holes, a hole appeared in the fence which surrounded them and the ropes which secured them were cut with no fuss, just a workmanlike quiet. Frankie was silenced with a swift blow to the head. He would come round soon enough, but his running commentary was unnecessary and a distraction.

Ralph roused Jack by the arm, indicating silence with a finger to his lips. Beckoning for them to follow, the four of them disappeared into the woodland, Jack and Charlie carrying Frankie between them.
The huge Welshman led them to a clearing in the forest some short distance away. It was not quite clear exactly what was going on.

'We cannot let them take the town!' Ralph hissed at Jack.

'What can we do with four of us and nae weapons?' grunted the wiry Scotsman. 'Even with weapons we have precious little hope. They have artillery, and numbers, ye ken!'

'If we could get close enough, we could spike the guns.' suggested Charlie.

'Hmm,' considered Ralph. 'Have you ever spiked a gun? We'd never get that close, and they never leave them unguarded. They move on the town tomorrow, early, now that the troops that cleared our trenches have caught up with their artillery. They are about fifty strong, but all seasoned men, I have been amongst them.'

'How?' asked Jack, not really wanting to know the answer.

'Don't worry about that, sarge, but we do need a plan and we need help! I can find the help. You make the plan!' Ralph started to draw with a stick on a bare patch of earth.

'This is how their camp is laid out, see, and it won't be too difficult to get away – here or here.' He pointed with his stick. 'They're too busy thinking about tomorrow's offensive but we don't have long before they'll notice you gone. They will look for you but they can't afford the men to search far or spend too long on you lot. They have orders. They're expected to move on Abbéville without delay.'

Jack looked at the layout and frowned. 'I din'nae think gettin' oot's possible, man an' we can'nae take them in the camp. Better we let them roll out. They can only take this route down the slope to the town. The track is narrow, and the guns are drawn by horses, you say. That will take time. The men will have to march either before or behind them or take the rough terrain through the woods. The best chance if we had twenty good men, is to hit them while they are strung out in a line and moving. But we don't have twenty men!'

'But, yes, we do!' Ralph waved a hand at the trees.
As the little band of desperados followed Ralph Owen's gaze, they began to make out the figures of men as they quietly rose from the shadows of

the trees, more than twenty of them. Charlie had never seen such beings before. These were not regular soldiers - local partisans perhaps, dressed as they were in green and white tunic, and armed only with longbows, and knives? They gathered shoulder to shoulder as if each one were an indivisible part of the whole. Ralph spoke in a language only Jack amongst them had heard before, Welsh. Frankie, who had just recovered his senses, lost them again in an instant as he saw medieval archers materialising from the trees around him, mysteriously rising from the bushes and forming up in ranks behind a singular, tall, imposing figure dressed in a Green and Buff tunic and carrying a longbow with a quiver of arrows slung on his back. There was complete silence. Then their leader stepped forward and introduced himself in eloquent English, finely contaminated with the aura of the mid-Welsh and a voice from the wild hills.

'Hear me! I am Gwyn ap Meredith. These men are sworn to me! They are from another time! They can be here because they fought in another war on this very ground! These are the Welsh archers of Crécy! These are my men, and we serve a mistress more powerful than you can know. Have you not questioned Ralph's presence amongst you – he of the knife? He too is one of us! We are not of your time. I was sent for a purpose, but the lines of time have become crossed. I should not be here. My time is four hundred years ago. The lady I serve will not be best pleased.'

'How can they fight modern weapons?' gasped Jack. 'They will be cut down like wheat at harvest time!'

Ralph replied. 'You cannot fight what you cannot see, Jack MacGregor! They choose to be visible to you, as do I. But, when the time comes they will be like wraiths in the mist!'

'Why would they help us?' chipped in Charlie.

Gwyn spoke. 'You, Jack MacGregor. I have news. My mistress seeks the services of a healer, a healer who can walk through time, who can see through its veil. She sees that that healer will come here to Abbéville, to the hospital. She will travel with her daughter, and another, to treat the wounded there. The daughter is your wife.'

Eyes wide with disbelief, Jack cried out, 'You are mistaken, my wife cannot come, she is at home, she is a woman, she will not be allowed to the front with the men!'

'Believe me, Jack MacGregor, she will travel. There is much about your wife you do not know!'

'We have a daughter. How can she leave our daughter and come here?'

'Your daughter is safe. Do not fear for little Agnes, she is well cared for, and do not doubt, your wife and her mother will be here.'

The action was reflex, one acquired from years of training. Jack's left hand removed Gwyn's knife from its sheath with the speed of striking snake, and with the point pressed into the huge man's throat, quietly bid him.

'Cease this nonsense! Sit down and tell me who you are. You know far too much for my comfort, and none of the rest makes sense!'

Gwyn's hands raised slightly, palms open in submission. He continued, quietly and with a distant look in his eye as if from a different life.

'Have a care Jack, you could injure someone with that. It is sharp enough to shave the moustache from your face and to remove the nose from above it.'

While he was talking, he motioned with his eyes and the men ranged behind him retreated into the trees, vanishing from sight in that uncanny way that Ralph so often used. Gwyn himself bent his knees and, taking Jack with him, lowered his huge frame onto a nearby log. He motioned to Frankie and Charlie to join them. Gwyn cleared his throat and began to speak.

'I was born in the year of our lord 1330 on a small farm in Wales. My father was a farmer, and I had a mother and a sister. In those times all men and boys were taught to use the longbow, and if required, they were called to fight for their king. Like all other boys, I learned at my father's knee. He had fought the Scots at Bannockburn, and he taught me well. I was sent to the Castle at Llantrisant to be trained further in warfare, and when war came, I marched with the Black Prince to France. On these very lands, at Crécy we fought a great battle. We were victorious and many men stayed with the army and fought on through France. Two days after the battle an arrow intended for another laid me low. It was tipped with a curse, and I lay sleeping until the healer, Sibyl, and the Lady Margaret, the mistress I must now serve, woke me. The price of the cure was that I serve the Lady Margaret in whatever she demands of me. She has the power to raise the souls of the men of Crécy, my men, and she has work for them. She has looked across the veil and sees all. Your wife will come, Jack MacGregor, and her mother with her, for they are not wholly of your world.'

Jack addressed his next comment to Ralph. 'So, you are asking me to believe that you are six hundred years old?'

'Aye man, and not looking bad on it, am I?' Then he, too began to disappear into the mist.

Jack grunted, a cross between a snort and a cough. 'I did wonder about you. You always were a strange bastard - I suppose the art of disappearance ...''

'Is part of the deal...., yes ..., amongst other things...' taunted Ralph, vanishing from view. 'Fun isn't it, but now we need to make plans.' Gwyn ap Meredith called into the darkness and Ralph Owen materialised alongside him, grinning.

CHAPTER 19. THE PRIVILEGE OF RANK – Lt. Montague Shipley

July 3rd, 1916
Second Field Hospital
Abbéville. France.

    Montague Shipley opened his eyes to find himself staring at the canvas roof of a large tent. Through a haze of pain and opium, his senses started to tune in to his surroundings. He moved his eyes and found that his field of vision was restricted by some form of bandage. Breathing in, he smelled the disinfectant smells of some form of hospital or field dressing station mixed with the smell of blood while his ears picked up the groans of men and calls of 'nurse.' He closed his eyes again and tried to recall the events which had brought him here. He could remember nothing except the word Abbéville and the name MacGregor. A lithe figure in a white apron covering her light blue uniform dress lifted the blanket which covered his arms, he felt the sharp prick of a needle and
drifted back off to a warm delirium, floating on a sea of poppies.
    Dr Samuel O'Connor pushed his sandy hair back from his thin, weathered face and sighed deeply, looking down at the man on the cot bed in front of him, wondering how the human body could survive such damage and still support life. The shrapnel had hit the lieutenant in the throat. His voice box was badly damaged, and they'd done a tracheostomy so that he could breathe, the chunk of metal he had removed had managed to miss every major vessel on its way through. Another bullet had shattered a couple of lumbar vertebrae, L1 and L2 to be precise, but that was of little immediate consequence. It was unlikely this man would survive in this hellhole, let alone walk again. The few years left to him before the toll of paralysis, immobility and lack of sensation started to cause his organs to fail, would be spent in a chair, and likely he would never talk again, with little functional larynx remaining and his jaw being so disfigured as it was. 'Fuck!' thought Sam.
    His colleague, Dr. Robert Jones, the officer in charge of the hospital, appeared at the opposite side of the bed and gestured to the tent flap. 'Are we expecting company?'
    An officer of some rank was striding towards the tent, a brigadier by his badges of rank and the entourage of hangers-on.

'Not that I know of.,' replied O'Connor in his soft Irish voice, 'We were inspected last week, and it's been busy on the front. I've hardly stopped for a piss in the last few days.'

'This can't be a social visit, can it?'

The General came to an abrupt halt in front of him. Jones threw up a very unsoldierly salute - drill was not a priority in the medical corps. Jones carried the rank of captain, but preferred 'doctor' as his chosen denomination. It seemed to say more about the situation.

'General Gerald Shipley, Captain. I believe you have my brother amongst your wounded - Lieutenant Montague Shipley.' The voice immediately indicated the speaker's county of origin.

'We do have a lieutenant sir. Brought in from the last offensive, badly wounded. Not good, I'm afraid. You'd better take a look, Sir. Frankly, I couldn't say if he's your brother or not. His uniform was that torn, and it was difficult to identify…..,' his voice trailed off. 'and we were that busy he was just left by the stretcher bearers along with the rest.'

'Show me, man, is he conscious?'

'He is under morphine and very sick. If he is your brother, he has taken shrapnel in his neck and a bullet through his spine. He is in a great deal of pain and a long way from any form of recovery.'

The doctor walked with the General back into the hospital tent, all bluster now gone. Gerald Shipley looked at the bed which held the bandage swathed body of the lieutenant. He took the left hand which was placed across the patient's abdomen and turned it over. Bending close to it he examined the base of the thumb and, seeing the two small star shaped scars, he turned his tear-filled eyes to Dr. Jones.

'He speared himself on a fishing hook as a child. I pulled it out, it left a mark, mother was furious, he was always her favourite. This is my brother, Captain. Please see he has the best care, fool that he is.'

'He will have the care we give every patient sir, under the circumstances. If you can help us get him moved home there is new surgery which could help him mend, reconstruct his face, that is his best chance. Mount Vernon hospital, that's the place, Hertfordshire, pioneering stuff, but it'll take time

'Thank you, Dr O'Connor but now to other matters. You need to prepare to evacuate or at least for some lively action. There's a battalion of Bosch artillery behind those woods on the hill. Our spies say they have orders to take the town. They are waiting for the troops my idiot brother conceded ground to, to catch up with them. You have a day or two before they move on you, at most.

'General, I have sixty bed bound casualties, including your brother. I have another forty, walking wounded. They could be moved out but the bed casualties, they cannot. Unless you can provide wagons for transport we are stuck in the line of fire and must hope they respect our status as a hospital. Few of the men are able to hold a rifle, never mind fire it.'

'I'll do my best for you, Captain, but no guarantees, resources are stretched. We have wagons but no horses, guns but no ammunition. The whole bloody shooting match has turned to farce. If no one takes a firm grip, we will all be overrun by the end of the month.'

General Gerald Shipley turned on his well-polished and very well-worn boots and walked away, shoulders slumped in thought. Dr Robert Jones was left feeling that Gerald Shipley at least was a man of his word and, if nothing else, would walk through the fires of hell for his brother. As Samuel O'Connor joined him, the two medical men turned to face each other. O'Connor spoke first. 'Time to send our nurses back then?'

'You can try, but they won't go, and Phyllis and Brenda at least can handle a gun if it comes to it. Ask, no, order Sister Delaney to start mobilising her walking wounded. Those who can fight can stay but she must be firm with the rest. Don't ask her Sam, order her. She must go with them, if we can get them out, and Sam, when was the last time you cleaned your revolver?'

'Don't worry, Cap' she's fine and dandy, ye forget where I'm from, 'tis always best to be prepared in the home country.'

Whistling as he walked, O'Connor went in search of his countrywoman Nursing Sister Josephine Delaney. He'd been sweet on her for months and getting nowhere. Sister Delaney's wit was as sharp, if not sharper than her scissors, and Dr O'Connor's bedside manner was not as sharp as his scalpel.

Dr Jones chuckled to himself as heard the piping strains of Tipperary disappearing towards the sacred canvas edifice where the off-duty nurses escaped to try and retrieve some semblance of normality. It was spacious and khaki, but still just a tent, adorned with all manner of drying underwear and other accoutrements of femininity. It was difficult being a woman in a warzone, but standards were there to be maintained, after all.

Propriety and decorum were their watchwords. Personal laundry must be done, but discreetly. Thus, on sunnier days, the guy ropes of the huge bell tent were often adorned with an array of knickers, corsets, underskirts, and aprons – quite a welcome distraction when all was said and done. Occasionally, the high winds blowing in from the sea would dislodge an item or two, and a red-faced private walking with a crutch or with his head bandaged would return it to its home. Some enquired after the owner. Most were just happy to return the item and lapse into revery of whose feminine form occupied it on a regular basis. Only one set of clothing was off limits for discussion, that of Sister Delaney. Sister Delaney's undergarments were fine indeed, mainly of silk edged with lace, and the finest Parisian at that.

Many a soldier, wounded or not, had harboured secretive thoughts about what, if anything, Sister Delaney wore when her laundry was pegged out in the wind. Dr O'Connor was among the most imaginative, and frequently considered the result of making any sort of enquiry in that direction. As he approached the tent the hospital had christened, 'Hell's Bell', because of its shape and the thoughts it generated, it was obviously washing day.

Sister Josephine was sitting at her writing slope updating the diary and making notes. In front of her was, also, a pile of letters home from her colleagues, She was required to read them all and censor their content, not to give any intelligence to the Bosch. It was the job she hated most, reading her nurses' thoughts and feelings, but most had learned to be discrete, in their writing at least.

Samuel O'Connor tapped on the tent flap and reinforced the dull thump with a jovial, 'Knock, Knock! Anyone at home?'

'And who might be enquiring?' came the lilting reply, dripping with sarcasm.

Thinking better of some inept attempt at humour, he replied 'Ah, tis only me, the green-eyed Derry boy!'

'Park it! Sure, you can see I'm a bit busy at present, Dr. O'Connor.'

She didn't look up just waved towards a canvas stool, or an empty ammunition box as alternatives to standing. He chose the stool, which promptly sank its back legs into the soft ground of the floor of the tent, depositing him in a thoroughly un-doctorly heap on the floor.

'Eejit!' Josephine stifled a throaty chuckle. 'And so, what can I be doin' for you?'

'All manner of things that I would never repeat even in private!' The chuckle came again.

'This is work then, not pleasure, I suppose?'

'Aye, sure, it is. You've to mobilise your wounded. There is threat of an attack in the next few days. Artillery have been sighted over that small, wooded hill, headed our way. The Bosch want Abbéville for their own.'

'I've about twenty fit to walk, the rest are weak as kittens, or they can't see. Are they sending wagons, if not I won't move them. The twenty are mostly Black Watch - they'd rather die than retreat. The rest are Welsh and just as stubborn.'

'This is not a request Jo! It's an order.'

'Well tell whoever issued it to cram it, as you paddies say, 'up their arse!' Unless there's transport, they'd be better either fighting or relying on the mercy of their captors. What are you doing with the beds then?'

'We've perhaps two we can move. The rest will be taken if it all goes to smash! We're not a fighting unit, Josephine. We have no formal arms training. We can defend ourselves, but we cannot make war. That is against the oath, so its self-defence only for us.'

'Then we bloody well defend ourselves, I'll not run. I'll not leave these poor men to be butchered by the Bosch!'

Josephine's blue eyes were dark with fire, her Irish accent becoming thicker with every word. 'That's my final word. Tell the Cap my nurses will be with him to the last!'

'Now Jo, if they send wagons, at least let the worst off go to safety and the younger nurses too. Brenda and Phyllis will stay, but let the others go. Who knows what the Germans may do, they are not all gentlemen. Their enlisted men are the same as ours, and you know what that could mean.'

'If they send wagons, you've a deal.'

He rose from his seat on the metal box, grasped her by both shoulders and kissed her firmly on the cheek, then left before her left hand whistled a slap past his uniform cap.

'Bejeezus, away with you man! Call yerself a doctor, do you?'

'Ah, but I love you, Josephine Delaney!' came the jaunty reply. Sister Delaney furrowed her brow in near exasperation, packed away her writing slope, picked up the pile of letters to be sent by the next messenger, then shouted into the back of the tent. 'Ladies, get out here! We have work to do, you heard the man!'

Out of the bowels of the bell tent, those few nurses who had been taking their ease appeared from behind the makeshift canvas hangings draped from the central pole that created at least an air of privacy. Aprons were donned, caps adjusted, and skirts twisted back into position and fastened.

'Right then, ladies, let's see which of this motley crew can be lucky enough to get sent home!'

The walking wounded were billeted in a separate tent to the bed ridden patients. Their treatment was mostly changing dressings, assisting them to the latrine when their comrades were churlish enough to refuse them, mopping brows and administering pain killers, acquiring cigarettes, and writing letters to their loved ones at home. Their war was over, theirs was now a waiting game, though the more able would gladly go back for round two, or in some cases round three, of the fight.

Those men who had been affected by mustard gas were billeted separately and kept together. Mustard gas was a new toy for the enemy. Sources said it was still being tested and refined, but the stuff they had launched at the trench next to Shipley's Mire had burned eyes, skin, and lungs. Some would never see or breath properly again.

It was a creeping deathly substance which rolled through the confines of the trench leaving the survivors gasping in pain. They had no protective gas masks, and most did not know to protect their eyes or try not to inhale the sweet-smelling stuff. It smelled strongly of garlic, but then to some, everything in France smelled of bloody garlic.

Sister Josephine walked amongst them. Those who were blinded, whether permanently or not, would ship out. If there were wagons, those who were breathing okay and whose burns were drying could stay, or they could leave on foot. She mentally made lists.

Amongst the others in her charge, the double amputees would go on the wagons, those minus an arm or who were mobile on one leg could stay. Her nurses made the rounds, checking bandages and giving each man notice of his destiny, provisional of course on the arrival of any form of transport. Captain Jones posted two of the more able men as lookouts, and the hospital at Abbéville settled for a watchful and nervous night.

It was well past midnight, and the sky was cloudy and moonless as Frankie and Charlie stole like thieves down through the woods. It was the sort of night that Frankie relished, and he had become a creature of the night-time. He moved like a cat and could see like a cat. Every move he made was cat-like. Faces blacked with forest earth, kit stripped down to a minimum of rifle, knife, and ammunition, they moved silently down the bank and along the hedgerows, Frankie occasionally chiding Charlie for his lack of feline talent, the smallest snapping of a twig being met with a hissed, 'Fuck's sake Charles, was your father an elephant?'

Charlie hated to be called by his full name, and Frankie Baker knew it. They entered the town by loping along the bank of the great river Somme, wading through it at the ford where, unknown to them, another, now unseen, army had crossed before. On the outskirts of the town, they found the hospital. Charlie grabbed Frankie by the belt, tapped his shoulder and whispered.

'Guards, they have posted a guard.' He pointed to the grey outlines of two khaki clad, half-equipped soldiers posted on the hospital's perimeter.

'Best we make an entrance then.' Frankie stood up out of the darkness, straightened his cap and with his rifle at shoulder marched up to the guard. He was met with the traditional,

'Halt who goes there?'

'Friend.' responded Frankie. 'Private Frankie Baker, Pancras rifles and my comrade, Charles Herbert Turner. Who is your commander?'

'We've no officers as such. The captain is a medic, so is the lieutenant, and the person in charge wears a bloody skirt mate!'

'The captain then, we have news for him.'

Private Flint signalled to his opposite number that he was leaving his post, then guided Frankie and Charlie towards a khaki tent with a pennant flying from its ridge pole – the stave and serpent badge of the Royal Army Medical Corps, alongside the Union flag.

The tent was lit by the amber glow of a paraffin lamp, and they could hear the muffled sound of voices. Richard Flint tapped on the tent flap and coughed. 'You have visitors, Cap.'

'What? More fecking visitors. Come in, be welcome.' The man who spoke was a sandy haired Irishman with a three-day beard and hands like shovels.

'Lieutenant Sam O'Connor at your service. You don't seem a bit injured, a bit grubby perhaps. So, what can we do for you? Don't mind the captain, he's planning the relief of Mafeking, it seems we are about to get more visitors - of the Bosch kind. He was in the Boy Scouts back home, would you know?'

The dark-haired man with soft hazel eyes raised his head from his writing.

'Lieutenant O'Connor likes his jokes! State your business, it's late, this war waits for no one. There will be more wounded in the morning, and likely fighting by the afternoon. I hope Shipley makes good on his offer.'

'Sir,' began Charlie. 'yes, there is an artillery division and supporting infantry setting up to take the town. We have a small company of men who survived the trench attack. We will try and stop their advance. Our purpose tonight is to warn you and to tell you to prepare yourselves. We have a spy in their camp. They plan to move tomorrow at first light and start their offensive the following day. They have heavy artillery and also a company of infantry, both conscripted men and some crack troops, and a small number of snipers. We are here to pinpoint and take out the snipers should they arrive.'

'Good.' muttered the medic, 'That'll help. We hope to have moved many of our worse cases out of here by tomorrow night, if General Shipley comes good, but then his main concern may be his brother.'

'Not Montague Shipley sir?' piped up Frankie.

'What of it? You know him?'

'He was our lieutenant, sir.'

'Do I detect a degree of disdain, Private? His brother was not over complimentary of his abilities.'

'Best he doesn't know we are here. Is he badly injured sir?'

'He will never walk again, likely he will never talk again. He is still under morphine, though he is coming around. His brother hopes to get him on his way to blighty tomorrow. We hope the General brings more than one wagon, and horses.'

'Can we help then sir? The local farms still have some horses, and surely even a hay cart would do. We passed several in the fields on our way here.'

'Anything with wheels will do, we have many who cannot walk.'

Charlie and Frankie ducked out of the tent. 'The farm by the ford, there was a hay cart in the field behind, they will have a horse to pull it.'

'Get all your London charm out, Charlie boy, and your best schoolboy French. We may get lucky!'

They left the hospital camp whilst it was still dark, but the dawn was starting to cast its light over the fields as they sat under the hedge and waited, watching the back door of the old stone farmhouse, its buildings ranged around it, as yet unravaged by German attack.

'We warn them.' said Frankie. 'Tell them what is coming. They hate the Bosch as much as us, they will help.'

'Look, there is life,' said Charlie, 'an old man, crossing the yard.'

'Come on then, ready yourself, 'Bonjour,' that's a good start!'
Charlie prepared his speech mentally, running the words of his elementary French through his mind, hoping what he planned to say made sense. He opened the gate to the farmyard and crossed to the cow shed where the old man was just getting started on the milking.

Charlie began in faltering French.

« Ah, bonjour, Monsieur ! Je m'excuse, mais je ne parle bien le français. Nous avons besoin d'aide s'il vous plait.
Alors, vous pouvez comprendre, nous sommes des soldats britanniques. Nous vous prévenons que l'armée allemande vient prendre la ville d'Abbéville. Ils ont de l'artillerie et des soldats juste derrière les arbres. Nous avons besoin de vos chevaux et de votre chariot pour sortir les blessés de l'hôpital. »
The farmer looked at them quizzically and replied slowly so that they'd understand.
« Je n'ai qu'un seul cheval de trait et un cheval de selle qui tirera un piège. Si vous emmenez ma fille avec vous en lieu sûr, vous pourrez avoir les chevaux et le chariot.

« Merci Monsieur, je vous en prie. » Charlie continued, as Frankie looked on, clearly impressed.
« Envoyez votre fille avec nous, nous veillerons à ce qu'elle soit en sécurité. »

The old farmer was white haired, short, with bowlegs and skin like a weathered walnut. His hands were gnarled with arthritis, the joints swollen from working outdoors in all weather. He was dressed in old black woollen trousers held up with both a thick leather belt and a pair of jaunty red braces over a linen shirt which sported a lively floral pattern. As he drew himself up to his full height of just over five feet, he saw Frankie's expression of amazement at his attire. His face broke into a wide grin and in perfect English he said,

'My daughter made it from the bedroom curtains - good cloth is in short supply!' He shrugged his shoulders in Gallic fashion and continued. 'Life must go on. Take the horses and anything else you need. The halters are on the wall, and the horses in the back field, there are three. Leave the white one, I'll have need of him. The cart and the trap are in the shed with the harness. When you have rounded them up, I will call Celine to help you - you do not seem like countrymen to me.' Now it was Charlie's turn to look amazed.

'Oh, yes, I speak your language.' the farmer rattled on. 'I worked in your city of London for several years, until my wife died. Now I prefer the peace of the country, but it seems even that is to be disturbed.' His hands, which had been busy under the small honey coloured milking cow, moved the bucket of creamy liquid from under her udder, slapped the cow on the rump in a friendly manner and shouted towards the house.

<<Alors, Céline, ici ! Des soldats Anglais. Il y a des choses à faire ! »

After a few moments, the kitchen door opened, and a woman appeared. Celine Dubois had long dark hair and olive skin, bright hazel eyes and a big smile. She was short and curvy and dressed in men's trousers, a leather waistcoat and a shirt made of the same material as her father's. Her feet were shod in wooden sabots.

Celine, cherie, take these soldiers to catch Old Pierre and Gryphon. Then, help them to harness the flat wagon and the trap. Leave Nuage for me, then you must pack a bag and go with them to safety, there is going to be trouble here, they say. I must stay to look to the farm, or they will destroy everything. Do not argue. I have decided. It will be for the best.'

'Papa, I cannot leave you!'

'Celine, you can, and you must! The Bosch will be no respecters of our property or your virtue. They are conscripted men. They have not seen a woman in months! I will have Nuage close by, he will carry me to safety. Do these things while I prepare some food for us and our guests.

And so, Frankie and Charlie left the farm, their stomachs full of good French bread smeared liberally with fresh butter and cheese and with two horses, a wagon, a horse drawn trap and Celine Dubois. Leaving her father Jean to face the onslaught to come, Frankie and Charlie drove the flat wagon pulled by the solid and ancient Percheron Old Pierre with Celine behind driving the trap pulled by the small black pony she called Gryphon.

The hospital was a hive of activity. It was nearly midday, by which time the captain had received word that General Shipley could send only one covered wagon and that was for his brother - no more could be spared. But, the evacuation of the walking wounded had been ordered, so one man was to travel in style and the rest would have to walk as they could. Rank has its privileges after all. No change there, then.

Sister Delaney looked at what Frankie and Charlie had acquired, her eyes filling with tears, tears of relief. She could fit at least twenty of her men on the flat cart, and her nurses could take the trap. She herself had no intention of leaving. She would fight on to the end, defending the wounded who were too Ill to make the journey to the coast and across the channel to Blighty.

The rest of the day and well into the night was spent preparing to evacuate the hospital encampment. General Shipley had sent a horse drawn ambulance for his brother, which arrived loaded with a small supply of rifles and ammunition, in case those remaining had to defend themselves. He had also included some Mills bombs and a small supply of explosives. Useful thought Charlie, just what the doctor ordered.

Frankie and Charlie went amongst the fitter of the men, handing out the rifles and a supply of bullets with each. Those who were remaining found themselves positions which they would take up, if and only if they were fired upon. Captain Jones raised the Red Cross flag high on the flagpole and by dawn the wounded were ready to move out.

As the sun rose over the Somme the motley band of injured men and their nurses flying the Red Cross flag from the front and rear of their wagons started their slow progress towards the coast, more precisely the harbour town of Dieppe fifty miles away. It would be a three-day journey, possibly more, in the hope of a supply boat to ship them home to safety.

CHAPTER 20. SABOTAGE

Mid July 1916.

Jack hunkered down in the thick undergrowth within the forest. He was out of sight of the Bosch artillery men, but he still felt very much alone. Charlie and Frankie had been gone for ages. 'Warn the hospital!' he had told them. They should have been back by now, for god's sake, but he knew to expect the unexpected. Who knew what they had come across?

He was well used to his own company. That was not what was disturbing him. It was the fact that he was hiding in company with over twenty men, but he could see none of them and only knew two by name. He couldn't even hear them when they moved – all very odd. In all fairness, Ralph had asked if Jack wanted him to stay with him. Jack's pride had got the better of him and he had pretended he wasn't worried. 'Don't be ridiculous!' he told himself. 'If you were alone you wouldn't mind. It's believing they exist at all which should terrify you.'

It was nearly midnight and the Germans had posted their guards. The guns they had with them were pulled by teams of horses, now tied in lines, and hobbled, in the same field as the men's tents. The guns themselves had been left on the dirt road on the other side of the hedge. Jack assumed that was because they didn't want to risk getting them bogged down in the soft ground or to make too much noise when they moved off. Gwyn had refused to harm the horses or even to steal them, so they planned to strike when the men were busiest, breaking camp and harnessing the teams to the guns. Then they would take out the men. The rifle company, which was now only a few miles distant, they would have to deal with when and if it arrived.

Jack had hoped to plot Charlie and Frank out in advance of the riflemen to pick them off as they came within range. Not possible with no Charlie and Frank and not possible with no rifles or ammunition. Nothing to do but wait.

The night drifted past, it was a dark night, the moon hidden behind towering black clouds. Night-time was never silent. The nocturnal wildlife which took refuge in the undergrowth scuttled back and forth seeking food and shelter. An owl called out across the fields, seeking answer from its mate. Is anybody there?

'No,' thought Jack, pulled out of his reverie and into instant alertness. 'That's no owl!'

'Whooooo, whooooo!' the call came again.

Jack raised his cupped hands to his mouth and blew through bent thumbs, an answering call, one long trembling, 'whooooooooooo!'

There was a rustle in the nearby bushes and a grimy face surrounded by unkempt spiky blonde hair appeared carrying a well stuffed rucksack. Frankie crawled into the hollow beside him, a hand appeared behind him passing him a rifle, then another, then another well filled pack. 'That's the explosives!' hissed Charlie 'Don't bloody drop it!'

'Where the……….!'

'What's the plan, sarge?' Frankie enquired, almost politely.

They waited, hidden in their hollow, silent, not even daring to eat the much-wanted food which half-filled Charlie's backpack, stuffed in alongside a metal box of bullets and half a dozen Mills bombs and all courtesy of General Gerald Shipley - brought in by ambulance, no less.

As quietly as he could, Jack briefed them. This is how it would be. They would wait until the camp started to harness the horses to the guns. Then, Gwyn and his invisible men, who could not be seen, would deal with the men and cut the horses free, as quietly as possible, please. No gunfire – we don't want to alert that bloody infantry division they have waiting behind the hill. Once the gun crews are dead, we spike the guns. Those should do nicely. He pointed at the Mills bombs, neat handheld grenades. Then, the detail.

'This is what you do to the guns. Pack the breech of each gun with nitro, and then drop a live one down the barrel. Then we withdraw, quickly, down to the hospital, or what's left of it. The blast will wake the dead - and the infantry unit. They will have lost many comrades and several artillery pieces. They'll be after us like wasps on a pot of jam, and they have orders to take the town.

Gwyn's men will meet us there. We man the hospital's defences and may God have mercy on us. We will be fighting well trained men, not only conscripts, but at least we can see them. Got it?'

Charlie reached into the rucksack for the food the nurses had packed for them: fresh bread, cheese, and cold meat. He passed it round and the three of them ate together for the first time in days. Digging deeper into the pack he pulled out a small metal flask engraved with a serpent and stave on one side and the initials S. O'C on the other.

'Have a nip of this! It's Irish, guaranteed to warm the cockles of Dublin, according to Doctor Sam. And he wants his flask back please, it was a gift from his Grannie back in Ireland. He makes the contents himself – Granny showed him how. Don't ask what's in it!'

He passed the flask round, and all three took a swig of the eye-wateringly strong liquid. Jeeesusss! Charlie slid the flask into his tunic pocket in front of his paybook, it might be needed later. He adjusted his position to relieve the pins and needles in his left leg and from the undergrowth heard the voice of an unseen warrior mutter,

'Diolch, butty, you've been sat on my bloody foot for ages! My toes 'ave gone numb!'

Charlie startled and flinched. Jack pinned him down, one hand on his shoulder. 'It's okay Charlie, they are all around us, you just can't see them yet.'

Frankie, sitting with his back against a fallen trunk, felt his resting place move behind him, and heard the distinctive grinding whoosh of metal on stone, a knife, no, numerous knives, being sharpened.

Around the sleeping guns, the crews started to wake. Men relieved themselves, leaning their heads against the great metal monsters while they took a long piss against the wheels. Mules and horses were fed with what feed was left. They had slept in their harnesses overnight, ready for a quick move at dawn. Men moved busily and with a semblance of German efficiency. Rations were swiftly eaten, uniforms hastily buttoned, and packs re-filled with equipment as the makeshift camp cleared itself to move out. An order was barked in German.

'Schnell! Aufsteigen!' 'Mount up! Quickly!'

The waiting mules and horses were backed up to the gun carriages, six to a gun, to haul the massive weapons to their muddy destination.

Gwyn did not need to utter a word of command. As if growing from the earth, behind each soldier appeared an apparition dressed in the soldier's garb of a battle five hundred years before, a wave of silent, throat cutting death, and those not dispatched by a well sharpened blade never heard the hiss of the arrows' flight amongst the shouting of orders, the braying of the reluctant mules and the neighing of half-starved horses. The dead fell silently, their final screams dying in the calloused palms held over their mouths and the massive forearms which lowered them to the ground.

Frankie and Charlie were quick about their work, the breach of each gun packed with nitro glycerine, carefully carried, and smoothly manoeuvred into the throat of each barrel.

Jack, armed only with a knife, cut the traces and what harness he could from the animals and, saving four of the horses, ushered them into the woodland to wait. Like clockwork, Frankie, Charlie, and Ralph tossed a grenade down each barrel and then ran as fast as they could to the waiting horses just time to vault onto their bare backs and begin a headlong gallop down the slope towards the river and, on the other side, the hospital.

The blast was massive, the grenades detonating the highly unstable explosive in the confined space of the gun barrel, then the explosions of the shells stacked ready for use. Behind the hill the infantry division heard the wake-up call and were scrambled into action.

Doctor Sam O'Connor and Sister Josephine Delaney were just finishing their early round of the wounded. They were suddenly aware that the ground was trembling beneath them and grabbed each other as the field guns met their end.

'Be-Jeezuss, that was fecking close – closer than feckin' usual! The feckin' earth moved!' Sister Jo was unphased and positively matter of fact about it, though she had winced at the blast.

'I'd love to make it move for you any day, Josephine, your tent or mine?' thought the doctor, but replied only a polite, 'Er, yes, and they are rather too close for comfort!'

'Is this the attack those lads warned us of, then?'

'There's no gun fire, and there are no shells landing, maybe we have some time, with a bit o' luck!'

Around the perimeter fence, they could see the walking wounded taking up positions on the makeshift defences, rifles in their hands once more, despite their wounds.

'Like feckin' Rourke's Drift!' muttered Sister Jo under her breath.

'Only we got away with that one!' replied O'Connor under his breath. 'My old granddaddy was there, so he said, had the medal to prove it!'

'You'd best get me one of those nice new rifles the General brought along.' Josephine laid her graceful, manicured hand on the erect hairs of his forearm. 'I shoot like Annie Oakley, not a rabbit was safe on our farm when I was around. Self-defence only, mind you. Fritz will have to fire first, but God help him when he feckin' does!'

Sam O'Connor's hand went to the well cleaned and fully loaded pistol he now carried with him at all times. It had once lived amongst the clutter in the ammunition box which served as a cupboard in his tent. He had hoped that he would never need to use it, but it looked like his dreams were over.

'I don't intend to wait to see the whites of their eyes Jo, oath or no oath.'

The pair had been walking slowly towards the boundary fence from where they could see the river and to the gate through which the wounded came.

'What in god's name?' He pointed at four moving specks in the distance.

'Horses!' replied Jo. 'And a white flag!' She saw Private Curry signal to his men not to fire.

Lying flat on his horse's neck, Jack felt the bullet whistle past his ear. It thudded into the ground beside him and was buried in the dust. That bullet was followed by several more, all wide of their target but getting more accurate with every round.

The piece of white cloth in his pocket was an afterthought when he tied it to the horse's harness. If the hospital had posted guards he didn't want to get shot by friendly fire. Behind the horses, emerging into sight over the brow of the hill like a line of Zulus, both Sam and Jo could see the outlines of armed men advancing in small groups.

In one Irish voice, both gasped,

'As we were sayin' - Fecking Rourke's Drift!' and ran to open the gates.

Three of the horses charged through, the fourth staggered and fell, its hind quarters hit by a round destined for the rider. Frankie was spilled from his precarious seat on its back and, landing heavily, lay still, the wind knocked out of him just out of range of the gun fire. The horse was down. It tried to get back to its feet, but its rear legs would no longer function. It grunted and lay still, whinnying and screaming pitifully in pain. As the other three animals cleared the gateway, Sam, and Jo of one mind ran out to the fallen horse and rider.

'Get the man!' shouted Sam, drawing his service revolver. 'I'll deal with the horse!'

It took all Josephine Delaney's strength to drag even the skinny form of Frankie Baker the ten yards to safety. He was dead weight, unconscious and bleeding from a head wound, his left arm hanging dislocated from the shoulder. As she handed his sagging body into the care of Ralph and Jack, she heard the sharp 'crack!' of the pistol as the horse was dealt with. Sam would not forget the look of trust and pain in its huge brown eye as he placed the barrel against the white star and the whorl of fur on its sweat blackened forehead and pulled the trigger. No time for sentiment.

A stretcher carried Frankie off to the casualty station. Charlie and Jack took up positions on the roof of the mess building, the only permanent structure available, but at least from there they had the advantage of height. From there they could pick off an enemy target as it approached. The rifles so kindly provided by General Shipley had come complete with optical sights. A little minor personal adjustment and they were deadly accurate.

Ralph seemed to vanish. In one minute, he was there, larger than life in battle dress brandishing a rifle, then he was gone. A shrill whistle was heard from somewhere along the boundary fence in between the shots fired by the walking wounded, as a rank of archers rose as one. To the cry of, 'Knock, draw, loose!', volley upon volley of arrows rained on the approaching German soldiers.

'Not Rourke's drift, this is feckin' Agincourt!' Josephine Delaney's laugh was slightly more hysterical than she wanted it to be, but she loaded her rifle, calmed her breathing, and took aim at a puff of smoke deep in the bushes to her left and another German sniper met his maker.

The exchange of fire lasted only minutes. Once close enough to see the nature of the opposing force, the arrows which pierced the cloth uniforms on bodies no longer protected by chain mail or even leather, the German advance had turned tail and fled. Crisis over, for now at least.

In the dressing station, Charlie and Jack teased Frankie for falling off his horse, and Frankie gritted his teeth while Brenda Higgins put her neat size five foot in his armpit and replaced his dislocated shoulder, then stitched the gaping wound on his scalp without the benefit of any form of anaesthesia apart from a threatening gaze. Charlie had drained the hip flask long ago. Jack straightened his tunic. His tie had long since been abandoned and now, he noted, he also had a button missing.

He would beg one from the nurses' quarters - he'd never known a gang of nurses who didn't keep everything they could salvage from a uniform, just in case. It wouldn't be the right button, but it would fill the gap.

With the archers still forming a guard around the perimeter they took stock of their situation. The threat of direct attack had gone, for now, but they all heard the sound of the artillery in the distance, felt the slight tremor in the soil beneath their feet, heard the blast of the whistle and the rallying cry of the officers as yet more men were sent 'over the top.'

Sam O'Connor cleaned his pistol. It was the first time he had ever fired the damned thing and he prayed it would be the last. He was a bloody doctor, he told himself. His job was to heal, or at least to do no harm. He had taken an oath. That was for humans, but did it apply to animals as well? He would never forget the look of trust in that animal's eyes. Had he betrayed that trust? He ran his fingers through his sandy hair, replaced the pistol into its leather holster and returned the weapon to his makeshift cupboard. Reaching into its depths he found a bottle of good Irish Whiskey, not quite the same calibre as Granny's munitions grade poteen he had given the men earlier, but good all the same. Now where was that little English bastard with his flask. They were all going to need a drink before the night was over, to be sure.

CHAPTER 21. A MAN WITHOUT HONOUR

Mid July 1916
Mount Vernon Hospital, London.

Nurse Fiona Cameron had just sat down. It had been a busy shift so far. Her feet ached with standing and her back ached with bending and on top of that her heart ached with missing Frankie. She worried for him, worried about him. His last letter had been so 'un-Frankie.' There had been no self-deprecating humour about life in the trench they had christened Shipley's Mire and the man they called Shipley Shambles. It had been a frustrated letter, a losing faith letter, a desperate letter, what of it, she had been able to read between the lines of censoring and crossing out.

She knew there had been action and massive casualties near where he was. The Bakers had heard nothing, they had not had a visit from the officer with that awful final telegram to say, 'We regret to inform you….'

There was no good way to break that news, fighting for his country or not. Dead was dead. But Frankie was not amongst the lost.

Through her idling thoughts, she heard the sound of wheels on the gravel drive outside the entrance to Mount Vernon Hospital. She rose from her seat, straightened the light blue linen uniform skirt and the long white apron which protected it from just about everything grubby, and peered out of the office window which had a view of the front door to see what was going on. There was a motor car outside, a rare thing indeed in this neck of the woods and its long, low profile with elegant running boards and large headlamps declared it an Austin. She heard a door close, out of her line of sight even if she opened the sash to look out further, then a male voice asking in an authoritative tone for the medical officer in charge. Without question the owner of the voice must be a man of some importance, perhaps a military man of some rank.

Intrigued, Fiona made the journey down the sweeping stairs with their ironwork bannisters and hovered outside Matron's office on the pretext of needing to reference Gray's Anatomy on the structure of the head and neck, perhaps. Dr. Bannerman, one of the two surgeons developing the techniques of reconstructive surgery, had his office next door to this little library. While perusing the anatomical tome she could not fail to overhear the animated conversation developing next door.

The owner of the car was attempting with some difficulty to make a case, but it was not going well.

'Doctor Bannerman, this young lieutenant is a hero of the trenches. He led his men into action. He deserves better!'

'General, it is not relevant to me who he is or what he did, and I am not refusing to look at his case, but he will be assessed the same as all our other patients, in his turn and not before.'

'Doctor, he is the son of a peer of the realm. His family would greatly appreciate it if.......' He was interrupted by Dr Bannerman whose tone began to get firmer and decidedly irate.

'General, if I thought you were trying to bribe me, or offer any other incentive, I could have you removed from my office. The lieutenant will be examined, but in his turn.'

'But surely, Doctor,' the officer's clipped voice was imploring, 'he is home, his mother cannot bear to see him as he is. She is distraught. She is doing her best, but she cannot look after him there. Could you not admit him? Surely, he could wait his turn here. At least she would start to believe he had hope.'

'General, assure her ladyship that where there is life there is hope. Bring him here tomorrow and we will find him a bed, but the rest, well he will need careful assessment and he will have to wait his turn. There are other men here who are just as deserving and in worse shape, I'm sure you are aware.'

'Thank you, Dr Bannerman, I am most grateful. I bid you good day and hope to see you tomorrow morning when I will bring my brother to your hospital.'

The office door shut firmly behind the General. Who did the shutting, Fiona was not sure, and she was not working until the afternoon tomorrow, so the patient would have to remain a mystery until then.

Fiona replaced matron's well-worn copy of Gray's Anatomy in the bookcase and left the office, softly closing the door behind her. As she turned the key in the lock to secure Matron's inner sanctum, a soft, slightly accented voice called her.

'Nurse Cameron, you know what curiosity does, d'you not? Please come in one moment, I have a task for you.'

Fiona stepped into Dr Bannerman's room. The smiling and bespectacled and gradually balding surgeon was sitting at a large mahogany desk, papers and books piled apparently haphazardly on either end.

'I expect you heard all that and what you did not will all become clear before too long. In the meantime, make up a bed in the side room off your ward. We have a new patient arriving tomorrow, so best we get ready to receive him. I'll talk to Matron about it. I fear from what I have heard there will be little we can do for the poor man, but we must try. They say he is a hero, but those that are not are just as badly damaged, as you well know.'

'Yes, Doctor, of course.'

'These are his notes, nurse, which were returned with him from the Front. You'll want to read them. They should help you get better acquainted with his needs.'

Fiona took the brown manila folder and returned upstairs to the ward where it was nearly time for the afternoon staff to start the late shift. Her good friend Jenny, 'call me Frances' Munro was due any minute and together they would make up a bed in the small side room for the mystery patient. First Fiona would read. She opened the front cover of the folder. The first few pages were taken up with the patient's personal details, name rank, service number, regiment and next of kin.

Name: Montague Simon Shipley
Born: 28th December 1884
Rank: lieutenant
Regiment: Kings Own Rifles
Service number: 45711
Next of Kin: Lady Elspeth Shipley – mother
Also: Gen. Gerald Daniel Shipley – brother

She turned the page.
The notes were made by a fair flowing hand, but obviously rushed, lacking in punctuation, and riddled with medical abbreviation.
They started bluntly with the letters N.L.T.L.

Received: 1st July 1926 4:45pm F. Hosp. Abbéville.
From: Trench Action nr Crécy en Ponthieu.

Stretcher. Unconscious. Bleeding.
Wound. Larynx. Jaw.
Wound. Left side Lumbar Spine
No Id.

Treatment.
Compression dressing, morphia.

J. Delaney, Nurse.

The next page was fuller.

Exam. Dr Samuel O'Connor

Catastrophic shrapnel wound to larynx.
Major vessels of neck and thoracic inlet miraculously intact,
Trachea intact,
Breathing partially obstructed at laryngeal level.
Right side mandibular ramus missing.
Teeth: pre-molars and molars right upper and lower jaw missing.

Bullet wound at level of vertebra L.1
Entry posterior aspect of left renal angle.
No exit wound.

Immediate surgery. Prog. Poor.

How this man still lives I do not know.

Lt Surg. Sam O'Connor RAMC.

Record of Surgery

Dr Capt. Robert Jones RAMC operating.
Dr Sam O'Connor RAMC assist.
Nurse J Delaney anaesthetics.

Tracheostomy under local anaesthesia. Silver Chevalier Jackson size thirty-six.
Airway secured.
Exploration anterior aspect of neck, slightly above level of larynx.
Shrapnel removed from upper throat area, resultant void in larynx and pharynx wall stitched – 2/0 catgut interrupteds.
All major vessels still intact.
Irreparable damage to vocal cords and Larynx.

General anaesthesia.
Right lateral position.
Exploration wound lumbar region.
Major damage to 1st Lumbar vertebral spine, transverse processes, and body.
Trauma to spinal cord and lumbar nerve roots.
Probable transection lower spinal cord
Wound packed with proflavine pack and dressed.

Supine position.
Laparotomy. Midline incision.
Liver and spleen intact

No detectable bowel perforation
Large haematoma muscles left lateral abdominal wall
7.92 calibre bullet removed from left peri-splenic region.
Spleen conserved.
Closure: peritoneum closed with catgut.
Mass closure of abdominal wall with interrupted silk.
Wound left open packed and dressed.

Prognosis – grim.
This poor soul will never walk or talk again, yet he maintains a determined grip on life.

Ongoing treatment

Pain relief, observation and what comfort can be given.

Re-examine and repack wounds at day three.

Notes.
3rd July 1916

FAO Dr Arthur Bannerman

Today we have been visited by General Gerald Shipley who has identified this casualty as his brother, Lt Montague Simon Shipley, an officer with the Surreys and Pancras Rifles.
The General has discussed with me his brother's prospects re: reconstruction of the damage to his mouth, jaw, and face.
I have advised him that such surgery is possible, but the techniques are very much in their infancy.
Should the patient survive transport home, he should seek an initial consultation with you at Mount Vernon Hospital, London.
General Shipley is arranging transport for his brother by horse ambulance to Dieppe.
Our position is currently precarious, we have had word of an attack on the town of Abbéville during a German advance. This has come from two lone riflemen who are detached from their unit.
The General has promised what transport he can muster for an evacuation and the riflemen are out foraging as I write.
Should we be evacuated home, I will personally follow up this patient at Mount Vernon on my return. He is an interesting case.
Until then I leave him in your capable hands.

He has shown some signs of regaining consciousness but is incontinent of urine and faeces as is to be expected with his spinal injury. He does not know the extent of his injuries.

Robert Jones RAMC

Fiona closed the notes. Shipley - the name rang all sorts of bells. Surely, if her memory served her, Frankie had mentioned Shipley in his last letter. When she finally finished her duties and was back in her room at the nurses' home, she would read his letters again. As she sat there wondering about it all, the ward doors swung open and Frances Munro breezed into work, her dark blue nurse's cape swinging from her shoulders, cap perched on the back of her head as usual.

'Hi Frances, when you've signed in, give me a hand over here would you.'

'Another admission! Don't we have enough already?'

'This one is a bit unusual. Strings have been pulled. I'll tell you as we make the room up. He's referred to Dr Bannerman from Dr Robert Jones out in Belgium somewhere. He's been pretty badly shot up. His brother came in personally this morning with his notes. General Shipley is his brother, does that ring any bells with you, Frances?'

Together they pulled the bottom sheet tight and folded the neat 'hospital corners' holding it in place.

'He'll need a draw sheet, rubber if we have one spare, or his mattress will be sodden in no time. I'll see if I can find one.'

Fiona disappeared to the sluice room where such things lived. Returning with the article in question, a reddish-brown thin sheet of rubberised material resembling a piece of someone's mackintosh coat.

'Cover it with a folded flannel sheet, it won't sweat as much.' She remarked to Frances as they worked together around the bed.

'I know, tricks of the trade, or he'll have bed sores the size of Bristol. Just a top sheet then, and a loose blanket, one pillow?'

'For the time being, until we sort his routines out.'

Fiona placed the pillow at the head of the iron framed hospital bed and smoothed the sheet one final time. Frances polished the cupboard and side table with a damp disinfectant cloth, then they both returned to the nurse's station where the other four of their number were assembled for Matron's briefing.

'Quickly ladies, you are late!' Matron chided them. 'No excuses! I know what you've been doing, but there are no special cases here, and I mean none!'

She continued to brief her staff on the other patients, studiously avoiding reference to the preparation of the side room, only used for exceptional cases. Matron was not impressed with any interference with her ward, even from the illustrious Dr Bannerman.

Duties completed for the day, Fiona crossed the courtyard to Mount Vernon House and ascended the stairs to her cosy attic room in the nurses' residence.

Taking off her uniform, she stretched out on her single bed dressed only in her silk dressing gown. For a few seconds she closed her eyes tightly and conjured up an image of Frankie, then opening her eyes she sat up and opened the top drawer of her dressing table. Frankie's letters were there, tied in a bundle. She undid the bow of cheap brown string which tied them, neatly ordered, the most recent on top. She selected the top one, the most recent.

June 1916

Dearest Fiona,

A note to say we are all fine. So far, we have been lucky not to be posted too close to the action though the next trench was gassed badly last week. The one survivor has now joined our company, making us four.

His name is Ralph, Ralph Owen, you'd like him.

We itch for work to do, but Shipley is like an old woman and refuses to deploy us for what we trained to do. Even Jack has become frustrated with him. He is afraid of his shadow and likes to keep us all about him for protection.

The rain when it comes is torrential and the mud gets deeper daily. The food is awful, but the company is good, and we keep our spirits up by joining the Welsh with their singing.

Must go now, Bosch has a sniper firing random rounds at the helmet Charlie is holding up on a broomstick. Pity we are not allowed to fire back. Will write again soon! Missing your pretty face and longing to kiss you. Say hello to the Bakers for me and give them my love -and Charlie's, too, in case his letter doesn't get through.
All my love

Your Frankie.

So, there he was – Shipley. Maybe he had news of the rifles, they were part of his command, weren't they? Odd, that bit didn't get censored. Then her mind cast back to what seemed to be a previous lifetime a night that had been drenched in blood and intrigue. Captain Jeremy Shipley - well, well. Fiona Cameron did not believe in coincidence, but she did believe in fate.

CHAPTER 22. A PROBLEM SHARED.

Fiona woke early, no need of the alarm clock which ticked loudly alongside her bed, armed, and waiting to chime its bells in her left ear at 5am, for the early shift which started at six. The clock was imported from America, had been a gift from her father before he died. He had contacts and friends everywhere, a fact she had found more than once since his death. Loud and brash like its country of origin, Fiona treasured the brass and nickel cased monster, with its three ornamental feet, Roman numerals and huge brass bell sitting ominously above the number twelve. It was even called 'America', just in case she forgot where it came from. There had been mornings when she had felt more like throwing it back there than getting out of bed. This was not one of them.

She pulled across the switch which disabled the bell, picked up the neatly pressed apron off the nightstand, straightened her uniform and descended the stairs to the kitchen in search of breakfast. Two slices of toasted bread with butter and Cooper's Oxford marmalade later, washed down with a large mug of strong tea with no sugar, she was ready to face the world and the ward and the day ahead. It was nearly half past five, the night duty nurses would be fidgeting now, waiting anxiously to get to their beds. She could almost hear the clack of their knitting needles or the tutting as they darned holes in stockings and socks. Dozing off at work was frowned upon, but the night staff had a myriad of ways to occupy their quieter moments.

One more day turn and then she had a few days off - she and Frances Munro actually had a day off together. They planned to go up to town, visit Agar Grove. Fiona had business with her father's executors and then they had planned a night out in the Duke. But first, to work.

Fiona was early, the night sister made her wait, she would not allow even one of her nurses to finish before time. The clock in Sister Veronica Battle's book, that is, her mind, was the clock, and things ran to it. Known as the Battleaxe behind her back she seemed a joyless, dried-up old prune of a woman, shaped a little like queen Victoria in later years, as broad as she was tall, about five feet in every direction allowing for her old-fashioned uniform skirt. Her hair was greying and curly and imprisoned in a net and topped with the starched headgear that told the world where she had trained. Her whiskered face and sharp grey eyes had seen too much death, had seen too much false hope disappear. Had there not been a war, she would have retired two years ago, but all hands were needed, and the Battleaxe would answer the call. She ran a tight ship and, had she allowed a little flexibility in its rigging, it may have weathered the storms better. Those nurses whose menfolk were at sea often referred to her as Cap'n Bligh and plotted mutiny. There was a veritable fleet of nurses applying to leave the night shift.

Fiona waited until Sister Veronica declared it time for hand over. She and her five colleagues and the lovely Sister Agnes MacDonald listened to the few events the quiet night turn had produced.

Bed one. Had been restless all night, fighting in his dreams, throwing off his covers. He was now asleep and sedated.

Bed two. Had been awake, because of bed one, he was now sound asleep, he was ready to be got up and about, later, or so he said.

Bed three. No change.

And so on until all twenty beds were accounted for. Those to be gotten out of bed and walking, those under sedation, those needing dressings changed, each member of the team had their role to play.

The keys to the office and the drugs cupboard were handed on, 'good nights' said, and the weary night staff went to their rooms across the yard and to their beds.

Fiona sat with the man in bed one for a few hours until her first break. He was calm at last. She changed his sweat-soaked pyjamas and sheets and made him comfortable. Coming round from his last dose of morphine, he started to talk.

'I'm sorry nurse, was I making a terrible racket, I can't help it. When I close my eyes, it comes for me, I can smell it, sweet smelling it is, like the smell of garlic, then I can't breathe, I hear the guns and bullets, men shouting. I am afraid to sleep nurse, lest I never wake up.'

Fiona read the name at the head of the bed. 'Nesbit Evans', is that really your name?'

'I've my father to thank for it,' the soldier smiled, 'and his father before him, and if I have a son, I shall pass it on. My middle name is David, the men call me Dai. Dai 'half cut' on account of the barber messed up my hair when we all enlisted!'

'Well Dai, there is nothing to fear here, you are home, you have done your bit. I have read your notes, your chest is clearing, a few days and we'll have you up and about in one of those smart new blue uniforms. Do your family know where you are?'

'Aye they do, but it's a long trip for them from Maesteg to London. My Morfydd can't afford the fare by train. Will they let me home with these bad dreams? I fear she would break her heart to hear me carrying on so.'

'Time and home are great healers, your war is over, rest now, I will be back after break.'

Break time came with a broken biscuit from a hijacked tin, a broken package purloined from the pile destined for the men at the front. A large mug of tea and a chat with Sister Agnes about nothing in particular, staring vacantly out of the window at the morning mist. While Fiona was washing her tea mug at the sink, she heard a vehicle pull up outside, a motorised ambulance. A door slammed as the driver got out, then the click as the passenger shut his quietly, then the sound of boots marching to the rear and the back doors opening.

'Careful now, Carter, don't bloody drop him!' The voice was brisk and used to giving orders.

'He's not so light as you'd think, sarge, and I've got the feet end.'
Fiona heard the big doors to the front hall open, and then the soft, Ayrshire burr of Dr Bannerman who was clearly aware of the new arrival.

'Use the trolley and the lift. Don't jar him by using the stairs. He's got enough on his plate.' A pair of porters arrived, rather smartly dressed in dark trousers and short, white jackets.

From the ward, Fiona heard the faint sound of the cage opening and the squeak of the trolley's wheels as it was pushed into the lift and then the cage door closing, the clunk of the brass and Bakelite control lever and the whine of the electric motor as the cage began its ascent. Then, the leather soles of Dr Bannerman climbing the one flight of stairs while the patient and his attendants made the trip vertically. In the still, warm atmosphere was an all pervading and almost reassuring smell of floor polish.

Fiona allowed herself a moment to savour it, explained to the young Evans that she'd be back in a few minutes, sighed and then made her way to the elevator door on the first floor.

'His room is ready, Doctor Bannerman, one of my colleagues is waiting for you. I'm at Bed 1 with young Evans if you need me.'

'Carry on with your duties, nurse Cameron. I am sure we can cope.'

Fiona broke free from the group, returned to the ward, washed her hands, and resumed her conversation with Corporal Evans.

'Tell me about your home.' she enquired of the soldier.

'Only a small, very modest house,' came the reply, 'a miner's cottage in a street just outside the town, one of three in a terrace, with a blacksmiths shop attached. My father was the farrier on the colliery for years. He was injured when the roof collapsed on his forge. Never went underground again, took to making things in ironwork to keep his hand in. Made all manner of things for our mam. My parents live in one house, my wife and I have the house next door, my brother and his wife live in number three.'

'What is the country like? I've heard Wales is a wild and beautiful place.'

'Where the collieries have not blackened it with spoil heaps, it is. My older brothers were kept in the mines for the war effort, my father never let me go down, said I had too much brain to hew coal. No offence to my brothers, like, but he wanted more for me.'

'What would you have done, if you'd had more of a choice?'

'My teachers said I had a talent for invention, designing things, engineering, and such like. I was to go to college in Pontypridd, then apprentice at one of the new engineering works.'

'You still could do that. You are still young. How old are you if you don't mind me asking?'

'I am nineteen, Miss.'

'You have a wife already?'

'Aye, we married before I was recruited, been sweethearts since childhood, she's a lovely girl my Morfydd, dark curly hair, dark eyes and a voice like a linnet for singing.'

He sat up in bed and rummaged in his bedside locker. Pulling out his battered paybook he produced a sepia photo of a young couple, dated 30th June 1915 by Emrys Roberts, photographer, Maesteg. They were a handsome couple indeed.

Until she saw the picture, she did not realise just how much bed space Corporal Evans occupied. He was all of six feet two, and though illness and inactivity had burned the flesh from his frame, his shoulders filled the width of the narrow hospital bed.

'What was it like in the trenches?'

It was the question they were told not to ask, but it crept from her lips before she could stop it. 'Sorry, don't answer that, I should never.... '

'My mother always told me a problem shared was one halved, maybe it would help me if I talked, it could hardly make me worse. I will tell you, but maybe pull the curtain round, I need a bottle in any case.'

Fiona scurried to the sluice room for a receptacle, then pulled the curtain while her patient filled it with healthy-looking pale-yellow liquid.

'Kidneys are working fine then, bladder in order, no trouble with the water pressure!' She laughed.

'It wasn't so bad at first, when we were first posted. It was all new and strange. It was tough, but we had each other, and no one had died yet. Then the Bosch set up a team of snipers. They made our life a misery, they did. They could see the back wall of our trench, and one spot, dead man's seat we called it. Sit there and one of them would have you. Got the supply man from the Watch, they did, the Black Watch. Huge Scottish bastard he was, 'scuse me swearing, came for a chat while they were dropping supplies. We told him not to sit there, but he was too busy rattlin' on to listen. His sergeant was friends with our sergeant. Bullet hit him straight in the 'ead. Instant it was. Our officer should have sent men to hunt them down, and we had four trained to do exactly that. They asked to be used, to go after these snipers who made life a misery for the rest of us every day, but he was against it, so we suffered, every day. Then it rained and the place became a quagmire, and the cold set in with the wet, and the supply couldn't reach us because of the snipers and the mud. It was terrible.'

He began to shake, Fiona took his hand and held it. 'But you survived, you are here, stop now, if you like, or why not write it down, I can find a notebook for you, that might help.'

Corporal Evans calmed and the shaking stopped. He breathed in deeply and held his breath for what seemed an age, then a long breath out.

'I think I shall sleep now for a while. Thank you nurse Cameron.'

He clasped the photograph to his heart and closed his eyes. For once, sleep came for him, with dreams of a green hillside and a pretty dark-haired girl singing for him with her feet dangled in a bubbling brook, stockings and shoes off and skirt hitched up to stop it getting wet, while a tall youth, his braces hanging around his legs and shirt off lay on the bank with a piece of grass between his teeth and listened to the voice of an angel. Morfydd played harp just as beautifully as she sang. As he drifted off, Corporal Evans started to hum in a fine tenor, filling in the descant as he slept in his peaceful woodland with his Morfydd.

Dafydd y Garreg Wen,

'Carice,' medd Dafydd, 'fy nhelyn i mi,
Ceisiaf cyn marw roi tôn arni hi.
Codwch fy nwylo i gyrraedd y tant
Duw a'ch bendithio, fy ngweddw a'm plant.'

'Neithiwr mi glywais lais angel fel hyn,
'Dafydd, tyrd adref a chwarae trwy'r glyn,'
Delyn fy mebyd, ffarwel i dy dant,
Duw a'ch bendithio, fy ngweddw a'm plant. [2.]

Fiona Cameron pulled back the curtains from round the bed in the side room and, curious as to the new arrival, enquired again of Dr Bannerman if she could be of assistance.

The patient in the side room had been neatly transferred from his stretcher to the bed by the two porters. The men who had delivered him had been dismissed and had left.

Dr Bannerman himself had settled Lieutenant Shipley's still sedated body into the first proper bed it had experienced since he'd finally got home and where the family had tried to make him comfortable on the chaise long in his bedroom overlooking the lawn and the fountain at the front of the elegant old house.

On seeing her head pop around the door, the doctor lifted his head from his examination of the patient's legs.

'Nurse Cameron, if you would.' he called her into the room.

'We'll start by removing the bandages from his face and neck, they may need soaking to release them. I need to see the extent of the damage for myself.'

Fiona made her way to the head end of the bed where the patient's mummified head lay on the one pillow, the thickness of the bandages giving his neck an unnatural upward kink. She undid the knotted end of the field dressing. There was obviously a shortage of safety pins, the ends of the bandage had been split and a knot craftily fashioned to secure the loose ends. Improvisation, well in these times of hardship, there was a lack of everything, it paid to be able to improvise. Make something of nothing.

As she unwound the bandages, then the dressing pads, she saw that the innermost covered the neat stitches which held the wounded throat together around the tracheostomy. They were soaked with seepage from the wound, but clean smelling, no infection. The silver of the tracheostomy kept bacteria at bay and the wound itself had begun to heal.
Dr Bannerman peered over her shoulder, spectacles balanced on the end of his long nose.

'Hmmmm, nice bit of work, Dr Jones. Pity I may have to undo it all.'
Neck uncovered, the next layer uncovered the young lieutenant's face. The right side was undamaged, a handsome high cheek boned face in profile if a little weak in the chin. The left side sagged as though its very foundations had been destroyed The cheekbone had dropped, the nose was pushed sideways the mouth turned down at the corner and the lips drooped open. A large piece of the man's jaw was completely missing. Fiona took a step away from the bed, her face a picture of mixed horror and amazement. One word escaped her lips. 'How?'

'How is he alive, you ask? I really have no idea. The human body is a remarkable thing and its grip on life can be tenacious indeed. We will need x-rays of his skull. I will see to it with Matron. The X-Ray technicians will have a mobile machine they can bring to the ward, I do not want this man moved. If he persists in living, he deserves the best chance to survive. Let's see what we can do to mend his face.'

'Shall I re-dress the wounds, Doctor?'

'No, nurse, thank you very much. Those stitches need air now, just a light bandage around his face. Should he come round, he may need to be introduced to his new profile gently, no need for anyone else to tell him.'

As if hearing the room stirring around him, the lieutenant raised his left hand from the bed, pointing skyward, a gasp of air rasped through the tracheostomy, some leaking around it and out through his mouth. It could not be a word, he should no longer have the means to form words, but Fiona was sure she heard the word, 'Charge!' and from the expression on Dr Bannerman's face, he had too.

That night Fiona broke all the rules of the nurses' home and drew herself a full hot bath of water. Water wasn't strictly rationed, but the water heater would only be coaxed into a limited amount. A full hot bath for one would mean cold baths for everyone else. Tonight, it did not matter, the night girls were at work, and everyone else had gone out. Fiona was alone to soak her weary muscles and think. Corporal Evans had been there. Would he tell her more? And Lieutenant Shipley, what did he know about the fate of the Frankie's unit? Tomorrow she and Frances would go up to town. They would visit the Bakers, and Charlie's parents and then they would have a little fun. After all, a trouble shared, is a trouble halved.

CHAPTER 23. ITS ALL IN HIS MIND

It was not the first night turn which Frances had worked. She sometimes filled in for Belinda Graham who hated nights and pleaded sickness at every opportunity. Belinda would have liked to make the swap permanent, but Frances was having none of it. She would cover for a friend, but a swap to the Battleaxe's team? Never.

The last round of medications had been done at midnight. Bedpans and bottles had been filled and emptied, drawsheets had been changed where necessary and all the patients settled for the night.

Frances and the other five night nurses retired to their common room, most to their knitting or mending and Frances to the letter she was writing to Charlie Turner's parents asking if they had any news of him. The letter wasn't really necessary, she was going up to town with Fiona Cameron in a few days in any case. She would see the Turner family then. She could ask them in person but writing it all down seemed to help. She was just completing the last paragraph when it started.

Stifled sobs coming from the last bed in the ward, the one by the window, the window the bed's occupant stared out of all day, watching, always watching, as if for some unknown enemy. Private Cole hardly spoke, his pale blue eyes were sunk into a cadaver-like face. Some relative or friend, a sweetheart maybe, had placed a photograph on his bedside locker. The picture was of a handsome if thin man in uniform, khaki cap at a jaunty angle, a wide smile showing the gap between his front teeth, a floppy fringe greased back out of his eyes, cigarette hanging from his lips. The photo had been taken at some seaside town by one of those photographers who plied their trade on the piers making money from the young soldiers and their girls out enjoying a few last days of freedom before the men were posted. Brighton possibly? No, Private Cole was Welsh. Penarth then, or Swansea? He had been quite a catch for some young lady. Very easy on the eye, and a charmer no doubt. That was then, before the horrors of war.

The sobs subsided, giving way to an anguished keening sound, the sound of an animal in pain, like a fox with one leg in a snare, pulling against the wire, unable to reason that to fight the trap was a painful road to certain death.

One of the older nurses, a hard-bitten woman who professed to have 'seen it all', looked up from her mending.

'Mad as a box of frogs that one, his mind is well gone. He'll be fighting with the fairies next, that's how it usually goes. Scream for hours he will, no peace for any of us until sun comes up.'

Frances rose from her seat. 'That is uncalled for, Katie Brown! I'll see to him - you just sit and ignore your duty why don't you. He's your charge, is he not? You could at least give him the comfort of being there.'

'Do as you please, child.' Katie Brown returned to the heel of the worn-out sock she was attending to. 'The man is broken, he has no life ahead of him, nothing will heal his mind. The sooner he ends it, the better for all, for that is what he will do, mark my words.'

Frances was not a young woman given to foul language, but having risen she made her way nearly to the door of the nurse's room, then turned on her heel. One long stride placed her directly in front of Nurse Brown. The slap rang out across the room, heard above the rising wails of Private Cole.

'You fucking cynical old bitch! You disgraceful old fucking hag! I hope his demons come for you one day for no man will ever pray by your grave and they say you've had a few!'

The room fell silent, a silence so large you could stab it with a foot long bayonet. Frances regained her composure just in time to hear the throaty cough which heralded the arrival of Sister Battle.

'I'm going.' Frances nodded towards the end bed. 'I'll sit with him, Sister.'

Sister Battle surveyed her staff, then, one eyebrow raised in question, addressed the oldest member of her team. 'Nurse Brown, a word at the end of the shift please.'

As Frances approached his bed, she could hear the cries becoming louder. Cole was lying on his side, curled into a tight ball as if trying to absorb his whole self, foetal position, knees hugged to his chest, head pressed between his knees. His whole-body shook. Sweat soaked his pyjamas. He had soiled himself but seemed quite unaware of the fact. Frances could smell it, fear, and faeces in one inhalation burned through the membranes of her nose.

He was talking now, if you could call it speech, repeating over and over, a name, just one name.

'Harri, Harri, I am coming Harri, wait for me, don't go, don't leave me.' Then more sobs, deeper and more heartfelt.

She swiftly drew the curtain round the bed, and stood watching for a few seconds, waiting for what seemed the right moment to approach. Her training told her not to rush in, to touch this man now might cause more distress, or he may lash out, injure her, kill her even, for he was, after all, a soldier, trained to kill and who knew what manner of demon he was fighting now.

So, she sat, in the chair alongside his bed, placed a hand softly on the pillow next to where his head should be. Picking up the photograph with the other hand she saw the writing in the back, 'My dearest Arthur, I will always wait for you.' And the initial 'A.'

Conjuring up a voice she had only heard mimicked by Frankie and Charlie, and sometimes by her good friend Fiona, she tried to sound like Rhianydd MacGregor, for Rhianydd was Welsh. The sergeant's wife, she mused, had been born in the wilds of Wales.

Frances cleared her voice and spoke. 'Hush now Arthur boy, Mam is here, tell Mam all about it, tell Mam what is wrong.'

The sweating form in the bed paused in its shivering, the legs relaxed slightly, the head drew out from under the covers, tears flowed silently down the gaunt cheeks. Frances placed a hand on the exposed ear, running her finger behind it pushing back the hair which had grown too long in the last few weeks. 'Talk to me then.'

There was a big breath in, and on the exhalation just one word, hung like a question in the air. 'Harry?'

A long-fingered hand reached from under the bedclothes and grasped hers, holding it as though it was some holy relic. The other appeared from under his body as if to join it. He sighed and relaxed and settled into an uneasy sleep.

Frances sat back in the chair, her left hand surrendered to being worshipped and she smiled to herself confident that she was the only person in the ward who knew that Private Arthur Cole sucked his thumb. The rest of the night passed quietly enough. She stayed with young Private Cole, cocooned behind the closed bed curtains, one side left open not to close off the view of the night sky through the window he stared out of all day. At some point she too had fallen into a fitful sleep dreaming of her own young soldier, unheard of for weeks, probably lost amongst the fallen.

When she woke, a pair of hunted eyes were staring at her. Private Cole was lying on his right side, still holding her hand like a lost treasure found. Frances jolted into wakefulness - it was unheard of for nurses to nap whilst on duty.

'Don't worry love, I won't tell. You were so peaceful like, has anyone ever told you, you talk in your sleep?'

He's a fine one to say that, thought Frances, yawning, and smiling back at him.

'He's alive, your man, he is alive! I know, the archers have seen him.'

Frances gathered her cloak around her against the chill that only dawn, and fatigue can bring.

'Archers? What have archers to do with it, don't talk, I ......'

'Then who is Charlie? Who is Frankie? I know them, I didn't see them, but the archers know! They told me! Last night they told me!'

The penny dropped, the look in those eyes was not hunted, but haunted. A voice that would stop a fleeing buffalo in its tracks assailed her ears.

'Nurse Munro, I won't have lateness, time for hand over, now if you please.'

'I must go. I am back this afternoon. We can chat then, but now, sleep, and please try not to dream.'

Pulling the covers over his hunched shoulder and picking up the soiled bedclothes and clothing she had coaxed him out of during the night, Jennifer Frances Munro (call me Frances) walked briskly to the nurses' station where Sister Battle waited. The last words she heard from private Cole as he drifted back to sleep and not to dream, were,

'Harry, only of Harry.'

All the others had gone to their beds. Sister Battle drew herself up to her full height of five feet and a smidge, then inflated herself to her full and similar width. She began.

'Nurse Brown, Nurse Munro, I will not have discord on this ward. Nurse Brown, I will speak to you in front of Matron Gunn later, be in her office by two pm sharp. Nurse Munro, you will apologise for your language and behaviour. You will never ever strike another member of staff again, no matter the circumstances. Am I clear?'

'Very, Sister.' Frances sucked up her pride. 'I am sorry, Nurse Brown, Katie. I should not have struck you and I am sorry, Sister, that my colleagues should hear such foul words from me. I let myself and my vocation down.'

'That is all, Nurse Munro. You may go to bed. Oh, and we all owe you thanks for a quiet night.' To Frances's astonishment, the Battleaxe winked at her. She shouldered her bag and made for the stairs, and bed. Still playing on her mind was talk of archers, and who on earth was Harry?

Frances fell into her bed in the nurses' home. Her room was at the back of the big old house which the nurses at Mount Vernon occupied. It was a pleasant room with a window which looked down the garden, a good room for a nurse working afternoons. The sun filled it at dawn along with the chorus of birdsong which went with it. A wonderful way to start a new day, full of cheer and hope and even when it was raining the sparrows would find something to chirrup about. This morning was a sunny August morning, the feathered choristers were in full flow, the sun was lighting up the dust shadows they found through the window. Frances wished dearly for a pair of heavy curtains as she pulled closed the shabby light cotton drapes.

Throwing off her uniform she fell into bed pulling the blanket and sheet and her cape over her head, trying her best to shut out the loud cooing of the pigeons which made their nest in the tree of the house next door. This was not the time for their love songs, damn them, she needed sleep. Curtains moved to the top of her mental wish list, and maybe a shotgun and not necessarily in that order. This thought amused her, and with her pillow wrapped over her ears she drifted off to thoughts of doves fleeing from her dead eyed aim wrapped in heavy blue velvet and falling into darkness.

She was woken by the cacophony from two floors above where Fiona Cameron's alarm clock was sounding twelve o clock. Fiona was working this afternoon, Frances had quite forgotten. Her friend had altered her shift so that they could travel up to town, as they called London, together. That bloody clock could wake the dead. The racket was silenced, and Frances heard the tread of feet on the floorboards two floors above. Mount Vernon House creaked as though it were about to fall around their ears.

Stirring herself from her five-hour sleep, she took her water jug to the tap in the kitchen and filled it with hot water from the boiler which lived on the range and was always hot. The newfangled water heater in the bathroom was far less reliable and only to be coaxed into action when the production of bath water was required. And then there was the large and hairy spider which lived behind it. This eight-legged beast either did not like the heat or had voyeuristic tendencies, for when the heater was on it loved to sit on the shelf alongside the soap, apparently staring at the naked occupant of the bath. Fiona had christened it Merve - Merve the Perve - and was quite content to let it look, it was only a spider after all. It ate flies, it was good for the environment, maybe even a bit of a pet. Frances had been known to throw her flannel at it, causing it to flee sideways back to its nest for surely, this creature commanded more than a simple web. Its name then changed to Merve the Swerve. Frances did not like spiders.

She poured water into the big blue and white china basin on her washstand and strip washed for the day, dressed in a clean uniform skirt, picked up a clean apron from the neatly pressed pile in her cupboard and wandered to the kitchen again where she could smell fresh bread toasting.

'One slice or two Frances?' Fiona greeted her. 'The butter is fresh and there's still a scrape in the bottom of the marmalade jar.'

'Two please, Fi, but I'll have honey, a visitor dropped a jar off before nights last night. I squirrelled it away before Katie Brown could get her claws on it, my god that woman is an old cow!' Frances placed the small brown stone jar of honey on the big scrubbed wooden table which occupied the centre of the big kitchen.

'What's she been up to now Frances?' I heard that Matron is looking to dismiss her. She's a good hand with stitching and bandaging but when it comes to the tea and sympathy and talking to the men, she is a right cold fish!'

'Well, last night I think she caught herself on a hook. She's up for a dressing down with Matron today, at two.'

'Oh, goodie!' Fiona chuckled. 'If we get in a bit early, we might catch a whiff of the brimstone! Nurse Brown versus Matron Janet, now that's a heavyweight battle of witches and with only one winner! Katie will quote age and experience, years of treating casualties, she will doubtless remember every battle since Bosworth Field and recommend that those that can't walk from the field be shot where they lie. Matron will tell her times have changed, the human body is remarkable, wounds will heal, minds will clear with time, where there is life there is hope, then she will tell her that taking one's own life is a mortal sin, and to assist it is tantamount to murder. Katie will lose her cool and probably mutter a pagan curse or two. Yes, I'd love to be a fly on the wall for that interview. No one crosses Matron Janet Gunn and gets away with it!'

Fiona and Frances turned up a bit early for their shift, just early enough to see Katie Brown, who did not live with the rest of the nurses, leaving Matron Gunn's office, her head bowed, her jaw stubbornly set, her old carpet bag hanging from her arm, and her eyes watering with tears. Speculation was that they were probably tears of anger.

That afternoon at briefing, Matron addressed both the morning and the evening shift nurses. They all gathered in the common room for it was bigger than Matrons office, if not so formal.

'Sit, if you can find a chair.' her broad Irish brogue began. 'Firstly, I would like to commend all you ladies on the excellent work you do. You all work yourselves to the bone. You give above and beyond what is required of you. I thank you all for that. It is down to you that men leave this place able to begin their lives again, scarred though they may be after their experiences of war. I would remind you all that there is hope for everyone. No-one is a lost cause in this building and that will remain so as long as I am in charge.

Today I have had the unpleasant task of dismissing one of our number. Nurse Brown is no longer a member of staff here. Nurses are valuable, and in many ways she is still effective. She has been transferred to the Field Hospitals division where her talents for stitching, bone setting and anaesthesia will be more useful. There is also another change to the staff. Sister Battle has been made Matron and is also to be transferred. She will be leaving us for the newly built hospital at Maesteg in the Welsh valleys. To fill these vacancies, Nurse Cameron, will you accept the post of temporary Sister on nights to start on Sister Battle's departure at the end of the month? Nurse Munro I would very much like you to join the night shift and replace Nurse Brown, and to continue the rapport you obviously have with Private Cole. Have you seen him this morning?'

'No, Matron I have not - why?'

'He is sitting at the table by his window, writing, and he has asked that you sit with him when you can, and he has eaten more than a bird for the first time since his arrival. I do not know what you did nurse, but please keep doing it, it seems to work. Make sure you write it down mind, others may learn from you, not all us oldies are beyond redemption.' Then addressing the room. 'Ladies I will speak with the night shift in due course, that is all.'

From the back of the room, they heard the slow clap of male hands and a deep voice sounding the words, 'Bravo Matron, Bravo!'

Janet Gunn leapt as though she had been fired, straight into the arms of Dr Robert Jones still dust stained and dirty, smelling of sweat, diesel and roadside pit stops, home from the front, but with only one patient in mind. Their kiss seemed to go on endlessly, her blonde head half hidden by his large, long fingered surgeon's hands, his head bent to hers. After a most unseemly time he came up for air and to a round of applause from the watching crowd.

'I can't stop, he gasped, but I had to see you! Supper tonight, I will pick you up after ten, I know you have orders to give!'

Then he was gone, down the stairs and out through the big front door and into the waiting car, the same car in which General Gerald Shipley had arrived.

Frances picked up her reading book and wandered down the ward to where Private Cole sat. He had turned the small side table around so that it faced the window. Wearing clean pyjamas, clean shaven and with a barber's appointment pencilled in for tomorrow, he had acquired a notebook and a pencil, and some sheets of what Frances could see was Sister Battle's own hospital note paper. His head was bent over the paper, and he was writing busily. He looked up from his endeavours, shyly hiding his work with his hand, like a schoolboy.

'Sister came to see me before she went home. She said she had read my notes, knew that I was to be a teacher before I was ever a soldier, said she had heard that I wrote poems, said was I the same Arthur Cole who wrote a book she had read.'

He paused. 'I told her I had written some old rubbish about my valley, and about the people and the mines. She said she had read it, asked me if it was true. I told her, aye it was. Why would she ask that, nurse, do you know?' The arm covering part of his writing slid away as his voice became more animated. Frances saw that he was now writing a letter.

Dearest, sweetest Harri, it began.

He had paused waiting for an answer. Frances was busily reading the neat writing on the sheet alongside the letter. She put a finger on the corner of the paper. 'May I?' she enquired.

'I don't suppose I can stop you, but please don't read it here.' He folded the paper in half and handed it to her. 'If I saw that you were moved by it, I might start crying again, and then I might never stop.'

'Deal,' she replied, placing the sheet of folded velum in her pocket. 'A poet eh! Published as well, at your age? Well, done you! It must have sold well for it to reach London!'

'I'm not so sure of that. Sister said she found it on the Paddington train from Cardiff. She had been visiting friends in Wales, but an hour later she came back with all this paper and told me to write more, told me it might ease my dreams to write them down.'

'Then I'll leave you to it, and just so you know, Sister Battle is now Matron Battle. In a month she leaves for the new hospital in Maesteg.'

'Well damn it all, Frances – nurse – miss, sorry,' – confusion overtook him, 'that's my valley! Maybe if I heal enough, I can go home with her, well not with her, at the same time, you know what I mean, if the hospital there will have me, my family are from near there. I can show her the ropes!' it came gushing out in one sentence.

'Let's get a few nights sleep in and a bit of weight on your bones first shall we. Finish your letter, I'll be back once I've done my round.'

Dearest Sweetest Harri,

Please forgive me for not writing sooner, but my mind has been absent without leave. For nearly a month all reason has deserted me, but last night I was visited by an angel, do not worry, she is spoken for. She sat with me through my dreams and found me a way home,

I know I can get well. It will take time, I know that, but with your help I know I can be what I once was.

I miss you so much, it seems so long since last I saw you, that day you saw me off on the train to the hell that is the war.

I long to walk the hillside above the house with you, to hold you in my arms again, to feel the touch of your hand in mine.

There is hope I may come home soon. I hear there is a new hospital in the town, one for servicemen, like me, who need help. There is a nurse being sent there, not just a nurse, the matron, she is a sister here at Mount Vernon, promoted to Maesteg. If I make progress, I may travel with her and recover better at home, or if not home, at least in our valley, nearer to you, my love. You are the only light in my darkness, a candle extinguished by the delusions of my mind. Nurse Munro has re-lit the flame, and Sister Battle has fanned the flame for me to live again. But the whole of the light is you.

I must sign off now as I am running out of the note paper Sister has kindly given me.

Missing you, my sweetest Harry
All my love Arthur.

PS: when you send your reply, please buy my kind nurses a pad of Basildon Bond notepaper. Mam will give you the money from what I send home.

He addressed the envelope.

Mrs Angharad Cole
8 Union Street,
Nantyffyllon
Maesteg.
Wales.

Folding the letter in two he slid it into the envelope, licked and sealed the flap and when Frances came back to sit with him giving him his evening meal of hearty pea and ham soup, and an extra slice of bread, he handed it to her with a big lopsided grin.

'Could I trouble you to buy the stamp, I'll give you the money.'

'Don't worry private, this one is on me, and I know where to find you anyway.'

She tucked the letter into her skirt pocket with his other writings. The name on the envelope cleared up a few things.

'Harri, short for Angharad then?'

'I have known her since we were little. Until she was seven, she couldn't get her tongue halfway around Angharad, so I called her Harri, it stuck. She will always be Harri to me.'

Then he started to laugh, and laugh until he cried, 'Frances Munro, what did I have you thinking of me?'

Frances blushed bright red. 'I shall go and post this directly.' She fled to Matron's office to purloin a stamp, then put the letter in the outgoing mailbox.

Sitting at the big desk she pulled out the other sheet of paper and read.

The poem was called, 'Ghosts of Bowmen.'

> *It was a day we'd all been waiting for,*
> *bellies churning, our first taste of war.*
> *To fight with comrades, so proud and bold,*
> *from that day on, I had lost my soul.*
>
> *A battle so bloody 'No man's land' slaughter,*
> *that stench of death, now with me forever.*
> *Our initial advance, victory we thought,*
> *short lived it was, as the battle changed course.*
>
> *Shells bursting around us, bodies piled high.*
> *my first taste of battle, I was destined to die.*
> *My head then exploded, shrapnel my downfall,*
> *a silence so eerie, that's all I recalled.*
>
> *'How are you soldier? don't speak just rest,*
> *your life has been saved, to this I attest.*
> *'Blighty' is calling, you've done your bit,*
> *your mind now is broken, soldiering unfit.*
>
> *'Sir, what of the archers?' I saw them appear,*
> *brandishing longbows, showing no fear.*
> *We were on the retreat, outflanked on both sides,*
> *on my belly I prayed, Lord please keep us alive.*

'Bowmen, you say son, it's all in your mind'
you probably dreamt it, that's what you'll find'
'No sir, I saw them, spread across 'No man's land,
arrows blotted out the sun, you do understand?'

'Your mind has been damaged, now this is the end,
no more 'Front' for you, of that you can depend.
'Sir, you don't understand they saved all our lives,
if they hadn't appeared, we wouldn't have survived'

'You've suffered a trauma, just empty your mind,
initially we thought, you were permanently blind,
once you get home, the scars they will heal,
but the battle you fought, by God that was real.

Frances held her head in her hands to steady her mind while her shoulders shook and the tears fell onto Matron's well used blotter, smudging the ink stains into patterns some of which looked to her distorted vision like archers, firing inky arrows at a paper enemy.
The only word and person she could bring to mind was Charlie. Where was he? Her scream echoed down the passage to the sluice room. Fiona who was emptying and cleaning bed pans ran into the room.
   'Oh, Frances, there is so little we can do!'

CHAPTER 24. SUB CRUCE CANDIDA

Katie Brown left Mount Vernon Hospital with tears in her eyes, tears of rage and frustration. Years of nursing men had hardened her - she knew that in her heart of hearts. Nursing had been her life, and she knew no other. Matron Gunn had been scathing, but right in what she had said.

'Nurse Brown, you have many talents, and a lifetime of experience, yet I feel they are better suited in a different theatre. I am transferring you to a role in active service. You are transferring to the Field Hospitals Division. I know you will be put to great use there. Don't take this badly. You need to refresh your bedside manner, nurse. In these times, all men's lives are valued. Do not get left behind.'

She had gone home to the small, rented room in the house she shared with her two cats, Smokey, and Smudge. She had eaten supper alone as usual and gone to bed, the cats curled on her feet. That night she had cried herself to sleep for the first time since she had been a child. In her heart she knew them to be tears of self-pity.

In the cold light of a new morning, she made herself a cup of strong tea with two sugars, lit a cigarette and inhaled deeply. She had the weekend to herself, then she was to report for her new role. A weekend to sort out her life. Maybe take a walk in the great park and feed the ducks and find a home for Smokey and Smudge, she was sure her neighbour Eileen would look after them. They did, after all, keep the house relatively rat and mouse free, and your feet warm at night.

On the bright side, active service pay was better. Katie Brown pulled herself together as her mother had always told her to do. She would do what she had been trained to do. She would show them what she was made of. She stubbed her cigarette out in the overfull ashtray, looked at it in disgust and emptied the contents into the ash bin, tidied her room, put on her coat, and headed for the fresh air of the park.

The fresh morning air cleared her lungs and she coughed hard, a deep racking, productive cough which concerned her slightly, she must cut back on the ciggies. Relaxing though they were, inhaling all that smoke couldn't be good for you. She mused on the fact that there were very few of the soldiers she saw who didn't smoke, it had become a stock phrase,

'Smokes like a trooper, swears like a trooper,' pretty much described herself, didn't it? Well, bugger them all to hell, she wasn't about to change. The country relied on its troopers, the troopers at the sharp end, let the lily-livered, brow mopping young ladies of the upper class try and mend men's minds, in her view it wasn't possible, she would do what she was good at, she would mend their bodies. Nurse Katie Brown would show them.

The weekend flew past. Affairs put in order, Katie locked her room and hid the key, said her goodbyes to her cats and to Eileen and, heaving her carpet bag onto her shoulder, headed for her future.

The train took her to Camberley and the tram took her the rest of the way. Katie walked up the steps of the Queen Alexandra's headquarters and in through the huge double doors into a hallway which smelled of mothballs, disinfectant, and Mansion Polish. The wood panelling which came to shoulder height glowed with a deep patina, the intricate diamond pattern tiles on the floor shone and stretched out before her as she walked down the long hallway and found herself at the bottom of a sweeping set of stone stairs, their wood topped iron banisters in the same state of highly polished cleanliness as the rest of the building.

Second floor she had been told, room four, Matron Wilshaw. Placing her bag on the floor outside the door, she knocked twice, firmly, she hoped without showing the nerves which were already forming a knot in her stomach.

'Come.' The voice on the other side bid her enter.

Katie lifted her bag, and taking a firm hold on the large white porcelain doorknob, pushed the door open and stepped into the room.

Matron did not look up. Her eyes were directed at the file of papers on the desk in front of her, reading avidly and highlighting certain places with a pencil.

'Sit.' She gestured to the chair placed opposite her, across the desk and about three feet away from it, just far enough to be uncomfortable.

Katie sat. Katie waited. Patiently. She had met the likes of Matron Wilshaw before, she told herself firmly. They didn't upset her. She knew it was just a power and authority thing. Katie would wait, she was good at waiting, she had nothing else to do.

Eventually a pair of blue eyes looked up from the desk, over the top of half-moon glasses which the wearer pushed back up the bridge of a long slightly Roman nose to a secure resting place.

'Sorry about that.' The voice that went with the eyes was cultured and well spoken. 'The paperwork is endless. The Front needs more nurses, I have none to send. 'No,' is not a word the army understands. I will not send untrained girls to war. It is an ongoing battle.' She closed the file in front of her, lifted it, tapped it square on the desk and replaced it in the basket marked 'out,' which was to her left.

'Nurse Brown, I have read a lot about you, good to have you on board.' A long fingered, well-manicured and scrubbed hand reached out across the desk. This completely took the wind from Katie's sails. She had expected frost and was receiving sunshine. Matron Wilshaw continued.

'They do excellent and pioneering work at Mount Vernon, but then you know that as well as I. Our world is changing, and faster than many can travel with it. Mental illness is not seen as it was and rightly so. I know the reason for your transfer, and I do not expect to hear of another such outburst, at least not from a nurse as experienced and capable as you obviously are. That is all in the past.'

'Thank you, Matron.' The words came out before Katie could stop them, all thought of remonstrating forgotten.

'Fact is, we need your experience and you will also need to learn. There are many new procedures used at the front. Can you learn, Nurse Brown?'

'Yes, Matron.' Was that all she could say.

'Good. The young nurses shipping with you will need your cool head. They will never have seen a war before, some think of it as a great adventure. I am sure you will guide them gently into the reality that it is not.'

'Yes, Matron.'

'Nurse Brown, Katie, I read your file, and apart from one incident, you have had an exemplary career. Your best skills are in sewing men back together. You are one of the few who has seen wounded men fresh from the battlefield. This country needs you. This matron needs you. And, before you say, 'Yes matron,' again, my name is Marion, I'm only Matron on the ward.'

Katie looked up from her hands which were making knots in her blue uniform skirt. She reached into her pocket for her handkerchief and blew her nose hard. Then she realised that the hardnosed nurse she thought she was, was crying.

Marion Wilshaw looked away, giving Katie time to collect herself, then reaching into her desk drawer she pulled out a requisition form and swiftly filled it in and signed it. Then wrote more instructions on a separate sheet of paper, pencil moving deftly across the page, she coughed to clear her throat and spoke again.

'Nurse Brown, the stores are situated across the courtyard. Go and draw uniform. Ours is slightly different from what you already have. Then, go to Sister Hunter at the dormitory, there is a billet waiting for you. I have drawn a map with directions. The barracks is large, and we are not the only occupants.' She indicated a series of boxes and arrows on the separate paper. A large arrow pointing to one box and marked NURSES DORM in capital letters. Janine Hunter will introduce you to your colleagues and show you round. Any questions nurse?'
Only one sprang to Katie's mind.

'When….?'

As if her mind had been read for her, the answer came. 'When do you leave for the frontline? In two weeks. You have an induction to complete, some techniques to refresh, or maybe learn, and then you go to Abbéville where you will at least try not to get shot.'

Katie Brown smiled for the first time that morning. For the first time in months, she felt alive, useful, wanted. She turned her brightest smile on her new boss. 'They'll find me a hard one to kill, them Germans will, I've seen their sort before.'

Matron's eyes twinkled when she replied. 'Just remember, Nurse Brown, you are now serving under the white cross, Sub Cruce Candida. I hold the rank of Major. Sister Hunter is a lieutenant. You are for the moment Staff Nurse Brown. It is a disciplined service. Without that discipline we lose everything. Dismiss.'

In an action recalled from a previous lifetime and a long-forgotten war, Katie Brown clicked her heels to attention and saluted smartly, did an equally smart about turn and marched from the office. As she closed the door behind her, she was sure she heard Matron chuckle.

Major Marion Wilshaw removed the file of papers she had so carefully placed face down in the OUT basket. The front bore the words, 'Personal Record.' The first page bore the name:

Katherine Elizabeth Brown.
Born 28th August 1880.
Date Qualified 31st March 1900.
Service. South Africa Boer campaign 1900 – 1902.
Discharged 1st April 1902.
Re enlisted 1st August 1914 posted Mount Vernon.

What had Katie Brown done for the twelve years after her discharge? Her record showed that she was capable, had served with distinction, shown a degree of calmness unusual for a young lady in the chaos of the South African veldt.

Reading on, she read that Katie Brown had come home to find that her father had died, her mother was frail and elderly and alone. Katie's parents had not been badly off financially and Katie had looked after her mother until that lady's death. This event had coincided with the outbreak of war and the end of the money from her father's meagre pension. Katie had re-enlisted. Had they read her record, they would have seen that her talents were for suturing, bone setting and anaesthesia. Her interview had documented 12 years of caring for a sick elderly relative suffering from the ravages of an apoplexy, a stroke in other words, and the onset of dementia.

Matron Wilshaw saw in her mind's eye a young woman struggling to cope with her mother's mental decline, with no hope of a recovery. Was it any wonder she saw no prospects for the damaged men coming home from the front.

Abbéville would be just the place for her, a refresher course in the basics and a few lessons in anaesthesia, she would do well.

Marion picked up her telephone and dialled Mount Vernon. She must thank Janet Gunn for sending her Nurse Katie Brown. She must also ask after Dr Robert Jones and the progress of Janet's love life. There was nothing like a spot of gossip to make the world go round, to alleviate the daily grind.

The phone rang several times then a male voice floated down the line, 'Mount Vernon, Matrons Office, Dr Robert Jones speaking.'

Marion replaced the receiver quickly without saying a word. He was home then. Her heart skipped a beat. She felt that empty feeling in the pit of her stomach. She did not want to speak to Dr Jones. He had broken her heart one too many times.

Rising from her seat, she crossed to the office window and looking out across the parade square saw the diminutive figure of Katie Brown emerging from the stores under a pile of newly issued uniform and heading the wrong way across square towards the male quarters. She thought about bellowing to her from the window, then thought better of it. Katie would find out soon enough that a rare breed of soldier was billeted at Camberley. She would be teased and subjected to all manner of male banter and then she would be turned around and pointed in the right direction. Modern warfare would be a sharp learning curve. The term, 'An Officer and a Gentleman,' seemed to have been deleted from the manual.

She had met Dr Robert Jones in exactly the same manner. He had made a lasting impression, but he would have to learn. She had little time for a man who changed his women more often than he changed his socks and treated them just as badly, for all his sophisticated patter. Robert Jones was an Officer, but, in the eyes of Marion Wilshaw, he was no gentleman.

CHAPTER 25. A BACHELOR FOR LIFE

Nant Ddu Farm
Maesteg, Wales

    Cefin Thorne liked to think of himself as a confirmed bachelor – and well he might. His farm was high up on the hillside above the small Welsh mining town of Maesteg. A track over a mile long wound its way up through the woodland from the nearest serviceable lane to where he farmed several hundred acres of mountain, mainly sheep and with a few fields of good pasture running alongside the stream which supported half a dozen milk cows, four goats and a motley selection of chickens, ducks, and geese.

    The Nant, as the stream was called, bubbled out of the mountain just above the house and was the farm's only supply of water. Nant Ddu farmhouse was a longhouse of stone and slate construction, built in the shelter of the hillside with a view down the mountain to the hamlet of Llangynwydd below. Cefin had been born on the farm and had lived there all his life with his father Maldwyn and his brother Hefin. Their mother, Mabyn, had kept her boys close to home and they had very rarely left the farm, only to attend school which they must, and on occasional trips to town to watch the local team play rugby. And chapel on a Sunday, always chapel on a Sunday, dressed up like the dog's dinner in stiff collar and shiny shoes, to stand on display in Bethania while the Reverend Edwin Davies preached the evils of drink and fornication and the values of hard work and sobriety. The brothers were two well-polished icons for the other mothers to admire, while their own children shunned the Sabbath, played in the street, and grazed their knees and elbows.

    Mabyn Thorne's two boys, they were raised how boys should be raised in the image of the Lord. Mabyn had died aged sixty in 1914 just before the start of the war which now took every available mother's son to fight for his country. After her death, Maldwyn had been bereft and seemed to have given up life. He no longer had any interest in the farm, rather spending his days sitting in his old chair by the fire, staring into the flames. His eldest son Hefin, short for Mehefin meaning midsummer, had been called up to the army. He had marched off in 1915, glad in his heart to get away from the claustrophobia of the valley and eager for experience of life. The report of his death in action had come only a few months later. Maldwyn had taken it hard and retreated further into his grief.

It was June 1916 and Cefin was now twenty-nine years old. He had no interest in women. His mam, when she was alive, had been a practical but not loving mother, but she saw to it that her sons and her husband were fed and clean and dressed appropriately. She had lived for the chapel. Her belief in the almighty pervaded their home, manifesting itself in the embroidered texts she stitched every evening by the fire after she had put her boys to bed. The almost Catholic statues inhabited every surface of the best room, reinforcing her constant belief that God and hard work would always see them right. Her God had seen fit to take her from them at the age of sixty, leaving two resentful sons and a grief-stricken husband, for Maldwyn had loved her for all she was more in love with God than life itself.

Cefin did not want female company, he had no time for the fairer sex. He was content to ride down from the farm once a week for a few beers in the Tyler's Arms in the village, to walk to the Rugby when the town were playing at home and there was no pressing work on the farm, and to sing in the choir, for he still sang in the choir on a Sunday. Though he despised the whole concept of religion, he sang because it made him happy. His life was a bastion of masculinity. Or so he thought. There were many in the valley who gossiped behind their hands and whispered in corners that he was, 'one of those,' a 'Nancy boy.' But as with all gossips none would ever say it to his face. Cefin Thorne might be a mummy's boy, but he looked as though he could probably punch his weight, if he were ever tested.

War had touched Maesteg in any number of ways. Most of the men had gone to war. Those men employed in the mines had been kept home as essential workers, keeping the coal supplied or, like him, tied to the farm. There had been a new hospital built. It was staffed with both local women trained as nurses and with nurses from all parts of the country. Many did not speak Welsh and were viewed with suspicion by the local population. There were soldiers too, injured and wounded men sent to a hospital in a peaceful valley to recover from their wounds. He saw them when he passed on his way to the Rugby Club or the Chapel, walking around the small town in their blue and red uniforms, different from the khaki clad serving soldiers on leave, but in a uniform which marked them as having served. They were not to be confused with the few who avoided joining up to defend their homeland. Or those who had deserted their duty, as Cefin knew some had.

It was a fine June day. The sheep were grazing the top fields high above the farm. The cows and the goats had been milked and the full churns taken down to the stand at the roadside to await the cart from Mervyn Collins' Dairy to collect.

Maldwyn was pretending to read the paper and staring into the fire in the kitchen, his mug of tea and his morning toast both growing cold alongside him.

'Dada,' Cefin called to his father. 'Dada, for heaven's sake man, at least dress yourself.'

Maldwyn was still in his old pyjamas and brown dressing gown. Maldwyn grunted. 'What's it to you boy, haven't you work to do, or find a wife to care for us? You know what they say of you boy?'

'I'm off up to the top, I'm taking the cob, the milk is gone to the dairy, you just sit for a while, I'll be back before tea.'

'What about my dinner, boy? I need my dinner.' The once strong voice was a pathetic whine. The sound of it grated on Cefin's teeth.

'You have arms and legs. Fend for yourself. There's ham and bread in the pantry and butter on the table, I'm sure you can make a sandwich!'

Cefin left by the kitchen, into the small yard, shutting the ledge and brace door hard behind him. He loved his father dearly, but it had been two years now since he had functioned as a person. Grief had him in its clutches and nothing would make it let go.

The sturdy black cob was tied up in the yard, broad backed as a table, with a kind intelligent eye, a large white star and four white socks. Boyo, the cob was the envy of neighbouring farmers.

Cefin loved nothing as much as to ride him up over the mountain, high above civilisation in the fresh air and usually the rain, but today under a fair blue sky he would ride over the tops behind the smoke of the collieries and up to Nantyffyllon. He needed no other company than Boyo and his own thoughts. He would count the sheep and check the fences and walls on the way, make a mental note of any that needed mending, for sheep could always find a way out, and be back to the farm before evening milking. His father would have to fend for himself today.

Cefin headed up the winding uneven path through the oak wood behind the house, Boyo walking with his usual bouncy stride as they navigated the steep bank and emerged onto the mountain top. Following the dry-stone wall along the edge of the field, Cefin placed two fingers into his mouth, under his tongue, and whistled shrilly. Among the ferns on the bank, white woolly heads popped up, looking round in search of Tan the sheepdog. Instinctively, they bunched together and ran to the centre of the field, but today there was no dog, just Cefin and Boyo. Sheep are not the brightest creatures. Easily fooled.

Riding the edge of the field, checking the wall for holes, and whistling the remains of the flock into the centre of the field, Cefin did a head count. Sixty-five ewes all present and correct. Turning the horse's head north, he headed along the parish road across the hillside, heading for Caerau. He would ride round the head of the valley, stop for a drink in the Masons Arms and then ride back through town. A good run out for Boyo, and an afternoon away from his father.

He had tried everything, humouring the old man, waiting on him, fetching and carrying for him, while he only became more withdrawn and reluctant to resume active life. Now he resorted to leaving him alone. Maybe if the old man had to get up and do for himself, he would do exactly that. His father was physically as fit as a fiddle, but the loss of his wife and his oldest son dragged him down. There seemed no way for Cefin to fix him.

Kicking his mount forward into a canter he swiftly covered the distance to the top of the valley. Turning down into Nantyffyllon he stopped at the back of the Masons. Tying Boyo to the metal ring outside the back door he stepped into the bar. As he entered, the bell on the door announced his presence.

'Be with you in a moment.' A lilting female voice greeted him, unusual for the Masons. The landlord usually worked the bar himself on a weekday. He rarely employed staff. A head popped up from below the level of the counter.

'What can I get you, sir?'

'Just a pint of Best, luv, and where has Clive put the horses' bucket, it's not by the back door?'

'One pint coming up, and the bucket is up the garden. Clive says folk are to put their horses up there, now. Tommy Torycoed's pony walked right through the bar from front to back last week, caused a right mess on its way through, so tie him up in the garden please..... I've not seen you before, you are...?'

'Cefin, Cefin, Nant Ddu - that's down the valley a bit.'

The barmaid placed his pint on the bar with a brief flash of a smile.

'I'm Angharad, but everyone calls me Harri, I've only been here a week, still finding my way, I am. Now get and move that horse of yours before I get in trouble.' She laughed, a pretty, tinkling laugh, and her dark brown eyes sparkled at him from under her fringe.

There was only one other customer in the bar, Old Jack Hall, sitting in the corner by the window. He nodded a greeting and Cefin excused himself to move Boyo to the new hitching post halfway up the garden. Returning a few minutes later, he took his pint from the counter and sat with a view from the bar window from where he could see his horse and keep a whether eye on him. Boyo was known to untie himself and wander. Being a horse on an endless quest for food, Clive's vegetable patch would be easy pickings, and he would eventually come looking for his master, though he was too wide to fit through the doorway into the building.

Halfway down his pint, he was joined by Idris Jenkins. Cefin had been in school with Idris who was one of five brothers, all of whom worked in the colliery. Idris also played rugby for the town and had once had ambitions to play for Wales. A mining accident which robbed him of two fingers on one hand had put paid to that. Idris also sang in the Bethania choir, on occasion, when his shifts at the mine allowed. Conversation soon turned from the day to day of their lives to girls, and in particular to Harri.

'Widow, she is, lives in Brown Street,' began Idris. 'husband missing in action, but Tom Torycoed saw him killed, poor bugger.'

'Was that before or after Tommy legged it?' replied Cefin.

'Bit strange why he legged it, Tommy told me he saw a huge man with a longbow and a big knife standing over him, then he disappeared. Arthur, her husband was, Arthur Cole. No-one has seen or heard from him for months.'

'Well, she seems a nice girl - bit too young to be a widow.'

'Fancy your chances do you, Cefin? She's not on the market just yet you know!'

'What, me? Idris, I've no time for women, there's nothing I can't do better myself, our mam put me off the fair sex forever. I have no need of another mythering God bothering hypocrite running my life.'

'That's harsh boy, your mam was a good woman.'

'I'm sure she was, Idris bach, a lovely kind God-fearing woman, but then you didn't have to live with her!'

Idris went to the bar and ordered two more pints. 'Met our Cefin have you, Harri?' He winked at the barmaid. 'Good catch is our Cefin. Own farm, own horse, and hung like one so I've heard.'

Harri blushed scarlet. 'Any more of that talk and Clive says I've to ban you! I'm a married woman, and best you all remember it, I shall be married until I have a grave to put flowers on.'

She turned from the counter, wiping her eyes on her apron, her full bottom lip trembling. 'Look, sort yourself out, Idris. Clive is back in half an hour, okay. He won't tolerate your nonsense, said in fun or no!'

Idris drank his pint in one, thumped the empty glass down on the bar and left, slamming the heavy oak front door of the pub behind him. Cefin finished his second pint in silence, thinking, time for him to go, perhaps. By the time he rode back to the farm it would be time for his evening chores. But maybe he'd just have one more. Well, why not? Harri had made him smile, laugh even. He liked her feisty attitude, and her voice was doing very unseemly things to the hairs on his neck.

'I'll go one more then. I'll keep you company until Clive puts in an appearance.' Cefin leant on the bar counter, eyes drawn to Harri's neat posterior gently stretching the seams of her thick black cotton skirt as she bent to pick a pint pot from the shelf. 'Will you have one yourself?'

'Just half of cider for me, thank you, I'm nearly finished after all.' She stretched up to the hooks above the bar to reach for a cider mug, showing off a dainty pair of ankles and a very slim waist as she did so, but quite unaware of the effect she was having on her customer. Cefin sat on a tall stool by the bar, his left shoulder wedged comfortably against the upright timber endpiece, while they drank their drinks in companionable silence, watching Old Jack shuffle back to his seat on his return from the outdoor privy.

'Clive's back.' he grunted to Cefin. 'Best you get gone.'

With this, a giant of a man appeared in the doorway, his bald head shining like a huge and well pickled onion and nearly touching the ceiling. Shoulders which filled the doorway, arms so muscled they hung away from his enormous girth as though he was permanently carrying a sheep under each arm, he glowered around the room, fixing his slightly porcine eyes on

Cefin and reached towards him with a huge hand. 'Is that your fucking horse that's destroying my veg patch?'

The huge hand swivelled bodily Cefin around on his stool and pointed his face toward the window.

'Sorry, Clive!' Cefin muttered, downing the remains of his drink as Boyo's large black head came into view, the evidence hanging from his lips. Three pints to the good and feeling brave, Cefin added, 'Don't be hard on him, Clive, he only went up there for a leek, man!'

Harri snorted as the bubbly cider ascended her nose as she was caught laughing mid-mouthful and leant her head on the bar in uncontrolled giggles, trying her best to compose herself in front of her employer.

'Ha, bloody ha!' Clive growled at Cefin. 'Get home, Thorne, before I put you and yer bloody nag in tomorrow's stew!' The voice was a threat, but Clive's eyes were laughing. Cefin retrieved Boyo from the garden, pulling the remains of a cabbage from the animal's lips, and led him out onto the road, just in time to see Harri wrap her cloak around her shoulders and come out of the front door.

'May I walk you home, mistress Harri?'

She turned and smiled at him. 'If it protects me from that idiot Idris, then yes, you may. It's only two streets away, but he gives me the chills.'

'Then Boyo and I will be glad to see you safe.'

They walked, either side of the horse's big black head. Neither spoke, Boyo's iron-shod feet thudded rhythmically on the hard dirt road and when they stopped outside the house in Brown Street, Harri scratched the cob's small black ears and rubbed his nose. 'You are a good old lad, aren't you.' Boyo nuzzled her softly in the shoulder. Cefin silently wished that he and his horse could swap places, just for a moment.

'He likes you, see. He doesn't do that to everybody.'

'Thank you, Cefin Nant Ddu, it's nice to meet a man with manners.'

'Goodnight, mistress Harri.'

'Goodnight, Cefin Thorne.'

She disappeared into the small, terraced house and shut the door behind her. Cefin swung himself into the saddle and rode towards home. Maybe women weren't such terrible things after all.

As he turned Boyo down the track through the woods, he was lost in thought, thoughts of Harri, damn she was pretty, she was intelligent too, but married, and obviously in love with her husband. But then he had no thoughts in that direction, would it hurt to have a female friend, just as a start? At the fork in the track where it branched right to the neighbouring farm, he noticed that there was no smell of chimney smoke, damn Dada, he had let the fire go out again. One more thing for Cefin to do when he got in. No kitchen fire meant no hot water to wash the cow's udders, no heat in the house, no nice hot cup of tea, no hot food, and no bath. Damn you, Dada!

He untacked Boyo, hanging his saddle and bridle on their pegs and rubbed him down, he would brush him later when he was properly dry, just to get the sweat marks out of his glossy black coat. He fed him a small scoop of oats and a fork full of hay and crossed the yard to the kitchen door.

The door was closed as he had left it. As he let himself in the strangely metallic smell of blood almost imperceptibly invaded his nostrils. Then the realisation that the ceiling was stained black with a congealing jelly of the stuff and, the walls were spattered with it. Dada was still in his old chair. Cefin could see the wisps of his grey hair above the chairback. The world stopped in a heartbeat as Cefin saw the shotgun wedged between his father's feet, the barrels under his chin, both had been discharged, and the old man's face was no longer recognisable as human. On the trivet by the fireplace was the remains of a ham sandwich on the blue and white willow pattern plate that he always used. Under the plate was a note written on a page torn from an exercise book, the one in which he kept the farm's accounts.

August 1916

Cefin my son,

I have gone to meet my Mabyn and your brother Hefin, I cannot be without them a day longer.
I have grieved too long, there is no respite. Do not grieve for me as I did for them, I am in a better place. Forgive your mother, she loved you dearly in her way, make a good life for yourself, this war will not go on forever.

Dada.

Cefin threw up outside the back door. What should he do now? With tears in his eyes and a choking feeling in his throat, he put Boyo's bridle back on the surprised horse and bareback rode him down to Tyler's Arms where he knew he would find Constable Blake.

The Constable was four pints the worse for wear but, leaving his bicycle outside the pub and riding behind him on Boyo, he accompanied Cefin back to the farm to complete the formalities. There would in time be a postmortem and an inquest. Until then, his father's body would be kept at the new hospital mortuary. He arranged with Constable Blake to take the body by cart in the morning.

He left the Officer to his work and fed his livestock then dealt with his father's bloodstained remains. For now, he laid him out on the table in the front room and covered him with a bed sheet. Then, once the Constable had finished his duties, he began the clean-up. It was nearly dawn before Cefin went to bed. An hour and no sleep later he went out to milk the cows, automatically making two mugs of tea and shouting to his father that it was time to get up. It would be many months before he stopped doing everything for two.

The coroner's report said suicide. No one disputed that Maldwyn Thorne had been lost in his grief since the death of his wife and then his son. The funeral took place the week after and Maldwyn was buried alongside his wife, Mabyn, his body clothed in his black serge suit and waistcoat, lest she berate him for not looking his best before the Lord. It was a small funeral. In the custom of the valleys, it was men who attended funerals and stood at the graveside, but all the men were at war or working the mines. Cefin was alone except for 'Edwin the Cloth,' as they called the priest, Jack Hall and Idris Jenkins, Tommy Torycoed who was still not picked up by the army, and Constable Blake who was not looking too hard for him. As he turned to walk from the grave, Cefin saw the dainty figure of Harri Cole waiting by the cemetery gate. She waved at him, shyly and he walked over to her.

She spoke first. 'Cefin, I am so sorry, is there anything I can do, you'll be needing help I think?'

'Thank you, Harri, but I've been managing alone for ages.'

'Well, let me walk with you at least, as a friend.'

'That would be very nice indeed, thank you.'

And so, they walked. They walked slowly, down the path from the cemetery which lay on a rise in the ground just outside the town. The graveyards of the individual chapels were long since full. Even his mother had not been buried within the stone walls and wrought iron of her beloved Bethania.

'It was not your fault, you know.' Harri spoke softly.

'I can't help but blame myself, I should have been there, I should not have gone out.'

Cefin ran through the events of that day over and over, like how could he have done things differently? It came down to one small act.

'I should have made his bloody sandwich!'

Harri actually laughed. She swallowed the laugh in her coat sleeve, but it came out anyway.

'Your father did not kill himself over the lack of a ham sandwich, he had lost his will to live.'

'I know that Harri. He hadn't been right since mam died, and then when Hefin was killed he seemed to shrink into himself even more, but I can't get it out of my mind. Perhaps if I had been kinder to him.'

'You were a good son to him Cefin, all the men told me that. You did everything you could, he needed help you could not give.'

'But if I hadn't gone out, I went riding, I went to the pub, I didn't want to be in the house, I....'

'Don't torment yourself, Cefin. It could have been while you were milking, or tending the sheep, his demons were calling him, there was nothing you could do.'

Without realising it, they had reached the farmhouse where the kitchen still smelled vaguely of strong soap, disinfectant and blood mixed with fresh lime wash. Cefin had repainted the walls and the ceiling. He had scrubbed the flagstone floor till his knuckles bled. The range in the fireplace gleamed with black lead. He had even scrubbed his father's old Windsor chair, washed the shawls which covered it, Mam's old Welsh blanket, the one she had nursed her boys in, the one his father had wrapped around his old shoulders to keep the draught from them. Cefin didn't have the heart to throw it out, but he would not sit in it. There were three ghosts sitting in it now, they didn't need more company.

'Tea?' he reached for the teapot and pushed the kettle onto the hot plate.

'Two sugars please, if you've got any.'

He reached two mugs, bright with the blue finish of the local pottery. They were mugs his mother kept for best, though he suspected she preferred the China cups which inhabited the dresser in the front room. Yes, he thought, his Mam was definitely a cup and saucer woman. They took their tea out into the yard and sat on the back step, looking up the valley to where Boyo grazed in the field by the stream. 'It's just him and me now.'

A big tear the first of many, ran down Cefin's cheek. Harri caught it with her finger, her left arm sisterly around his shoulder. 'At least knowing is better than waiting.' she whispered to herself, 'You know they are gone. You have a place to visit them, the sadness will heal in time. I must wait.'

'Then I will wait with you, if you will let me, if you do not feel he is dead then he is still alive, somewhere, and he will return, I shall wait with you, and it will help me.'

She took a mouthful of tea, the deep breath in that went with it producing a most unladylike noise.

'Pardon me!' she laughed. 'Now Cefin Thorne, who is to do your cleaning and your washing while you have a farm to run? I have time to occupy. Clive pays me for one shift a week behind his bar and while my husband is missing it seems his money is suspended. No pay, but not yet any pension. I have received nothing from the army in weeks.'

'I will manage.' he replied.

'No, you will not. I will catch the dairy wagon down when it collects on Tuesday and Thursday, I will walk the rest. I can clean and keep you tidy, and you and Boyo can take me home when you check the top fields in the evening.'

'All planned then, is it?' Cefin laughed.

'Of course.' She looked at him, one eyebrow raised.

'Do I get a choice in the matter, Angharad Cole?' He used her full name, rolling it across his tongue where it left a sweet taste like the toffee which old Mrs Tinter made in the back room of the shop.

'Cefin Thorne, enough of that, only my mother called me Angharad and then only if I had misbehaved. I've been Harri since I could walk.' I am also Harri to him, she thought.

'Oh, and I will bring little Myrddin with me. The fresh air will be good for him.' The clock above the fireplace chimed three. Cefin stood and began to shrug his shoulders out of his black overcoat,

'Duty calls, the cows won't wait, nor the goats, and Boyo will want his feed.'

Harri helped him. She fed the chickens, and she caught Boyo and brought him in to his stable for his feed. Then she set to work in the kitchen. In the pantry she found bread and cheese and a quarter of a fruit cake which Cefin had bought from the shop the week before. There was always butter and milk but there was little else in his cupboards.

Cefin finished his chores, sat down while Harri watched him eat what she had prepared, then gestured to the door. 'Best I take you home, it will be dark before I get back, and the tongues will already be wagging.'

'Let them wag, everyone needs a friend, that is all we are, friends. I like you Cefin Thorne, you are like the brother I never had.'

He saddled Boyo and with Harri sitting behind him they rode across the mountain and back to her home. Cefin rode back with a pleasant fuzzy feeling in his gut, a smile on his face and for the first time in years he looked forward to the future. He was nearly thirty, a confirmed bachelor, he had no interest in a wife, but now he had a friend, a kindred spirit, and she was waiting, he would wait with her. As the sun dropped behind the mountain, he felt the burden of guilt and expectation lift from his shoulders. He whistled cheerfully to himself and smiled as the black ears four feet in front of him pricked forward and his mount picked up his stride and turned down the path for home.

Angharad Cole was confused. She had not felt like this in years, no, not years. She had never felt like this before, sitting astride the wide back of the horse, her arms wrapped tightly around the man in front of her, feeling every move of his muscles with either her arms or her chin or her breasts. Her new friend had muscles like whipcord under that shirt, there was no fat on his belly. She wondered was it true, what Idris Jenkins had shouted across the bar, or was it true what the gossips said.

She had slid down from the horse, a stray hand glancing off his left thigh as she lowered herself as gracefully as she could muster onto the ground outside the house. Her legs were slightly wobbly from the ride, so she leant a few seconds on his leg, while she caught her breath. Then she had turned away from him and with a half wave of her hand had let herself into the overcrowded cottage that was her home.

Just in time for her mother-in-law to thrust a red faced and screaming child into her arms.

'About time girl! You can't go galivanting about the valley with that man, you'll be the talk of the place, and your son has been mythering all day.'

Brought back to reality, she eventually soothed and fed the fractious teething baby, murmuring into his silky hair and singing softly to him. Then she took both of them up to her tiny room in the eaves of the house, settled Myrddin for the night, then stripped down to her shift and lay on the bed watching the stars through the tiny window, gazing at the mountain. Pulling the thin patchwork quilt over her she let her hand wander down her body and imagined another life.

1st August 1916

Harri had dropped into a routine. Each Tuesday and Thursday she rode down the valley with Mervyn Collins the Dairyman who collected the full churns from the farms on his way back up the valley. She walked up the track to Nant Ddu Farm in time to catch Cefin when he came in from the yard after milking. She spent the morning cleaning, polishing, and cooking. If she had brought young Myrddin with her she would leave him in the crib which Cefin had found in the loft under the eaves of the house. It had been his and his brother's before him. He had re-painted it and made it good for its new occupant, Myrddin, who would soon be out of it and crawling about under his mother's feet.

On this fine summer morning, Harri arrived without Myrddin, he was teething again she said. She had left him with her mother-in-law, he would be fine with his nanna Cole. She was excited and over their morning tea she reached inside her cardigan and pulled out a velum envelope. 'I have a letter, from London, it came with the post yesterday. I was too excited to open it then, worried about what it might say. Sit with me while I read it, please Cefin. It is news, pray that it is good.'

She sat and looked at the handwritten address for at least five minutes, running a finger over the words as if trying to feel the writer. Then she slid the back of a clean dinner knife under the seal and opened the flap and pulled out the folded sheet of paper. With a shaking hand she unfolded it and began to read and as she read her hand leapt to Cefin's wrist and she gripped his hand tightly where it rested on the big, scrubbed table. 'He is alive, thank God, he is alive, and he is getting well, Cefin, he is coming home, soon.'

She flung her arms around his neck, nearly knocking him out of his chair, took a handful of his unruly curly black hair in each hand and kissed him firmly on the mouth.

'Cefin Bach, my waiting is nearly over, I must write, I must write now, do you have paper, you must have paper, and a pen, I must catch the post when I go home!'

There followed a great search through his mother's desk in the best room, there he found a goodly supply of the lavender coloured paper his mam had used for her church correspondence and a pretty, enamelled fountain pen, and a bottle of Hibberts ink which with the addition of a little water became useable.

'Use the desk. Aye, mam wouldn't mind a bit.'

'No, kitchen table for me, I shall think better there.'

For half an hour Harri sat and scribbled, then crossed out and started again. Eventually surrounded by a pile of half used paper she was finished, the letter was addressed, and a stamp affixed.

'If we go now, you will make the post.' Cefin had already saddled the horse, Boyo stood ready in the yard. 'Hold tight Harri, we will be going as fast as the old boy can manage!'

CHAPTER 26. A CONSULTATION

August 1916
Mount Vernon Hospital..

    Dr Robert Jones sat with Doctor Bannerman in the wood panelled office, second on the left of the front door, matrons' office being first on the left, in the position of doorkeeper and guard dog. All entrants needed to get past Matron's door before gaining access to anyone's inner sanctum. Either side of the huge wooden kneehole desk, which took up most of the room, was piled with manila folders labelled with patient's names and containing their notes.
    Jones was poring over the X-rays of Montague Shipley's jaw, alternately holding them up to the light which streamed through the big sash window and to the rudimentary light box which the two doctors had contrived. A structure made like a small cucumber frame from a sheet of frosted glass, it was illuminated from behind by that most modern invention, the electric lightbulb. This was propped up on easel style legs and the developed X-ray image held in front of it.
    The hospital benefited from electricity but only in certain areas, the rest still being lit by gas lamps. Electric light was unreliable and expensive, but very helpful in some circumstances.
    'Hmmmm, it's a bit of a mess in there,' muttered Dr Jones into the air.
    'The left side is shattered. The nurses tell me he is taking his food through a straw.'
    'Whatever I try, it's going to be fixed, or have very little movement. I can fashion a prosthetic implant which will give more stability. It appears that the remains of his temporomandibular joint are still in place. If I can fix to that and to the right side of his jaw at the other end, we may be in with a chance.'
    Bannerman folded his papers on the desk. 'Rather you than me, Bob, but you have all my assistance, who on earth is going to make this 'prosthetic' and out of what?'
    'That, my friend is something I will have to work out. His bloody brother the General must have pulled all sorts of strings to get me home to do this, whatever the cost.'

Bannerman pulled his white coat off the hook on the back of the door, straightened his waistcoat, checked the time on his gold half hunter pocket watch. 'Time to go upstairs. Lock the office when you leave. My writing paper has been disappearing in remarkable quantities in the last few weeks, so has matron's, nurse Munro has them all writing diaries and letters home! Says it does wonders for their mental health, and I have to say she may have something, Private Cole is so recovered I'm thinking of sending him home!'

'What, the lad who saw the archers?'

'Yes, that's him, he came up from Abbéville after that disaster of an offensive. His C.O. saw fit to put a note in his file.'

Dr Bannerman rummaged amongst his folders and pulled out a scruffy scrap of paper, slightly stained with some bodily fluid, he thrust it under Dr Joneses nose 'Here, read this,'

Memo......

Private Cole is delusional, of that there's no doubt,
he's a brain damaged warrior, along with so many
others. It is recommended that he be returned home to
England at the earliest convenience to undergo a full and thorough
psychiatric assessment.
He will never be fit for active duty again.

'Well, there's a lot of truth in what he says. Matron says he kept the ward awake with his nightmares until the advent of Nurse Munro. I must meet this ministering angel,'

Dr Bannerman was halfway out of the door when Dr Jones added.

'Strange things happened at Abbéville. if he says he saw archers I wouldn't be too sure it was all in his mind.'

Robert Jones took a fresh sheet of Dr Bannerman's treasured velum paper, a set of dividers and a ruler and pencil and started to draw the structure with which he proposed to mend Shipley's face.

Leonard Bannerman ascended the stairs and began his ward round. All was very much the same as the day before, except for the bed by the window where Arthur Cole sat in his chair, dressed in his new blue uniform, hair neatly trimmed, clean shaven, and smiling. He was still looking out of the window watching the world go by, but now not blankly, with a sense of purpose.

'Private Cole.' The doctor smiled broadly at the seated figure 'Expecting someone?'

'Only the postman doctor, I'm hoping for a letter from home, see.'

'Sister Battle says your nights have been peaceful for nearly a month now.'

'Yes doc, writing things down helps a lot, and talking,'

'I can see that, Arthur, so much so that I'm going to recommend you are sent home, or at least to continue to mend at the nice new hospital in your hometown, ideal in fact, as Sister Battle is being posted there at the end of the month. You can travel together,'

'I wrote home about it, Doc, I actually wrote to my Harri to say I was on the mend, it's her reply I am waiting for, there he is now, the postie.'

Dr Bannerman reached into the deep pocket of the leather case he carried with him on his ward rounds and produced an exercise book and a pad of Basildon Bond paper and envelopes. He placed both on the table in front of the distracted Private Cole.

'Here's a little something for you, the book for your poems, and paper to write home, it will help to prevent the nursing staff raiding my best headed velum. Lord knows why they take the trouble to cut the heading off with matrons' guillotine, then leave the evidence in their common room bin.'

Arthur watched the distinguished looking figure walk back down the ward and waved a thank you at his departing back. He was sure the medic was chuckling by the way his shoulders were moving under his coat.

The postman had let himself in and left the hospital's post in the basket marked 'Post In' on the table in matrons' office.

He picked up the pile from the basket marked 'Post Out.' There was no one in the office so he announced his presence loudly and cheerily up the stairs, 'Anything more for the Post!'

Not receiving a reply, he went cheerfully on his way. In the last few weeks, the number outgoing letters from the patients had more than doubled, all of them it seemed were writing. Most were writing home, to addresses as far away as Aberdeen and a few to Wales.

Doctor Robert let himself out of Bannerman's office, locked the door behind him as requested and let himself in to Matron's office next door. 'I'll sort it.' He called up to the ward on the floor above, 'the post I mean.'

Picking up the pile, he started to separate the official mail from the personal, then the staff personal from that of the patients, then into piles for the individual nurses, which they could collect from their pigeonholes. They also had pigeonholes in the nurses' home, but mostly their mail came in mixed with that for the hospital. Then the mail for the ward, he dealt it into piles.

Nesbit Evans 4, Arthur Cole 1.

Private Cole had a reply then. The letter was addressed in a neat hand and smelled of lily of the valley. Good news, he hoped.

He tucked the drawings he had made from Shipley's x-rays under his arm together with Shipley's notes and with the post in his hand ascended the stairs two at a time.

Nesbit Evans was also sitting his new blue uniform alongside his bed. Dr Robert handed him his letters. 'Four for you, you are popular, or do you owe money.'

Then further down the ward to Cole, who was waiting expectantly for the arrival of any missive addressed to him.

'Just one for you Cole.'

'Only one I want Doc Robert.'

'I hope it's good news then.'

Cole took the letter in both hands, held it to his nose and inhaled deeply. Then his hands trembling slightly he broke open the envelope and slid out the sheets of paper covered in the same neat hand as the envelope.

6th August 1916

Dearest Arthur,

I was told that you were dead. I wrote to you in June and received no reply, some of your unit had been sent home, their families had news, but no one had seen or heard of your whereabouts, we had no word that you were missing or wounded. Tommy Torycoed who is on the deserters list came to your mam's door and told us that you were dead. He said he had seen you, lifeless, hit by a blast, and a man standing over you with a huge knife. Tommy said that the big man leant over you, then you both disappeared. He was certain, even though he was running away. We had heard nothing from you, so we believed him. Da said not to do anything until we had a telegram, but no telegram came.

We have all moved home. The house in Brown Street became too small for all of us, so when the house behind in John Street became vacant, I moved into it along with your brother and his wife for a few weeks, but his wife and I do not get along, so I am now lodging across the road from your ma and da. Maybe the telegram went to John Street. Your brother's wife Tegwen would not get out of her way to pass it on, so we went on believing you dead.

Imagine my surprise when I received your letter, I was fit to burst with happiness. You are safe at least, and coming home. I have been to the new hospital, just to see what it's like, it is half way up the Neath road, looking out over the municipal park and the valley. It is so new it is not yet shrouded in coal dust like most of the other old buildings. If I could find the train fare I would come and visit, but the fare would be too much and it would be a journey for two. I cannot wait to tell you, it was in my last letter, the one which never found you. You are a father, a dear little boy. I have called him Myrddin Robert Arthur for your father, but he is not yet christened so you can change it if you like. Who is Nurse Munro of whom you speak so well? I am glad she has taken you under her wing and you are writing again. I laughed so much when you said she thought Harri was a man! Oh Arthur, soon the old you will be back. I cannot wait, neither can your son. He has a fine mop of curly hair just like mine, but he has your eyes, your long legs and surely is as stubborn as all your family. I fear he was also born to be a collier; his favourite game is counting the coal in the scuttle. I must end now if I am to make the post.

All my love, cariad,
Your ever loving Harri.

Arthur Cole had not walked more than a dozen steps since he graduated from his bed to the chair. So buoyed up was he by this letter that he rose like a phoenix from his seat, face alight with joy.

'I'm a father boys, I'm a bloody father, I have a son!'

Dr Robert Jones was just sitting down alongside the bed of Montague Shipley when he heard the commotion.

Good news indeed he thought to himself, no doubt a cake would appear at teatime. Cake seemed to arrive on the ward as if by magic, it disappeared as quickly, he must make sure he was present when it landed.

'Now, Lieutenant Shipley, this is what I have planned for you.'

The lieutenant was now sitting up in bed. The surgery to his neck had healed well, though it had left an indentation on either side big enough to insert a finger into. He could not talk but communicated quite well using a quite modern form of sign language, though only sister Agnes was proficient in understanding him. He also wrote notes, copious notes, and summoned the nursing staff by means of a bell. He still had no sensation below his waist and was incontinent of urine and faeces. This was his main source of discomfort and frustration. He listened intently as Dr Jones explained that he intended to replace the missing section of the left side of his jawbone with a specially made metal implant which would be attached to the existing stable section of bone with screws. The unstable fragmenting section would be removed and a further metal implant would hold the roof of his mouth in a stable position until the rest healed. This he believed would give Shipley a jaw with some movement, the ability to eat more normally and would drastically improve the cosmetic appearance of his face by giving the left side its structure back. The lieutenant nodded enthusiastically. He was still under a great deal of sedation. Today had been a rare trip into consciousness.

'I need to take a few measurements inside your mouth, if I could.'
It was obviously painful for Shipley to have his broken face examined, and the resultant tensing of his muscles resulted in a discharge of faeces onto the draw sheet beneath him. Shipley's face told the tale of humiliation. Dr Jones called for a nurse to change the bed clothes. Once your face is healed, we can think about a colostomy, that should give you more control over your bowel movements.

Leaving Shipley in the care of Nurse Fiona Cameron, he left the lieutenants letters on the night table and wandered into the nurses' common room in search of cake.

CHAPTER 27. SURGICAL INTERVENTION

St Marys Hospital,
Sidcup.
August 1916

Dr Robert Jones scrubbed his hands for one last time and knocked off the tap with his elbows. He worked methodically, drying them on a pristine rough white towel, fingers first, palms, backs and on up to the elbows. A tight-fitting cotton cap over his cropped hair and cotton mask concealed his rather anxious features. Pick up the gown by the edges. Arms into loose green sleeves and tight cuffs, left then right. A theatre auxiliary pulled the insides of the sleeves so that the cuffs arrived at his wrists, then the edges of his green gown abruptly towards the middle of his back and tied them. He took a step towards the shelf where his gloves lay waiting. A brief dusting with talcum powder, then don the gloves with a snap, blinking away the dust. Take a breath and relax. All will be well. The patient lay on the operating table, draped and ready for surgery, peacefully anaesthetised, his wrecked face awaiting reconstruction under the surgeon's hand.

Montague Shipley's future once again in his hands, he had been transferred to St Mary's Hospital in Sidcup for the surgery where the operating facilities were far superior to the basic room at Mount Vernon. The technical experts at the hospital had engineered the silver gilt intra oral splint which would be inserted into the roof of the patient's mouth. This would give stability to his upper jaw and allow his lower jaw to be lifted and screwed back together, fixed with small gilt screws, and specially made plates. The young man would at least have a facial structure which was stable, and eventually he would be able to chew effectively on one side of his mouth. The kit had all been made from moulds taken by Dr Jones of the inside of Shipley's mouth using a basic form of putty, and measurements taken from the x ray images of his skull. The putty moulds had been difficult, painful for the patient who had resisted the intrusion into his injured mouth at every turn. Dr Jones hoped to keep the visible scarring to a minimum. He would try and hide his incisions under the jaw line. He hoped Lieutenant Shipley would be happy with the results if he survived the operation.

Jones walked towards the anaesthetised patient and the team who would work with him. They had all been involved in the discussions regarding this rather novel procedure. Arriving at the side of the table he nodded a greeting to a similarly clad nursing sister and her assistant and towards the anaesthetist, partially in shadow at the head of the table, offering a reassuring smile.

'Everybody happy in here?' he enquired. 'May we begin, please, Sister?'

'When you're ready Dr Jones.' she nodded. 'Dr McCann is the patient going to stay asleep?' he enquired of the shadowy presence behind the draped head.

'Don't you worry about that, Jonesy, you can get started when you're ready. It's all going to be fine.' Tilting the patient's head back and to one side, Jones swabbed the area well with alcohol and draped up the remaining exposed head. The young anaesthetist, Dr McCann had developed a new technique, administering the anaesthetic gases through a circuit of pipework which mixed ether and nitrous oxide and oxygen and fed them down a distinctive orange rubber tube he had placed in the trachea allowing the gases passage straight into the patient's lungs. So much easier, thought Jones, having the whole of the patient's face visible for the whole of the operation. The level of anaesthesia could be adjusted easily exposing the patient to much less risk. The anaesthetist could monitor breathing, and blood pressure using a sphygmomanometer.

'That's a new bit of kit you have there, Ivan.' the surgeon spoke to his colleague.

'Where have you been hiding Rob, I've been trialling it for some months now.'

'Down at the sharp end, my friend, dodging the bullets. Have you lost many with this thing?'

'Not one so far, but there's always a first.' He winked an eye at the theatre nurse and saw her blush over the top of her muslin mask, right to the roots of the blonde hair pinned down by her tight head scarf which held it back off her face.

Dr Jones picked up his scalpel and, stretching the skin beneath his fingers, began the delicate work to reconstruct Shipley's face.

Conversation continued between colleagues, it served to lighten the tension in the room, as Jones cut and stitched, and grimaced at the puzzle of half healed bone which was Shipley's mandible.

'Like a good jigsaw do you?' Ivan McCann commented on observing the layout of the mandible exposed beneath the skin.

'Thrived on them as a child, the more pieces the better.' quipped Jones. 'I loved the ones with pictures of trains the best, this is more of a train wreck, sadly.'

McCann checked the patient's vital signs and pumped a little more anaesthetic gas into Shipley's lungs.

'That should do nicely, we wouldn't want you waking up just yet would we now,' He addressed his sleeping patient then turned back to Robert Jones. 'How did you get sent back, may I ask?'

'Our man here has friends in very high places, his brother had me travel with him from Abbéville. I'm glad to be home, but I left Sam O'Connor expecting a visit from the Bosch. I hope they survived, the men we couldn't evacuate I mean. If they were captured, I pray they are treated well.'

'Was that your hospital then?'

'For our sins, yes it was.'

'Then ye'll be knowing Josephine Delaney.'

'How could anyone forget. Sam O'Connor has been sweet on Sister Jo for months, and she's been fending him off for longer.'

'I was in school with the lovely Josephine, she's a character so she is. My first kiss behind the bike shed, too, met her again when we were called up. Turned into a classy lady, fond of her silks and such,'

McCann chuckled to himself as if in the middle of a fine memory.

'That's the way to her heart, you tell Sam, a little bit of silky luxury goes a long way with our Josephine. Sister now, is she, well she was always going places.'

Several hours later, with a long exhale of breath, Dr Jones tied off the last neat stitch and surveyed his work. If infection was kept at bay and all went smoothly it was not a bad job.

'Ye should apply for a job under Mr Gillies, that's as fine a piece of work as I've seen him perform, being as yer back in blighty.'

'I intend to go back to the front once I'm done here. This is only temporary and I've some personal business to attend to with Janet Gunn before I leave.' He stood back from the table and surveyed his work. Shipley might never be able to talk, his larynx was beyond repair, and he would always have a large indentation on either side of his neck, but he would be able to chew his food and swallow it, and his breathing was unobstructed. Once the scars had healed, his rehabilitation could begin in earnest.

'I'm finished, Ivan, it's over to you, bring him round, don't lose him for goodness's sake, his brother is a General. Do you have time to give him a catheter, less painful to do it here, I'd say, it would save a lot of bed changing for the nurses and make his life easier in the long run, poor bastard.'

He watched as McCann started to remove the curved orange pipe from the patient's throat and then stop.

'One catheter coming up. Nurse, one catheter please,'

The nurse exposed the patient's lower body and went about the process of inserting a urinary catheter. McCann went back to his tubes.

'Say, Ivan,' added Robert Jones 'where did you find those? They seem just the right size and the right curvature do you have the budget to have them made to order?'

'Well, you have to improvise, man. I found these in the shop which sells sporting goods on the Tottenham Road, they use them to inflate footballs. If it does the job, I'll use it, these have just the right bore, and the right amount of flexibility.' He picked up a spare from his box of implements and demonstrated. 'I've requisitioned all their stock - it's not as if we've a great need for footballs now, is it?'

Dr Robert Jones smiled. 'I don't suppose even The Arsenal can raise a full side these days.' On that note he turned and walked from the operating room leaving his patient in the hands of the anaesthetist and the theatre nurse to be brought back to the land of the living. His head re-swathed in bandages, he would be transferred back to Mount Vernon by private ambulance in the morning. He found a quiet room and wrote up his notes.

It was just over a month since Shipley's injury. He had spent much of that time under heavy sedation, it was time now for him to face his future. His hold on life was remarkable, as though driven by some hidden purpose.

Shipley's return to Mount Vernon was marked by a reception committee of Dr Bannerman, Matron, and his brother the General. He was reinstalled in his private room away from the main ward and it here that Fiona Cameron found him. The patient was now sitting up in bed, his lifeless legs covered by a blanket, his face still bandaged like an Egyptian artefact.

Bright and breezy, she opened the door.

'Good evening, lieutenant.'

The figure in the bed raised a hand from his mattress in greeting and emitted a harsh grating noise from the healing remains of his throat.

'Time to settle you for the night.'

She busied herself with tidying his bed, emptying the bottle which took the contents of his bladder straight from his newly installed catheter. That's a relief, she thought to herself, at least he won't be wet all the time. She offered him a bedpan, the patient grunted, and the bandaged head shook, which she took for a refusal. Calling on Frances Munro to assist her, they lowered the lieutenant into a comfortable position for the night. Whether he would sleep was doubtful. Frances offered to sit with him for a while until sister morphine took effect.

Shipley's sleep was restless. As far as he could, he tossed and turned and cried out through his wrecked voice box, producing only harrowing gasps of air. Frances took his hand and talked to him. She spoke to him quietly of his company of men thinking that her quiet voice might calm him, but this seemed to agitate the lieutenant greatly, especially any mention of the name MacGregor.

Frances and Fiona crossed the yard to the nurses' residence after their shift, curious as to why the name MacGregor should mean so much to their very important patient. There was still no news from the front, their men were still missing, but not officially so. The only comfort was that they were not listed amongst the dead.

Life at the hospital ticked along to the beat of Fiona's alarm clock. Days came and went and there was no news.

Private Cole made his recovery in leaps and bounds, spending his time sitting, writing at the table he had positioned by the window, his nightmares becoming less frequent and less intense in their nature. Private Evans, too, was up and out of bed, both men, comrades from the same company and the same town, talked of going home. Cole was already listed for transfer to the rehabilitation hospital in their hometown. He had been heard saying he would keep a bed warm for Nesbit Evans and a pint of beer on the bar of the Masons Arms for when he arrived.

Within a week Shipley had his bandages removed, he could eat food which was more solid and was looking forward to having dentures fitted. He, like the others, had asked for a pad of paper and a pen. For him it was his main means of communication. He gestured with his hands, indicating most of what he wanted, and when he sat out of bed he wrote. His brother had acquired for him a lovely mahogany writing slope, an old campaign model, with a drawer for paper and a tray for his pens and beautiful blue glass ink wells in silver holders.

Shipley wrote letters, endless letters, all addressed to General Haig himself, and several to a Captain Jeremy Shipley, based in Military Intelligence, Room 40, Admiralty, London.

The letters were always several sheets thick and never left for the nurses to post, they were handed personally to his brother for delivery and marked **'CONFIDENTIAL BY HAND.'** Apart from his brother he had had no visitors, though he had also written to his mother, but she had not replied. In fact, Shipley had received no replies to any of his letters. His frustration was evident.

It was several weeks later when it arrived, a thick wad of paper in the form of a military dispatch. Matron Gunn handed it to him and he dismissed her from his room with an impatient wave of his hand and broke the seal. It was from Jeremy Shipley. Matron watched through the round window in the door to his room and could have sworn she saw him smiling, as well as his distorted face would allow. That night Shipley slept like a baby, peaceful, relaxed, contentedly snoring through his stitches.

CHAPTER 28. BAD NEWS TRAVELS FAST

August 1916
London.

It was 6.30am on a wet London morning in August and Sergeant Lloyd of the Metropolitan Police stood in front of the battered front door of 3 Agar Grove. There was no need to knock, the door, as always, was open. The Baker family did not believe in keys, they had nothing in the house worth stealing.

He could not count the times he had come to the house in search of Frankie. It had become a game of cat and mouse. Frankie was a clever thief, a slippery little customer, and Sergeant Lloyd could never pin anything on him. He had a grudging respect for the lad. The boy had volunteered, hadn't he, he hadn't waited to be called up. He and his best mate Charlie had done the right thing and marched proudly off to war. It was with a heavy heart he called in through the open door.

'Letty, I need a word.' he called out to Mrs Baker.

She answered the door, hair still up in papers on her head, apron tied round her waist in a business-like manner.

'Come in Gareth, social call is it, our Frankie has been away these past few months.'

Then her face dropped. 'He's not….'

'No, Letty, he's not. It's worse than that, he's on the deserters list, is he here?'

'He's in bloody France fighting the Bosch, him and Charlie, too bloody young he was to go and all, but I couldn't stop him.'

Sergeant Lloyd pulled the scruffy, dog-eared printed list from his tunic pocket and showed her the entry.

'We get the list every month, the list of deserters, in case they make their way home. See, he's here,' He pointed to the name. Then he pulled out another page, 'and Charlie with him.' The finger pointed to the name of Frankie's best friend.

'Not them, Gareth, this is wrong, they are brave boys, they would never have run away from a fight, whatever that says. They ain't here, do you want a cuppa while you're here?'

The policeman wandered through into the Bakers' kitchen and viewed the table which was covered with oil cloth, the sugar bowl and milk jug ornamenting its centre, the one available teaspoon stuck vertically in the sugar which had partially congealed itself into tea-stained lumps. Maybe he would pass on tea. He did however know Letty Baker well enough to know that the cups would be clean and the milk fresh. A nice fresh brew would go down well, and Letty made a good brew. He swatted the residual detritus of living from the seat of the wooden chair to protect the seat of his well pressed uniform trousers and sat down.

'Funny,' he said. 'there's two others on the list from the same company, a Sergeant MacGregor and a Welsh boy called Owen. Seems like they all went together.'

'Jack MacGregor?' Said Letty Baker pouring the tea. 'That's their sergeant, they worshipped him, the men would follow him anywhere. No way Jack MacGregor has gone AWOL or run out on his King and Country, or his men. Your list is wrong, Gareth, I'll bet my next week's housekeeping on it! And if they turn up in the street, I'll bring them to you myself!'

Sergeant Lloyd finished his tea and rose from the table, scraping the chair back across the flagstone floor. 'I hope I don't have to hold you to that, Letty, you take care now.' He stepped out of the front door onto the rain-soaked street, his hobnail boots crunching with official familiarity on the pavement, only to turn through the next gate to have a similar conversation with Jesse Turner, but without the benefit of tea.

As the officer left the Turners' house, Ethel Turner pulled her old coat around her shoulders and headed off across the park towards the Cameron's house. She still worked there, employed by the lawyers to keep the place clean and tidy once a week, still had a key to the kitchen door. She needed to speak to Fiona Cameron. She knew that Fiona visited the old house on her days off from Mount Vernon. She still had a pipe dream of opening it as a home for the wounded. She would take a chance that Fiona might be there today. Ethel didn't believe a word of what she had heard, but before she spoke to Letty Baker on the matter, she would speak to Fiona Cameron. Fiona still had friends in the War Office, and if anyone knew anything about Frankie's whereabouts it would be her, and as far as she knew, no one else knew about Fiona and Frankie.

How wrong she was. She was within a few yards of the Cameron's house when she saw the dark shadow and heard the clicking boots of

Sergeant Lloyd stepping up to the big front door. Taking the key from her pocket she ducked in through the door to the kitchen garden and let herself in through the servant's door.

Fiona Cameron was dressed for work, her neatly pressed and starched nurse's apron folded and ready to slip into her portmanteau, her warm woollen cloak hanging over the back of the kitchen chair, her blue nurses uniform hanging just to the top of her flat black button boots. Her head was bent over a steaming cup of what smelled like Earl grey and a slice of toasted bread and marmalade on a plate beside it. As Ethel entered the kitchen by the back door, there was a loud knock on the front door.

'Miss Fiona!' She called under her breath.

'Ethel, Mrs T, it's your day off…… what the….?' There was confusion in Fiona's voice.

'Don't answer the door, it's the police!' Ethel whispered urgently.

'Why ever not, I've nothing here to hide.'

'They are looking for the boys, Frankie, and Charlie and their Sergeant, Sergeant MacGregor!'

'Well best they look in France. They aren't here, Ethel, are they!' Fiona went and answered the door,

Half an hour later, Sergeant Lloyd left the house feeling as though he had been interrogated by a professional. Fiona Cameron had extracted from him far more than he was meant to say about the Deserter List.

He had told her that the list of deserters and men gone AWOL was mostly concerned with those who had not returned to their units. There were a few on the list who had deserted from actions with the British Expeditionary Force, but not many. Sergeant Lloyd had said that most who deserted whilst on active duty were rounded up, court-martialled, and shot before they ever got back to Blighty. Yet, someone had taken the trouble to post all four of the missing riflemen as deserters, not as missing in action. Before he ever made his rounds, he had done some homework. They had been entered in the list by Lieutenant Montague Shipley who alleged that the four riflemen had deserted their posts and absented themselves from action when their unit went 'over the top.' If this was right, then they were damned as cowards indeed. They were all trained as snipers, not a coincidence. Sergeant Lloyd did not believe in coincidence. Four elite snipers go missing before an action? Unlikely. Maybe they were active, but not where Shipley thought they should be. His gut feeling was that there was, 'More to this than meets the eye.' Those had been amongst Sergeant Lloyd's parting words. 'Shipley, he's the key, anyone called Montague is bound to be an ass!'

Fiona watched as he strode down the path and out onto the road, walking the measured strides of a man deep in thought. Her gut told her that Sergeant Lloyd would dig further. She knew that her own digging had only just begun, but she could do nothing until after her shift at the hospital. She could not cry off her duties. She would look up some of her father's contacts, see if she could find out more about Shipley.

In the meantime, more and more casualties were being shipped home from France. Men with horrific wounds or suffering the effects of gas and shell shock, men too damaged to ever be themselves again, all trying to forget what they had seen, heard, and smelled. Shadows of men, many so encased in bandages they were unrecognisable. Some so injured all she could do was hold a hand and talk to them.

Then there was Charlie's girl, Frances. She worked the same ward as Fiona. She had two brothers on the front line, twins, one of them already lost, Jeffrey Munro. Fiona had only met him once, the big slightly sinister Scotsman, a private in the Black Watch. They had all been out to the Duke for a night before the boys were mobilised, their last night of leave. She remembered the other twin more clearly, all six and a half feet of Neville Munro, dancing the sword dance over crossed walking sticks, in his kilt, in the bar of the pub. Now that was a sight she would never forget, his brother sitting strangely quiet on the wooden settle, just watching proceedings, eyes blank and slightly brooding. Twin brothers, but so different, one the exuberant extrovert, who loved life, the other the brooding and sometimes dangerously introverted. Well, Jeffrey was amongst the fallen, one of many killed by sniper fire in a trench in France. Frances had been bereft at the news. Her mother had received the telegram at their home near Inverness only last week. Neville had written home the week before with word that he had been promoted sergeant and they were together. He could not say where or what they were doing, but it had been good news - only to be wiped out with the next knock at the door.

'Mrs Munro, we regret to inform you……….,'

Fiona gathered her wits, gathered her belongings, and headed for the tram. She would see her friend Frances tonight. At the end of her shift, she found Frances in the sluice room washing bedpans and tidying up to hand over to the day nurses.

'We need to talk.'

'Have you heard from the boys then? Have they written home?' replied Frances, polishing the last bed pan and placing it in the rack and taking off her apron.

'I have bad news, Frances. I need to tell you.'

'Not....., no, no one is dead, at least I don't think so, but it's Frankie and Charlie, Sergeant MacGregor and one other, I may need your help.' Fiona told Frances all she knew, all Sergeant Lloyd had told her.

'My brother,' said Frances, 'he was killed by a German sniper. He was running supplies to the trenches. His Sergeant, Malcolm Ferris was with him. He told Neville the trench was being targeted. Neville wrote home after Jeffrey was killed. He told mother that the riflemen in the trench wanted to send a party out to disable the snipers, but they were ordered not to. He couldn't write much, it would be censored, but he said enough.

'Shipley!' murmured Fiona under her breath. 'Shipley is the key.'

Rhianydd MacGregor answered the door of 3 The Parade, Cardiff, young Agnes in her arms, teething and red faced from crying.

'My husband is with his men.' she told the young constable who dared to accuse her Jack of cowardice. Then she slammed the heavy door of 3 The Parade firmly on his size twelve boot. The young constable stepped back from the door. Maybe discretion was the better part of valour in this case. He had other calls to make and finding Jack MacGregor was not his priority this morning, and he valued his toes, and his testicles. Young Mrs. MacGregor was not one to be trifled with, clearly. He was not a fool, not quite. The Parry's, whose house it was, were well respected. He would check his facts again and come back later, perhaps when Moses Parry was home.

Rhianydd was stunned. She had not heard from Jack for weeks, but that was not unusual. Letters home were rare, and those that got through were usually heavily censored. Jack was brief and to the point in what he wrote. When his last letter arrived, he had been in good health, up to his knees in mud, surrounded by idiots and beset with sniper fire. His letters talked of Charlie and Frank a lot. Rhianydd had not met them but knew they were from London, and Jack had been their sergeant since they joined up. From what Jack wrote of them, they were brave lads, if frustrated by a lack of action.

For once Rhianydd wished she had her mother's gift of sight, or at least had not been so hard on her about their family history and all that went along with it. Her mother had tried to tell her about her real father, about her true heritage, but she had refused to listen. William Rees was *her* father. She didn't need another. Maybe it was time to build bridges. She could start by taking Agnes to see her grandmother.

Rhianydd settled Agnes in her crib, then sat at the kitchen table, head in her hands and tried to picture her husband. 'Jack MacGregor, where on earth are you?' she whispered She tried to bring him to mind, but she could not. Was it just that she did not have the gift, or something more sinister?

Her fiercely practical side wasted no more time on such things, things she could not believe in wholeheartedly. Instead, she pulled out the railway timetable and began to plan the tedious journey from Cardiff to Mid-Wales. The trains were few, the service cut back due to the war, a lot of the rolling stock had been commandeered for troop transport. What little was left was pulling the coal trains from the mines to the ports, to supply the war machine. It was Uncle Moses' business, he talked of little else than keeping the engines of war turning. The anthracite steam coal from the pits of the Rhondda was a valuable commodity these days, more valuable than gold in the eyes of many.

The Constable returned later in the evening accompanied by his sergeant and she and Uncle Moses had listened to what the sergeant had to say, Moses urging Rhianydd to remain silent and keep her counsel. Moses assured them that a man in his position would not be in the habit of harbouring deserters and asked them if they would like to search his house from attics to cellars. The officers politely refused and were ushered back out through the big front door, satisfied that they had made 'thorough enquiries.' Neither of them intended to make a return visit.

Rhianydd planned her route. The train could only take her from Cardiff to Newport and then north up to Monmouth then across mid Wales to Llanidloes and Newtown. From there she would need to hire a pony and trap to take her to St. Harmon. Was her mother even there? Her last letter, the one she had hardly read, had mentioned a telephone. She recalled thinking, 'Why does the old witch need one of those?' before filing the letter away in the old wooden box she had brought with her from the apothecary's shop. It was a cheap packing box which once held the perfumed soap William Rees loved making so much and the wood still smelled of the exotic perfumes of his greenhouse blooms. She pulled out her mother's last letter.

Hengwm
St Harmon
1914

My dearest daughter Rhianydd,

I wish you well. I always knew you would follow your own path in life. You are as fierce and as stubborn as your father. I hope your betrothed realises what he is taking on. I have not had the privilege of meeting Jack MacGregor who you say is a soldier. In times of war that is not a comfortable thing to be.
Travel safely to Scotland, look after Helena, she is not so robust as you. She will need her sister.
I am heart sorry for the rift between us and hope that one day all will be right again.
If you need to contact me, I have had installed a telephone. It is useful if I am needed in the village, for I still act as nurse, healer, midwife and occasional vet to the folk and the animals who live in St Harmon. I am sure Uncle Moses has a similar device. My number is St Harmon 3, the Priest and the Pub being numbers 1 and 2, respectively.
Please I beg you do not be a stranger.
Give my love to Helena.

Your mother
Sibyl.

Her mother was always concise with her words, no change there then. It was late, she would try the telephone in the morning.

CHAPTER 29. A TANGLED WEBB

London 1916

Doctor Robert Jones stretched his naked body. Like a small boy he wriggled further into the warm depths of the massive bed, under the cover of a massive eiderdown. God it was good to be warm.
From the steam filled bathroom of the hotel suite which had cost him an arm and a leg in pay, and a few raised eyebrows, Janet Gunn emerged long legged as a thoroughbred racing filly, her blonde hair darkened by the steam and piled in an unruly heap on the top of her very pretty head.
  His body could still feel the touch of her fingers on his skin through the washcloth, smell the lily of the valley soap as she had washed the ingrained dirt of from his skin, he had not had proper bath in months. He closed his eyes and re-conjured the feel and the smell of it all, banishing the smells of blood, death, and disinfectant from his nostrils at least for tonight.
  The bedclothes at his feet stirred and he felt the caress of lips on his ankle, and gentle hands massaging their way up his legs towards his groin. Dear god, what was the woman doing to him. The brush of silk, slippery up his thighs and from there all sense left him, all his senses descended, focussed on the one point of his anatomy where Janet Gunn was ministering the tender caress of her tongue. Then she was hovering like an angel above him, silken wings of her peignoir brushing his freshly washed skin, 'Dear God,' were the last words he remembered as he felt his heart miss several beats and his mind dissolve into stars behind his eyes. Then sleep.
  When he awoke, his first sight was into a pair of blue green eyes, chin resting on his chest, one finger making patterns in the thick mat of curly hair which covered it, a pink catlike tongue searching for a nipple and flicking over it, and round it, slowly. Sliding a hand around the lithe body still attached to his, he swiftly reversed the situation and peering down at her, lowered his mouth to her skin and began to give Matron Gunn the full benefit of his comprehensive knowledge of the female anatomy. Now it was her turn to cry out. He wondered what forms of blasphemy he could draw from her sweet lips. 'Oh, Janet Gunn, I love you.' His voice was a

whisper amongst the silk and the skin. Her next movement caused him to call his maker again.

It was just before lunchtime and several acts of mutual worship later.

'I'm starving, Robert, I think we missed breakfast.' She looked at him entreatingly.

'You are enough breakfast to last a lifetime.' he winked at her and pulled the eiderdown back over his shoulders and over her head.

'Well, it must be time for lunch then. Food I mean.'

He looked at her with the expression of a disappointed puppy.

'I mean it Robert, I need food, I haven't eaten since breakfast yesterday.'

On cue, her stomach growled loudly, to emphasise the point.

'Pie, mash, and peas in the park it is then. Get your clothes on if you don't want stale pastry and cold liquor!'

Robert threw off the bedclothes and with a suggestive wiggle of his nether regions and a flex of his shoulders reached for his newly laundered underwear and uniform trousers.

No uniform for Janet today, she had a whole weekend off, her man on her arm and she intended to forget the whole damned shooting match, at least for the time being. She did indeed look stunning in a lilac-coloured ankle length dress, hair worn pinned up, with her wide brimmed hat perched on top and secured with the deadly sharp hat pin she used for testing patients' reflexes, her only pair of button boots on her feet. He held out her old, classic camel hair coat for her to shrug into, buttoned his tunic, and they were off, away from the hotel and out into the green expanse of Regent's Park.

It was Saturday. The park was busy with couples out walking, mainly men in uniform home on leave, or waiting to go to war for the first time. Nannies in uniforms pushed perambulators containing the children of the wealthy, and Marion Wilshaw played with her young son on the grass under one of the huge chestnut trees.

From the corner of his eye, she was sure he saw her as he walked past, arm draped about his new lady friend. That blonde bitch, Janet Gunn.

The pie stand in Regent's Park was more of an outdoor café than a stand, small tables clustered around the serving hatch. Rob seated Janet at a table and then went to the hatch, returning with two small plates loaded with a meat pie in crusty golden pastry, a scoop of mashed potato which on first inspection appeared on the lumpy side, and a drizzle of the parsley flavoured gravy referred to as liquor.

The pair were too hungry to comment on the consistency of the mash, it was delicious to taste in any case. The meat in the pie was obviously affected by rationing, as was the consistency of the liquor, just a bit more liquid than was usual. But, it wasn't the cold stodge he had become used to in the hospital mess, it was a delight to his numbed taste buds and his empty stomach.

Replete, they walked across the park and out through the Primrose Hill gate passing the great villas which lined the edge of the park.

'See that one there.' Janet pointed to one with the shutters closed, obviously empty. 'Would it not make a fine rehab for your men coming home?'

'That must be the Cameron house, 'Fernleigh,' isn't it called?' he replied.

'That's what it says on the gate, I can read it from here.' she remarked. 'What a lovely looking place it is.'

'Funny you should mention it, the daughter wants it to be exactly that, but the old man's wife has challenged the will. They say that she has disappeared. It'll be stuck in the courts for years. Hell hath no fury like a woman scorned!'

As they let themselves out of the park into the hustle and bustle of St Pancras heading for, 'at least a pint of good beer before I must go back,' Marion Wilshaw took her young son by his hand and, muttering the words, 'arrogant bastard' to herself, started her long tram and bus ride back to her sister's house in Paddington. There she would leave her son, the boy who called his mother, 'Aunt Marion.'

The Duke of Clarence was busy. The usual array of railwaymen and porters sat in the snug cradling their pint pots of ale, a few soldiers clustered around one end of the bar, young men enjoying a last weekend before mobilisation. One stood back to allow the couple through. This man, he noticed, was wearing an officer's uniform but the badge was not familiar. Should he salute him? The young private was in a state of confusion when Doctor Robert spoke.

'Captain. Medical corps. No need to salute. Not here anyway.'

'Th..th..thank you, sir,' the private stammered through his words.

'When are you going across?'

'We leave on Mmmonday, ssssir. Just a weekend to say goodbye to the folks.'

'Good luck, look after each other.'

'We will, sir, all in the same school we was, just round the corner, got to get our name back, after them deserters shamed us.'

The private pointed to a broadsheet pinned to the underside of the bar flap: The Deserters List.

'Pass me that, let me see it.' Robert Jones demanded slightly sharply.

The private pulled the list from its pin ripping the edge as he did so, handling it as though it were used toilet paper, he handed it to Robert Jones. Two names were ringed in red on the list, with descriptions of the men concerned. Frank Baker and Charles Turner, both riflemen listed as privates. The description of the one fairly distinctive - very slight and very blonde. Alarm bells rang in Robert Jones's head while he subtly folded the broadsheet and slid it into his trouser pocket. He was sure he had met those men, and they were certainly not cowards. Half the regulars in the pub knew Frankie and Charlie but they weren't about to say anything, not to anyone. 'Not seen them since they went to France.' was the communal answer. No one was telling lies.

At the bottom of that same pocket was a small leather box. The ring was old, it had belonged to a great aunt of his, one small ruby set between two diamonds, the setting unusual in that it was rather like a signet ring with the stones pressed into the gold. It was the ring he had once thought to give to Marion Wilshaw.

Looking at Janet Gunn over the rim of his pint and her wine glass, he took his heart in his mouth and spoke the words he never had the courage to say to Marion.

'Janet Gunn. Will you marry me?'

The reply was instant, 'I will!'

A cheer erupted from the gathered soldiers, the railwaymen and the man behind the bar, there was not much to celebrate these days. More and more young men being fed into the war machine and never returning, the shortages of everything imaginable. A bottle of bubbly was produced courtesy of a man called Black Eric who occupied the dingy smoke filled back room of the pub and from who you could get most things. Had they wanted to know, it came from the wine cellar of a house called, 'Fernleigh,' stolen earlier that year along with five others in a box. The dirty looking

Welshman even proposed a toast to the bride and groom, and to Ethel Turner.

'Who,' thought Janet Gunn, 'was Ethel Turner?' But she raised a glass in salute and savoured the bubbles as they drifted up her nose. The ring had slid easily onto the third finger of her left hand, a perfect fit, as if it were always meant for her, and her alone.

Across town, Marion Wilshaw sat in a slightly care worn kitchen and was pouring out her heart to her sister Alice, damning Robert Jones to hell and back in one breath and declaring her love for him in another. Alice was losing patience, and she poured her sister another gin. Marion would be staying the night, no doubt. She took a large gulp of her own drink and spoke.

'It's not all his fault, Marion, is it! You never told him, you just told him to go away, well you told him to fuck off, and you said it like you meant it, and you said it several times. I was there, remember! A man like him won't beg. You made your bed, now you must make the best of it. Put out the candle you burn for him. Do it now and quit crying in your drink. You have a life and a career. I have a husband who drinks and three kids to look after. One more is nothing.' Alice Ford harangued her sister in frustration.

Marion drew in her breath and answered. 'The money I give you for Alfie keeps more than my boy, it keeps you all. That man took advantage of me, but you will never see that, will you? You've an arrangement which suits you, that's all that matters. You are nothing but a selfish bitch, no sister of mine.'

Without thinking twice, she threw the remains of her drink in her sister's face and slammed her glass on the table. She left her sister's home taking nothing with her, her bag and her coat still hung in the hall. The coloured glass leaded window in the front door shook as she slammed it shut behind her as she half fell down the flight of steps at the front of the house, stumbling half blind with grief and gin into the gutter.

The chilly night air closed around her as she walked, every step taking her closer to the park, drawn there by some unseen cord. She was more drunk than she had ever been. The gas streetlamps were no longer lit, it was darker than pitch, she stumbled blindly into walls and doorways finally completely lost, coming to rest under a bridge by the canal where her legs gave way under her. She sat with her back against the damp stone wall and wiped her face on her sleeve. What was it with gin, it always made her cry.

She threw a stone at a movement in the darkness beside her, and as if by magic several large black humped shapes grunted and ran into the night.

'Fucking rats!' She shouted after them as they disappeared.

Back at her sister's home, Alice was dealing with the tearful boy, woken by the shouting, asking in his high-pitched sad voice, 'Where Aunt Marion? Want Aunt Marion.' Alfie Ford had heard it all from his seat half way up the flight of stairs.

She made him a drink of warm milk and added a tot of whisky from her husband's bottle. That should get him back to sleep.

'Don't fret now, young Alfie. Auntie will come back, she always does.'

Sunday passed in the Ford household and there was no sign of Marion. Alice assumed her sister must have flounced off back to her life in uniform, hoity-toity matron of the hospital. Marion would call when she was ready.

On the other side of town, Robert Jones and his fiancée spent a final day together, mainly encased in the bedclothes of their hotel suite.

On Monday, Robert caught the train to the coast to meet the troop ship at Southampton along with the young men of the rifles who sought to regain the honour of their regiment, thought to be besmirched by deserters.

Janet Gunn returned to Mount Vernon with the rosy glow of a woman in love. Mr Bannerman would swear he heard her singing to herself all day. It was a day when she would have given anything to anybody he thought, she was so buoyed up on life. It was good to see.

The telephone in Marion Wilshaw's office rang, the receiver lifted. 'Major Wilshaw's Office.........'

CHAPTER 30. STOP PRESS

'.........I'm sorry the Major isn't at her desk, no, she was away for the weekend. She's probably been delayed in town. Can I take a message?'

'Tell her Doctor Robert Jones is home.'

The young nurse who had answered the phone in passing scribbled the message on the Major's pristine white blotter and hastily left the office.

Constable Whitehouse often walked the tow path, especially on a Monday when he was an early turn. Like as not, he needed to clear his head after the weekend. This morning was no exception, and it was drizzling, that fine misty rain which soaked through his heavy uniform coat eventually making his shoulders damp. He left the station after the usual mug of tea, a briefing from his sergeant and a raised eyebrow with the attached offer of a peppermint to mask the smell of his breath. Turning left, he walked the short distance to the steps which led down to the canal. In a few hundred yards he would be under the long bridge which took the railway lines over the width of the waterway and its towpaths either side. A sheltered, dark place, the floor dry but the walls running with damp. It was like looking down a tunnel it was so long, but the green expanse at the end was well worth the walk. His excuse for the deviation from his patch, 'I've been checking the vagrants sarge.' was his usual reply when questioned.

The bridge was the summer haunt of several of the area's older tramps, the veteran soldiers too old to re-enlist who drank their pension and lived in a cheap gin-soaked haze, unwashed, unshaven, in a sometimes violent but mostly well-meaning world of war stories and camaraderie, punctuated by petty squabbles.

This morning was different, strangely quiet. There were no sleeping humps covered in assortments of old blankets and great coats. There was no embryonic fire in the wire cage burner that they hid in the darkness. For one or two to be missing was not strange, but for no one to be 'at home,' was unheard of.

In the next few steps and with the help of his new battery-operated flashlight he found out why. On an instinct, he found himself thigh deep in the canal's green surfaced, slightly murky water, wading out to its centre. Reaching with his free hand he grasped the hem of a blue serge skirt and pulled it towards him. There was no response from the attached body.

Holding the flashlight in his teeth and finding it too large to let him breath as well he stuffed it between the buttons of his tunic. Enough light for him to see what he was doing at least.

'Turn her over,' he told himself. 'she may be alive.'

Albert Whitehouse had found one of his old soldiers in a similar condition several months ago. Instinctively, he had pressed on the old man's chest. This had pushed the water out and the air in and his heart had started to beat again. He turned the woman over and dragged her still form onto the bank. Frantically he examined her. She was not breathing, that was evident. Her upper body was clad in a white muslin high necked blouse. She wore no jacket and the white cloth had gone partly transparent in the water. Her breasts showed in shadow through the cloth. 'Sorry love,' he spoke to her, then he ripped the blouse open and started to press on her chest. There was no response, the face remained an awful grey blue colour. The eyes did not regain their colour or their life. This woman was dead. But how? Was her death the reason for his soldiers being AWOL? There was no sign that she had been violated, but she had no bag, no belongings, no coat even.

Innocent they may be, but stupid they were not, those old soldiers. This would be thought a murder, or a robbery at least. They would all be suspected and none of them wanted even one night in a cell. He adjusted his trouser legs and walked to the end of the tunnel, back towards the station, his boots squelching, full of canal water and heavy wet navy-blue serge sticking to his legs. He took out his whistle and blew. It was unlikely to be heard, so he made a mental note of all he had seen and sprinted back to the station to find assistance. He reported to his sergeant, Sergeant Hills, and then ran back to wait with the body in case any passerby should try and tamper with it in any way.

The woman carried no identification. She was a little above average height and appeared respectably dressed - Button boots, serge skirt, blouse buttoned up to her neck, not the dress of a prostitute. Under the grime from the canal water, she was clean, her nails manicured, not grimy. Her hands were used to work, not soft as a lady's hands, but not calloused from manual labour. This woman looked after herself. Constable Whitehouse stayed with her until she reached the mortuary. Then he returned to the station to complete his report.

This done, he went in search of his vagrants. Someone must have seen something. They would not want to tell him, but it might save their skins if they did.

Tuesday's newspaper was delivered to Mount Vernon Hospital. It was thrown in through the big front door and into the porch by the paper boy. It landed with a thump on the big, rough coconut fibre doormat. Janet Gunn bent to pick it up on her way down the hall. She pushed open the double doors as she unfolded it to see the front page. She froze. There on the front page, was a banner headline BODY OF UNKNOWN WOMAN FOUND IN CANAL and beneath it a grainy photo of a woman she knew. The dead woman was Marion Wilshaw.

Janet Gunn had not known Marion well. They had spoken on the phone. They had met briefly once or twice socially, though not so much in the last four years. About eighteen months before the war, Marion had taken a job in the training hospital at Camberley. They had kept in touch for a while, meeting when work drew them both into London. She had liked Marion, found her to be a bit of a gossip, overly fond of a drink after work, and sufficiently like herself to look at that they had sometimes been mistaken for sisters.

Janet continued to read the article and then picked up her telephone and asked the switchboard to connect her to the Police Station at Paddington Green.

Five minutes later, Sergeant Hills was with Constable Whitehouse on their way to 7 Formosa Street, Paddington, the home address of Alice Ford, nee Wilshaw, and her husband Reginald.

They arrived to find a heated argument in progress. The cause, a letter which had arrived in a brown, official looking envelope requesting Reginald's attendance at a recruiting station where he would be enlisted into the army. Reginald was not under any circumstances going to enlist. He was against the war, not for any particular, moral reason, but because he was a coward. He had ignored the letters requiring him to attend reservist training, always crying off pleading illness. He had researched and found out that the occupation of type setter did not make him necessary for war work. Now the authorities had finally caught up with him. There was a uniform with his name on it in the stores. Reginald had other ideas.

The two Constables arrived to hear him arguing loudly with the lady of the house, if she could be called a lady. 'They can't take me Alice. I'm a married man and I have children. I am exempt.'

Alice Ford shouting loud enough to be heard in the street, 'No, you stupid bastard, we aren't actually married.' had no influence.

'We are! I went to the church! I was there, you were there, in a bloody white dress with a big bulge in the front and yer father playing hell!'

She looked at him with a look that should have withered him into the unwashed hall floor. 'And you were too drunk to stand, and the priest refused to marry us until you were sober. You didn't sober up. You've been drunk every day since. We said no vows. We signed no papers. I use your name and tell no one of that day. Folk round here believe us wed but in truth we are not!'

Sergeant Hills reached the doorstep and coughed. 'Everything alright here, folks?'

Reginald spat viciously on the front steps, narrowly missing Sergeant Hills' very shiny boots. Constable Whitehouse took his thumbs from their resting place in the waistband of his trousers and prepared for action, loosening the strap on his truncheon from its place tucked in his belt and pulling the body of the well-turned piece of oak wood further up the long pocket which ran down the outer seam of his trousers. They had dealt with Reginald Ford before. Come quietly? He never came quietly.

'Who the fuck called you lot?'

'No-one, Reg, calm yourself down, it's your wife we've come to see.'

'I've done nothing!' shouted Alice. 'Nothing, except have kids with this lily livered, cowardly, idle bastard!' Alice spat out the words with a venom acquired from years of practice. Her face was red, and her hair stuck out like a stork's nest on the top of her head.

Albert Whitehouse took her by the arm and guided her back into the house. Her anger was subsiding and disappearing into tears. He left Sergeant Hills to deal with an overheated Reginald.

'Put the kettle on, Alice love, and sit down.' They were in the lean-to kitchen at the back of the house. Alice did not respond. Albert pulled out a chair and sat her on it, elbows on the oilcloth which covered the rickety table. Albert found the kettle, filed it with water and placed it on the gas cooker then lit the gas.

Alice began to talk. 'It's not that he hasn't a job, Albie.' She had known the Constable for years. 'He works at the printers, he's a typesetter. That's how it started, the drinking.' The words flowed out of her like water. 'Drinking with the others in the mornings after shift, he'd come home drunk, leave me with the kids while he slept it off all day, then he'd be back to work and drunk on the way home again. Some weeks he drank the rent money, most weeks I had nothing to feed the kids.'

'Alice, we haven't come about Reg, we've come about your sister.'

'What about her, stuck up cow that she is. She's back in Camberley by now.'

'When did you see her last?'

'Saturday night. She stormed off. She went back to her own place, didn't she.'

Albert looked around him and saw what he needed on the mantelshelf above the fire, a picture of a happy, smiling, pretty young woman in a nurse's uniform, with Alice, and between them, just learning to walk, a little boy.

'Is that her?' he asked.

'Yes, why?' Something in Alice's brain registered that bad news was coming. 'What's wrong?'

He reached into his pocket for the photograph of the woman he had fished out of the canal. He placed it on the table.

'Is this your sister, Alice? Your sister Marion?'

Alice went white, her whole body shook into racking sobs.

'I should have followed her. I was angry. She was angry. She was very, very drunk.'

'Alice, I need you to identify her. Get your things, we can talk on the way. I'll bring you home afterwards.'

It wasn't a long walk to the hospital. Alice calmed herself and walked alongside the tall blonde-haired policeman, somehow keeping up with his long, measured stride.

'I'll need a statement,' he said, his voice matter of fact.

'Was I the last person to see her?'

'It looks that way.'

'Where did it happen?'

'In the canal, where it goes under the railway.'

'Silly cow, she never could learn to swim.'

Slowly, the events of the day emerged. Marion's day out with her son, the happy way she left the house, the argument they had had over her infatuation with the boy's father. Alice swore she didn't know the man's name. Albert did not believe her, but that could wait. The boy Alfie was cared for well with his aunt. No need to open another can of worms.

On the way back to the police station to make her statement, Alice pondered on how they would survive without Marion's money. If Reginald refused to take orders, he would either be imprisoned or sent abroad with the army and eventually shot. Likely, there would be no pay either from the army or from the printers. A world of destitution raised its head, for though Marion had a pension, officially she didn't have a son with a claim on it. They were Alice's details on Alfie's birth certificate - father unknown.

She arrived home to four hungry children, no food in the cupboards and a note on the kitchen table from Sergeant Hills. 'Reginald is spending the night in the cells. He'll be out in the morning.'

Albert Whitehouse reached into his pocket and handed her a shilling. 'Go and get some food, I'll hold the fort until you get back.'

Well at least she had peace and quiet for the night.

CHAPTER 31. BACK TO FRONT

August 1916
Abbéville, France.

Dr Robert Jones was back. He strode across the central square, past Hells Bells where there was no doubt it was washing day from the array of smalls pegged on the guy ropes. He bid a jaunty, 'hello' to Jo Delaney who was sitting on an upturned crate soaking her feet in a bowl of water. Still floating on his own personal cloud of happiness, his broad smile seemed infectious. Jo Delaney looked up from massaging her sore feet and smiled back at him thinking, 'The doctor had a pleasant leave then, he looks smugger than the cat what got the cream.'

Pulling back the tent flap of his own shared canvas abode, he saw the familiar sight of Sam O'Connor stretched on his cot, hands behind his head, shirt open to the waist and bare feet wiggling in the air.

'What news Sam?' he asked.

'Oh, it's all been happening here, pull up a crate, I'll tell you all about it. But yours first, you look chirpier than a hedge full of sparrows, my friend.'

'She said yes!'

'Who said yes?'

'Janet. She actually agreed to marry me!'

'Sure, there's one born every minute. I thought you were asking Marion.'

'No, my Irish friend, she blew me out years ago, told me right where to go, and with a mouth like a sailor.'

'Well, whoever it is, I'm glad for you. How did Shipley turn out?'

'He 'll never walk again, and he'll probably never talk again, but at least now he doesn't mind looking in the mirror, he can chew his own food and his piss goes straight into a bottle. They'll sort a colostomy out for him later. Did you have visitors after I left.'

'You could say that. Sit down and I'll fill you in on the detail.'

Dr Jones sat down. Dr O'Connor sat up and began to tell him of the defence of the hospital. The description in all its detail took a while, Sam O'Connor left nothing out. Eventually he pulled out his dented hip flask and two tin cups from his metal cupboard.

'If I hadn't seen it meself, I would never have believed it. And then I also found this.' He reached under his cot and produced an arrow.
Dr Jones chuckled, 'I believe you, old man and there's a lad in Mount Vernon who would believe you too.'

'Robert, I'm telling you, they were here, a whole army of them.' O'Connor took a swallow of his whiskey.

Dr Jones cleared his throat. 'Tell me more of the two soldiers, the ones who warned us, the ones without a unit.'

Sam O'Connor took another drink. 'After the evacuation was ordered, they left, they took half the guns and all the explosives with them, the stuff General Shipley brought for us. Then they disabled the artillery and came back. In fact, they are still here. Why?'

Jones reached into his trouser pocket and spread a broadsheet on the bed in front of O'Connor. He pointed at the names circled in red.

'Yes,' replied Sam, 'they're here, and these two with them.' He pointed at two other names further down the list. 'What will you do? You're the senior officer round here.'

'Find them quickly, I need to speak with them.'

Sam O'Connor buttoned his shirt and tucked it hastily into his trousers. He pulled on boots and socks and without tie and tunic the two medics walked quickly over to the ward where Frankie Baker, head swathed in a bandage, was sitting up in bed, arm in a collar-and-cuff sling. His bed was surrounded by his three comrades and they were all deep in conversation. At the approach of an officer, they all stood. Dr Jones pulled the curtain round the bed, surrounding them all in what privacy the canvas created.

'At ease.' Jones addressed them. 'Which one of you is Jack MacGregor?'

'That would be me, sir.' Jack identified himself.

'And Turner?'

'Me, sir.' replied Charlie.

'I know the one in bed is Baker so that makes you Owen.' He addressed Ralph. 'Am I correct?'

'Yes,' growled Ralph 'what of it?'

'Well, private Owen, and the rest of you, best you read this.'

He spread his copy of the Deserters List on the bed on top of Frankie's legs.

'You can't stay here. You aren't safe here. I travelled from England with young men who know you, young men who have been told that you are cowards and traitors, young men who seek to cover themselves in glory and find you.'

'But they will surely be sent straight to the trenches, they are conscripted men.' Jack MacGregor spoke.

'And they may be wounded, and brought here, where you are. You cannot stay. For us to harbour you and say nothing will endanger us, and for you to be discovered, well you know what happens then.' Sam O'Connor said his piece.

Jack MacGregor stood. He straightened his tunic. 'Doctor, we half expected this to happen. We will make our plans, there are woods between here and the coast, we can hide up there, maybe cause a bit more chaos for the Bosch. Can we stay until Frankie's arm is healed? At least give us that long.'

Robert Jones looked at Sam O'Connor. 'How long Sam?'

'The sling can come off now.' He removed the sling from Frankie's shoulder and spoke to the patient. 'Start to use it. It will ache at first, go slowly with it and keep it warm, it should be fine in a few days. Stick to shanks pony, not the four-legged variety. Oh, and as far as your head goes, it is as hard as a cast iron pot. Very little sense and definitely no feeling.' Jack MacGregor addressed his men and Dr Jones.

'Until the end of the week then.' It was a statement and a question rolled into one, answered with a quiet, and reticent, 'Until the end of the week,' from Dr Jones.

Frankie's shoulder healed quickly. The stitches in the wound to his head were more of a problem. The wound to his scalp had become infected. Treated with gentian ointment, Nurse Brenda had it under control and she would pack him a supply of the violet-coloured salve and give Charlie instructions on how to remove the stitches when the wound was no longer weeping. 'Cut on one side of the knot, Charlie, then pull the knot, which will drag the loose end through, don't try and pull the knot through the skin! You can use the scissors to pull them if you're careful.' Those had been her instructions when she handed him her own a small pair of nail scissors in a leather case to keep in his pocket with the rest of his personals. But then Charlie didn't smoke, so his tobacco tin was empty, plenty of room there.

Dan Curry and Richard Flint donated tobacco. Frankie was the only smoker of the four of them, but they hadn't had a tobacco ration for weeks. They hadn't had any rations for weeks. They couldn't exactly walk into the stores and ask, could they?

At break of day on the Friday of that week, packs bulging with supplies, Frankie's blonde hair tinged a delicate shade of lilac and spiked up around his stitches, his shoulder aching like the devil under the weight of his rifle and the pack he carried, the four men left the confines of the hospital. It was raining, steady heavy rain, but the sky in the distance was blue. It would clear by midday. 'Rain before seven, fine before eleven.' Sam O'Connor gave his meteorological prediction before they left.

They crossed the river back into farmland. In the distance, Jack could see the remains of Jean Dubois farm, still with a wisp of smoke emerging from the chimney. The stubborn old man was still there then, him and his horse. His daughter had left with the evacuation, where was she now? As if reading his thoughts, Ralph spoke. 'Aaah Celine. She was heading to London, where the streets aren't paved with gold, but she's doing well for herself, don't worry about her, sarge.'

'How do you do that, Owen, read my mind, I mean.'

'It's a knack I have sarge, the missus hates it.'

'You never mentioned a wife before, Owen.'

'Didn't I sarge, well you probably never asked.' Ralph remained tight lipped. If this particular wife ever found out she was referred to as 'the missus,' his nuts would end up in a bucket - nothing more certain than that.

They were walking now, in pairs, Ralph and Jack in front, Charlie and Frankie behind. The open countryside along the river gave way to woodland, the trees summer green, not yet decimated by war. As they disappeared into the cover of the trees, Ralph began to talk.

'Did you never wonder sarge, how I manage to hide so well?'

'Is that another knack you have! Along with disappearing for ages and reappearing when least expected but most useful?'

Ralph snorted, a very Welsh noise, indicating humour.

Jack spoke again. 'Any other sergeant would ha' put ye on a charge by now, ye' are disrespectful, scruffy, yer uniform is a mess, yer hair is too bloody long, but ye can fire a rifle and kill a man at a distance with a knife, and ye may wander off now and then, but ye always come back. Who exactly are ye?'

Ralph snorted again. 'Let's just say I'm Welsh, for now, and I have certain talents which are useful, in exchange for their use, you won't mind if I disappear for ....'

When Jack turned to answer, Ralph Owen was gone. Jack shrugged his shoulders, there was little he could do. They were all on the missing list. He could hardly turn him in. Behind him, Frankie and Charlie were so deep in conversation it took them several strides to notice that one of their number was missing. Then Jack heard Charlie's broad cockney accent

'How does he do that, here one minute, gone the next? Will he come back this time do you think?'

And Frankie's reply. 'He'll be back, he's one of us now, he won't let us down. Where do you think those bloody archers came from, they didn't go through the recruiting office now did they?'

'Hey sarge, what's that over there, looks like a cave or something?'

Charlie pointed to his right into the woodland and towards a rocky outcrop which towered above their heads. About twenty feet above the ground was an opening. There was a narrow ledge in front of it, an easy climb for one like Frankie. He dropped his pack and stared up at it, mentally seeing hand and foot holds. He hadn't climbed since his ascent up to the balcony of Fiona's house on the park. This would test his shoulder. He wiggled it about under his tunic, then removed the restrictive garment and then his boots and socks. Frankie began to climb. Just as he was pulling himself over the final ledge, his shoulder gave way. The pain shot down to his fingers and they let go. He felt himself start to slide. He heard Jack's sharp intake of breath. His chin hit a ledge with a snap that jarred his teeth into his tongue, and he felt the sharp metallic tang of blood in his mouth. Then he felt a pull on his belt, his trousers pulled up between his arse cheeks and he stopped falling. Some invisible force guided his right foot to a convenient gap in the rock face. Instinct told him to use it. He pushed down on his right foot and swung his left leg onto the ledge and rolled towards the cave entrance. As he regained his breath and his composure and adjusted his underwear, he was sure he heard a Welshman laughing and a mocking voice in his ear whispered, 'You are a little out of practice, Frankie!'

Frankie looked into the darkness of the cave and whispered back. 'Thanks, you Welsh Bastard.'

The flippant voice returned, fading into the distance, 'My pleasure, you English Cock.'

A rope was thrown up to him from below, their packs were hoisted up, closely followed by Jack and Charlie themselves, climbing with the rope's assistance.

'That was a close one, are you okay mate?' Charlie hugged his old friend round his good shoulder.

'I'm fine, just a bit of slippery moss, that's all, it happens!' he replied, brushing off the incident, knowing full well that the fall could easily have killed him. Catching Jack MacGregor's eye, he saw the Scot raise an eyebrow at him. Jack MacGregor had seen it all and didn't seem surprised by it, not one bit.

The sergeant spoke. 'Let's see where this goes then, it's dry at least. It could be home for a few days. Time to test those flashlights Jo Delaney liberated for us from the stores.'

He undid the side pocket of his backpack and pulling out the required article pressed the 'on' button. The bright beam of yellow light illuminated the walls of the cave and revealed a passage leading backwards into the rock. The passage led upwards, over fallen boulders and rough stones, a natural cleft in the rock which had been enlarged. It was just wide enough for a man's shoulders to pass through. Jack was puzzled. Whilst going upwards, the passage was also progressing backwards. The outcrop of rock was surely not that large, they had seen the back of it when they left Abbéville. The distance they had walked into its depths, they should have reached its extremity by now, but the passage went on, winding upwards until, with a twist of his shoulders, he emerged into another cavern, this one lit by daylight which drifted in through a natural vent in the roof. At the back under the vent was a shallow hollow in the rock, its surface blackened with ancient soot. In a recess in the rock was a pile of sticks, again blackened by age and when he shone the flashlight upwards to the flat expanse of wall behind him, he drew in a breath.

'Would ye look at these?' Frankie and Charlie squeezed through the gap into the cave and saw in the light of Jack's torch, paintings, paintings of a battle. These were not the cave paintings he had been taught about, there were no woolly mammoths or buffalo being hunted, no pictures of stick men with spears. Here were pictures of archers dressed in cream and green livery, men on horseback wearing brightly coloured tabards, volleys of arrows being fired, and amongst them two figures, larger than the rest. One looked suspiciously like Gwyn ap Meredith. The other was noticeable by his highlighted shock of untidy black hair and his pinpointed green eyes.

Surely not, Jack scratched his head, this was all too convenient, the cave, the paintings, a place to hide, and a man who was one of them, but not. In the fireplace, Charlie had lit a fire, its embryonic flames licking upwards in a plume of smoke twirling towards the fissure in the rock. They would be warm here, and dry. He turned the flashlight off and stepped further towards the daylight filtering in from the front of the cave. As he rounded the shoulder of the rocky wall, the tops of trees spread out in a hundred shades of green before him, and in the distance, he could see the grey waves of the sea.

All of a sudden, the world seemed completely back to front.

CHAPTER 32. CONFESSIONS OF AN OFFICE CLEANER

August 1916
London.

Ethel Turner pulled her overcoat around her, pulled her hat down over her ears and closed the door of 4 Agar Grove behind her. Her husband had retired to bed after an evening in the Duke of Clarence. He was due in work early in the morning and was lying on his back in the marital bed snoring loudly. He would not notice her absence. The girls were sleeping peacefully in their bedrooms at the back of the house and Charlie – well, he was the reason for her mission. She felt the comforting shape of the large iron key in her pocket and walked briskly towards the park, destination Fernleigh House.

Letting herself in by the kitchen door, she found the kitchen a cold quiet place, no smell of cooking, no warmth from a banked-up fire, the house was empty. Fiona visited every few weeks, but rarely stayed, preferring to sleep in Frankie's room at the Baker's.

Ethel opened the door into the main hall. She could see that the furniture had been covered with dust sheets, like herds of strange, humped animals grazing in the parlour and the dining room. The door to the gun room was locked, and running a hand around the top of the door frame she found the key. No change to that hiding place then. The gun room was still as it had been, the General's precious Purdeys gleaming in their racks, the old double barrel gun still loaded but hanging broken by the door. She could see the metallic glint of the cartridges in place in the barrels.

Her eyes were still growing accustomed to the dark as she felt her way to the cupboard where the General stored the cleaning kit. It was not locked - it never had been locked. She felt into the back of the cupboard for a small wash-leather pouch, yes it was still there. She placed it in her pocket and left quickly and silently the way she had come.

Back at home she tidied her hair and changed her clothes and readied herself for work. Then she opened the pouch and examined the contents - the keys to the General's office at the admiralty. He had employed her to clean it for him once a week. No doubt his superiors had taken his own set of keys back when they collected the safe, but they wouldn't know about the spare set. Ethel just prayed that they hadn't changed the locks.

Ethel caught the first tram across town to the imposing double fronted terraced townhouse now converted into offices which had housed the late General's former place of work. She arrived before the smart uniformed young lady with the very red lipstick who guarded the entrance, she who flirted unmercifully with the young intelligence officers as they came and went. She knew Laura Davies, and Laura was well used to seeing Ethel coming and going. Laura would not remark on her presence, she was confident of that. Ethel had far too much dirt on Laura for Laura's ongoing employment.

Bold as brass, she climbed the two flights of stairs and, using her keys, let herself in to what was now the office of Captain Jeremy Shipley, the brass plate on the door declared it so. General Cameron would never be so foolish as to advertise his presence. Those who needed to see him knew where he was. But times had changed. Shipley was one of a new breed, all for show, anything for the next notch on the greasy pole of promotion.

The filing cabinet was easily unlocked, the bent spoon she had fashioned was easily slid between the frame and the lock. She had seen a similar spoon in Frankie Baker's house. Frankie's spoon, no doubt.

There it was, filed neatly under M for MacGregor. Ethel lifted the folder from the cabinet. A clock somewhere chimed seven o clock. She had an hour.

Sitting at the General's old desk, where she had sometimes sat before, she had a rest before she opened the folder. The hand-written letters from Montague Shipley to his brother and to General Haig himself had been typed in triplicate, one on velum and two additional copies on thin, see-through copy paper. No one ever used the third copy. The General had often told Ethel he was surprised the typists made three. The third was usually so faint as to be useless. Ethel swiftly removed the second more legible copy, folded it, and replaced the rest as she had found them. She pulled a seemingly redundant and empty folder from where it had become lodged underneath the neatly ordered files and re-locked the cabinet. She tidied and dusted the top of the desk, stuffed her hoard into the folder and the folder under her ample coat. She was on her way back down the stairs and out through the door just as the lovely Laura was taking her seat for the day. Laura was already fending off the attentions of a handsome looking lieutenant in the Guards who had come to see Captain Shipley on some urgent matter. Ethel lifted a hand in greeting and left without interrupting the lieutenant who was regaling Laura with some tale of derring-do, no doubt. She disappeared down the street, her presence quite unremarked and hopefully to remain so, a file full of papers under her coat, mission accomplished. She arrived back at Agar Grove just as Jesse was returning from his shift. He would no doubt have a quick wash to remove the surface grime and adjourn to the Duke of Clarence Public House for the afternoon, leaving her with time to read her stolen letters. The girls would occupy themselves until teatime, Sophie would prepare their meal, and they would all be out in the street, playing hopscotch until dark. Once her husband had slammed the door behind him, Ethel sat down at the dining room table and started to read.

Each letter was neatly written in a firm hand in fountain pen and was written from Mount Vernon Hospital. They began on 15th August 1916. The typists had typed the body of each letter verbatim. The first was addressed to General Haig himself.

To General Sir Douglas Haig
From Lieutenant Montague Shipley. Queens Own Surrey Regiment and St Pancras Rifles.
Sir,
I write from Mount Vernon Hospital following surgery to repair wounds sustained during the advance from the trenches at the Somme near Abbéville on 7th July last.
I write to report an incidence of desertion by a whole unit of men who were at the time under my command. The men I will list below are guilty of an act of the utmost cowardice in that the deserted their posts before the order came to advance.
These men were the best trained of the battalion. They were respected as soldiers and their desertion was infectious. To inspire the men, I personally led the advance and was severely wounded. Nothing has been heard from these men since. They may be dead, or they may be still Absent Without Leave either in France or on home soil. I ask that they be added to the deserters list, their records marked with dishonour and should they be captured, the ultimate penalty paid. They are:

Sergeant Jack MacGregor, Private Frank Baker, Private Charles Turner, all St Pancras Rifles and one other, Private Ralph Owen of the Monmouth Regiment.

Signed: Montague Shipley.

The response had been brief and not even addressed to Shipley himself.

August 1916
Office of General Haig.

Memo

To Major Colin Harper, intelligence.

Please read enclosed and deal in an appropriate manner,

Signed
Douglas Haig.

  From here a paper trail showed that Major Harper had caused the men's names to be added to the deserters list. He had then allocated the case to Shipley's brother to make further investigation.
Jeremy Shipley had obviously spoken to his oldest brother, the General. The typists had religiously typed what must have been a brief note between siblings, about their injured brother.

Gerald
What do you know of our brother's state of mind? Knowing him as I do, I am reluctant to condemn these men on his word alone, though Major Harper has set those wheels in motion. Please call at the office on the matter.

Yours
Jeremy.

And the response typed on the same page.

Jeremy

I have had charge of our brother's care and treatment since he was rescued from the battlefield. His pursuit of vengeance regarding these men is what has kept what is left of him alive. I have spoken with those who were also there that day. Montague, it seems, did not cover himself in glory in the lead up to the advance.
Several of the enlisted men have reported arguments approaching outright dissent on MacGregor's part, between him and our brother.
Their trench was targeted by snipers, a problem MacGregor's men were trained to solve. Speak to the Black Watch.

Yours
Gerald

What had happened next was not clear, but Montague Shipley's next letter was written to Major Harper who had in turn referred it on to Captain Jeremy Shipley.

Sir,
Whilst I am gratified that you have added MacGregor and his men to the lists of deserters, I must stress, in response to your further enquiry, that MacGregor's conduct was insubordinate in the extreme. Our orders were to hold fast until instructed to advance. The loss of men to sniper fire was unfortunate but could not in my view have been avoided. The loss of the Black Watch supply officer was again most unfortunate. I am not aware of any authorised operation undertaken by MacGregor and his men which sent them out of the trenches, I certainly cannot recall signing any such order.

Signed
Montague Shipley.

Then followed medical reports which documented Shipley's injuries and treatment, observations as to his state of mind and his progress. They did not make good reading. They painted a picture of a man hell bent on revenge. Maybe the lads had left their trench, but why, what were they doing, and more to the point, where were they now?

Ethel needed a second opinion. She would sleep on it and tomorrow she would speak to Letty Baker.

After Jesse had left for work at the sidings and the girls had gone to school, Ethel knocked on the door of No 3. The door was open as usual, she called out a greeting and let herself in.

'Get the kettle on Letty, or a gin if you have one, though it's a bit early for that yet.'

'What's to do Ethel?' Letty answered from her kitchen. 'Come in, take a load off.'

Ethel did as she was told.

'What's up Ethel, how can I help?'

'I've been doing some digging, about the boys.'

'And?'

'That officer, Shipley, certainly has it in for them, wants them all shot he does.'

'Our boys are no cowards, he must be making it up, what have you found?'

Ethel spread the type-written sheets on Letty's table.

'Bloody hell, Ethel Turner, where did you get these?'

'I still have my contacts,' Ethel winked, 'and a set of keys, no one notices the cleaner, do they?'

Letty was busily reading. She talked as she read, filling in the gaps as she went along.

'So they were in their trench, being shot at by snipers, and not sent to do anything to stop it?' It was a rhetorical question. 'My Frankie wouldn't sit still for that Ethel, nor your Charlie. And from what they said of Sergeant. Jack he wouldn't stand for it either.'

She hummed to herself and sucked on her bottom lip. 'So, Jack argued with him after the Scotsman was shot. I'll bet that was one of the Munro brothers, they were all close to the twins, they are Frances's brothers ain't they Ethel?' Ethel nodded the affirmative.

'What would Jack do, what would his men want to do?'

Ethel answered for her. 'He'd plan something, rather take action than sit and get shot at, that's for sure.'

'That's what has happened, and someone knows it, but who, and what? Maybe the girls have heard something. Shipley's in their hospital, isn't he?'

'I think they're coming home this weekend, Frances mentioned something. Best you air the bed for Fiona, her father's house is cold as the grave, she won't want to sleep there.'

With that, Ethel made her excuses. Her girls were home, and duty called. Letty was still leafing through the stolen pages, reading and re-reading. She idly picked up the manila folder and shook it. Stuck in the folded edge was another sheet, one which was smaller than the others and had become stuck in between, it was not typed like the others, it was handwritten. There was a letter, and attached to it was another document, on old piece of paper. It bore the marks of having been folded and into a small square. It was dirty brown and also possibly tinged with the stains of human blood. Letty read the letter first.

21st July 1916
Inverness

To whom it may concern.

I have today received my husband's personal effects from the commanding officer of his regiment, The Black Watch. Whilst going through the package which contained amongst other items letters sent to him at the front, I have come across a document which does not relate to my husband who was Sergeant Malcolm Ferris. I have not read it other than as far as to see that it was written by Sergeant Jack Macgregor, who was a friend and comrade of my husband. I feel that it belongs other than in my personal possession. I attach it for its correct disposal.

Yours Sincerely
Ellen Macdonald Ferris.

Letty read the attached paper and rubbing her chin thoughtfully reached into the drawer of the sideboard which contained all manner of oddments and finding the stub end of a pencil which Frankie had brought home from camp, she found what she wanted in the rest of the file and then began to write. Looking up satisfied, she held two pieces of paper to the light, tipped a small amount of tea onto the tablecloth, just enough to stain what she had just written the same delicate shade of brown. She replaced Ellen Ferris's letter and its companion in the folder with the rest of the letters and went next door.

The following morning Letty heard the slam of the Bakers' front door and, as she looked out of her window, saw the overcoated figure of Ethel Turner, hat pulled down over her ears once again heading for the admiralty offices.

CHAPTER 33. ECHOES OF WEDDING BELLS – Rhianydd MacGregor

August 1916

    I undressed slowly, shedding my clothes into an untidy heap at my feet, poured the hot water I had fetched up from the kitchen from the jug into the basin and using a bar of dada's best orchid scented soap I washed the dirt of the day from my skin.
    I dried myself on the thin sheet which acted as a bath towel, then used the rest of the water and dada's shampoo to wash the smell of the hospital from my hair. Night shift was exhausting, and that bloody policeman had caught me at a bad time, not that I would have told him different if I had been less tired. I had only just walked in through the door to a fractious grumpy teething baby needing her mother's attention. How dare he call my husband a coward. I could see him there now, standing on the doorstep, his size twelve boot positioned just to stop the door closing, his ill-fitting uniform hanging like a scarecrow's rags from his skinny shoulders, his scrawny spotty neck emerging like a curious turtle from the high collar of his tunic. How dare he darken my doorstep with such an accusation. Why was he pointing at my husband's name on his filthy list? Why had he not volunteered himself to die for his country? I left him in no doubt as to who was the coward in my eyes.
    I had not slept at all that day, surely my body would switch off now. I needed rest, most of all my mind needed to stop thinking. I climbed into my nightdress, pulled the warm brick from the foot of the bed and climbed in. Lydia would see to Agnes when she woke, I would be left to sleep, she had promised me, and she was a girl of her word. Pulling the blanket and eiderdown over my ears I closed my eyes and willed myself to sleep. Instead of sleep, I found Jack.
    He was standing naked before me as he had done on our wedding night, and many nights after. Broad shoulders tapering to slim hips, and a very firm behind, he was not a tall man, but he had the long athletic legs of a runner. His chest was dusted with dark curly hair which grew in a tapering path to his navel and on down to the thatch below. In my exhausted haze, my hands became his hands, they wandered over my

body, travelling lightly down my belly through the still bath damp curls and further into the moistness beneath.

'Jack, I need you!' my mind cried out as fingers worked their magic. My body cried out in response seconds later, blood pounded in my brain and round my body, I cried out to the darkness, 'Jack where are you?'

As my heart beat steadied and my vision cleared, I was sure I heard him answer, 'Help me!' Then there was silence.

I heard the clock ticking in the hallway downstairs, so like the old clock in Pen y Banc. Mother had that timepiece now. It was one of the few things of father's she had salvaged from the wreckage of his life. Could she help me, I wondered? Would she help me? I had said terrible things to her before I left to get married. I had accused her of so much, but did I really think so little of her?

If what she tried to tell me was true, then her life had been remarkable, unusual yes, but remarkable just the same. Had I not seen him, the being who she said was my real father, and the brother who was wholly of my blood? Did that mean she loved Helena my dear sister less?

I closed my eyes again, focussed on the Tick! Tock! rising from the hall and tried to conjure sleep. Instead, I heard a voice, a mellow low-pitched voice, not Jack's Scottish tones, this was different, more melodious. 'I hear you, daughter, do not fear me, come home.'

I sensed he was near, in the room maybe, but I had heard no one enter. No tell-tale creak of boards, no rattle of the doorknob. Opening one eye, I was sure I saw the figure of a soldier standing by the window, taller than Jack, bigger by far, his eyes luminous in the dark of my bedroom, rifle held by his side, cap tilted back on dark curly hair, face heavy with stubble. Not old enough surely to be my father, but then he was not from anywhere where years mattered, for him time was not important.

I tried to sit up, but the bedclothes pinned me down, and when I freed myself from my eider prison, he was gone, as silently as he had arrived. I climbed from my bed, wrapped myself in my dressing gown and crept downstairs to Uncle Moses' study. I found the key under the blue glass inkwell on the desk and opened the walnut corner cupboard. Taking a crystal tumbler from the shelf, I unlocked the whisky decanter from its tantalus and poured myself a large dram, drinking it down in one swallow. I felt the mellow buzz of Aber Falls run down my throat, warming my chest and vocal cords. I poured another and carried it back to my bed. As my head hit my pillow, I heard the clock mark the hour of four with his best baritone voice ringing out for all wakeful inhabitants to hear. No one stirred. Suddenly I felt very alone.

My mind drifted back to the day I had met Jack in those months before war had been declared. We had met at one of those functions in a London hotel ballroom where hospital staff and the military were invited to socialise together. There was dancing and drinking and lively conversation.

I had stood out in the crowd, I suppose. I am taller than most women I know and have hair you can see from a distance, such is its colour and mass. That evening, I was wearing a long dress of sea green voile, cut to flatter - it showed off all my better attributes. I had been crossing the dancefloor to find a refill for my drink from the bar when he had collided with me. He was walking backwards, still in conversation with a colleague. When he turned to face his obstruction, he was staring me straight in the décolletage and I was looking down into a pair of the darkest brown eyes I had ever seen, simmering at me with a mix of embarrassment, mirth, and appreciation. The fine black moustache above a wide mouth had twitched and he had taken my hand and asked me, 'tae dance.'

Those were the only two words I understood of what he actually said. Thinking back, it was me who made the first move towards the dance floor, and months later in a moment he considered safe, he told me what he had actually said was, 'Hey, ye great braw lassie, wi a frame like that, yer surely tae huge an' cumbersome tae dance!'

But we had danced, him in his regimental kilt and short jacket, nimble on his feet, whirling me around the floor until I was breathless, then steering me into a quiet corner, 'fer further inspection.' he later told me.

I was no slouch on the dancefloor myself. Aunt Blanche loved a party and she had taken trouble to see that both Helena and I were taught all the social graces. We could dance a highland reel and the Dashing White Sergeant with the best of them.

Obviously, I had passed inspection because Sergeant. Jack MacGregor had appeared at the nurse's accommodation where I was living with a bouquet of flowers the following week.

We had been out walking in the park several times after that and he had told me he was being posted to a training battalion in London. War was imminent, everyone was predicting it. Would I marry him?

The ring he produced was simple, three diamonds in an unusual setting, a thick plain band of gold with the stones pushed into indentations. Like currants into the surface of a bun. 'My grandmother's,' he mumbled as I said yes, and he slipped it onto my finger.

We met in the April of 1914. May, June, and July had flown by and then on 5th August 1914 as Jack had predicted, war was declared.

Meanwhile, I had arranged to transfer my final year of studies to a London hospital. We had decided to get married in Scotland and once I was qualified as a doctor I would return to Cardiff, as I had a home there. And I had Helena my little sister to care for.

I had fallen out with my mother just after my father's death and the awful incident in the cemetery, I had said some unforgiveable things to her, and I had not even told her that Jack existed. All she knew was that I was taking Helena with me to Scotland, and when I returned I would be a married woman. All she had ever seen of my husband was a photograph.

All Jack knew was that I had a sister who depended on me and that we both lived with my uncle and aunt in Cardiff. I had not told him about mother until later, and then only that we were estranged.

Jack and Helena and I had travelled to Scotland by train, it was his last period of leave before returning to his unit. He told me that he was attached to the training battalion for the foreseeable future but if or when war broke out that would change.

The journey was a long one, made more bearable by Helena and her observation of the other passengers and of the changing countryside as it passed.

Our train passed through the industrial Midlands and through the wild countryside of Yorkshire, and on over the border to Scotland, then further North to the Highlands near Inverness.

We married in the church at Grantown on Spey on 15th August 1914. Helena was bridesmaid. Jack's father, Graham MacGregor, walked me down the aisle and gave me away. The ceremony was witnessed by his brother Samuel and his childhood friend and fellow Sergeant, Malcolm Ferris of the Black Watch, who was also his best man. The only other persons in attendance were Jack's mother Agnes and the priest. The bride wore a simple dress of white satin with a high neck and leg of mutton sleeves in a very Edwardian style.

The festivities afterwards were held in the Claymore Bar in Grantown where we had booked a room upstairs as the bridal suite, Helena having been billeted with Jack's parents for the night at least.

It was a night of exploration, and we were both eager to explore. Released from the boundaries of propriety, clothing was shed in an unceremonious heap, dress falling like an off-white waterfall around my ankles once released from its fastenings by his trembling hands. I fumbled with belt buckles and sporran, and eventually the kilt fell the same way as the dress, tartan merging with the stiff silk like the two naked bodies which merged together on the rather lumpy bed. My virginity was lost that night, I did not even feel it leave, but it went with a flourish and an outpouring of joy which was echoed several times before the dawn broke.

We spent a week exploring the Scottish countryside, we both loved the hills. Jack maintained that the Welsh and the Scots had a thing about mountains and neither a true Welsh person nor a true Scot could ever live without having sight of a hilltop.

We climbed to the places where he had climbed as a boy and lay in the springy heather, exploring each other. By the time we had to say our goodbyes to Scotland, we were both thoroughly acquainted with each other. It was a magical time. Helena too was in love with the place, and a little smitten with Samuel who was only two years her senior. They promised to write to each other and if Samuel did not follow his brother into the army, she would visit again next year.

The journey back to London was quiet, it was a journey back to reality. Helena and I would return to Cardiff, she to her school and life with Uncle Moses and Aunt Blanche and of course her good friend and cousin Lydia, me to my studies and to an eventual transfer to a London Hospital.

Within a few weeks I was transferred to London as a final year student and with a few strings pulled by Uncle Moses, who had friends in some very high places, I was transferred to St Thomas' Hospital. Despite being married I would have to live in the nurses' accommodation at Thomas' House. Jack's regiment had no fixed billet, they lived in tents. Their training camp was outside of the city. It would not be possible for me to stay there and commute back and forth to the hospital.

Jack and I spent the next few months meeting at weekends and on days off, making the most of our nights in the bedrooms of inns and boarding houses, tents, and open countryside.

In April 1915, Jack enrolled for training with the St Pancras Rifles. New recruits, most of them youngsters, he was tasked with finding out those who were suitable and training them as sharp shooters. He was over the moon with his role and took a pride in instilling in his men his own ethics: work hard, play hard, fight hard and never give up.

During this time, I had become pregnant with our first child. Agnes May Macgregor was born 21st April 1915. I had qualified and returned to Cardiff to take up a post at the infirmary.

On 6TH June 1916, Jack and his battalion had received their mobilisation orders and been sent to France. I had only received a few brief letters from him since that day.

I heard the chiming of the clock in the hall marked five o'clock but in my head its echo sounded like wedding bells ringing a new bride out into the world.

Tomorrow I would use Uncle Moses' telephone and ring my mother, Sibyl.

FLASHBACK

CHAPTER 34. DECLARATION OF WAR – Sibyl

5TH August 1914
Hengwm, Wales.

It was Wednesday after the bank holiday, not that it made much difference to me as life went on pretty much as normal in sleepy mid-Wales. Farmers do not benefit from a day of holiday just because the banks are closed. The cows still need to be milked, the other livestock fed, sheep counted to make sure they haven't wandered. It was about nine o'clock in the morning and I had finished my first round of chores. I had milked Rosie and Branwen, our last remaining milk cows, and Genevieve the goat at six o'clock, fed the chickens and let them out for the day to scratch in the back field. The ducks had waddled out of their house down their established path to the brook in the opposite direction. Mammon the sow had her snout firmly in a trough of vegetable peelings and making a tremendous noise over it. Her piglets were squealing happily beside her, no doubt learning their piggy table manners from their mother.

Time then for a quick mug of tea and a slice of toast and marmalade before I began the pile of laundry in the wash house.

I was standing at the white stone sink in the kitchen and had seen the blonde head of Dickie the paperboy riding his bicycle along the path at the bottom of the valley. Faster than usual this morning, the open flap of his news bag dangling dangerously over the spokes of his heavy old black butchers bike.

No matter, he didn't venture up the hill to Hengwm. It was a standing joke in the Sun Inn, down in the village, that he was terrified of me and of the house. So, I would walk down to the village later and collect my own newspaper from the shop myself. I placed my old blue and white striped pottery mug upside down on the drainer. Through the window a few white fluffy clouds drifted in the breeze, the lilac tree in the garden swayed gracefully and dropped a few petals on the grass beneath and the sun began to warm the earth. I adjourned to the wash house to warm the water.

I was just attending to the fire under the laundry boiler when I heard the blue gate to the front garden creak on its hinges, open so far, then stick on the hump of that uneven stone in the path which was just in an inconvenient place. A muttered, 'Damn it!' as the visitor cursed the noise he had just made in opening the gate and no doubt stubbing his toe on the stone, and then the sound of footsteps on the side path heading for the back kitchen door.

I recognised the voice, it was Dickie! What brought him to my door I wondered? Hand on the latch of the back door I counted his steps in my mind, envisioning him standing with his fist raised to knock, and with my sternest face set, the one I keep for Mammon and the piglets, before his teenaged fist could make contact with the wood, I opened the door before him.

'Good morning, Richard!' I addressed him by his full name.
'What brings you up the hill this fine morning?'
He stuffed a copy of the Monmouth Gazette into my hand. 'Dada said you should read it straight away.'

Then he spun on the heel of his well-worn boot and fairly sprinted back down the path out through the gate, leaving it open for Floss, Uncle Edward's old sheepdog, to wander out. She was old now and nearly blind, she would not go far. Her wanderings were confined now to whimpering, tail wagging dreams before the fire where her seniority allowed her to warm her old bones in the evening, or the sunny spot just outside the back door where she still habitually lay, waiting for his return.

Her young replacements were still tied in their kennel in the yard. They had not yet learned restraint from constantly working my sheep. They had been fed and now lay at the extent of their tethers, heads on paws, waiting for the call to work.

Newspaper in one hand, I dragged the kettle back onto the grate with the other, for some reason took Uncle Edward's huge brown mug off its hook, made a fresh pot of tea and, once it had brewed, unfolded the Monmouth Gazette.

The headline registered first!

GREAT BRITAIN DECLARES WAR ON GERMANY

As I spread the newspaper with one hand, I pulled Edward's big carver chair away from the end on the table, sat down and started to read. All the while my mind drifted back to the last time I had seen my family. Family was important in these unsettled times. I felt a deep sorrow at the way we had parted. I had not seen either of my daughters far too long.

    I could see Rhianydd as she had been that awful evening. Her face had been white with rage and her hands shook. Her eyes had glowed a terrible shade of blue which sparked with anger.

    'Why?' she spat at me. 'Why did you do it?'
    'Do what?' I replied perplexed.
    'Any of it, MOTHER! You have the morals of an alley cat! You have more faces than the town hall clock! You lie continually and you expect EVERYONE to believe you! I have just had THEM marauding through the ward of my hospital, scaring everyone half to death! One claims to be my brother and the other, well MOTHER I think you have some explaining to do!'
    I turned on her. I should not have done.
    'I need explain nothing to you. You need to accept that William Rees was not your father. You have different blood running in your veins. Embrace it and all it can do for you.'
    'Mother, admit it, you are a fantasist and a witch, you do not live in the real world, you inhabit some sort of fantasy world, not even children believe in fairies these days, you cheated on father, admit it! I am in no way related to that thing!'
    'Rhianydd Rees do not say another word. Go now! Come back when you can apologise and when you can listen to what I have to say to you, and when you can accept who you are, for one day you will have need of

your father, your true father, and you are more like him than you will ever know!'

She had turned on her heel and stormed out. Doors had slammed, windows had fairly rattled in their frames. I had packed my bag and sat in that impersonal lonely hotel room and waited for daylight and stuffed in my pocket the note which was slid under my door in the few hours in which I had dozed.

I had returned to Hengwm and had not read her letter until days later. My daughter was now a married woman. I had never met the groom, though I had seen a picture of him. Must I accept that I have indeed lost my daughters, that they have built their lives without me.

I think of what I was like at their ages and tick all the mental boxes. Stubborn, yes. Headstrong, yes. Foolish, sometimes. I can only wait and hope that at least one of them will come back. Blood is, after all, thicker than water.

Uncle Moses kept me abreast of the fact that Rhianydd now had a child Agnes May Macgregor. That was in 1915. It is now 1916 and I have never seen my granddaughter. I have not seen either of my daughters for nearly two years. I have written to her, but I have received no reply, neither do I expect to. She is stubborn and proud as her father - I have not seen him for a similar period of time. Maybe, when I do, I should remind him quietly of the damage he has done before he has a chance to do more.

Hengwm seems to be a very difficult place to find, most who do find it seem to be lost.

Since my return from Cardiff much has changed. The Monmouthshire Regiment has been called up to the war and most of the able men who are not essential to farm work, or the mines, have been conscripted into the army. Many of the young lads volunteered, climbing over each other in their haste to sign their lives away for King and Country. They have a romantic vision of war. They see it as glorious and themselves as invincible.

Uncle Edward soldiers on in keeping the farm running smoothly. I help him where I can and have also taken on the running of the Sun Inn and a small healer's practice in the back room. I am already called on as midwife and it is a small step to treating minor ailments and setting broken bones, both in humans and in animals. I am kept busy.

The far-off echoes of artillery fire from the practice ranges at Trawsfynydd are carried down the valleys on the North wind and amplified by the landscape, they reverberate off the mountains like distant thunder, but I know they are not.

In the last month I have had a telephone installed at Hengwm and there is also one at the Sun, so, together with the one at the vicarage, there are now three in the village. It replaces Richard the paperboy who is no longer around to run errands and take messages left with his father, Tomos the Shop. He, like the others, has volunteered and marched off to war with the Monmouth Regiment.

I hear the shuffle of boots by the back door and feel the draft on the back of my neck as the door opens and Uncle Edward comes in from the yard for breakfast.

'Get the kettle on, girl, I am parched.' He can see Rhianydd's letter on the table, its folds worn from opening and closing, the writing nearly worn from the paper with handling. 'Brooding on it won't bring her home, only time will do that, she is more like you than you know. Now where's that tea, and pour one yourself, you look as though you need it.'

I pull the kettle from the range. It is always full and always boiling. A farmer's capacity for tea is only matched by that for beer. I add water to the waiting leaves in the big brown china pot, cover it with its crocheted cozy and fetch the mugs from the dresser, pondering why Edward still calls me 'girl' when I am forty-five years old. I suppose to him, age is just a number.

I catch my reflection in the glass of the kitchen window, straighten my hair and my dress slightly, straighten my back and think, 'not bad for an old one.'

I pour my tea first, not out of any quaint etiquette, but I can't drink mine at the shade of brown which Edward requires. Edward likes his strong, strong enough to bend the spoon, as he says. We sit in amicable silence, both lost in our own thoughts, Edward usually in the price of sheep at market, the weather and the hay making, or the fact that the cow may have a touch of mastitis, could I take a look at her later? He will ask me, I'm sure, after all I am cheaper than the veterinarian.

I am staring at the telephone. The black Bakelite and brass well dusted ornament sitting on the end of the dresser, its cables run neatly out of the kitchen window to the pole they sited on the path down by the garden gate. Part of me is willing it to ring, but like a watched pot…….

I practically leap from my seat, the wooden legs of the kitchen chair scrap back along the flagstone floor as I practically throw myself across the room in a most unladylike manner, my hand reaches for the receiver on the third ring and I place the earpiece to my ear, holding the mouthpiece by its candlestick like stalk. I listen for a voice, but no one speaks, then the operator at the exchange in Newtown comes over the line.

'Connecting a call from Cardiff 652.'

I wait for the clicking to stop and the connection to be made.

'Hello, Uncle Moses, is that you?'

There is silence for a moment then a woman's voice brings joy to my ear. 'No, mother, it's me, may I come home?'

Tears fill my eyes, they run unobstructed down my cheeks. Edward passes me what purports to be his handkerchief, an old piece of rag stained with who knows what, and smelling of horse and hay and farmyard, tinged with axle grease and bacon fat. I should confiscate it for the next wash.

Through my tears she tells me train times and travel plans. Is she bringing Agnes, will I meet my granddaughter at last? I sense that there are things she won't say, but to have her with me will be a start.

CHAPTER 35. AN AWKWARD CALL - Rhianydd

Uncle Moses had left for his offices on the coal dock early that morning. I had heard the big front door close behind him. He would walk the half mile along the canal bank from the house at The Parade, taking in the morning air, listening to the sounds of the ships waking up to be loaded and unloaded by the great overhead cranes, the cries of the seagulls overhead as they swooped low over the water in search of scraps thrown overboard, the smell of sea water, fish, and industry. He would buy a paper from the Western Mail boy who sat at his newsstand at the dock gates, tuck it under his arm to be read over his first cup of tea at his big desk.

He would call his brother William in Pontypridd about the production coming from the mine at Tonypandy. How many tons, what quality? Then he would start to organise the shipping for the day, juggling ships, and tides and all the other variables. Moving them like pieces around a chessboard.

Aunt Blanche would not rise for at least another hour. She liked to take her breakfast in bed, starting her day in a leisurely manner before her round of visiting. It was barely eight o'clock when I lifted the mouthpiece of the telephone which was on a table in the hallway. Uncle Moses had a separate line in his study, for his use only. I pressed the switch to contact the exchange and asked the operator for a connection several exchanges away. I heard the click of switches and the sound of the lines coming to life, then the voice of the operator in Newtown. 'I am connecting you, caller.'

Through the static on the line, I heard, 'You have a call from a Cardiff number.' I felt a nervous knot form in the pit of my stomach and not a little trepidation at the thought of the conversation I was about to have. Then a husky female voice which I had not heard for over a year replied, 'Uncle Moses, is that you?'

'Mother, it's me.' I replied tears welling in my throat. 'Can I come home?'

There was silence on the line then I heard a long exhale of breath and an equally emotional voice, trembling with tears. 'Call me from Rhayader, I will pick you up. Oh, Rhianydd, I have missed you so much!'

Then she was all business as we exchanged train times and dates and said our goodbyes. As the line cleared and I replaced the receiver I realised that I hadn't told her about her granddaughter. I replaced the mouthpiece on its hook and went to pack my valise. The hospital owed me leave, I needed to take it. I had been waiting for Jack to be home, but now he was missing, no not missing exactly, absent and thought a deserter. Matron granted me a week, no more she had said.

'Good Luck!' had been her parting words.

A week would hardly be enough. I decided there and then that I would not return without him.

CHAPTER 36. THE PRIODIGAL'S RETURN – Sibyl

Augst 1916

    I left Hengwm at lunchtime, driving the pony and trap at more than a sedate pace. It was a little over an hour's drive to the station at Rhayader where I would meet my daughter for the first time in several years. By the time we had reached the next village, the old pony had objected to my haste and reined himself back to a gentle jog mixed in with a brisk walk. I allowed him his leisure and let the reins hang slack over his rump as we journeyed through the leafy lanes of mid-Wales. I was early, and to pass the time left the trap tied outside the little railway station and went to wander around the shops in the town. Something for Agnes, but what would Agnes like? I picked up and discarded dolls and dresses and other toys. These? No. Not if my granddaughter was anything like her mother. In the window of the haberdashers I saw just the thing, it was a felt hobby horse, with a bright ginger head, just like her mother's hair and a white mane made of wool. It had wooden handles either side of its neck and a broomstick for a body. I was certain that she would like it. For Rhianydd, well that was more difficult and, in the end, I chose several yards of dark green ribbon. With hair like ours one can never have too much ribbon, and it all gets lost or goes missing eventually. I have found lengths of my own being used to mend fences and tie gates shut. Uncle Edward has no scruples in these matters.

    I made my way back to the platform just in time to see the two o'clock train pulling into the station. It stopped in a cloud of smoke and steam and to the accompaniment of the guards whistle the doors started to open and close with a crash and a bang. As the smoke cleared, I saw them standing just behind the engine. She had not changed but her face looked a little strained and worried and her hair as usual was escaping capture. I held out my arms and the small figure standing alongside her stumped towards me on unsteady legs. I knelt on the flagstone floor and a small child with black curls and bright blue eyes flung her chubby arms around my neck with a joyous shout of, 'Gannie.' It seemed I had been given a name already! 'Gannie.' I could live with that.

The porter lifted Rhianydd's bags into the trap, and she held out her hand, never one for big demonstrations of affection. 'Mother, I am sorry, can I ever make it right?'

'You just did.' I embraced, her squeezing her thoroughly. 'You are thin, does Uncle Moses not feed you?' I added.

In the light wind which blew down the platform I was sure I heard his voice, just one word quietly, 'Daughter.' It flew away in the noise of the steam and the train pulling away and the squeak of the gate as we closed it behind us.

The old pony, refuelled with a nosebag of oats while he was waiting patiently at the station, valiantly hauled his much bigger load back to Hengwm. We said little. Agnes chattered on about her hobby horse, comparing it with William, who was pulling the trap. He too was ginger with a white mane and tail.

'William,' she said. 'My horse William too.'

Rhianydd was far away, withdrawn into her thoughts. I let her be. She would tell me all when she wanted to. For now, it was enough that she was home.

By the time we arrived at Hengwm, Uncle Edward had moved my belongings into the little room under the eaves and made a room for Rhianydd and Agnes in the little room attached to his own which was over the kitchen. He had moved himself into my bedroom and Rhianydd into his. Hengwm was not large house, any more visitors and I would be sending Edward to sleep in his cellar. He had tidied the kitchen of farming bric-a-brac. No longer was there a hammer on the sideboard and a sheep shears in the pantry along with the whetstone. There was also a delicious smell of herbs, rosemary, and thyme and, yes, lamb stew in the huge cauldron over the fire. He had laid out the dishes on the big kitchen table, and his old eyes glowed with pride as he announced, 'Dinner is served.'

Tired from travelling, Rhianydd and Agnes retired early to their beds. In the morning, I was called out to stitch a wound in the shoulder of one of the neighbour's plough horses. I left Uncle Edward in charge.

When I returned, Hengwm was quiet. Rhianydd had taken little Agnes up onto the hillside. They had set off hand in hand, Agnes toddling along on her chubby little legs. Their mission was to find and pick blackberries. They were equipped with my gardening trug, a flat wicker basket, which Rhianydd had lined with a tea cloth to protect the fruit from the basket, and vice versa. The two of them, I was informed, had left just after breakfast, Uncle Edward was in the top pasture checking the flock for lameness and signs of maggot infestation and I could see him from the house.

The humid weather had led to an unusually high fly population and, as Uncle was fond of mentioning, they didn't need a second invitation to feast on a sheep's scabby backside. A maggot infested sheep was a dead sheep unless caught quickly, and even then, there were few of my herbal remedies which would kill off the fly larvae once they started to hatch. The goats needed milking, there would be eggs to collect and the hay in the barn needed to be stacked. Edward had unloaded it from the trailer late last night and the bales were piled in a haphazard fashion near the entrance, partially blocking the door. It was not like Uncle Edward to leave things in such a slipshod fashion. He had been distracted these last few days, in fact ever since Rhianydd had come home. He sensed there was something amiss. The mountain was talking to him again, as it had in years gone by. I had no doubt he had visited the druid's cave on the way to check on the sheep. He seemed perhaps weary of life, his never-ending years weighed heavy on him, and he feared being called to their service again.

I had got as far as stacking the hay in the back of the small barn. Edward had fetched enough down on the trailer to fill one section. The rest was in the big stone building halfway up the hill, enough to last several weeks once the weather broke and the grass no longer provided enough nutrition for the beasts. Hay bales needed to be stacked right, like bricks in a wall needed to be laid right. If they were not, then the stack would belly out and fall down. I was religious about it. Wedging in the last one, I stood back and flexed my shoulder and back muscles, leaning back, hearing my joints pop and admiring my work. Then I leant forward, hands on the top of the bales, and wiped my headscarf across my face. It was warm work. I adjusted the old linen shirt I wore for yard work, re-belted the old pair of britches, and turned to head for the kitchen and the kettle.

He was leaning on the door jamb, legs crossed, propped there at a jaunty angle. Watching me, hair dishevelled and untrimmed, hanging in a loose dark wave to his shoulders, its curls making it bounce as he shook his head. He was dressed in khaki, a soldier's uniform.

'You have such a nice arse, Red.' His face broke into a boyish grin. 'I love to watch you working, especially bent over like that.'

'How long have you been here?'

'If you mean here, the place, then several hundred years. If you mean now, today, well about twenty minutes, I'll not have you saying I'd watch you struggle.' He crossed the dirt floor with three long strides and gripped me by the waist.

'Christ, woman you're getting thin, well thin in places.' His hands slid to the portion of my anatomy he had previously admired. 'Never let this change.' He squeezed one cheek and pulled me against him. His next words got lost in a kiss which smothered any chance of my replying. 'I need you, now!'

His other hand had undone my belt and the britches descended inelegantly to the floor. I stepped out of them and my work boots, fighting with the ankles and trampling the cloth into the ground. I was hungry with want for him, it had been too long and, as much as I pretended otherwise, my body needed his like boiled eggs need salt. He was naked. How did he do that? I knew damned well how he did it, one thought was all it took. Was I that out of sync with his ways, or just out of practice. I fell face first onto the hay bales and felt him mount me roughly from behind, my hips thrust back towards his to receive the shock of penetration. I reached beneath me and grasped his balls, soft haired spheres fitting neatly into my hand.

'Not yet you don't!' I growled into the forearm, which was under my mouth,

I felt him gasp, and his onslaught slowed. I felt another hand move, caress me, and opening my thighs slightly pressed down onto it. I screamed into the muscle of his forearm as the spasms overtook me, stars appeared before my eyes and in a stolen moment cleared, and I lay pinned beneath his weight, face down, scent of man and meadow hay in my nostrils and a sense of peace all over my body. We rolled together, clinging like limpets to each other. 'I miss you, Merch Goch.' he whispered.

'I love you, Adain Eryr,' I replied.

We were roused by the sound of loud singing coming down the track, and the yard gate creaking as someone swung on its hinges. The singing was in a piping child's voice, the lower alto of my daughter and the tuneless baritone of Uncle Edward who was the exception that proved the rule that all Welshmen could sing. It was a song about goats. Colourful goats called,

Oes Gafr eto?

Oes gafr eto?
Oes heb ei godro?
Ar y creigiau geirwon
Mae'r hen afr yn crwydro.

Gafr wen, wen, wen.
Ie finwen, finwen, finwen.
Foel gynffonwen, foel gynffonwen,
Ystlys wen a chynffon, wen, wen, wen.

Gafr ddu, ddu, ddu.
Ie finddu, finddu, finddu.
Foel gynffonddu, foel gynffonddu,
Ystlys ddu a chynffon ddu, ddu, ddu.

Gafr goch, goch, goch.
Ie fingoch, fingoch, fingoch.
Foel gynffongoch, foel gynffongoch,
Ystlys goch a chynffon goch, goch, goch.

Gafr las, las, las.
Ie finlas, finlas, finlas.
Foel gynffonlas, foel gynffonlas,
Ystlys las a chynffon las, las, las.

Gafr binc, binc, binc.
Ie fin binc, fin binc, fin binc.
Foel gynffonbinc, foel gynffonbinc,
Ystlys binc a chynffon binc, binc, binc. [3.]

They had not yet got as far as pink goats – they were traditionally left until the last verse. I heard the tramp of feet stop by our own goat shed where my afternoon of distraction had led me to quite forget to milk our two goats, Merry and Myrtle. I heard Edward, 'tutt' in his Welsh way and call to Rhianydd,
   'I don't know what planet your ma is on these days, but the girls aren't milked yet. Put the kettle on Rhi' love, while I sort them, and wash those berries, we can have tart for tea if you can fettle some pastry.'
   I heard the bolt pull back as he let himself into the goat shed, and his whistling to the goats as he set about my neglected chores.
   Tidying my clothes, I went and leaned on the half door. He looked up from Myrtle. 'Where the devil have you been, Sibyl? Things are going to the dogs here.' I felt Eryr lean on the door beside me blocking out the light into the shed.
   'Oh,' said Edward, 'it's you, back, are you? I knew there was something amiss, felt it in my water I did. Go inside both of you, you are blocking my light.' He turned back to the goat muttering, 'Talk of the devil and one will appear.'
   'He was never going to be pleased to see you, was he.' I said to Eryr, as we negotiated the path to the kitchen door. On the threshold he stopped and turned me to face him. 'The child?' he enquired.
   'Our granddaughter. But then you must have known that.'
   'I came because I missed you, not because I was called. Tell me all and tell me now.'
   I pushed open the door, into the cosy clutter of the kitchen with its black iron range and grate and massive scrubbed wood table. Rhianydd was just lifting the kettle off its hook over the fire, her hand wrapped in a protective cloth. She poured water into the pot, swished it round and poured it down the sink, then scooped two spoons of tea into the warmed

pot, as Agnes, who was sitting in Edward's Windsor chair, cried, 'Man, mummy, big man.'

The boiling water missed the leaves and splashed onto the table, its steaming flood heading for Agnes lap.

Then it stopped, at some invisible barrier, and cooled, and then ran in a cold stream over the edge of the table where Rhianydd now stood with a frightened Agnes in her arms.

I noted the direction of Eryr's eyes, green lasers fixed on the trail of water. He hadn't lost his touch then. Edward appeared in the middle of this domestic idyll.

'Why don't we all sit down and find out what this is all about, young lady?' He patted Agnes on the head. 'My chair please.'

She slid down from her perch to allow its owner rightful possession. They sat around the table while I busied myself making pastry, rolling it on the stone slab in the pantry and quickly forming into a blackberry and apple pie using the contents of my trug, freshly picked by Agnes and Rhianydd and some of the apples from the tree in the orchard.

'Daughter, how are you?' The question hung in the air. 'You look well.'

'That must be fresh air and the joys of motherhood, it certainly isn't my circumstances.'

'And my granddaughter, it is good to know of her existence, and to meet her. I am sorry I have not been here for you.' He sounded formal, overly polite. Rhianydd responded angrily.

'My father was an apothecary from Newtown, but he is dead. Even so, you have no claim to me as a daughter, and none to my child!'

'So be it,' he whispered, half to himself and barely audible, looking at his hands, eyes full of sadness and not a little remorse.

I spoke quietly, but firmly, the words meant for him, for though she did not realise it now, Rhianydd would need him in the days to come.

'Eryr, Rhianydd is married to a soldier, a sergeant in the rifles. Last week she had news of him, bad news.'

'He is dead?' The expressive eyebrow raised again.

'No, in some ways worse than dead. He is posted missing and his name and that of his unit has been placed on the deserters list.'

'The man is a coward?' The words left his lips before he could bite them back.

'No, he is not!' Rhianydd spat at him. 'He has a name, he is called Jack, Jack MacGregor, and he is one of the bravest men I know. His unit are snipers, elite men, but have not been used as such. In his last letter he was frustrated, annoyed even. Something was badly wrong.'

'So, you have come to your mother for help?'

'Yes!'

'What do you believe that she can do?'

'I know that she can see things. If she has a mind to, maybe she can see him, see where he is, if he is in danger.'

'And if that were possible, what would you do then?'

'I would go and find him. I am a doctor. I will enlist and get myself posted with the army. They need doctors. I can pass as a man, then I can seek word of him, find him, and his men, clear his name.'

'You love him very much then?'

'More than life. He is my daughter's father, he is the other half of my soul, I must find him, or I will die trying.'

Eryr rose and walked around the table, placing a hand on her shoulder. He spoke to her. 'You are more my daughter than you know. Your mother may find him, but you will need my help to get him back. Accept who I am, daughter. You are of the blood. You just choose to ignore it.'

Rhianydd burst into racking sobs, head on her folded arms, resting on the table, the heat and the stress of the moment finally manifesting itself. I picked up Agnes and took her to bed, with a story and the end of the goat song. When I came back to the kitchen, Rhianydd had gone for a walk, to clear her mind she said. Edward had produced the whisky and poured four large measures into the weird assortment of glasses he had found in the cupboard. He held Eryr with his still piercing blue eyes and shook his white whiskers.

'It will be a steep curve for her, she is stubborn, like her mother.'

'Yes,' replied Eryr, suddenly all business. 'We start tomorrow. Do you still have your stone, Red, and your cloak, we will need both.'

The door opened and Rhianydd reappeared, 'I cannot call you, 'father'.'

'I have a name, it is Eryr. Call me that if you will.'

'Tomorrow then.' Then she threw back her whisky in one gulp and took herself to bed.

Edward shuffled his way up the stairs, I covered the unbaked pie with a cloth, and joined Eryr in the front of the fire. We sat like two old bookends watching while the embers died.

'Strange,' I said to him over another measure of whisky, 'Edward was afraid this week, I sensed it. Let him stay here, he is needed here.'

'He need not come with us, and neither will you, or her. This is not war like you have seen. There is no place for a woman there, not even behind the lines. Do you recall you dreamed of horses screaming, men dying in their thousands?'

'I still have that dream, more often than before.'

'That is where we seek this man, this Sergeant MacGregor. It will be hard to see him, Red, he is not one of us.'

We spent the night in my small bed in the bedroom in the eaves, the same bedroom where I had stitched his wounds many years before. That night I dreamed the dream of the screaming horses again, this time mixed with the crack of rifle fire, the screams of wounded men and the shrill blast of a whistle. But I saw no one, maybe my gift had left in the years I had not used it, maybe I was just recalling the past in my dreams. Tomorrow I would try and see through the mist.

CHAPTER 37. TOMORROW – Sibyl

A farm wakes at dawn. I woke as usual to the familiar sound of Uncle Edward's ablutions, the grunts and groans which accompanied his bodily functions.

Eryr and I lay squashed together, me between him and the bedroom wall, thoroughly woken by the noises from below, and thoroughly aroused by our own particular needs. We tried our best to keep from laughing, aware of Rhianydd and Agnes in the bedroom directly beneath us, and Uncle Edward who was making enough noise to wake the dead.

The old, narrow bed creaked and groaned as if crying out in sympathy as we tried to make love to each other, Eryr with one foot on the floor and me with one hand behind the headboard to muffle it's banging on the wall. As if on cue, uncle shouted up the stairs,

'Kettles on! I'm going up to the top field, I'll leave the goats for you, Sibyl, mind you don't wake the neighbours.'

Hengwm's nearest neighbours are several miles away. Uncle Edward has a strange sense of humour. The sun was starting to rise. I could see its glow through the gap in the thin curtains covering the tiny window of my bedroom. It was going to be a fine day. The mist which hung over village would clear by mid-morning, leaving a clear blue sky. Eryr helped me with the milking and the morning round of feeding while Rhianydd took Agnes up to see the ponies in the top field. Old Ginger had long since died, but the wild ponies were still there. Agnes was fascinated by them, and one bay roan foal seemed fascinated by her. Edward already had plans to break it in for her to ride, when they were both old enough of course.

'She has a way with them, you can tell a mile off, it's a certain quietness, she has no fear of him, and he has none of her, she will be a rider, and a good one, no doubt of that.' he had told Rhianydd.

Our conversation with our daughter had not gone well. It had been a hard conversation to have. Rhianydd shouted, I shouted, and Eryr had stood inscrutable as a Chinaman in the corner, waiting for us to calm down. The angrier she became the more I saw her father in her. This was not the time for anger, it was time for her to listen, and if she could, to accept who I was, who her real father was and that without that acceptance, he, for it would be he who would provide it, there could be no help.

Eventually she had stormed out through the back door of Hengwm into the yard, stood with her hands on the stone wall for several minutes, head bowed and obviously thinking, then she shrugged her shoulders and returned to the kitchen.

Then he spoke. 'Sit.' it was a command, and she obeyed it.

'Now, are you ready to listen?'

'Can you help me?' she asked. 'I need to know if you can find him.'

'Your mother may find him, she may see where he is, she may see things you find hard to know, but what she sees is the truth. Her sight will not lie to you, you must be prepared for this.'

'I know he may be dead, or injured, or captive. However he is, I must know.'

'Once he is found, I can take you there, but only if you believe what I am, and if you are accepting of my world. What I create is an illusion. Your mother has learned to use her blood, her power. To do this, you need to use yours, to focus what is in your blood.'

'But I have no.....'

'Have you ever dreamed, daughter, dreamed of places which you have never even been to, and known them, seen people who you were sure you had met before but could not place, have you been to a strange place yet known exactly where you were?'

'Yes, but.....'

'Have you ever healed someone who was beyond healing, and not known how, just by instinct, by the feel of them under your hand?'

'Yes, I have.' she replied uncertainly.

All these things you get from that part of you which is not human. Embrace it. It will not make you any less a mother, or a wife, unless you wish it, you need never again acknowledge it's presence. Your mother chose to live in her own place and time for most of her life. I have missed her sorely, but it was her decision. Your brother Calon chooses differently. You should meet him. He is very much like you in many ways.

After lunch, when the table had been cleared and the dishes put away, I went to the door at the back of the cottage, the one which led to the steps down to the cave, the cave where Gwyn the archer had been left sleeping, all those years ago. The ancient box bed was still there, the entrance which had been walled up had been cleared by Edward years ago. He knew his father was no longer there. The cave still gave me chills, but not today, today it was warm. I went to the back wall, to the big oak coffer, which was the only other piece of furniture. I opened the lid and reached in.

The gazing ball made from my birthstone was still there, wrapped in the old cape made from the deep dark velvet of a medieval curtain and lined with the furs of forest animals, a remnant of a previous life it seemed, and full of memories of departed friends. I lifted out both and shaking the dust from the cloak swung it around my shoulders. As I was shutting its lid and turning from the room, my eye caught was caught by an item lying in the box bed. It was a P14 Enfield rifle complete with khaki webbing and an optical sight. Must be Edward's, I thought, he kept guns on the farm, but usually shotguns. He had no real use for a rifle, maybe he was expecting an invasion of rabbits from the west. With the cape wrapped round me, I cleared my mind and climbed the steep damp stone steps and stood in the hallway, just for the fun of it. One by one everyone filed past me into the kitchen, and no one saw me, except Eryr who smirked and winked at me and with one of his special looks, imagined me naked, a look which made my clothes disappear before me, and him. I pulled a face at him and wrapped the cloak closer and imagined clothes. He hadn't lost the knack, then, but I found neither had I. A little practice and focus of the mind and all was returning.

I strolled into the kitchen unseen and then unveiled myself to the audience now seated around the table. I stood before them in the uniform of a First World War nurse.

Eryr smiled in approval. 'Getting into character, I see, Red.'

I sat down at the table with the gazing ball in front of me, and I saw.... nothing. The ball remained a mist. I placed my head in my hands. 'He is not one of us.' Eryr's words rang in my head. 'I need a connection, a common link, where is Agnes.'

'What do you want with her?' Rhianydd snapped.

'She is one of us, she has our blood. She also has Jack's blood in her veins, maybe she will find him.'

Rhianydd fetched a sleepy child from her afternoon nap, and I sat her on my lap. 'See nanny's magic stone, darling, can you see through it?'

I placed her hand on the gazing ball, her baby clear blue eyes focused on its shiny surface, and she smiled at her reflection in its depths. I closed my eyes and focused my mind. Slowly and steadily the mist started to clear. I had never met Jack MacGregor in the flesh, I had only seen a photograph of a dashing young soldier with dark hair, darker eyes, a lopsided grin under a well-trimmed and businesslike moustache. I did not even know the names of the men in his unit. Agnes had never met her father. He had been posted only days after her birth and had been in a holding camp and unable to take leave. The child's other hand reached out to the polished sphere on the table, her face lit up and she spoke, only one word. 'Daddy.' Then she said it again, and again. She did not yet have the words to say more, but her whole face was alight with smiles, and she was wriggling on my lap like a demented worm.

'Rhianydd, come here, stand behind me.'

'Mother, I can't do this.'

'Yes, you bloody well can. Place your hand on mine and think of him. Call Jack with your mind.' For once in her twenty-one years, she did as she was told. It was she who saw Jack, and heard him, the man I found I knew well, but did not expect to find.

'Gwyn,' I mouthed, speechless.

PART 2
1471 THE CLOCK GOES BACK

CHAPTER 38. PETRICHOR – Gwyn ap Meredith

April 1471
Wales.

    I had long stopped feeling the cold. My body seemed to float above itself and, on the occasions when I seemed to be approaching consciousness, I could see that I lay in a small stone room, in a wooden box bed, that the door was sealed with rocks and there was no way out. Sometimes my eyes would become transfixed by the sparkling light cast by the crystalline rock of the walls. Where the light came from to make them sparkle like they did was a mystery, for the room had no window and no obvious connection to the outside world other than the sealed-up door. My body was wrapped in some sort of cloth, but not a shroud. No one came, there was no one to come, they had all gone. Who had gone, I could no longer remember their names. Today was different, today I felt warm.
    Slowly the warmth crept back into my bones. I did not know where I was or how long I had been there. All I knew was that I started to feel again. I could remember little except the small cave behind the house, and Marged.
    Marged was gone, long gone, so was little Arianrhod. I no longer felt them close to me. And my son Edward, what had the fates decided for him? I smell smoke in the air, strange sulphurous smoke, like the gunpowder of the cannon at Crécy. I hear footsteps, light footsteps approach, but I cannot yet see, everything around is tinged with red.
    'He is waking. Good, not before time.'
    It is a female voice, haughty, a strange mixture of courtly English and Welsh vernacular, it is she, the witch, the Lady Margaret. Who does she talk to? She is not one to talk to herself, or to waste words for effect.
    A cup is placed to my lips, it is cool fresh mountain water. I can taste the freshness of the stones over which it has flowed, imagine it bubbling from the earth in its excitement, flowing down the valley past Hengwm, yes, it is the same water, I would know it anywhere.
    'Drink. Gwyn. Drink your fill, recover your senses, then you will eat. You are needed and there is not much time.'
    My eyes opened. I felt the pins and needles clear from my hands and moved my fingers slowly, the flow of blood and warmth to my extremities

painful at first, but then rather pleasant as life came back to sleeping flesh and bone. Above me the walls of a great cave stretched upwards. Stalactites grew down from above like great limestone teeth, some had grown so long they joined to the floor like the bars of a great stone cage. Where was my box bed? This was surely a different place, nothing was familiar. Dim light entered the cave from some unseen aperture, casting light on the dust particles in the sulphurous smoky air. Add the presence of fire or a dragon and this was surely what hades looked like.

Sitting up, I found that my movement was cramped, a huge weight across my shoulders and chest. I felt it move, sinuous and muscular, easing its weight away from me, releasing me from its prison. It moved, uncoiling itself, and as I opened my eyes, I became aware of a huge amber eye returning my gaze.

Jesu Grist, a dragon, a red dragon. It breathed deeply through its nostrils, stirring my hair with a gentle warm breeze, further warming my bones. Then it turned, and on its massive clawlike feet walked heavily from the cave, wings folded along its back, its footfall shaking the ground and its bulk blocking the only source of light from the passage.

It was then that I saw her, tall and stately as she had always been, long hair, now silver, hanging in a tight braid down her back, her robes long and cleverly tailored of deep burgundy velvet, shot through with silver thread. She held out a hand toward me and beckoned me towards her.

'Welcome home, Gwyn, you have been a long time away. There is much for us to do.'

'Where am I?' I asked her in a voice hoarse and croaky from lack of use. 'And when is this, what year are we in?'

'So many questions. Come, sit, eat. While you eat, we will talk.'

She provided me with food. My body had not eaten in years. She had kept me suspended in a place just before death for nearly one hundred years. She made it clear that it was she who owned me, she who had command over my life until she chose otherwise. She had work for me to do. I was to assist her to raise an army and make a new king for England, put a Welsh born King on the throne of England. My journey would start, as it had started last time - at Hengwm.

Her talk was animated, fanatical, the light of a zealot in her grey eyes. Whatever she was about, she truly believed it to be right. Her course was set and all I could do was obey - obey or be eternally damned.

In between the threats of damnation were promises of release and freedom from her curse, promises of a return to my family, images conjured of Marged and the children. Lies, lies lies, Marged was gone, Arianrhod was gone, the fever had taken both of them. Not even Red could save them. They had died a mortal death, not one that could be reversed. Yet she would offer anything for my services in her world of promises and lies.

The Lady Margaret, for despite her own rebirth she was still Lady Margaret de Clare, de Audley or Beaufort, she was the same mind in a different body. She had followed the prophecy, waited patiently, and kept me for a purpose. So here I was, now dressed in the garb of a wandering soldier, back from the one hundred years' war, searching for employment for my longbow and sword, for sale to the highest bidder.

My sword and bow had been kept with me, wrapped in the flea-bitten cloak they had placed over me when the sleep had taken me back to its bosom. My destination was the great castle at Pembroke, to seek audience with Jasper Tudor, Duke of Bedford. My purpose, to be recruited as tutor to his nephew, Henry.

I was again on the hill above Hengwm. I followed the track down the valley, through the overhanging bog oak trees, between the green mossy banks covered with low growing berry bushes and late flowering daffodils and crocuses. They would usually be gone by now. The winter must have been harsh to keep them below ground so late.

A light rain had been falling, wetting my hair, and running down my face, damping the old cloak round my shoulders, which now smelled more pungent than a wet dog. I turned my face up to meet it. I had not felt the misty Welsh rain for years or smelled the petrichor rising from the warm mountain turf beneath my feet as I walked.

The rain clouds towered up into the heavens like giants peeling onions in God's kitchen, raining tears down on the earth below. I rounded the bend in the track and there was Hengwm, seemingly unchanged. The yard gate still swung easily on its hinges, and I could hear the sound of animals penned in the yard. As I approached, a dog began barking and a horse whinnied. A dark grey head marked with a white zig zag stripe and a pure white forelock appeared over the loose box door. The horse whinnied again and stamped, prompting a gruff but kindly shout of, 'Quiet lad!' from a male voice, and as I pushed open the gate, I heard the shuffle of boots on the path and saw Edward emerge from the kitchen garden, a bunch of greenery in his arms and a pail of water hanging from his left hand.

Edward had changed little since I saw him last. His hair was still a shocking shade of red, he had grown his beard, but it was neatly trimmed. He wore homespun breeks and old leather boots with a brown tunic and neck cloth, topped off with a slouch hat.
He looked up as the gate swung towards him and fixed me with a sharp blue stare.

'Dada! I was told to expect you! Come in and welcome!' He embraced me, excitement in his eyes, my son and I had not seen each other in several years. 'The Lady messenger arrived last week and gave me silver. He'll need a good horse, she said. You must have a good horse and there he is, a bit flashy for my taste, but he is sound, and he is swift, not battle hardened, but he is sensible, and he comes when called. The rest of his nature I'm sure you will find out in time, his name is Llwyd.' Edward was walking and talking at the same instant, his words cascading out of him like a waterfall in the spring thaw.

I followed him into the house. All was as it had been all those years ago, one hundred years had brought little change to this part of Wales. There was a new chair in front of the hearth and some new ironmongery over the fire to carry the pots. Everything else was as I remembered. I stepped back across the yard to see my new mount in the flesh, on the way stopping to view my reflection in the water butt. I had been forty-six years old last time saw myself. Now I should be one hundred and forty-five by my reckoning. But no, there I was, changed not a bit, hair still dark if a little grey around the temples, in need of a trim, beard a little overgrown and peppered with ginger and grey, eyes, two, still green and still as sharp as ever. I had not run to fat, though my muscles tired easily. A few weeks on the road and a few practice sessions with the bow, all would be well.

As I approached his stable door, Llwyd poked his head out again and whickered, thrusting his grey nose into my jerkin and pushing me in a friendly manner searching for food. I opened the stable door and stepped in. He was a fine animal indeed. Iron grey, about sixteen hands to his shoulder. White mane and tail. Eight inches of bone easily but none of the feathers of a heavy horse, broad and deep chested with large, powerful hind quarters.

'Where did you find him?' I asked Edward, he is too much quality for these parts.

'A passing Irishman owed money in the village. I cleared his debt and kept his horse in return.'

'And what did he look like, this Irishman, in case he should try and take his fine horse, back?'

'He had the look and build like yourself, but you can't miss his eyes, he had the eyes of the devil, I am sure he has been here before, but I can't place him, he gave his name as Owain. He left as sudden as he came, seemed to vanish into the hills towards Aberystwyth. Had a strange air about him, he did. Nothing to put your finger on, but if I were to meet him again, I would not trust the man.'

A knot had formed in my stomach at the mention of that name. Surely, he could not be in league with her ladyship, not after all that had gone before. I kept my counsel. If it were him, surely Edward would have recognised him. I had enough to think about without dealing with the Faeries, and that particular Faerie had a habit of inserting himself into my life welcome or not.

Edward brought me back to the present.

'There is a practice target in the bottom field. You have a week before you need to leave. You can practice there tomorrow. In the meantime, there are rabbits in the wood and deer on the hill, and nothing yet for supper.'

He slung his own weapon over his shoulder, picked up a quiver of arrows from behind the kitchen door, handed me my bow, called the dog, a wire haired and vicious looking mongrel called Floss, and set off towards the woods at the rear of the house.

It was late afternoon, and the rabbits would be grazing, easy targets for a practiced bow man with his eye 'in.' But not for one as out of practice as myself. After four missed shots I adjourned to the bank of the stream where I had tickled trout as a boy. Two hours later, the light was fading, and I was two trout up and, courtesy of Edward's better shooting, four rabbits to the good. Edward and I walked back to Hengwm where I tended the yard and the animals while he prepared supper.

Tomorrow I would again make my longbow part of my arm, and my sword an extension of my wrist. Tomorrow provided blisters where there had once been hard skin. My arms ached and my fingers were raw. I strapped them up with gentian salve from the pot Edward kept for treating the animals. He seemed to use it for everything from cows and goats with sore udders to his own cuts and grazes. The Healer we had called Red had planted gentian in a corner of the field just outside the garden wall. It was not a native plant, but it thrived there in the mountain soil, Red had had a way with plants. This pot of ointment had never seemed to empty, its contents never drying up, a thick, slightly sweet-smelling concoction mixed with grease and beeswax. There was still plenty left, and Red had not been seen at Hengwm for one lifetime at least.

It took a week for my fingers to harden with the help of the salve and rubbing with raw distilled spirit to harden the new skin, another trick Edward used on harness galls. Very useful for sore fingers.

While my body was becoming accustomed to itself once more, I took the time to accustom myself to Llwyd and he to me. We rode for miles over the tops towards the coast, the comforting sight of his long grey ears flicked forward to the going in front or twitching backwards to listen to my voice. He was a fine horse indeed, soft mouthed, willing, and kind. I could guide him with hands or just by pressure of my legs. He was not feared of anything I could find, and he jumped like a stag over obstacles in the woodland. Edward had done well! He had even stabled him next to the pigsty to get used to the grunting, squealing occupants. Horses were not enamoured of pigs. I chuckled to myself as a memory surfaced of a large chestnut horse and Hugh de Audley in confrontation with a large sow just outside Llantrisant. His charger Blondell had been terrified of pigs. What became of her, I wondered. Maybe she had found a home with the French and bred many fine foals, all with her fine temperament and fear of all things porcine.

The bond between horse and rider is formed in the small things, rubbing him down, cleaning dirt from his coat, making him comfortable after a long ride, talking to him softly, a rub behind his ears, a soft word and a bucket of warm mash and hay. The routines I had been taught in Llantrisant came flooding back. Llwyd and I became firm friends. As Edward had told me, he came to a whistle and did not stray too far if left to his own devices. I was well pleased with him.

At the end of the week, I mounted up, saddle bags filled with food for three days, and began my trek to Pembroke Castle. Light rain moistened the ground and damped my skin and my clothing, but it was the rain which brought life, and I was feeling more alive each day. Better this than being kept as a sleeping dog in the old witch's kennel. I would do her bidding and then see what opportunity came to free myself of her claws. I took the whole of the three days to reach Pembroke. I did not rush Llwyd, we had time to spare, time for me to re-acquaint myself with the land I loved.

Pembroke Castle loomed in the distance, a great stone statement of intent. A stronghold built to keep the occupants safe and its enemies out, home of Jasper Tudor created Earl by his half-brother King Henry VI and now also home to his sister-in-law Margaret Beaufort and her son Henry. I approached the great gates with a little trepidation. I was admitted by a liveried gatekeeper who greeted me with a brusque, 'Enter and state your business.' Once satisfied that my business was with Sir Jasper and Lady Margaret, he directed me to the stables. The stable lad took Llwyd from me, with instructions to rub him down well and feed him. I was further directed into a small room alongside the great hall. The room was sumptuously furnished, the walls hung with tapestries depicting hunting scenes and the narrow windows looked out over the estuary towards the Haven, as the mouth of the river was called. The smell of the river rose up to meet me, a combination of marshland, fish, and effluent from the castle, which was thrown daily into the water to be washed out to sea on the tide. Below me was a quay with small boats unloading their contents. Coracle fishermen sculled out in the channel making their way back to the nearby village of Milford. The porters, scurrying like worker ants, disappeared with their burdens of bales of cloth, sacks of grain and barrels of ale and wine into what must be a cave or a storeroom under the main hall, probably with access to the kitchens above.

I leant on the wall and peered out through the window, absorbed in the view until the piping voice of a page boy, smart as paint in his lordship's blue livery, with a large Fleur de Lys to the front and rear, bid me enter the great hall with a cheery, 'Sir Jasper will receive you now.'

The great hall was a fine room indeed, not over large but with a high vaulted ceiling hung with banners and painted with murals. Wood panelling covered the walls which were otherwise lime washed. Long oak tables and benches were arranged down either side and a huge fireplace occupied the centre of the outer wall. At the far end of the room a handsome brown-haired man of about my age sat on a large throne-like seat. He beckoned me approach him.

I swept a low bow to Jasper Tudor, Duke of Bedford, and Earl of Pembroke, Lady Margaret being noticeable by her absence.

'Gwyn ap Meredith at your service my Lord.'

'Be at ease, man, I am not one for ceremony. I take it you apply to train the boy in use of arms?'

'I have some experience in that field, my Lord, both in sword and longbow. I was trained by Sir Kenneth Fitzsimon at Llantrisant.'

'You have experience on campaign?'

'I have sir, I fought alongside the king on the fields of France.'

I did not specify which king, or which fields, and he did not ask.

'You will dine with us tonight and meet the lad. He is a fine boy, but his mother mollycoddles him, he needs to toughen up. Tomorrow I will test your skills, then I am sure his mother will decide if you are suitable. In the meantime, Gwyllyn here will show you to your quarters.' Jasper Tudor was a hospitable man,

She was not there at supper, neither was the boy. Jasper and I dined alone. The meal was fine, lamb spit toasted and juicy, flavoured with rosemary, accompanied by roasted vegetables and fresh bread, all washed down with a very good but strong ale. The conversation was lively. An educated man, he talked of the wars between York and Lancaster, every turn of the conversation loaded, seeking information on my own loyalties. I am neither York nor Lancaster. How could I be. The witch who is now his sister-in-law has kept me dormant all these years. In truth I should be dead, but he is not to know that, and she will not tell him. Jasper Tudor still idolises Margaret Beaufort. He knows not what she has become.

I slept that night in a soft bed, blessed relief after sleeping with Llwyd in fields and under hedges for three days. I woke refreshed and to the sounds of humanity waking, the clang of pots and buckets, the calls of the cook to the kitchen maids, berating them for some minor misdemeanour, and the smells of bread baking. Chickens clucked happily about the kitchen yard, a goat's bell clanged merrily in the distance and the familiar scent of the stables permeated the air as hay was shaken out, the stamp and whinny of horses eager for their breakfast. My stomach grumbled, awakened by the combination of noise and smell and the scent of bacon cooking.

It was not much past dawn, but I dressed and made my way to the kitchen in search of sustenance. The broad hipped, ample breasted cook flexed her forearms and appraised me with a grey eyebrow, assessed me as in need of food. I was seated at the end of a bench, a culf of bread spread with fresh butter perched on a pewter plate and balanced on the corner of the table. I was just finishing a last chew and swallow of the two slices of thick smoke cured bacon which had accompanied it, a dribble of grease attempting to run down my chin, which I mopped up with my sleeve, as Jasper burst into the kitchen.

'Come then, Gwyn, no time like the present, the Butts, let's see what you are made of!'

'My bow?'

'Is here! I took the liberty.'

'My Sword?'

'Yes, that as well, come, the boy is waiting for us.'

I followed him through the confines of the castle to a broad expanse of grass alongside the outer wall. Here there was a practice ground complete with targets. Waiting patiently by the gateway was a tall figure of a man, grey haired with a neatly trimmed beard, this was not possible surely? It was Sir Kenneth Fitzsimon. His merry brown eyes connected with mine and he shook his head imperceptibly. Lady Margaret had been at work again. His hand was on the shoulder of a slight framed boy of about fourteen years, brown haired, slightly thin featured and with a wary, worried expression.

'This is Henry, son of Margaret Beaufort and her husband, my late brother Edmund. Teach him well, one day he will be king, if his mother has anything to do with it.' Jasper introduced his nephew.

Kenneth raised an eyebrow and spoke. 'We have little time my lord, two weeks at best. Then we must leave for France.'

Jasper Tudor regarded me with an appraising look, then handed me my bow. 'Are you as good as he says you are?'

Three arrows to the centre of the furthest target silenced him. Half an hour later, my sword arm was aching from use, and I was sweating profusely and exhausted. Jasper Tudor was a rare fighter with a sword. Battle hardened and canny as a fox. I held my own, but barely. We both leant on our swords, panting, and dripping with perspiration.

'You'll do fine.,' he grunted. 'Teach the boy all you can. Yes, we leave for France in ten days. There are those who live in fear of his claim to the throne and will not rest until he is dead.

I could see that the teenage Henry revered his Uncle Jasper, here was his father figure. His true father had died of disease in the dungeons of Carmarthen Castle. Edmund Tudor had fought to suppress the Welsh rebellion, fighting for a Lancastrian king but the tables had turned and a York King had imprisoned him, leaving him to die of the plague. His young wife, still only a child, had miraculously survived a childbirth which should have robbed her of life. She was too young to bear children. She had birthed Henry at the tender age of twelve. Henry Tudor had been born to be a thorn in the side of the warring factions of York and Lancaster. He had a legitimised claim to the throne through both his mother's and his father's line, a threat to the now ascendant house of York, indeed.

I placed a hand on his slim shoulder, subtly feeling there for any strength of muscle beneath my hand. I found little. Sir Kenneth saw my actions, he read them well and spoke. 'I have taught Henry the basics of the sword, he is quite proficient. I'm sure he will surprise you.'

I addressed the boy, 'Well then,' I tossed him a wooden practice weapon, 'show me!'

A timid voice replied, 'What should I call you, master?'

'Call me Gwyn, for that is my name, and I will call you Henry for that is yours. Titles will attract attention so, we will not use them, will we Kenneth.'

He proved to have an arm stronger than it appeared, a sinewy strength, good balance, and timing. I doubted he would ever draw a longbow, but as my role seemed now to be that of both tutor and bodyguard, and he was destined for kingship, I doubted he would ever need to. He could learn on a less powerful weapon that would suffice if his lordship ever required to go hunting.

That evening she made her appearance. Kenneth and I were already seated at table, though the serving boys had not yet appeared with the food.

The great doors to the hall opened and she appeared. A regal entrance on the arm of the man Margaret Beaufort loved, her son walking ahead of her, he finely dressed in the blue velvet colours of Bedford, she in the deep green and red of the house of Tudor. Her eyes flashed grey when she saw me, a look which reinforced my subservience to her power. Gone was the benevolent caring lady of Llantrisant. Here was an arrogant, cruel, and self-serving woman. I would get no merciful treatment of that I was now sure. One look was all it had taken.

'Ah, Meredith, I see you answered the call.'

'I am yours to command, milady.' I replied, graciously.

'I trust you will not forget that fact.' The words dripped slowly from her, landing like ice to my veins. 'Are you long back from France?' She changed tack, and the conversation moved to news of the politics of France and the French, then to the training of her son. She spoke mainly to Sir Kenneth or to Jasper, occasionally to Henry. I was largely ignored, I was after all only her son's henchman, a paid lackey. At the end of supper, she rose and announced her intention to retire. 'Meredith, I would speak with you alone. Come.'

I followed her out of the hall and up the winding stairs to her rooms in the Tower. She invited me into her inner sanctum and closed the door.

'Sit.' she commanded. 'I have work for you Meredith. You will train the boy. Jasper will see to his welfare and his education. He has the contacts who will house you until it is safe to return. You will train him in combat. He must be proficient in the use of arms. He will need to show his strength on his return. You will do that?'

'Could I refuse?'

'No, you could not. There is more, he will need an army. You will find them, those you took before. I will raise them, all of them, and the red woman, I need her most of all, find her for me and once your work for me is done I will release you.'

There it was, the offer, but there was treachery in the price. Would I be willing to pay it?

'Now, go, teach my son well, I am weary, I must rest.'

Indeed, the candlelight of her rooms showed her as she was, an ancient crone, white haired and haggard, not the regal, still young woman who had taken supper with her son.

CHAPTER 39. EXILE – Gwyn

1471,
Pembroke Castle,
Wales.

Life at Pembroke Castle proved similar to the regime at that other castle which had been my home in my youth. This time, though, I was the tutor and responsible for the training of a boy of royal blood.
Edward IV the Yorkist king had regained the throne and was savagely ridding his country of all threats from anyone perceived to be Lancastrian. The red rose of Lancaster was to be eradicated. Dangerous times to be a teenager with a direct bloodline to the throne of England, for such was Henry's lineage, whether made illegitimate by law, or not. As many Kings had found out, you may make as many laws as you liked, but the only certain way to remove a threat to your throne, was to kill it. Bloodlines remained on paper long after blood had soaked into the ground.

Pembroke is remote from London and the hub of the Yorkist Court, but he would not go unnoticed, his mother trod a fine line between professed loyalty to whatever Crown was in place and treason. She had made a marriage for position to Sir Henry Stafford not long after Henry's birth. This had ensured her social position and kept her to some extent safe from the wrath of the king. She hid her Lancastrian sympathies, swore loyalty to the York King and kept her son in Wales, leaving Henry for long periods with his uncle Jasper. It was little wonder they were so close. In the meantime, she plotted his course to the throne. Every move made with care.

I came to like, even love Henry, was he not after all young enough to be my son. Once the ice was broken, he proved to be a quick-witted intelligent boy. Witty and good humoured, well educated, Jasper had engaged the best tutors for him. He spoke French, English and a little Welsh which his nurse had taught him when he was a very small boy. For now, though, Wales was not safe. After three weeks of lessons with sword and bow, proficient with one but still wayward with the other the decision was made. The net of Edward's court was growing tighter, it was time to sail for France.

Jasper was no stranger to life there, he had spent many years in exile himself. Over mugs of ale after lengthy suppers in the hall, after an exhausted Henry had gone to his bed and his mother retired to her chambers, he had told me of life in exile. Sir Kenneth and I were no strangers to war, or to its stories, but Jasper had truly lived a warrior's life, and in times when no man's back was safe even from a friend.

Jasper's father had led an army raised from the men of Wales in support of the deposed Lancastrian King. Jasper had been with him and on the losing side of the Battle at Mortimers Cross. This had seen his father Owen Tudor, and their men fight their way across the river Lugg and then flee as far as the city of Hereford only to be captured and beheaded, his head displayed atop the market cross for all to see. Dawn of the morning of the battle had been strange indeed. Three suns had been seen in the sky. The victorious Edward of March had taken them as his emblem, rallying his terrified troops to the sign of a holy trinity, and taking for himself the emblem of the sun in splendour.

Jasper himself had fled into exile in France, sheltered for six years by Louis XI who, despite making a peace with the now king Edward IV of England, refused to surrender to those he considered kin, even if somewhat distant. After six years, Jasper had returned to a country in complete turmoil. His estates, and the very castle we sat in at Pembroke had been lost, confiscated by York King Edward IV, and given to William Herbert along with guardianship of his sister-in-law and her son, only to be regained when his half-brother Lancastrian Henry VI was returned to the throne three years later. The tables had now turned once again, and it was once more time to take refuge across the channel.

Preparations were swift. Three riding horses, Llwyd amongst them, two pack animals loaded with enough supplies to get us to Tenby and across to Saint Vaast la Hogue. It was several days voyage. The ship would be required to navigate Land's End and Lizard point and then a run up the English Channel in front of a stiff south-westerly. The weather was turning, La Manche was not known for its calm waters in the best of weather, and we were heading into Autumn's storms.

The town of Tenby was two days ride from Pembroke and we broke the journey at Manorbier, where the de Barry family were sympathetic to our cause. The castle at Manorbier was a fine structure and them most welcoming, with no great fuss. A welcome for ordinary travellers, no one of note.

We rode the last five miles to Tenby along the cliff tops, arriving to take ship on a substantial two masted trade ship called Y Gwylan, the Seagull. Jasper sold off one of the pack horses, his load now carried by the other animal, and we boarded ship in the harbour. We were still settling the horses when the captain ordered the lines cast off and under light sail edged out into the short, blue-grey chop of the bay.

Tenby was a thriving international port. Its fortified walls had been newly built with a fine five arched gatehouse leading to the town with elegant merchants' houses, storerooms, inns, and hostelries, all nestled round the harbour and the two, fine sandy beaches where the fishing fleet pulled their shallow draft boats ashore to rest. Tenby had been rebuilt by the generosity of Jasper, Tudor Earl of Pembroke. His estates had paid for the walls, which had been razed by the raiding parties of the Welsh uprising, to be restored. He had made the town safe. True it had its share of thieves, pickpockets and the usual posse of whores who entertained the sailors ashore, but it was a jewel on the Welsh coast, one we now saw disappear over the stern of the Seagull as she sailed westward out into the grey swell of the Irish Sea. The wind was fair, the clouds scudded across a grey sky, but it was not yet raining. A long day's sailing took us south to the far point of Cornwall. The waves crashed white over the reefs off Land's End and then, off to our port side, Lizard point. Looking westwards there was only sea and the faint shadows of the Isles of Scilly. As we turned northeast to run up the south coast of Cornwall and then out into the channel towards northern France, the weather changed.

I felt the wind harder on my cheeks and pulling at my hat, ruffling my hair and pulling it back from my face. Our ship started to pitch and roll, the westerly ebb tide against the following wind tossing her sideways and forcing her bows ever higher out of the water over each oncoming wave. Jasper held tight to the rail and, above the howl of the freshening wind, shouted and gestured to go below.

I saw him head for the companion way and the stairs down to the cabin, holding Henry firmly by the arm, a very green looking Henry, most of his substantial breakfast having been deposited over the side.

The horses corralled and hobbled on deck, tied securely to their hitching posts, and fenced in by the guard-rail, whinnied nervously as the floor beneath them creaked as it rose and fell. They braced themselves with their hooves and leaned against the rails. Llwyd at least had the shelter of the cabin wall beside him, our other mounts leant into him, the calmest of the three, seeking comfort in his shadow. Pulling my knife from its scabbard I cut their hobbles. If the weather worsened, at least they would be free to move themselves.

The deck was now empty of all but the necessary crew. Passengers had taken refuge below decks. This was the wreckers' coast, a stretch of water and coastline known for its treacherous rocks, unseen sandbanks, and unpredictable weather.

For six hours the captain tried to make way up the English Channel against the tide. We made little headway. The wind had backed to the north-east and the tide was still against us. In the face of the imminent storm, our gallant crew reduced sail. Attempts to bear away out into the channel were unsuccessful and we heeled over to an impossible angle throwing cargo over the side into the maelstrom. Squalls of freezing rain blasted through the air like grapeshot. Waves crashed over the deck. Our horses lightly tethered somehow kept their footing on the sea washed boards. Those in the forward pen were not so lucky. Brought to their knees by a crashing wave they were unable to rise and were swept overboard taking the deck rail and hitching posts with them. Three huge waves later, the top section of the foremast followed them into the sea, hastily cut loose by the crew.

Jasper appeared on deck, grabbing me by the arm he pulled me below, 'Horses can be replaced man, but not you!'

Protesting, I was dragged into the fetid confines of below decks. Passengers clung on to any available object that did not move. Sailors weaved between them, and the captain barked orders to further reduce sail to a storm jib, almost bare poles. The sky was almost pitch black and the wind a steady screech. The ship shuddered and groaned as we ran down cavernous green troughs and then up over unending peaks. Somewhere to starboard there was a light in a window - a granite cottage on the little isle of Ouessant, some leagues off. Somehow, we had come through Le Raz without wrecking. That was no place to be. The storm had blown us south and west, out into the channel, further from Cornwall and ever closer to France, but with no hope of making the harbour at St Vaast. After six hours the wind abated, and the sky began to clear. Where were we?

A battered Seagull, sails in shreds, foremast missing, bobbed in the calm after the storm, the captain, Clive Bowman, assessing the damage with the eye of a father inspecting his son after a tavern brawl.

'We must make land, and soon!' On one mast and a little canvas he limped the ship into the small harbour at Le Conquet on the edge of the Rade de Brest.

Brittany, not where we had planned to land, but it was land at least, and the sun shone. It was far further south and indeed west than we intended for Jasper had contacts from his fighting days who still lived in the lands around Caen, now a long way to the east. I, too, was familiar with that part of France, the valley of the great sleepy river of the Somme, and a small town called Crécy en Ponthieu. Would the grave of Morwenna the laundress still be marked after all this time? Were the souls of the fallen peaceful in the ground or were they restless for another war?

Soaked with sea water and still walking wobbly legged like drunks from the voyage, we led our remaining horses onto the quay. Local seafaring folk arrived and offered help in a brogue not unlike that of the Welsh who had bid us farewell a day or so ago. Jasper left Henry in my charge while he went into the town to find lodgings for the night. I tied our animals to a ring at the dock wall and went with Henry to fetch our packs from below deck.

Bundles shouldered, we were just emerging from the bowels of the ship when Henry shouted, 'Hoy you!' He dropped his burden and hand on the knife at his belt ran towards where the traveller whose horses had been washed overboard was untying Llwyd from his tether.

I ran after Henry, knife drawn. The man had flung himself into the saddle and had the reins of our remaining pack horse in hand. This thief dug his heels into Llwyds iron grey sides, the horse grunted and sprang forward into a canter, the dark brown solid little pack pony dragged in his wake. Our other horse had been left in peace. Only Llwyd was being ridden away and was now at the end of the street, the pony having been abandoned, not being able to keep up with his companion. Henry began to sprint after them. My hand on his shoulder stopped his progress.

I pulled myself to my full height and as Llwyd reached the fountain in the middle of the town square, I placed two fingers into my mouth, under my tongue and whistled, two shrill blasts, then I stopped.

The fleeing grey shape came to a sudden stop. The metal of his iron shod feet sparking off the flint in the cobbles. The rider displaced by the sudden lack of forward motion fell sideways into the lily pond which surrounded the fountain. I whistled again and heard an answering whinny, and Llwyd trotted across the town square and back to his master, coming to a stop in front of me and nuzzling my pocket for food. Back at the fountain a huge man rose from the water, like Neptune from the deep. He climbed out over the ornate carved gargoyles of the rim and sat, dripping on its edge. As we approached, I recognised a horse trader, a Welsh born horse trader, now from Ireland, with the looks of the devil and eyes to match.

He spoke first. 'I'll not be getting my best horse back then.'

'That you won't, you'll find he's mine now.'

'That old farmer struck a hard bargain, but I'd a debt to pay and the law on my tail, if you ever want to sell him, I'll give yer a fair price mind.'

'Over my dead body, Owain, don't push your Irish luck! What brings you here anyway, tis a long way to journey to steal a horse, fine as he is!' I punched the cheeky Irish bastard in the shoulder in a friendly way.

'I come to join your cause. I'll be the first of many. I'm Ralph now, Ralph Owen.' A conspiratorial wink was aimed in my direction. 'Let me buy you an ale, these Breton lads make a decent brew and there's a fair tavern around the corner.'

I suspected that Jasper may have found it already, it being the only lodging house in the town. Indeed, he was just emerging from its dark but welcoming depths, 'We have beds at least for the night, there are stables next door, Henry go with Gwyn and see to the horses. Where did you find this reprobate, I've not seen him since Pembroke assizes!'

He also poked our newfound friend in the shoulder. 'Is there still a price in your head, stolen any good horses lately?'

Ralph's face cracked into a wide smile, and he laughed, a deep belly laugh. 'I never give up trying. Ha, the look on your face when I leapt from your castle walls, I'll never forget it! Nor the stench of that liquid midden I landed in. But I settled the debt, I'm a free man now.'

'I don't doubt you are, so, will you join us?'

'Well now, Sir Jasper, I thought you'd never ask!'

And so, our number became four. We shared our two rooms at Le Coque Rouge. I slept with Ralph in one the two rooms, sharing the lumpy and bug infested bed. Henry shared with his uncle in the other - no doubt a room with cleaner linen and more frequent visits by the chamber maid.

The morning dawned bright and blue with none of the chaos of the previous day. After a good breakfast, Jasper announced his plans.
We would travel south. The Beaufort family were, after all, related to the Dukes of Brittany through the de Montfort's. Someone there would be bound to offer us shelter, at least until we found our feet.

CHAPTER 40. A VOICE IN THE DARK- Sibyl

1916,
Hengwm.

    I turned over in the cramped and creaky bed, his breathing in my ear echoing through the turmoil in my mind like the soughing of the wind through the ash trees outside. The thin curtains were open as was the tiny window of my attic room. Opening one eye I looked out from under the quilt and saw the face of the moon sending its unearthly white light towards me. I closed my eyes and the soughing noise changed, like a radio set tuning itself in, seeking a clear channel through the airwaves.
    I felt his arm around my waist pull me back against him, and his leg wrap itself over mine like a giant anaconda. I dug an elbow into his ribs to make room to breathe. The voice of the night became clearer, not Eryr's quiet but persistent snoring, which had faded into a warm, contented rhythmic breeze down my back. This was a voice, it was calling me, faint at first but becoming louder and more persistent.
    'Red Meredith, Merch Goch, hear me.' A woman's voice draped in the folds of time, shrouded in death. 'Hear me, do not fight me, come…….'
    My mind conjured a picture, a stone room, a tower, a figure clad in blood red, white and silver hair blowing in threads around a gaunt, life worn face. A face in reflection, its edges blurred by the ripples of water framed in the ornate rim of the vessel she used. I closed my eyes and banished her from my thoughts, I turned my face into Eryr's warm chest with its light dusting of hair. I felt him rise to my touch and groan in appreciation as I pressed myself closer to him. The leg which had entangled mine moved and I was imprisoned beneath him, I opened my body to him and felt myself float away, rocked by the music of the night and the creak of old wood. The white of my internal moonlight flashed with an accompaniment of stars. His arms encased me, his legs held me, my own wrapped around his.
    I came around on a mountain top. I felt bouncy heather and mountain turf under my back, it was dark, very dark, except for the full face of mistress moon and her attendant. The black curls resting on my belly stirred and those piercing green eyes looked up at me then lowered themselves to their work. It was not him that cried out to the moon, but I.

We lay there, spent, my head on his shoulder, and counted stars until the dawn said there were no more stars to count.
Then I walked, barefoot and naked back to reality.

As we approached the turn in the path, I heard him cough, and hastily thought about clothing. The yard gate squeaked a little on its hinges, and Edward's head appeared at the kitchen door. He emerged carrying his iron bucket of warm water and headed for the cowshed.

'I've poked up the fire girl, a brew wouldn't go amiss, when you have a minute.'

I saw his white whiskers shake along with his shoulders as he opened the door to the dairy and whispered soft endearments to his own harem of softly lowing ladies.

'Get over, girl.' The soft lilt came over the door with the slap of a calloused hand on warm cow hide. 'Mind my bloody bucket.'

The thump of the stool being set in its place, the groan as he lowered himself onto its seat and the scrape of metal on stone as he adjusted the pail and slosh of water as he prepared to start milking.

'Get on with you, Sibyl, put that fiend down and get the breakfast on.'

Uncle Edward had the ears of a bat. They had not yet heard the kitchen door close behind us, he knew exactly where we were, and likely exactly what we were doing. I pulled away from the lips that lingered too long on mine

'You take the feed round, and I'll be in the kitchen.'

Eryr grunted his assent, Edward rested his forehead against the cow's side and snorted with laughter and I closed the kitchen door firmly behind me.

I heard tread on the stairs, and a bleary eyed, 'Good morning, mum' herald Rhianydd's entrance into the room. 'Agnes is away with the fairies this morning, must be the mountain air.'

I poured water into the big brown tea pot and stood it to warm, then pushed the black iron kettle back onto the range to boil. The tea was in the tin caddy which was on the mantelpiece above the fire.

'Just toast please, no bacon for me. Oooh, is that honey I see, in that case, just bread and honey.' Rhianydd picked up the bread board and lifted the cob loaf from the stone bread bin, tucked the board under her arm and picked the butter dish up with her free hand and placed them on the oil cloth which covered the big kitchen table. With the addition of cutlery, the milk jug and sugar basin breakfast was assembled.

I heated the big frying pan and began frying bacon for those who wanted it. Edward would be good for a few slices with an egg and a slice of toast. Eryr the same, faerie he might be, but his appetites were all human. I smiled to myself at the thought. Rhianydd caught my eye and raised a dark red eyebrow. 'That bed could do with oiling.'

I feigned innocence. 'I don't know what you mean, child.'

'Between that and Uncle Edward snoring my looks are suffering from lack of sleep.' Rhianydd pulled an imaginary wrinkle flat. 'I'm sure between the pair of you, you pulled the moon closer.'

'Rhianydd dear, ladies do not snore.' I countered.

She looked at me appraisingly and with her father's twinkle in her blue eyes replied. 'It's not the snoring I'm referring to.'

I spooned tea into the warm tea pot and added boiling water and placed it on the table under its padded cosy.

She picked up the wire toasting fork and speared a thick slice of bread, then held it to the fire to brown. The kitchen door opened and Edward and Eryr left their boots in the step. 'Smells good, girl, is the tea made?' Edward pulled his big chair out from the table and sat. Rhianydd poured a splotch of milk into a big blue and white striped mug, added brewed tea and two sugars, sliding it across the table with the teaspoon still in place. He stirred it several times, the 'diolch yn fawr' was hidden in the sigh of appreciation and the slurp of the first mouthful.

'Uncle!' She reprimanded him.

Eryr sat, plate of food before him, mug empty and expectant.

'You can pour your own.' Rhianydd still hadn't quite come to terms with Eryr, maybe she never quite would, and maybe that was my fault. Eryr gracefully lifted the teapot and poured for himself and for me, and then for his daughter.

'Two sugars, no hemlock?'

Despite herself she laughed, 'Just one sugar please, I'm sweet enough, save the hemlock for yourself!' Then addressing Edward, 'Can I take Agnes up to the top field later, to see the ponies?'

'Aye, why not, she's got a feel for that little roan one, maybe I'll fetch him in when he's off his mother, never too early to learn.'

'She's already named him, he's called Zak.'

'Zaccariah, which is a very long name for one so small. Where is the little one?'

As if on cue the passage door opened, and a bleary-eyed Agnes stumped into the room dragging a ragged fur lined cloak behind her.

'Where did you find that, darling?' asked her mother.

'In Gannie's room,' came the reply.

Rhianydd looked at me and at Eryr, a question on her face, I shook my head quietly. Rhianydd spoke. 'Shall I give it to Gannie then, I think she looks a bit cold, don't you?'

She took the cloak from her daughter, and I draped it lightly round my shoulders, trying not to think invisible thoughts, now was not the time or the place for Gannie's magic.

The day passed quietly, Rhianydd took Agnes up to see the ponies, Edward pottered about in the yard, mending broken harness, oiling the gate and any other hinge which needed it. Eryr mucked out the small stable next to the cow shed and bedded it down with thick straw for a new occupant. Tomorrow Edward had resolved to catch Zak. His mother was halter broken. Edward would lead her down from the mountain and young Zak would follow, the separation from his mum would be made as easy as possible, it was in Edward's view long overdue. After a few days without her, young Zak would be happy in the tiny paddock along the stream and in his own small stable at night.

I wrote lists of what we might need to do to find Jack. We knew he was alive, we knew he was in France, but where, was a mystery. We needed more. Rhianydd must go to London. Uncle Moses could pull in some favours, get her an interview with someone who knew what had really happened, for someone must know, mustn't they?
It was mid-afternoon. Uncle Moses would be in his office. I picked up the telephone and asked for his number.

'Connecting a call from the Newtown exchange.' the operator spoke.

'Yes?' spoke the gruff voice.

'It's me!'

'Of course, it's you, who else would it be? You are the only one who has this number, except the ministry bods and they don't phone from the back of beyond.'

I explained what I wanted. He hummed and ha'd for a minute. 'Send her to see me in Cardiff first, I will make a few phone calls. I know Gerald

Shipley, he's a sound fellow, a man you can talk to, but let me do the talking, aye.'

'Call me when you have word.'

'I will, I'm due in London tomorrow for a few days. This war can't get enough coal, and they keep enlisting my colliers, I'll see if he's available.'

'Thank you, Uncle Moses.'

'No trouble. Goodbye Sibyl.' Uncle Moses hung up before I could enquire about my younger daughter Helena. If anything were amiss in that direction, he would have told me, wouldn't he?

Two days later Moses had been as good as his word. Rhianydd boarded the first of several trains which would get her to Cardiff. Moses had set up a meeting for her with Gerald Shipley. She would get the details from her uncle and catch the train to London. Agnes would stay with us at the farm, distracted with the excitement over Zak and her infatuation with Uncle Edward and also with Eryr. She would be kept well occupied while her mother was away.

Every night while Rhianydd was away, the voices called me. Every night I took refuge in Eryr's arms, the only place it seemed I could not hear them.

'She wants something from me.' I told him.

'You must not answer her.' he replied. 'There is no good in what she wants, her soul turned black when they burned her.'

'But she did not burn.'

'Magic like that will burn a soul, it leaves its mark. She is up to no good, Red, do not answer her.'

He had called me by my pet name, 'Red'. Red for the colour of my hair, Merch Goch, the red maid. 'Stay close by me, Red, she will not drag me to her. There are many under her power, but I am not one of them, she holds no grip on me.' So, Eryr became my refuge again, with me, rarely out of sight or sound of him, I felt safer and more whole than I had done in years. Within the week Rhianydd returned. She was alone and no wiser.

CHAPTER 41. BOY TO MAN- Gwyn

We would spend twelve long years as guests of Francis Duke of Brittany at his summer residence the great castle of Suscinio situated on the French coast at Sarzeau. The internal politics of France and that of England would make Jasper and Henry diplomatic pawns, valuable to Duke Francis in his fight to retain the independence of Brittany from the rest of France. Their situation was also valuable to the French King, Louis XI, who sought to gain favour with Edward IV by eliminating Henry on his behalf and therefore ridding Edward of a threat to his throne. However, Duke Francis II insisted that both Jasper and Henry were in his protective custody and would remain so, and with that, Edward had to be content, for a time.

The years passed by, and the teenager became a handsome young man, dark haired and with deep-set blue eyes which sparkled when he spoke. He was finely built and well-spoken and educated. Despite both mine and his uncle's ministrations, he would never be a warrior, for although proficient with weapons he had neither the temperament nor the inclination to be ruthless in battle. We lived under the great Duke's protection and bided our time.

In the years that followed, his mother, ever the politician, had contrived to become friendly with Elizabeth Woodville, the beautiful Lancastrian widow who had married the Yorkist Prince. She had born Edward many children, all of royal blood and all of whom would be good matches for her son. Was it the feminine wiles of two witches that had contrived to find young Henry a bride amongst her flock of daughters? Henry's mother wanted her son by her side, by now it was 1476, and had engineered his return. Duke Francis agreed to let Henry leave Suscinio and return to England.

Whether he was counselled against this by his uncle Jasper or whether he sensed that Edward would renege on his word, Henry feigned illness on his arrival at the coast and, pleading a sickness of the bowels and a fever, made his way back to Suscinio where Duke Francis welcomed him with open arms.

Henry's mother Margaret Beaufort and King Edward continued their political machinations. Periodically each tried to lure Henry back to England each for differing reasons, Margaret to have her son by her side and Edward to have better control over the perceived threat to his throne.

Things came to a head in April of 1483. Duke Francis was facing an unstable time and was no longer able to guarantee the safety of his political refugees. Then, Edward, who was usually of robust health, died unexpectedly, leaving his twelve-year-old son as his heir under the protection of his brother Richard Duke of Gloucester, a man who had aspirations to take the throne of England for himself.

Edward's reign had been relatively stable. He was well liked by the populace. When Richard seized the throne for himself, his claim to it and his grip on it were tenuous indeed. The French nobility, Duke Francis and King Louis saw in this an even bigger bargaining chip in the form of Henry and his uncle Jasper.

In the shadows, Lady Margaret still planned her son's return to England and perhaps to more than a Welsh Earldom. To add fuel to the political and diplomatic flames, the twelve-year-old Edward Vth and his young brother Richard were held in protective custody and had not been seen since their uncle's usurpation of the throne. England was once more in crisis. Margaret Beaufort's husband, Sir Henry Stafford, had been killed fighting for Edward IV at the battle of Barnet. Margaret had then married Sir Thomas Stanley, another highly political man who had managed to remain on the right side of the axe for the duration of the wars. The response of Richard III to these uprisings was swift. All perceived traitors were eliminated.

Meanwhile, Elizabeth Woodville remained in sanctuary and plotted the return of her line to power. Her sons, she feared, were dead. This left her daughters. A strategic marriage to a male claimant was the only way forward. She and Margaret Beaufort resurrected the proposed match between her daughter Elizabeth of York and Henry and their conspiracy began in earnest.

A messenger was sent to Brittany to broker the marriage and with the support of the treacherous Duke of Buckingham a rebellion was started. This rebellion was ill planned and swiftly put down by Richard III's army and the Duke of Buckingham captured and on 2nd November 1483. He was executed.

In December 1484 at Christmas time, Henry found himself in the cathedral at Rennes in Brittany where his mother's political machinations with Elizabeth Woodville came to fruit. Henry swore that he would marry

Edward IVs daughter, Elizabeth of York. This effectively declared his intent to eventually make a move on the throne of England.

This had an unexpected effect. Many of Buckingham's men fled to Brittany to avoid execution and swell the cause of Henry Tudor, under whom they thought they stood more chance of survival. The lands around Sarzeau were filled with displaced Lancastrians willing to fight for a cause.

The politics of the French court is, if anything, more unpredictable than even the greatest vagaries of its English counterpart. King Louis XI died leaving a thirteen-year-old heir. The resulting power struggle drew Henry's protector, Duke Francis, into the fray, resulting in unrest between Brittany and the rest of France. By this time, Henry and Jasper had left Brittany and were sheltering in the protection of the King in Paris.

Like pieces on a chessboard the English nobility positioned themselves for or against King Richard, those who were for him open in their declarations of loyalty, those against being naturally more subtle in their moves.

Margaret Beaufort's husband, the Lancastrian Thomas Stanley, who had cleverly walked between all the fires, travelled north on the pretext of visiting relatives. The King, suspecting his allegiances were not as firm as they should be, took his son as hostage and kept him a prisoner.

Amongst these times of unrest, there was seen a window of opportunity for Henry to leave the unrest of the court of France and return to England and make his advance on the throne.

With an army comprised of the displaced Lancastrian supporters and French mercenaries Henry set sail from Hon fleur, soon arriving in Wales.

CHAPTER 42. MATER QUERCUS – Gwyn

Mater Quercus custos animarum aperi cor tuum mihi.

Mother oak, keeper of souls open your heart to me.

Ralph and I left the castle at Sarzeau before dawn, he riding one of the Duke's finest horses. As usual he had 'business' of his own to attend to, but we rode together as far as Caen, making camp just outside the now thriving town which had been razed to the ground at my last visit. A hundred years had rebuilt its walls but not the trust of its people. We were now in France, a country which had lost count of the armies which had fought on its soil, but whose people always kept score. France is a fine country, but the French, well they would always be French!

After a week's ride, mostly sleeping under hedges or in abandoned barns, we had spent the last of our coin on beds and a hot meal. The meal had been delicious, some form of fowl cooked until the flesh fell from its bones, in a concoction of red wine and mushrooms, washed down with more red wine. We had talked long into the night, neither of us very honestly, both skirting around the truth and the purpose of our respective journeys.

Ralph Owen seemed an enigma, he was sworn to Henry's cause, yet always with a hidden agenda, guarded in his words, in his actions, as if walking a fine line between fires, not wishing to get burned by either. He gave the impression that he knew either everything or nothing at all. The only things which gave away his passion were those eyes. Eyes so green they pierced your soul, but with remarkable flecks of other colours which highlighted his mood.

We had talked in careful circles. 'Had I travelled through France before?' he asked.

'Yes, but not for many years.' I answered.

'Is it much changed?' he asked.

'Well, the people have.' I replied, to which he laughed, and his face darkened in reflection.

'Well, people die, don't they?' was his eventual response as he took another glass of the very passable red wine.

'Men and women die, but a people lives on, and they have changed. They have lost trust, they do not know who to believe, so they believe no one.' I was rambling, my tongue becoming loose, yet he seemed remarkably sober.

'Do the dead live on?' he asked, 'Or is there truly nothing after life?'

'If there is nothing, then there is nothing to fear. If there is eternal salvation, then why is there no rush to get there?'

He laughed at this. 'You speak as though you have experience.'

'Me?' I responded. 'I am just a poor soldier, bound in service to a higher authority. I have much experience of life, but not yet death, and I intend to remain with the living. And you?' I floated the question out. 'Who do you serve?'

'I serve no master and no mistress,' came the reply, 'but I do know there is a wave of change coming. We must be careful it does not wash us away, Gwyn Meredith.'

We staggered up the rickety stairs to our room, both mindful not to forget our weapons which the proprietor had insisted we leave at the door. Of necessity we both fell into the one bed, I slept like the dead and when I awoke, I was alone. Ralph Owen was gone - to catch his own tide to shores of his own, no doubt.

Before we left, a messenger had arrived at Sarzeau, a messenger who searched for Ralph and came with news from Abbéville. He and Ralph had gone out that night. They had not been seen in the taverns of the village where the displaced Lancastrians spent their days. The following day they had returned, buoyant, almost euphoric but exhausted. Ralph had taken to his bed and slept for several days after his return. The messenger, his face dark shadowed and grey with lack of sleep had been ushered into Jasper Tudor's inner sanctum. On a fresh horse, he rode out the following day with instructions to travel swiftly, at night, and to stop for no one.

Much time had passed since we arrived at this great fortress. Henry was now a man, my work was done. He had been well schooled by the best tutors in academia, Jasper had mentored him in manners and etiquette and chivalry. I had taught him to fight like a warrior. The only lessons he lacked were those in life. Of necessity he had spent much time on his own, devoid of the company of his peers. He knew little of life in the world outside the castle and I had been forbidden from taking him with me on my forays into the forests of France. Things were stirring in the ether. Henry was as ready as he ever would be. The York king Edward was dead, his young sons were imprisoned and declared bastards, his wife the Woodville witch had fallen from favour, if she was ever in favour to start with. Only Edward's fixated love for her had kept her alive on many occasions. The house of York was weakened, the Lancastrians had no candidate for the throne. Was there ever a better time?

In the villages around the chateau, the Lancastrians gathered, a rag tag band. Though great in number they were not fighting men, they were refugees, ordinary folk who were loyal to king Henry VI.

The time had come for me to gather the spirits of Crécy, but were they still there, would they come or were they bound to one soil forever?

With the comforting strength of Llwyd beneath me, his grey ears pricked forward, I left the town of Caen, putting Ralph to the back of my mind and headed north towards Picardie. It was a long ride. I had travelled the road before on foot. It had not changed much in a hundred years. The trees overhanging the road were larger, the fields still neatly farmed, the cottages still low stone-built humps sheltering from the wind which swept over the land carrying with it the scent of the sea.

I followed the coast to the mouth of the river Somme, turning eastwards and following the river to the crossing at Abbéville. The road took me through woodland with thick undergrowth, banks rising on either side of the road, thick with bracken. The last of my coin spent in Caen, I foraged for my food in the plentiful woodland, reconnecting with the land, rediscovering my inner senses. I found my eyes becoming sharper, my reflexes quicker, I sensed where there was danger more acutely, the old Gwyn was returning. Maybe it was that bloody Irishman, or was it something else, as I went to sleep each night, wrapped in my cloak, on a bed of bracken piled into a scraped-out hollow in the ground. I drifted off to the sounds of marching feet, and the haunting chorus of men singing a strange incantation about, 'a long way to Tipperary.'

Crécy en Ponthieu had changed little in a century, and there in the corner of the churchyard was a plain stone marker, the women had been good to their word then. One word carved into the rock, Morwenna. I would remember her, as I remembered all the others I had lost along the way, Marged, Arianrhod, and even Edward in some respects. Ralph's talk of the nature of death had stirred feelings and thoughts I had licked away years ago. I was destined to have no family, destined to wander, tied to my mistress by invisible chains, always at her command, from wherever or whoever she might be.

I entered the Church where my Prince Edward had said mass with his father many lifetimes ago, I prayed for Morwenna and for Marged, for little Arianrhod and all the others I had lost. Then I went to the river and called on the ones I hoped to find.

One day's ride outside the town, into the forest, there it was, the small hill where it had all begun, two days after the victory, when all should have been celebration. I rubbed my shoulder. There was still a dead spot where the arrow had pierced my flesh. In the summer it buzzed like a hive of bees but felt no pain. In the winter it itched like a fiend, sending waves of numbness down my arm and into my fingers. Marged and Red had tended me well. If it had not been for them I would have been left among the dead. Them and a Prince, a boy who had refused to believe what he could not see for himself, who had learned not to act without reason. We had both been only sixteen then. I sat on the grassy hillock to get my bearings, Llwyd grazed peacefully alongside me, no need to hobble him, he was not going to go far. The sunshine on my face dazzled my eyes, it held me in its glare, and there she was, standing on the edge of the forest, Marged, her hunting bow over her shoulder and her quiver of arrows hanging at her waist, fletched with black, red, and white feathers. She was calling me, but I could not hear her. I tried to follow her, but I was frozen to the spot. When I stirred again it was dark, the nocturnal forest was waking, owls called their eerie call over the treetops, navigating across the sky always in search of prey. Deeper in the trees wolves stirred and organised themselves for the hunt, and I listened, ears tuned to the sound, unafraid. Behind me Llwyd blew softly on my shoulder, his warm breath and soft nostrils massaging the tingle in my shoulder.

This was her work. The hand of my mistress was in this night. She used me like her mule, carrot and stick, promise of a reward that never quite came. What crumb of hope did she dangle in front of me now? The answer was plain, that which I had lost and had hardly known, my family. I cleared my mind, shook my head, opened my eyes and there it was, where it had been before, older, greater but still the same, it's great trunk and sweeping branches standing like a welcoming mother.

Mother Oak. The voice of the witch invaded my mind, I did not speak, she spoke for me. My words and my limbs controlled by her, my thoughts only hers. I was walked to the arms of the tree, my hand reached out to its gnarled bark, and I spoke the words she gave me.

Mater Quercus.
mater quercus custos animarum aperi cor tuum mihi
Mother oak, keeper of souls, open your heart to me.

It kept repeating, each time more insistent, but nothing happened. The voice was not mine. Mother oak did not listen. I turned from the great tree. I realised that I had tears streaming down my face, then falling on my knees with my forehead pressed against her I called again. I was not calling a tree, I was calling my wife, my oak, the stout hearts of those I had loved, knowing that they were all dead.

Mater Quercus custos animarum aperi cor tuum mihi.

I felt the bark become as soft as Margeds apron front. Giving way in front of me, she opened up her door and let me in, I was home.

CHAPTER 43. THE LIGHTS ARE ON – Gwyn

The keeper of souls kept her secrets and her occupants well hidden. I wandered for what seemed like miles, following the trails cut in this hypogeal world by the great roots which anchored her to the earth. I found no one, the souls I was searching for were gone. Had they truly fallen like the leaves of this great tree, to be taken back into her soil, reused to form the next crop of greenery in life's cycle.

Then I heard it, the singing, again, sounds of men singing, Welsh voices, singing hymns. Voices mixed with the crash of cannon fire. But canon louder than any I had ever heard. The earth shook with the vibration, the sounds of a whistle, another explosion, a grenade, and rapid bangs, not canon, smaller than canon. Then another shout.

'Gas! Gas! Gas!' A pause, a silence, ungodly, unearthly silence, punctuated by the screams of men in pain.

'My eyes, man, I can't see!' followed by the last rasping breath of one who could no longer breath. A sickly-sweet smell soaked down through the soil. My own eyes began to itch. I tied my kerchief over my nose and mouth and was drawn towards the noise.

In the mid-distance there was light drifting into this subterranean world. I walked toward it and into the madness of warfare like I had never seen before. I had seen the cruelty of the horse pits full of spikes. I had seen men hacked to death with swords. I had fired volleys of lethal arrows from a distance at my enemy, but always, always I had been in sight of my foe. There was something human in the seeing of the consequences. Here was death at a distance, mass death, thousands of men killed within minutes. I emerged from one tunnel into another, but this one had no roof. Gone was the clean smell of the earth, replaced with the stench of mustard gas, the reek of blood, vomit, and liquid brown fear. I climbed the ladder in front of me, my longbow drawn but now slightly unwieldy to move with. In front of me was a man. I tripped over his legs, I fell, my body arched over the top of his. Instinctively I rose up over him, aware of the threat in front of me shielded by a grey wall of mist generated by the sweating earth. I fired one arrow after another until the quiver was empty, I felt their small metal darts which came out of the mist pierce my flesh passing straight through my leather gambeson, but I felt no pain. I saw men fall, arrows embedded in their dirty grey coloured jerkins. These men wore no colours. Where were their standards to draw to, where were their leaders? They wore no armour, no mail, not even leather like my own. The fallen man turned over, he started to crawl back towards that stinking pit of gas filled death. I dragged him away. I hid him in one of the holes made by those huge cannon balls which fell like rain on us. He mouthed something at me, his face white with shock.

'Arthur.' That was it, he was telling me his name, or maybe it was 'Archer,' he was muttering. What of it, he fell backwards into the mud. I fell with him, his body protected by mine. We lay there, entwined until I felt a stretcher bearer pull him free. I heard them muttering between them,

'He's alive Harry, he's bloody alive. You take his feet. I've got his head.' They busied themselves with a stretcher, unrolling the canvas and expertly rolling the casualty onto it.

'Look at this, Ivor, look, it's real I'm telling you, look! It was sticking out of that German, the one over there!' Harry pointed across the wasteland from whence they had come. 'It's a bloody arrow, I'm telling you!' It was then, as I sat up in the mud, that I realised that I was sitting within feet of them, and they could not see me. The casualty opened his eyes once more and looked straight at me. He reached out his hand in thanks, or something more.

'Harry, find Harry.' The stretcher bearer tucked the arm into the stretcher and fastened it down with a strap. 'I'm Harry you idiot. You made it son, your war is over, just lie back and let us take you home.'
I was dragged by the leg by unseen hands, over the edge of what seemed like a precipice, I lay there for a moment before opening my eyes and staring up into faces I knew well and into the green eyes of Ralph. It was not him who spoke, but a youth called Delme. 'Well, bloody hell, man, if it isn't Gwyn Meredith. What kept you so long man, we've missed you?'

Looking round I saw that, while they all wore the green and fawn livery of Llantrisant, Ralph wore the uniform of the man I had saved, a dirty green, brown tunic and what passed for breeches. One by one the archers faded into the background, disappearing miraculously from sight. Ralph spoke then.

'Go with them, they are your men. They need you and you stick out like a bloody sore thumb.'

'And you?' I queried, 'You aren't exactly invisible.'

'I have work to do here, but listen for me, I may have need of your skills.'

He pointed to the corner of the trench we sat in.

'Round there – that is your way out. Mind the bodies, and don't breathe the gas.'

He seemed completely at home, unconcerned by the chaos which went on around him.

'What place is this?' I hissed at him.

'We are in 1916.' he hissed back. 'You should not be here.'

I followed his instructions, back into the underworld, the safe, subterranean underbelly of mater. It struck me that I was visible, too visible to some not to be remarked on. I had found my army and I, too, had my orders, from her. But this was not her time, and the man who served no master would get his work done.

Meanwhile, in the field hospital at Abbéville, Private Arthur Cole raved about archers, his mind, in the view of all who tried to heal him, deranged. Dr Sam O'Connor pronounced him unfit for duty, for though he was physically whole - he had only a small knife cut to the palm of his hand, his mind was not. The doctor wrote his notes up and, as he moved the patient off the stretcher canvas and onto a cot bed, his hand disturbed a long thin object left on the stretcher under the man's thigh. Pulling it clear his jaw dropped in amazement, for in his hand he held an iron tipped arrow about two and a half feet long, the feathers at its notched end the red, black, and white of what he recognised as the spotted woodpecker. Maybe the young man wasn't so mad after all, but he was going home. Dr O'Connor placed the arrow under his bunk. What the eye didn't see……

Private Cole would be on the next transport home. He continued to mutter about a man called Harry, and rave about an archer, and stare into the distance. He did not eat, and he screamed of gas in his sleep. His lights were on, but there was no one at home.

In mater's bosom we were all home, but there was only the dim light of the iridescent stones which were found in her soil. We heard the chaos above, but this was not our war, our time would come. The men of the army of Crécy had lain dormant in the earth for long enough.

We heard the endless fighting above and around us, the cries of the men, the screams of wounded horses. Where was Llwyd? I felt bad that I had left him. Was he still standing by the oak tree in the year of our lord

1486. A good horse will always find a home. I salved my conscience with that thought.

The whistles were blown, men were sent to their deaths, no thought to the numbers of the dead. The bodies lay unburied and those that were, lay in shallow graves just deep enough to cover them and give them dignity. In the bosom of Mother Earth, we waited for her call. In the meantime, I assessed my troops.

In the end it was Ralph who called. Ralph who had become detached from his unit, Ralph whose comrades would need our help.

CHAPTER 44. TIMES ARE CHANGING

June 1485,
Pembroke Castle,
Wales.

The Lady Margaret wrapped her cloak about her and shivered. She was standing on the ramparts of the great castle at Pembroke. She stared south across the bleak Welsh countryside and the grey swell of the Irish Sea. She missed her son as only a devoted mother could. He was her all, her reason to exist, through him she would live her life, regain her power.

She unhooked the huge iron key from her chatelaine and unlocked the tower room. The huge wooden door creaked open. She parted the curtain of age-old cobwebs and the remains of the tapestry hung to keep out the sea wind. Once bright with the colours of birds and fish, intricately stitched by the ladies of the French court, it was now faded and brittle with the corrosion of many years of salt spray, friable to the touch and liable to disintegrate with a breath.

The room was undisturbed for nigh on twenty-eight years. Once the sewing room of Margaret Beaufort, it had become her own private space. Margaret Beaufort was gone, though all believed her living. Margaret de Audley occupied her space now, in every way and more. She would see that the child with his tentative claim to a throne would fulfil his potential. She felt for him as a mother to a son and more. He would be her future.

Brushing the age-old dust from the cupboard, she reached inside for the ornate silver, jewelled charger she used for her work. She poured the water she had carried to her roost into it forming a shallow dark pool, then blessed it, reciting an ancient prayer to gods more ancient than the Christian god to whom she made pretence of service.

Staring intently into the black waters she watched them clear, watched the figures emerge from the darkness. It was nearly time for him to come home, her Henry, her fine boy, he had spent enough time now in exile, Jasper and France had taught him all they could. The houses of both York and Lancaster had fought themselves to a standstill. Richard of York had declared himself King. There were rumours around the court that the rightful York Princes were murdered at his behest. On that subject she knew different.

The Woodville Queen would never have placed both her sons in danger. Two young lads had disappeared, but one was not of royal blood. It was time for a new line, a new house, the house of Tudor. She stared into her gazing pool and called him home.

He would need an army. The people of Wales had little stomach for more conflict, they were kept poor and servile by the marcher lords and the barons. Yet if he could return with men at his shoulder, and Welshmen at that, maybe others would join his cause, take up arms for their freedom, for a release from the taxes and impositions of the current regime. Surely, they would fight to place one of their own on the throne.

There were those she could call on, one in particular whose talents she needed and whose soul she already owned.

Where was he now? His home was not in this time, not even in this place. Would he serve her willingly or resent her calling him to her again? She sensed they had become close, her warrior and those that had fought the great victory at Crécy with him, those who had rid her of her murderous husband. Fate had cast them to the four winds of time. Could she reunite them? She sensed that they had battles of their own to fight. Well, she would aid them where she could, but as always there would be a price to pay, and always to her benefit.

She froze for a moment. There were footsteps on the stone steps outside, she hastily covered the silver vessel with a shawl, a knock on the heavy wooden door.

'Margaret, there is news from France.' The deep rich tones of Sir Kenneth Fitzsimon called her from her reverie.

'What news, my dear, is it news from Henry himself, or from Jasper, is the messenger still here? I must speak to him, I must send word to my son, but first I must seek the Lord's advice, for it is his work I am about. Come to the chapel with me, we will pray together.'

Margaret opened the door to greet the grey-haired old knight who had been her only love since her teenage years. He, too, had sacrificed much for her happiness, in fact he had walked through fire for her. He had left his life behind to follow her on her journey. She stepped into his embrace, kissing him full on the lips, her body alight from the thrill of her secret activity, she pressed herself against him.

'Come, let us say prayers of our own, my love.' Theirs was a love which had survived centuries. She felt the need of the man who tried to keep her from darkness.

'Margaret, the messenger waits, you must write now in reply.'

'Feed him, make him welcome, rest his horse while I am in chapel. Then I will write, he will not catch the tide until the morrow.'

They descended the steps to the courtyard together.

'Margaret, be swift in your devotions, I fear this messenger will not wait!'

Sir Kenneth strode through the archway leading to the kitchens where he had directed the messenger in his hooded cloak, with his letter, only to be handed to Margaret herself. The man had a familiar look, but Sir Kenneth could not place him. The eyes, yes, that was it, the messenger's eyes were an uncanny shade of green but tinged at their centre with red. The black curls were wet from the rain despite the cloak's ample hood and the face chiselled and arrogant. A face he had seen before, yet different, somehow younger.

Lady Margaret prostrated herself on the stone floor before the altar in the small chapel, feeling the cold of the Welsh earth rising up through the floor and into her thin wasted body. She pressed her lips to the flagstones and prayed to the Christian gods she had forsaken but an hour ago, 'Holy Mary, Mother of God, hear me in my hour of need, tell me is it time, is it time to bring him home? His cause is a just and righteous one, if it is time then please be his guide, do not let him fail.'

For an hour or more she lay there, listening to the sound of the Lord's silence, and extracting from it what words of comfort she could find.

Meanwhile the messenger sat by the great fire in the kitchen hearth, cloak removed and hung to dry, his leather breeches and boots steaming in the heat from the fire, a warming mug of mulled ale in his hand. Despite these ministrations from Sir Kenneth and the cook, the messenger was restless, impatient to leave. He paced to and fro,' constantly looking towards the door as if expecting danger, not trusting his host, not letting down his guard. A groom had taken his horse to the stables to be fed, a fine black animal, well-bred and likely as swift as the wind.

'You are eager to leave, my friend.' Sir Kenneth commented, his own mug of ale half drained.

'There are those abroad who would kill me, I know I am followed. To linger anywhere is risking death.'

'How are you known, then? You came via the port at Tenby did you not? Surely there is no one on these shores who knows your purpose?'

'Richard of York has eyes everywhere, he fears everyone. I have felt his spy on my collar since we left France. He does not know what my purpose is, but he will know I have come here, he will wait for the Lady to write a response.'

'She writes as we speak. She will ask you to carry what she writes.'

'Then she must write with guile, not with the tongue of a mother.'

The kitchen door opened, and Lady Margaret made her entrance.

'Do not ask my name, milady, I am called only Calon. I have no written message, save to say your son is well and sends his greetings. He grows weary of his exile and sends you this from his uncle in Vannes.'

The messenger reached into his jerkin and produced a leather pouch which he handed to her. She emptied its contents into the palm of her hand.

The green stone was about the size of a bantam's egg and polished to a shine, the white veins spiralling through it like the lines on a page. She felt the stone cool in her hand, Jasper, the stone meant protection, endurance, and strength. What else had her rock woven into this simple gift?

'Calon, you will stay with us tonight, we will have you on your way at dawn.' Without further words she left the room in a swirl of cloak and skirts, the keys of her chatelaine rattling at her thin waist. The two men left at the kitchen hearth heard the slam of a distant door many feet above them.

'Give her time and you will have your message. It will be for only one man to read. This master serves two ladies, but I feel you know this already.' Kenneth prepared himself for a long night. He had a feeling that this messenger would not allow himself the luxury of sleep, not while there were Yorkist eyes everywhere and sorcery afoot.

High in the Tower room she placed the Jasper egg in the water of the gazing pool and watched as the message unravelled before her.

'We are four thousand strong, we are ready, the time is now, make your plans.'

From round her neck, she unfastened the great pearl pendant he had given her when she had birthed her son, a gift for another Margaret, a Margaret replaced in body, but not in his heart.

She placed it alongside the Jasper in the water. 'I will summon my army. I have faith they will answer my call. I await your arrival. God bless you, and my son.'

She placed the great opalescent pearl pendant against her breast and folded her love around it, sealing in the message which another had woven into its depths. That night she slept on the small couch amongst the tools of her trade, absorbing into the Pearl and the Jasper the magic of the stars above. Tomorrow the messenger would need no ship, but then she knew that from the time of his arrival. Calon, son of Eryr, a messenger of some importance. Times were indeed changing.

CHAPTER 45. A CHANCE MEETING

1916,
Nant Ddu Farm,
Maesteg.

The leaves had started to turn on the trees heralding autumns arrival, yet summer was hanging on to her wide brimmed hat against the stiff breeze which lifted the dust from the ground and swayed the long grass in the top meadow.

Nant Ddu basked in the remnants of warmth and prepared to batten down the hatches for winter. The hay crop had been late but good, the barn was full, the animals would not go hungry. Harri had been busy stocking Cefin's pantry with preserves and pickles. The hillside around the farm held a glut of berries for jam and the resurrected kitchen garden had produced a fine crop of tomatoes in its lean-to glass house. The crop was shared with the Cole family and even young Myrddin who was now walking had been recruited to pick fruit, smearing more on his face than he put in Harri's basket.

The windfall apples from his mam's trees had been pressed and made into a very drinkable cider, while the edible ones had been set to dry in the storeroom Harri had made out of one of the coal sheds. The farm burned more wood than coal on its fires, and most of the coal was needed to fuel the war. Cefin had chopped and split a large stack of logs for the winter, creating a neat pile in the corner of the barn next to Boyo's stable.

The other acquisition was Charm, a sturdy black and white pony, handy for pulling logs out of the wood, and also handy for pulling the trap. The trap, which his mother had driven down to chapel every Sunday and which, since her death, had been kept by his father like some religious icon under a tarpaulin in the yard. A coat of paint and some attention to the shafts and the padding in the seat, and Harri could drive Charm down to the village to run her errands with little Myrddin sitting alongside her as she drove. Harri was buzzing with excitement, and while Cefin shared her joy it was with a tinge of what he didn't like to think of as jealousy. Arthur was coming home, well as far as the hospital anyway, for the time being. Harri had opened the letter last week and read it to him. Hardly able to contain herself, she had stumbled over the words, hands shaking as she held the sheet of paper in front of her.

Dearest Harri,

Dr Bannerman has said I am well enough to come home. I have gained weight and am sleeping well at night. I feel well in myself, and he says I am so improved that he is happy for me to continue my treatment, such as it is, at the Maesteg hospital and, if all goes well, I may be home properly for Christmas.

My travel warrants have been arranged. I am accompanied by Sister Battle, Veronica, who is taking up a post as Matron at the hospital in Maesteg. She is a fine nurse and will be a great asset to the community, I am sure, though she is very strict and likes everything, 'just so.'

I should not speak out of turn, Harri, but I must tell you that such is her reputation that she is known as 'the battleaxe' to both patients and staff alike. If she is aware of it, then she says nothing and bears it with a sense of humour.

Anyway, it is all settled, and we travel from Paddington to Cardiff on Thursday next, to connect with the valley train to Maesteg arriving at three thirty in the afternoon. Sister Veronica, for that is her given name, has arranged for the porter for the Hospital to collect us and our luggage, though where she has several trunks, I have one small bag and the clothes I stand up in. I will then be settled in the ward, where I understand there are other recovering soldiers. I wonder if I shall know any of them.

Oh Harri, I am coming home, I cannot wait to kiss your sweet lips and to meet my son Myrddin, a fine name, you have chosen well. I cannot wait to hear all your news.

All my love forever

Arthur.

Arthur and his companion and escort had fought their way through the chaos of Paddington Station, through the soldiers travelling home on leave, heading for the West Country, through those leaving loved ones and returning to their units. Now they sat opposite each other in a private compartment, each with a view out of the window, Arthur looking forward and Veronica looking back. In Arthur's poetic brain he wondered to himself if there was some hidden significance in their choice of seats. He had not made the journey home for nearly two years. There was an anxious feeling in his stomach, a kind of knot, which ached a bit and bobbed up and down when he thought of Harri and home. Would he cope, he prayed he had left his demons behind him, he also knew that they could return at any moment. Would Harri understand that he was no longer the same Arthur she had waved off from the station to fight for his country.

Veronica smiled at him.

'You will be fine, Private Cole, it will take time, but I'm certain you will be fine.' Her voice was soft and kindly, and made him believe that, yes, all would be just that.

Arthur looked with fresh eyes at 'The Battleaxe.' Dressed in an ankle length skirt with button boots and a neatly tailored jacket, the whole outfit was a colour best described as the colour of fallen leaves, a reddish brown, which brought out the colour in her salt and pepper hair which was not so severely pulled off her face as usual. Off duty, Veronica Battle had a pleasantly pretty, round face, hazel eyes which sparkled at him from under her slightly wavy hair and the cloche shaped hat she had pulled on over it. Out of her uniform she seemed to be taller and more shapely, but just as perceptive and efficient as ever. She was seated looking backwards, looking back towards the London they were leaving behind, but he did not think she did it with regret. Was he looking forward with an equal amount of anticipation.

The guard strode briskly along the platform slamming carriage doors, checking that the door to the guard's van was closed and secure. He blew his whistle, two long shrill blasts, the second turning up at the end, and waved his flag to the driver. Arthur felt the grind and heard the screech of metal on metal as the engine took the strain, the shrill whistle as the driver announced the departure of the 06:30 train from Paddington to Swansea, stopping at Reading, Didcot, Newport and then Cardiff. Shrouded in a cloud of smoke and steam which hung heavy in the damp morning air, the huge wheels began to turn, and the engine gathered speed. He leaned back into the corner and comfort of the bristly seat, getting his best view of the countryside as it rushed past at ever increasing speed.

'You will like the valley, Sister. The folk are friendly enough, once they get to know you, and you know some Welsh. Most of them only speak English when they must. They are happier in their own tongue.'

'I think I remember most of what you taught me,' she laughed, 'but it is still a daunting prospect, new job, new home, new people. I never expected to leave London, but I am not sorry to go. I like a challenge.'

'Do you think I will be home by Christmas? I should like that very much.'

'Arthur, with you it will be time, if writing keeps your ghosts at bay, keep writing, it will help your mind heal, work will help as well, but work in the fresh air, not in the mines. Your mind needs peace, not more turmoil. As for Christmas, no promises, then no disappointments, what will be, will be.'

He shrugged further into his uniform jacket, royal blue, not khaki now. The uniform of the army hospital was blue, with white lapels and a jaunty red tie. It marked him as a wounded soldier, no longer a fighting man, a man awaiting his discharge papers. What did his future hold after that? Closing his eyes and listening to the rhythm of the train, he nodded off to sleep. They had had an early start after all, and both his body and his mind tired easily. Veronica Battle reached in her carpet bag for her book of Welsh poems and started to read, but within minutes, like her charge, she fell into a doze with her head and shoulder against the window and her book open on her lap.

It was a journey of just less than three hours from Paddington to Cardiff, then another hour or so to Bridgend and a change of train to Maesteg. Veronica dozed to the sounds of the train, the hypnotic pounding of the pistons driving the great wheels, the rhythmic clunk of the wheels on the track, the whoosh as the train passed a building or under a bridge, the muffled chatter of other passengers heard through the compartment wall, the soft tread of the conductor progressing along the train's length checking tickets, opening, and shutting sliding doors, making polite enquiry of the occupants of each compartment. Some passengers were still finding suitable seats as the train left the sprawl of London and entered the countryside of Berkshire.

The compartment door slid open, and an enquiring head looked in. Seeing two free seats, the body attached to the head stepped into view, hoisted a multi coloured carpet bag much like Veronica's own up onto the luggage rack, nodded a greeting at the two sleeping occupants and sat down, facing the engine. His inner sense of self-preservation made Private Cole open one eye, and from the shelter of a half-closed eyelid, he observed the new occupant of the seat next to Nurse Battle

The woman, for this was a woman, was young, in her twenties maybe. Tall, much taller than average, she was slim, athletic in build, broad shouldered and long legged with unruly curly dark red hair pinned under a wide brimmed hat. She stretched her long legs out in front of her and rested them on the seat opposite, exposing a pair of very long and shapely calves which were connected to a pair of feet which were on the large side for a woman, or so the observer thought. Sensing that she was being watched, the woman removed her feet from their resting place.

'Sorry, it's been a long few days, my feet.'

'At least remove your shoes, my dear.' cut in Veronica, in her best nursing sister's voice though she did not open her eyes.

'I would,' replied the woman, 'but my stockings – there is a big hole in the left toe. One can't get thread these days to mend anything properly, and the cost of new. Well ….!'

The soldier who was now more or less awake reached into his own bag and pulled out yesterday's newspaper, spreading it on the seat opposite the young woman. 'There you go, no mess on the upholstery now miss, no harm done.'

'Rhianydd MacGregor.' The woman held out a hand to the soldier, a large hand encased in a black leather glove.

Private Cole met a dark blue stare with his own dark countenance,

 'Arthur Cole, pleased to meet you. Where are you headed?'

'Cardiff, to see my uncle, and then to my mother's home further west. And you?'

'I thought I could detect a hint of Welsh in that voice. I am headed for home in Maesteg.'

'With your wife?' nodding towards Sister Veronica.

'No, this is Sister Veronica Battle. She's accompanying me on the journey and will be Matron of the hospital in Maesteg when I get there, I am a patient you see?''

'Oh, sorry for the confusion, I'm pleased to meet you.' blushing a little and nodding more formally towards the out of uniform Sister Battle,

'Actually, I have been studying to be a doctor, I'm in my final year, but the war has messed things up. I am to finish training in London instead of

Cardiff. I expect I shall end up treating the likes of you and your comrades, though I would dearly love to be sent abroad,'

'You can do more good at home, my dear. I would not be on this train at all if it were not for the good doctors who treated me first and the nurses who have helped me since.

Rhianydd listened politely as Arthur Cole related his story but without paying much attention. It was an interesting tale, but he was not her patient. She mentally screened out much of the story, appearing to listen politely and nodding and saying 'yes' in appropriate places.

'Yes,' he concluded, 'I am certain, I will not be shaken from it, my life was saved by an archer, a medieval archer, with a bow and arrow. My commander says I am deluded, but time will tell. I know what I have seen.'

Rhianydd's eyes flew open, and she sat up straight in her seat.

'When were you wounded?'

'First day of July, why?' came the answer.

'And where?'

'Just outside Abbéville, on the river Somme, in the big push forward, thousands killed, I'm not surprised.....'

With this, Arthur began to shake uncontrollably, he started to sweat, and his hands began to shake. He curled himself into a ball and began to sob, calling out the same name over and over again. His nurse woke from her sleep.

'Do not, I beg you, upset him again. He has a wife, a new baby, let him go home and forget.'

Rhianydd started. 'Have you heard of the battle of Crécy? Did you study it in school?'

'I did, but not in great detail, why?'

Veronica took hold of the soldier's hand and began to talk to him, soothing words about home and a life and a future. Rhianydd continued regardless.

'The army which fought at Crécy marched through Abbéville. They fought a battle there. Some died there. Do you believe that men have souls?'

'I do, but what relevance has this?'

'The battle is fought on common ground. Men have fought there before. The souls of the departed seek to join those of the living and rise from the ground to meet them. They fight on the same side they did before. The archers were Welsh, that is why we were taught about it at school. He is Welsh, is he not.'

'Clap trap! Rubbish!' declared Sister Battle. 'I will not hear more of this. You are as deluded as he is. Archers my foot, it will be the Black Prince he sees next!'

Rhianydd murmured to herself, just loud enough for anyone else to hear. 'Well, he was there, but he came home, didn't he.'

Sister Battle adopted her most assertive tone. 'Young lady, I do not know who you are, but you must not continue like this, it only does him harm. Now, help me here for a few moments.' She produced a pre-loaded syringe and, with the practice of years, stabbed Private Cole in the thigh through his trousers. That should calm him until we reach our destination.'

Veronica rose from her seat. 'I must use the conveniences, please don't wake him, he needs his sleep.' She disappeared out of the compartment.

The figure in the corner stirred, fidgeted slightly, and became more drawn in on itself. The soldier and his nurse changed trains at Cardiff, leaving Rhianydd to continue her journey alone. She did not even know the nurse's name, though she was sure that she would recognise her again. And who, she wondered, was Harry?

CHAPTER 46. BOYS NEED A FATHER

1916,
Maesteg.

He was a lovely little boy. Angharad had brought him up to the farm most days. Ever since his first steps he had toddled his way around Cefin's kitchen, played with the small animals, fed the chickens and the ducks and the pet lambs which had been rejected by their mothers. He idolised Cefin. Cefin in turn idolised Angharad. She had held him together since his father's death, it was she who had made sure he ate when he forgot to, who reminded him when he forgot to do things, she made lists of the jobs he needed to do round the farm.

Cefin Thorne had lost his whole family and Angharad Cole was now his rudder. Their friendship became remarked on. Up and down the valley from Caerau at the top to Llan village at the bottom, tongues wagged, generating a breeze of snippets of information gleaned from a word here or a word there. The gossips in the chapel drinking tea and sitting around their kitchen tables talked, they talked over the garden walls and fences when they pegged their washing out to dry.

'Her husband is alive you know, poor man, what must he think?'
'But they say he has lost his mind, better that he were dead.'
'But he is still her husband, shameless she is with that Thorne boy.'
'Behaving like a right floozy, no good can come of it, you'll see.'
'And that little boy, growing up with no father.'
'Mervyn the milk says he has a father alright.'
'Mervyn the milk should know, he drops her off at his gate most every day, the boy too!'

Angharad heard them, the valley gossips, swift to pass judgement on everything and everyone. She tried to ignore them, but the words were hurtful, and the hurt grew like a festering sore in her mind. Damn them all, she had done nothing wrong, let them talk around their tea kettles, had they so little in their small-minded lives that she was all they could talk of?

Arthur would be home soon. He was at least back in the valley now, but he was changed, so changed. Valleys are small places and hospitals are hotbeds of gossip. Arthur heard, he heard it through the silences of conversations paused as he entered a room, he heard it in the pitying looks from the nurses. He heard it in the sadness in the voice of his friend Veronica Battle, busy with the running of the hospital. Too busy now to spend much time with him.

Angharad had been so excited when he arrived, she had not seen him for over a year, from the day he had boarded the train in Cardiff. His letters home had been few, not his fault, it was not as if they had a regular postal service from the front and a letter could get just as lost between Cardiff and the valley as from the trenches of France to Cardiff. She was sure the postmaster read some of the letters home, she could see him now, the ferret-faced weasel-like pale-faced goblin of a man who ran the sorting office. She imagined him steaming open letters over his tea kettle and reading the loving words sent by soldiers to their wives and sweethearts.

What she imagined he also did she banished from her mind. 'For shame on you, Angharad Cole,' she told herself. 'You will go to hell in a handcart for such thoughts.'

She couldn't look at Thomas the post in the same way ever again. She tried not to look at him at all, but she was sure he had read her letters. She could tell by the perverted leer which inhabited his face when he greeted her in the street.

Arthur himself was delighted to be back. He spent his days walking in the municipal park across the road from the hospital, dressed in his blue and red uniform. He grew physically stronger daily, the weeks of lying in bed were behind him and he soon progressed from the park and would walk on the hillside behind the hospital building. He knew the hillsides well. If it was too wet to go out, then he would write. He wrote poems mainly and some short stories.

Angharad visited him three times a week, she was working she said. He didn't like to think of her working, but times had changed, women had needed to work with their menfolk away. The jobs the men did still needed doing. Life went on despite the war.

The Arthur who had come home was different. Where he had been outgoing and loving, he was quiet, withdrawn, as if he were afraid to touch her. He would not talk to her about the war, he would not let her read his poetry, it was too personal he said. They no longer had anything in common. He seemed afraid that she thought him deranged for he heard the gossips too. He had also read what the army had written about him.

Angharad felt as though there was a wall of glass between them, they could see each other, but they could no longer touch each other or even hear each other, something had disappeared. Something which she feared she had now found in someone else.

She had told him all about her job in the Masons Arms, told him all about the customers and Clive the landlord. He knew many of the regulars there, those who had been too old to fight, and those who had now grown old enough to drink but were still too young for the army. Then there were the men who stayed in the mines, essential work it was called, feeding the war machine an endless supply of coal.

Her other 'job' on the farm, she talked less about. She had told him that she kept house for a farmer who lived alone on one of the farms on the hillside above Llan. He had known Maldwyn Thorne and he had met Hefin Thorne on the train, the day they travelled to London as soldiers to fight for their country. He was sad that Hefin had been killed. He had known Mabyn by reputation, a great one for the chapel. He did not know Cefin. Until now.

The little green worm of jealousy turned. He asked himself what his Harri was not telling him, for there was more in what she did not say than in what she did say. And then there was little Myrddin, his boy, but the boy who had a dada called DaDa Cefin.

Arthur's progress was good. Physically he was becoming stronger every day. Fresh air and exercise and food had strengthened his body, but he was still haunted by his ghosts. He slept little, his nights disturbed by the faces of dead comrades and the screams of the wounded. He wrote daily, putting his feelings in verse or prose, as the mood took him. He desperately wanted to go home, but those final few steps to get there seemed to be taking a lifetime.

He must face the problem, grasp the nettle, or the thorn. This raised a smile in his thoughts, 'grasp the Thorne,' he turned the words over in his mind. Well, he needed to meet this man, needed to find out who his son called DaDa.

From the little Harri had told him, he had worked out that Nant Ddu was on the hillside above the village of Llan, lower down the valley, outside of the town. He could walk there, it would take him most of the day, but it was possible. He was strong enough. He could always catch the bus back, or hitch a lift, it was easy enough for a man in the blue uniform of a wounded soldier to flag down a passing cart, or sometimes an automobile, though there were few of those in the valley.

Harri was due to visit tomorrow, he hoped she would bring little Myrddin with her, but the boy was a boisterous child, and while he would sit quietly, he was bored easily and disturbed the other patients. Maybe they should walk outside this time, go across to the park, let the child run off his energy. Tomorrow came, and with it a fine fresh day, a day full of hope and enthusiasm.

They walked in the park, but Harri seemed distracted. The child had played on the swings, Arthur had pushed him, held his hand as he climbed the steps of the big slide and then caught him at the bottom. He had asked Harri to tell him about Nant Ddu, but she avoided the question, wanting to talk more about his finding work, finding a house of their own. She had fetched sandwiches for their lunch, homemade bread she said and ham, from the farm, fresh apples, he heard the unspoken 'from the farm' as he sank his teeth into the crunchy green skin, sweet but slightly sour, refreshing, clean tasting. Then they had walked back to the ward, holding Myrddin's chubby hands between them. Harri had kissed him but only on the cheek, 'There's people watching,' she murmured, 'and Myrddin.' Then she pulled away from him and he bent to kiss his son. The child was having none of it. The little lad shocked all who heard him with his parting scream of, 'Want dada Cefin, want him now, want go now!'

Harri had taken him away then, with no parting kiss for his father, a red faced tearful and screaming child had left a bereft man crying unshed tears of his own. Arthur was in shock, this was not the Harri he had left when he went to war, this Harri had become distant, the doctors said it might take time to get back to civilian life, back to living as a family, but the Harri who had just left him taking their son with her did not seem to want to try. Everything she did was about, 'the farm,' yet she could not bring herself to talk openly about it.

That night had been awful. No nurse had come to sit with him when his nightmares started, and in the morning he had come to his senses in the midst of soiled and sweat soaked sheets for the first time in weeks and also to the cheery voice of Nesbit Evans.

'Arthur, bach, you kept the whole valley awake last night, had a bad one, did you? I've come to say farewell, I'm off home to Morfydd, my discharge came through, pensioner now, no more fighting for me. You get well man, your boy will come round, more of you he needs to see! And your wife, she needs you, look to your wife, Arthur.' Then Nesbit Evans was gone.

After checking with the nurse on duty, Arthur drew himself a bath and gently lowered himself into the steaming water. He had filled the bath, what could they do to him if he exceeded the proscribed amount of water. The water level was at least four inches above the tide mark which was the demarcation line. He scrubbed himself clean of the night's events and cleared his mind as best he could. If he continued like this he would never get back to his family, for Harri and Myrddin were the only family he had.

'Get a grip, Cole.' he told himself as he towelled himself dry. Today he would not wear his uniform. He had acquired some civvies on his walks on the mountain and down into the town. The second-hand shop had gladly provided him with a serviceable pair of worsted trousers, a cotton shirt with no collar, a waistcoat in a slightly faded burgundy, a quality garment none the less, its back made of black silk, complete with adjusters to adjust the fit. His army boots would have to do. He topped it all with a tweed flat cap and his army great coat.

Just after breakfast he stuck his head around matron's door and informed Matron Battle that he was going out. She grunted acknowledgement, it was not unusual for Cole to go walking, but he rarely told her personally, maybe there was no one else to tell. Lifting her head from her interminable requisition forms, she saw him walking down the drive with a spring in his step and a kit bag over his shoulder.

Arthur headed down through the park where he had played with his son only the day before, out of the gate at the bottom of the hill and onto Neath Road, down through the town and down the valley where the winding towers of the colliery stood like huge iron beasts against the mountainside. If he could only remember where the footpaths went.

The narrow tracks which criss-crossed through the woods, they would lead him out onto the mountain top, onto the fields above, where no doubt Cefin Thorne grazed his sheep. Today he would pay Mr. Thorne a visit, try and find out a bit more about his wife's involvement with the farm, and the man who lived there. Try and put his mind at rest.

It was early when Mervyn the milk dropped Angharad off at the bottom gate and lifted the two churns of milk off the stand onto his cart. He climbed back onto the driver's perch, clicked, and whistled to the horse and flicked the reins over his back. The horse took the strain and the wheels turned and Mervyn continued his round of collections. As he pulled away, he admired the rear view of Angharad Cole forging her way up the steep track to Nant Ddu. 'Fine woman,' he thought to himself, 'despite what they say.' His mind filled in.

Harri was puffing and blowing like a steam train when she let herself into the kitchen. She threw off her cloak and draped it over the back of a chair. Resting her hands on the table she breathed deeply, in then out, regulating her breath until she could talk. 'That hill doesn't get any easier!'

Sitting at the table, Cefin Thorne was sewing a button back onto his work shirt. He was stripped naked to the waist, his belt undone and his braces hanging over his hips.

'Give me that! You are making a right pig's ear of it. You sew like a cow with a toothpick.' She took the shirt, and the needle and thread from him with one deft swipe of her hand.

'Tea, Harri?' He asked, raising an eyebrow. 'What's brewing under your bonnet this fine morning?'

'Do you need to ask?' came the reply.

Deft fingers plied the needle swiftly in and out of the button, sharp white teeth bit through the cotton, then held the shirt up by its shoulders to inspect for further defects. Finding a small tear in one arm she re-threaded the needle and began to effect repairs. Cefin rose from his seat, scraping the chair back across the flagstone floor. He crossed the room to the fire and lifted the teapot from the top of the range where it was keeping its contents nicely warm. Taking a mug from a hook under the shelf on the dresser, he poured milk and then added the dark brown brew. 'It's a bit strong girl, shall I water it more?'

'No, I like it strong - like my men!' she quipped.

He placed the mug in front of her as she rose from her seat with his shirt in her hand. Holding out the shirt, her hand brushed against the hard muscle of his shoulder. Cefin Thorne was a man who carried no spare flesh, a torso lean from hard work, muscles toned by the swing of the axe chopping wood, the lifting of hay bales and animals and all browned to a deep tan by the summer sun. She felt his strength, it was all about him like an invisible charge, her whole body sang with it. The hand which should have draped the shirt over that shoulder and resumed drinking her tea, dropped the slightly grubby item of clothing onto the floor, her hand recoiled and she gasped, but with a life of its own the hand returned, it travelled down over a chest spattered with dark curly hair.

'Don't, please Harri, don't.'

Now standing square in front of him, her chin level with his chest Angharad Cole turned her face up to his.

'Dark,' she giggled, 'like my tea.' Then she pulled his face down to hers and kissed him.

She had expected him to pull away, expected him to respect the boundaries they had drawn, the boundary of friendship which she sometimes pushed to its limit. His hands were like vices on her hips, one flat in the small of her back pressed her against him. The buttons of his trousers were straining, she could feel it even through the thick layers of her dress between them. Her mind was telling her this must stop, but her body betrayed her, her hand slid down between them, undoing each button, slowly. She heard him groan, his teeth now nibbling on her ear. Then his hands were under her skirts, lifting them, and lifting her, she found herself carried up the narrow stairs to a bedroom.

'Cefin!' she gasped through his kisses. 'We…….' It was a token protest, she realised too late that it was she who had removed his clothing and her own. It was she who now lay euphoric, her head on his chest and her fingers trailing pathways through the hair of his chest down to his flat belly.

He was the first to speak. 'That must never happen again, Angharad, I hope what we had is not spoiled forever.'

Her response was lost in the pounding of a fist on the front door. Cefin lifted the bottom sash of the window. 'Who is it? Come round the back, I'll be there in two minutes.'

As he watched from above, a figure dressed in a strange mix of clothing turned and made its way towards the kitchen door. Who did he know who wore an army great coat and a cap. 'You stay here, Angharad. Don't leave this room, this caller can bring nothing but trouble.'

Hastily dressing himself in his working clothes, Cefin made his way back to the kitchen where the caller was waiting patiently on the step of the open door.

'What can I do for you, my friend?' Cefin began.

'My name is Arthur, and I have come about my wife.' Arthur was all politeness, his sad eyes fixing Cefin with a determined gaze.

'Angharad?' queried Cefin, feigning ignorance.

'Yes, that's her, I hear she keeps house for you. I hope that is all she keeps.' The reply was quietly spoken.

'Sit down man, I'm expecting her soon, she's told me all about you. Have you walked all the way across the valley this morning, can I get you a brew or a beer perhaps?'

Cefin swiftly cleared the two used mugs from the table and replaced the kettle on the fire. The blackened iron receptacle was just coming to the boil when the kitchen door opened again and there was Harri, breathless and glowing, hair escaping from its once neat and seemly bun.

'That hill never gets easier, Cefin, I'll have a tea if there's one going.' Her hands rested on the table as she got her breath back. As she raised her head, all colour left her cheeks as she recognised the visitor.

'Arthur!' She flung her arms around his neck and kissed him full on the lips. 'You must meet Cefin!'

He could taste man on her lips, he had seen the two mugs on the table, and he saw her cloak on the back of the chair. He had seen all he needed to see, images of lost days of happiness spun through his mind, images of a small boy playing with his mam and dad, the voice of that child calling for dada Cefin. Arthur's eyes were burning with tears and his chest tight with pain as he spun on his heel and made for the door. There were no more questions to be asked.

He crossed the farmyard in half a dozen strides, let himself out through the gate and before Angharad could gather the courage to follow him he had vaulted over a nearby stile and was lost in the woodland. She would never see Arthur Cole again.

Dusk fell quickly over the valley. Veronica Battle picked up her bag and her coat and walked briskly towards the exit door, her work done for the day. Pausing before she left the building, she retraced her steps and walked into the ward. Nesbit Evans had gone home, that she knew. He had told her so himself when he left the card and bunch of flowers on her desk. Arthur should be back by now. He knew the rules. In by dark.

'Is Arthur back from his walk yet?' Her enquiry was cloaked in a reprimand for the young nurse who had not yet thought to miss one of her patients.

'He's never back until the last-minute, matron. I'm sure he'll be back in a few minutes.'

'He's a grown man.' she told herself. 'He knows his way around, don't worry about him, have a little faith.'

Veronica Battle was going home this weekend, visiting friends up in the 'smoke,' as the locals called it. Arthur was flying the nest. She would see him on her return. In her carpet bag she still carried his book of poems. She knew he was working on another, until then she would continue to thumb through well-worn pages, reading words she has read a thousand times, and which still spoke to her soul.

Every night she mentioned Arthur in her prayers, asking that he may find happiness again, wherever his road took him. In her heart she knew he had gone, and in her soul she prayed he stayed safe.

CHAPTER 47. LONDON CALLING - Rhianydd

Mother had organised it all in the time I had taken walking with my Agnes to the top field, armed with a pocket full of carrots. Agnes had tempted Zak with them, and he had summoned enough courage to take one and then another from her outstretched palm, before being chivvied away by his mother. The rest of the herd had been more suspicious, remaining several feet away, blowing down their inquisitive nostrils, not quite brave enough to venture closer.

Agnes had insisted we stay for most of the day, she was fascinated by everything that lived and breathed on the mountain. She loved nothing more than to pick bunches of the meadow flowers and then ask me to name them and tell her stories. She quite innocently told me that Uncle Edward had told her that every flower had a fairy which lived in it and that the fairies looked after the mountain. I had just finished a completely made-up story about the Bluebell fairy when she piped up in her contralto voice

'Mummy, when I grow up, will I be a fairy, too?'

'Of course, dear, all little girls grow to be fairies.' I told her, making a mental note to have a word with Uncle Edward about his tuition methods.

By the time we returned to Hengwm, the men had finished the day's farm work and mother had been in the kitchen making plans and phone calls.

We were to wait for Uncle Moses to call back. Mother was sure he would find and talk to Gerald Shipley. Shipley was loosely connected with the supply department and whilst more concerned with men, food, and ammunition, all of those needed coal to get them across the channel and Uncle Moses needed men to mine his coal. At the outbreak of war, miners had left to join the forces in their hundreds. The practice of digging tunnels under the enemy trenches as a tactic made them a valuable resource. There was also a shortage of pit ponies. Many had been requisitioned as draft horses for the army and were pulling heavy artillery to the front instead of coal drams. They would never return. Those that were not killed by enemy fire would die from starvation. Those that survived would not be brought home, they would be sold off in France to save the cost of transportation. Uncle Moses was in London to negotiate, along with the unions, to stop the conscription of miners to the front.

The phone call came two days later. Mother had already looked up train times and plotted my journey via Cardiff to 'the smoke' as she called London. As it turned out, Moses was detained in London for longer than he expected but he had arranged for me to meet with General Shipley.

The train pulled out of Cardiff General on time, to the whistle of the guard. Running late after a short reunion with my sister Helena and our aunt Blanche, I had made an undignified run for the train, legs pumping and skirts flying, one hand holding my hat on top of my curls to stop it disappearing down the platform in the cloud of smoke laden steam being belched out of the engine like dragon's breath. The guard was visibly laughing as he held the door open for me to throw my valise into the carriage and leap on after it. The door slammed behind me, another blast on his whistle and a wave of his red flag to the driver, and I felt the train stir into motion.

Searching for a seat, preferably on my own so that I could collect my thoughts together about the questions I needed to ask, I found myself in a compartment occupied only by a middle-aged lady with salt and pepper hair, a slightly plump heart shaped face and a slightly stern smile.

'May I?' I indicated the vacant seat.

'I don't see anyone else there.' she replied, turning her smile on me, and then returning to the book she was reading. I placed my valise beside me on the seat and opened the newspaper I had partially read over breakfast at The Parade. The train gathered speed and we were soon approaching Newport. The compartment door opened, and the ticket collector put in an appearance.

'London is it then, Ladies?' he asked in a friendly manner as he clipped out tickets and examined them to see that they were all in order.

'Yes indeed,' answered the lady with the salt and pepper hair, 'is there a problem?'

'No ma'am not that I am aware of, though there are works on the line at Didcot which may hold us up for a time.,' he answered.

'Will there be much delay?' I queried. 'I have an appointment for which I cannot be late.' I folded the newspaper deliberately and looked out of the window, watching the wetlands travel by as we left Newport and headed for the tunnel which took us under the river Severn and into England.

The ticket collector braced himself to the motion of the train. 'We should be delayed less than an hour. Don't fret, miss I'm sure your beau will wait!'

I became conscious of his eyes alighting on the wedding ring on my left hand and his embarrassed cough as he excused himself and firmly shut the compartment door as he continued his round. The train fell into darkness as we dipped into the two miles of tunnel, and I heard a subdued giggle from the seat opposite. When we re-emerged into daylight, my companion was wearing a broad grin.

'Oops!' she commented and smiled broadly at me over the top of her book.

'Oops, indeed!' I smiled back at her. 'What are you reading? If you don't mind my asking?'

'It is a book of poems written by a patient of mine. He is a remarkable man, invalided home from the war.' she answered. 'I take it everywhere with me, I find his work very restful in its way.'

'Well,' I replied, 'it must be more entertaining than the news. I'm Rhianydd MacGregor by the way.' I introduced myself. 'Dr. Rhianydd MacGregor.' I held out my hand and a firm handshake was returned.

'We have something in common, then. I am Veronica Battle, Matron Battle.' She raised an eyebrow. 'Yes, they do.' she added.

I looked at her confused. 'Call me the Battleaxe, but only behind my back and in fun. What takes you to London?'

'My husband is missing in action, he, and his whole unit. I have a meeting with one General Shipley about it. He may have information which would help to find them.'

My bottom lip began to tremble, and my eyes filled with tears. I wiped my eyes on my sleeve not having easy access to a handkerchief, and the one which was stuffed into my valise was one of Edward's huge spotty affairs, not exactly ladylike or to be produced in company.

'Shipley?' she queried. 'I know Shipley. Gerald Shipley. A gentleman if ever I knew one, and a fair man. His brother was a patient of mine before I was promoted to my current post.'

'Promotion to Wales?' I was surprised.

'Oh, yes, to the rehabilitation unit in Maesteg. We do great work there with men who are shell shocked from the trenches and those who have been affected by the chlorine gas.'

She went on to add. 'I was a ward sister at Mount Vernon. We became known for our results after serious head and neck injuries in the field. The Maesteg hospital is new and is dedicated to helping such men recover. I love it there. I am only travelling to London now to attend a small celebration, rather welcome in the midst of all this gloom. My good friend and colleague Janet Gunn is to wed Dr. Robert Jones when he returns from the front, but she insists we will celebrate their engagement. She has been pursuing the poor man for years.'

It was then that I realised that I had met this lady before, several weeks ago on the same train only travelling in the opposite direction. She remembered the journey and told me of her charge on that day and of how, eventually, his demons had gotten the better of him and that he had disappeared, discharged himself from the hospital and left.

I asked her what she knew of Lieutenant Montague Shipley, and she told me of a man who she believed would never walk again, who had been lucky to survive at all if you classed his present predicament as lucky. She told me chapter and verse of his treatment and his brother's insistence that he had nothing but the best.

Then we talked of Wales and her life in the valley town that she now made her home. I told her of Hengwm and the hills of West Wales and of my daughter and by the time the train pulled into Paddington we were nearly three hours late. As we stepped out onto the platform into a chilly damp London afternoon, she took me by the arm and with a very direct look offered me advice. 'Take great care who you trust. Montague Shipley is a very bitter man, but all will be well. I feel it.' Then she handed me the book of poetry. 'Read it on your return journey and, if you can, return it to me in Maesteg when you are done. Take care Rhianydd MacGregor.'

Before I could reply, she had shouldered her own large carpet bag and was lost in the crowd and the smoke of the platform.

I stepped out of the station to find a spotty faced private who did not look old enough to wear the uniform which hung from his slim shoulders and swamped his skinny neck. He looked agitated as he approached me. 'Dr. MacGregor?' he stuttered.

'Yes.' I answered, trying not to terrify him further.

'You must come with me. The General is called away and can give you only a few minutes of his time. He is in his car, around the corner.'

He shepherded me away from the station and into a side street where a large Austin car was parked, its engine running and a smartly dressed chauffeur seated in the driver's seat. The soldier opened the door to the passenger compartment and ushered me in.

General Gerald Shipley was all old-fashioned good manners. He profusely begged my pardon for the manner of our meeting. He told the soldier to sit up front with the driver, pulled the glass screen across to separate us from the outside world and then told the driver to drive.

'This war stops for no man, my dear. I understand why you have come to see me but as I told your uncle, I really cannot give you much more information than you already have.'

'Sir, I beg you to listen. Surely there should be further investigation, the word of one man cannot condemn the lives of half a dozen brave soldiers.'

'My dear lady,' came the reply. 'I am not a complete fool, but I have the advantage of having been to the front myself. I have seen what goes on there. It is surprising that more men do not break under the pressure, so, until I have substantial evidence to the contrary, I must believe my brother, he was after all their officer. What else would you have me do? My car will drop you at your hotel. I wish you a quiet trip back to Wales. I can do nothing without evidence my dear. Nothing.'

'But?' I started......

'Give my regards to your uncle, assure him I shall try and get him more miners.'

The car stopped outside an elaborate stone building, now used as offices and Gerald Shipley left me in his car and strode inside, baton and leather briefcase under his arm.

Without thinking, I jumped from the vehicle as it started moving and followed him in through the double doors into the long, tiled passageway. I caught up with him before he reached the security desk and thinking to save myself an ignominious ejection from the building, I flung my arms around his neck and kissed him full on the lips under his thick black officer's moustache.

'Oh Gerald!' I exclaimed. 'Yes, I will, of course I will, when will it be?'

He blustered and blushed uncontrollably but without pause swept me up in his arms and carried me up two flights of stairs. I was carried into an office which smelled strongly of mansion polish, and which was decked out with noticeboards and wall to wall filing cabinets. I was deposited uneceremoniously into a wing backed armchair, upholstered in oxblood leather. He spoke first.

'This, my dear is totally outrageous. If it was not for my friendship with your uncle, I would have you ejected from here immediately.'

'Please, General Shipley, I have been told that you are nothing if not a fair man. I beg you do not condemn my husband and his men out of hand. They are still alive I am sure, and they will account for their actions themselves. And I am sure, in fact I have heard, that there are those that will vouch for their bravery. Do not brand them cowards. This war needs heroes, not villains.'

'My dear Rhianydd, you are as passionate as you are beautiful, and your husband is a very lucky man. Your Uncle has nothing but praise for you. If you were free to marry, then I may well have accepted your back handed proposal. I will review the case. I will read all the paperwork I promise you and I will act appropriately. Can you have that much faith in me at least. Trust me that I know my brother well. Now you must leave. I will walk you to the front door.' He looked down into the street from his window. 'I see my driver is still holding up the traffic.'

I left London the following day not sure whether my visit had done more harm to our case than good.

In Cardiff, I thanked Uncle Moses for his help and did not stay. Hengwm was calling. It was time for us to take action. On the journey home I pulled Veronica Battle's book of poems from my bag and immersed myself in the surreal world of Arthur Cole and his dreams of the Ghosts of the Archers. Matron thought them fanciful tales formed in a disturbed man's dreams. I knew different.

CHAPTER 48. FLIGHT INTO WAR - Sybil

1916,
Hengwm and France.

We left the mountain above Hengwm unseen, Rhianydd and I clinging tight to Eryr. There was no time for conventional travel plans. Neither of us would be accepted for enlistment to go to the front. I was too old and had no recognised formal qualifications and Rhianydd would simply be sent to a British hospital on home soil. Around the big table it had been decided. We would join the enlisted when they got off the train in the town. The hospital itself would not send us back, they needed every man they could get.

Fiona and Frances would follow the paper trail in London. They would find out what they could from Fiona's contacts in the Admiralty and, subtly, from the men who had come home, they would be our collectors of information. Along with Letty and Ethel we had quite a proficient network.

Rhianydd and I would find the men and get them to safety. Where that safety was, was not yet clear. We at least knew they were alive. If they were dead, I would not see them, or hear them, yet I had. I had also seen and heard others who confused the picture.

Then there was The Lady Margaret, why was she there, for I could sense her at my shoulder watching, waiting, slowly pulling her invisible threads tighter around their target.

Flying with Eryr or indeed with any of his folk is at first terrifying, then exhilarating and then just plain addictive, especially if you are physically drawn to them. Rhianydd clung on to his back in terror. He would not let her fall, the power of his mind would keep her safe - she had yet to learn all these things and she still balked at the thought of him being her father. Agnes on the other hand had come to adore him, wooed by a variety of conjuring tricks and a child's cloak of forest furs, just like Gannie's, which was invaluable for playing dress up or for hiding at bedtime. Agnes was a very precocious child, far more advanced than most two-year-olds, her mother won't believe it's a Faerie thing.

He hadn't taken Agnes flying yet, there are boundaries with Rhianydd that even he won't cross, but it's only a matter of time.

Me, I just allow myself to be taken. Sometimes the space between the earth and the stars is the only privacy we get from Uncle Edward and the creaky bed in the loft.

It's a bit like falling off a cliff, although I admit I've never actually fallen off one, to trust another being implicitly with your life, surrender yourself totally to their care. To step into infinity and then soar upwards faster than the climb of an eagle in flight, to be held on the pinnacle of ecstasy for moments and then drop, faster than a stooping falcon, your heart and stomach weightless, all cradled against a wall of muscle and sinew, wrapped only in nakedness and starlight. I'll take that over a lumpy mattress and a creaky bed any day.

No time for such reminiscences. Eryr was all business, we were now a military operation. Travelling high above the clouds, unseen to anyone but the birds, we flew over the grey seas of the channel, landing on a hilltop just outside the town. The view from above was terrifying, the small dim lights of the hurricane lamps where soldiers huddled together in the mud of their subterranean homes, the great ruts firmed where the field guns had been pulled into position. From either side, the occasional crack of gunfire, a single shot, then silence, another desperate man finding his own way out of his personal hell. And a horse, galloping, nostrils flared, terrified by the sights and smells around it, saddled and bridled in a way no modern horse would be, iron grey, with a white mane and tail, the only parts visible through the coating of mud on his sweat-soaked coat.

Something made us follow that horse, saw it safe as it ploughed through the woodland, and summoning a last burst of energy leapt the wooden fence into a small farmyard, landing with a clatter of iron shod feet on the cobbles. Head down and flanks heaving, the animal came to rest, its handsome head against the door of the house.

A curtain twitched, a light was visible, the farm was waking, the door opened, and a boy's voice called back into the bowels of the house.

« Papa ! Ici, 'y a un cheval. »

Taking the exhausted animal by the bridle, he led him unprotesting to the barn, talking to him in rapid bursts of French, ending with the word 'Tonnerre,' a rough translation that his name must be Thunder as he was the colour of thunder clouds! As we dropped down onto the hill behind the farm, I sensed that a life had been saved, one poor horse at least would be kept from the cruelty of war.

Eryr left us on the hilltop, not far from the small rough road which led down through the woodland and across the river to the town.

'Keep out of sight until daylight, the train coming in from the port arrives at eight o clock. There are nurses travelling on that train, follow them, you will not be noticed in the crowd.'

'You are leaving us then?' I asked him. The thought of being without him in this awful place scared me slightly.

'I have work to do, I will be close by.' He kissed me full on the lips and Rhianydd on the forehead, then turned and disappeared into the woodland, his parting words to his daughter, 'Look after you mother, child, she is not the fighter she was, though she will never admit to weakness. Now, go.'

We went, stumbling forward in the darkness down what was little more than a rough track, my stout hobnailed shoes slipping on the moss-and mud-covered stones. I tripped and fell, my outstretched hand landing on what felt like cloth. I would know the feel of serge anywhere, rough wool cloth. I pulled back, gasping, and the object I had fallen on turned over, the death bloated face of a dead soldier inches from my own, an arrow protruding from his neck. I vomited, the contents of my stomach mixing with his body fluids as they soaked into the soil of 'la belle France.'

'Get a grip, mother!' I heard Rhianydd behind me. 'There is death here, and lots of it.'

I did not argue, picking my way back to the pathway, and in the increasing light of day we saw what we had walked into. All along the grassy verge alongside the track were bodies, everyone wore the uniform of German artillery, and everyone had his throat slit, or an arrow in his gullet.

'Iesu Mawr!' I muttered. What manner of man did this? In the adjacent field were the remains of several huge field guns, no horses stood in the traces, they had not been harnessed, the great barrels of each one open at the breach, the firing mechanisms blown apart. Useless lumps of scrap iron, and dead men surrounding them.

In the distance I saw their intended target. In the distance I could just make out the red and white flag which denoted the presence of a hospital.

'Bastards.' I heard Rhianydd behind me. 'How low will they sink?'

In this theatre of war, not even a hospital was safe.

I counted the dead men, thirty in total, and four artillery pieces.

Rhianydd meanwhile was intently staring at a small gold item lying half buried in the moss on the bank. Her jaw was twitching, and I saw her swallow hard. Then she went down and working the item loose with her long fingers looked at it more closely, as if to be sure.

'They were here.' she spoke. 'He was here, I am certain of it, look!' She thrust the object under my nose. 'It's a tunic button, a Rifles tunic button, I should know, I sewed them on.'

'There are no British dead here, all these men are German, look at their uniforms.' I pointed around us. There was not a British soldier's khaki dress amongst the grey of the German dead.

'It means he is alive, at least he left here alive. Come away, we must get into the town to meet the train.'

We walked the two miles further in silence, Rhianydd gripping the button like some newly acquired lucky charm, or at least a sign from above. Those men had been dead a few weeks, anything could have happened to Jack by now. But at least she saw hope, and that counted for a lot.

We had all travelled wearing khaki battle dress, that way at a distance we would pass as soldiers. Rhianydd posing as a male doctor would require her to dress in the appropriate uniform. I had cut her hair, uncle had offered to trim it with his sharpest sheep shears, an offer she had refused, so I had cut her luxuriant auburn locks with a pair of kitchen scissors. It was a bad job. No army barber had ever done a worse one. We crossed the river and then made our way into the centre of town. The long, low, slightly gothic railway station was quiet, the clock on its tower announced that it was seven o'clock, marking the hour in time with the town hall clock nearby. Good old France, their bells had not been melted down to make bullets for guns and mess tins for the men. We had lost most of ours two years ago.

We ducked into the waiting room and found it empty. 'Best you do your clothes thing, mother, I'll keep watch.'

Thinking of Eryr and nurses' uniforms I eventually managed to mentally clothe myself in the pale blue dress and navy shoulder cape of an army nurse. We stayed out of sight and waited for the arrival of the train, to all appearances a middle-aged nurse and a young ginger headed medic.

At half past eight the train pulled in and amongst the hundreds of soldiers swarming onto the platform and concourse I spotted three figures dressed similarly to myself. I pulled Rhianydd's sleeve. 'Let's go, there they are, let me do the talking.'

We crossed the concourse and fell in several yards behind them as they paused to cross the road, apparently heading for the horse ambulance parked by the central monument, a vehicle easy to recognise by the large Red Cross on its canvas sides and another on its roof. I hailed them. 'Nurse!' I called in my most authoritative voice.

The older figure turned round and stopped. By this time, we had nearly caught up to them.

She spoke. 'I thought there were only three of us or I'd have waited at the station.'

'Not to worry, we only received orders at the last minute.' I replied.

'I am Sibyl Meredith, but, and I pointed to my hair, everyone calls me Red.'

The older nurse held out a friendly hand. I took it and felt a firm, cool answering grip.

'Katie Brown,' she replied. 'This is Sally, and this is Elspeth.' She introduced the two young ladies cowering alongside her.

'Pleased to meet you all.' I replied.

From behind me, a deep voice rang in my ear. 'Dr Jack Rees.' Rhianydd introduced herself. She held out a gloved hand to Nurse Brown, who eyed her suspiciously.

'This must be our transport.' muttered Elspeth.

'Next stop the hospital!' An over cheerful male voice heralded the arrival of our driver, a short stocky man in his mid-thirties with a shaven head and one eye, a black patch covering the other. He walked with a decidedly bad limp in his left leg though did not use a crutch or a stick. He lowered the tail board and rolled up the canvas.

'All aboard for Abbé Ville!' We climbed in, Dr Rees last as he assisted all us 'ladies' onto the tailboard in very undignified fashion. The driver, who introduced himself as Private Daniel Curry, unhitched the horse from the hitching post and climbed onto the driver's perch. Flicking the reins over the beast's back, he clicked to it and told it to walk on. We jolted into motion and were driven the short distance to the edge of town and the arrangement of canvas tents and ramshackle sheds that formed the No 3 Field Hospital.

Our transport stopped outside a huge canvas bell tent, its guy ropes bedecked with drying laundry, and a makeshift hand-painted wooden sign declaring its name as 'Hells Bell.'

Our reception committee was a statuesque blonde nurse in the uniform of a senior sister in the Queen Alexandra's which equated to the rank of Captain, one to be saluted then. I followed Katie Brown's lead and saluted her smartly, as did Sally and Elspeth.

'No need for that crap.' The voice, soft but authoritative, conveyed that it would not tolerate dissent and was very broadly Irish.

'I am Sister Josephine Delaney, or Sister Jo as the men call me. Despite what Doctor O'Connor and Doctor Jones, when he's here, think, I run this show. Daniel,' she gestured to our driver, 'take the wee Doctor to O'Connor's surgery will ye, he'll want to be showing his new man the ropes.'

Dr. Jack Rees obediently followed the limping figure of private Curry across what passed for a central square to a small rectangular tent with an RAMC pennant tied to the top of the tent pole. The tent flap flew open, and Sam O'Connor welcomed her aboard.

Sister Jo showed us where we would be sleeping: a section of the tent curtained off with canvas sheets, a small cot bed and a wooden crate for a cupboard. The other occupants made use of the tent poles and guy ropes for hanging space. There was a communal mirror hanging from the big central pole for those who did not have their own. Such things were apparently acquired from occasional trips into town, but these had been stopped since the arrival of Fritz as she called the Germans. Sister Jo expounded at length in broad Irish about life with Fritz.

Today, she said, was quiet. They were usually woken by the first pounding of the German artillery several miles away, then the response from the British guns, this would make the ground shake for most of the morning, then there would be sporadic bursts of machine gun fire from either side. There was, she said, a system of field telephones to signal the imminent arrival of wounded, but more often than not the stretcher bearers and the field ambulances just turned up, they had learned from experience that this would usually be about half an hour after the shooting had stopped. Yes, she said, they had been attacked, she told of the attack on the hospital some weeks ago, the aid given by two troopers who had come to warn them, the evacuation of the more serious casualties, and some of the walking wounded, the defence of the hospital by those that remained, and the unusual soldiers who had helped them, bejeezus, whatever next?

CHAPTER 49. OUR COVER IS BLOWN

August 1916,
Abbéville,
France.

Dr Sam O'Connor looked at the young lieutenant standing before his makeshift desk and could barely resist the urge to laugh. He straightened his face, took a breath in, and looked up from the space he was staring at, which was midway between his hands, which were placed about three feet apart palms down, on his blotter. He himself was standing up.

The enlistment papers and paybook before him belonged to Dr. Jack Rees, aged 22yrs, qualified from Cardiff medical school in the last year, enlisted two weeks ago in London and posted to Abbéville.

He examined the lieutenant from the top down, taking rather more time than was absolutely necessary because he was not sure what he was going to say. The oversized uniform cap sported the RAMC cap badge with its serpent and stave. It was pulled down over short-cropped dark red curly hair, badly cut in a short back and sides, the top slightly longer, its curliness threatening to break out in rebellion from its khaki prison. About two inches of line free forehead and pale complexion lay beneath the cap, then came distinctive auburn eyebrows arched over a pair of dark blue eyes, the eyebrows not quite meeting, but neatly plucked into separation in the middle above a narrow aquiline nose. To complete the picture, high cheekbones, a wide mouth, and a firm chin remarkably free of stubble.

The rest of the uniform was suitably baggy, baggy enough to hide a multitude of sins. He'd seen worse fitting tunics, but not often. And the trousers, well they fitted in all the wrong places, even though the creases were razor sharp and the boots polished to a high shine.

'Should I be callin' you Jacqueline then?' O'Connor's Irish lilt only served to highlight the sarcasm that dripped from every word. He grinned, raising his eyebrows quizzically. Lieutenant Rees looked at him in puzzlement. He tried again.

'Look, yer not foolin' anyone. I have no doubt you are qualified. I have no doubt you can do a job, but I can't be having a woman this close to the action.'

'I was sent to serve my country. Would you send me back then - sir?'

O'Connor was perplexed. He needed all the staff he could get, the evacuation a few weeks ago had taken several of his best nurses. Then, General Shipley had had his commanding officer ordered home purely to operate on his brother. Dr. Robert Jones had returned only a week ago and seemed completely distracted ever since. He had, it turned out, been offered a very attractive post under Dr. Gillies at the hospital in Sidcup but had preferred to return to his comrades on the frontline. Then, the young Jones had become engaged to be married. It would be a shame to lose a skilled surgeon, whose talents were somewhat wasted in the butcher's shop of Abbéville, to either warfare, or wife, or both and at the same time, but what could he do. He pushed his huge hands through his sandy hair before speaking.

'You'll billet in with the nurses, find yourself a cot. Now, hear that?' He cupped a hand to his ear. The young lieutenant listened hard but could hear nothing.

'Exactly!' O'Connor continued. 'That, that you're standin' there listenin' to, is the joyous sound of silence. Fritz is having a day off! Stow your kit and then come and find me, I'll show you round. Oh, and ditch the cap, it makes you look like a simpleton and I'm sure yer not.'

As the imposter left the tent, kit bag over her shoulder, Sam O'Connor watched and admired her from the rear. Tall for a woman, broad shouldered, long legged, what had she done to that hair, that haircut was criminal. The cogs of his mind whirred back to a dance in an officers mess several years ago, it must be her, the tall redhead who had been dancing with the Scotsman. They had not been introduced formally, but the Scotsman had bought him a drink at the bar and declared that he intended to marry her. Strange name she had, Rhian..., no, longer, more Welsh, Rhianydd that was it. Rhianydd MacGregor. His mental tumblers began to turn again, why was she here? He did not believe in coincidence.

He kept his counsel and read through her record, then hooked his stethoscope round his neck, picked up his bundle of notes, tucked his pen behind his ear and went to begin his round. She caught up with him about twenty minutes later, the cap removed, the rest of the uniform cinched in tighter at the waist and apparently much better fitting. He looked up from the dressing he was checking on the unconscious patient in the bed.

'Rhianydd Rees or is it now MacGregor, it is you, isn't it?' She smiled at him, not sure of what would come next. 'You may dance like a man, and you may drink like a man, but sure ye'll never look like one. There's bits of you that, well they'll never be male as long as there's a god in heaven, so I'll say nothing if no one else does. Did ye marry yer wee Scotsman? And why in god's heaven did ye cut yer hair off? Whoever did that needs shootin,' now let's get stuck in, shall we.'

He showed her round the beds, having her check dressings, assess the progress of injuries, chat with the patients. He found her knowledgeable and competent. He subtly questioned her, sought her opinions on treatment. As long as she did not crack under fire and was as handy with a scalpel as those long nimble fingers promised her to be, she would do well. Round completed, he retired to his tent to write up notes, leaving her to her find her feet amongst the nurses in Hells Bell as they called the huge tent they occupied. Had she met sister Delaney, yet he wondered?

Josephine Delaney had called her staff for their daily briefing and sent them on their rounds. Then she addressed the new recruits before sending them off with Brenda and Phyllis to find their feet. Only four of them, but better than none. Two were very young, barely out of school. She doubted they were old enough to be sent to a field hospital at all. She had read their training records. They had all the right training, but could they use it in practice? When the shelling started, the ground shook even if they were a few miles from the guns. Hiding under the covers they would be no use to man nor beast.

Then there was Katie Brown, old school Katie Brown. She smoked and, from what she had heard so far, she could swear like a sailor. Her record said she had been to war before. She had experience under fire. Sister Jo hoped she would be a steadying influence on the youngsters.

Last but not least, Sibyl Helena Meredith. She too had lied about her age, or Jo Delaney was a fool. From her attitudes and her way of talking she was a woman in her fifties, though she looked much younger, and she had no formal qualifications, at least none that she could produce. Her record was bare. A brief background history declared her as some form of healer from a small rural village where she acted as doctor, midwife, and veterinarian. There were places, thought Jo Delaney, especially in Ireland, where 'witch' would have been added as well. She spoke well, carried herself as though she owned the place and was obviously friends with the new doctor. They looked so alike they could be mother and daughter, for the young doctor's disguise fooled no one. But Jo Delaney would let Dr O'Connor deal with that.

Jo Delaney made her decisions. Katie Brown could mentor the youngsters, Sally, and Elspeth. She herself would keep an eye on Sibyl.

The new doctor had been billeted in a curtained off section of the tent, given 'his' own space with a cot bed and a stool, all the spare furniture they could find. By rights he, who was really she, should have taken over Dr. Jones' bed, but O'Connor in his wisdom would have none of it. If he gave Robert's bed away, then the man would not return. He was superstitious like that! Jo Delaney went to make herself a drink and eat her lunch. She was worried, it was too quiet, Fritz was up to something, and they were too close to it, whatever it was.

Dr. Robert Jones walked into the town of Abbéville. He made a bee line for the building on the corner of the town's square which had been commandeered by the Chiefs of Staff. He held the now ragged copy of the Deserters List in his hand. He strode up to the young Corporal positioned like a guard dog outside the door to the General's Office. Under the pretext of news about the General's brother he demanded an audience with General Gerald Shipley.

'Tell him it's Dr. Robert Jones, Corporal, he will see me.'

Two minutes later he would address the General from the other side of his desk. He laid out the broadsheet and stabbed his finger forcefully into the names circled in red.

'These men are dead, sir. My second in command says they came to our aid when Fritz attacked two weeks ago. It was they who destroyed the German artillery. Their bodies are in the wood north of the hospital. The one wounded man who was treated told us this before he died of his injuries. Dr. Jones hoped that this would at least buy MacGregor and his men some more time and distance to decide what they would do next.

General Shipley raised an eyebrow.

'Why such a concern with these men? They are on the list for a reason.'

'I read the list when I was last in London, sir. The hospital was unaware that they were deserters. We treat any wounded no matter what their status. We do not have time to read these lists, even if we were in receipt of a copy. I did not want a bad reflection on my staff.'

'Come now, doctor, from what you have said, these men are not cowards, they did not hide themselves away from a fight. MacGregor was reported as missing by my brother. I take it you are aware of that?'

Dr. Jones lied. 'No, sir, I was not.'

General Shipley continued. 'And your second in command has seen the bodies?'

'Of Owen, yes,' Jones lied again, 'he has. The others no, he has not. The woods they lie in are not safe to investigate. Fritz now has an infantry unit poised in the fields behind.'

'Convenient that, isn't it.' replied the general, raising an eyebrow. 'Best I mark them as dead then?'

'Thank you, sir, and your brother is doing well. I must get back to the hospital, the wounded usually start arriving in the next hour or so.'

As he spoke the deafening report of the massive guns shook the building to its foundations. 'Are we making any ground sir?'

'None that makes a difference, doctor, but things may change tomorrow.'

Dr. Jones ran all the way back to the hospital, just in time to hear the distant sound of the whistles and the cry of the men as they hurled themselves into another wall of bullets. He hoped that new doctor they were expecting had arrived. They could desperately use another pair of hands.

CHAPTER 50. JUST LIKE THE O.K. CORRALL – Red

August 1916.

    British guns had woken us at dawn, the usual ground shaking, ear jangling pounding, then the German response. The barrage continued until after breakfast, then the sound of the whistles and the rallying cries of the men sent over the top to face the hail of bullets. Bursts of gun fire, more shelling, the smoke, and the smell of cordite drifted over the hospital on the breeze. By lunchtime all that could be heard was the plaintive cries of the wounded of both sides.

    By mid-afternoon the field telephone in the corner of the operating tent had rung, casualties were on their way. Within an hour the wounded were stacked up in a reception area to be triaged by nurses Sally Higgins and Elspeth Cherry. Those awaiting surgery would be taken straight into the operating tent. Doctors Jones and O'Connor ran two tables, Jo Delaney served as anaesthetist assisted by the new Doctor Rees. Lit by two huge paraffin storm lamps, equipment was laid out on scrubbed tables covered in clean drapes, all boiled to an inch of their lives. We waited for the onslaught to arrive. Phyllis and Brenda who had returned following the evacuation acted as scrub nurses, one for each surgeon.

    That left Katie Brown and me to assist with the triage and deal with the walking wounded. Some wag familiar with our talents had provided our tent with a large sign which was made from a section of packing case nailed to a piece of fence post and painted in big red letters announcing, 'WITCHES and STITCHES.' Anything to lighten the mood.

    As darkness fell, no one had eaten since breakfast. The tarpaulin holding the surgical waste was nearly filled with amputated arms, legs, and fingers, there was even the occasional ear. Those who did not survive lay shrouded under stretcher canvas in the makeshift mortuary in the next tent.

    The wounded kept coming, the stretcher bearers and the field ambulances exhausted by their efforts. It was gone six o'clock before the flow of wounded relented. Then the shelling started again. I was taking a short break looking out through the perimeter fence towards the river. Rhianydd came and stood beside me, enquiring,

'Coffee?' although it arrived as a statement. She handed me a tin mug full of what passed for coffee, heavily laced with chicory, and had she splashed some of Sam's whiskey into it? The mug was so hot it nearly burned my lips, so I inhaled the fragrant steam blissfully and waited for the contents to cool to drinking temperature. As I waited for my coffee to cool, my eyes and ears became accustomed to the dark and to the silence which had descended.

'Something is out there.' The hairs on my neck were tingling, my sense of danger on full alert.

'Nonsense mother,' Rhianydd poo pooed me, 'it's pitch out there. If we can't see, neither can anyone else.'

I saw one of the band of walking wounded who patrolled our boundary fence stop. He shone his flashlight out into the darkness. The dim yellow light produced by the failing battery cell hardly illuminated a thing, but he moved it carefully in a slow arc. All it revealed was grass, and more grass. Daniel Curry, who was on guard duty propped up against a sandbag wall, beckoned me over.

'You're right.' he whispered. 'Go and warn the tent. We are about to have visitors.' He had had the presence to look down the optic sight fitted to his rifle. As he spoke, I saw a flash of torchlight flicker off a silver hat badge, a mistake there, and a fatal one. Experienced men painted their buttons and badges black. Daniel saw it too. There was a sharp 'crack' of his rifle and the shadowy figure slumped into the darkness. But, before he could reload, a return of fire caught Daniel in the shoulder, and he fell away from the sandbags, groaning in pain.

Then they were on us, running out of the darkness, vaulting over our pitiful sandbag defences, crashing through the tents, no regard for the wounded or those caring for them. Shots were fired, nurses screamed, then there was silence. With organised efficiency they rounded all the staff into the operating tent at gun point. Robert Jones stood scalpel in hand, midway through removal of a bullet from the leg of an unfortunate sergeant. There was a German pistol held to the back of Robert's head. In heavily accented but good English the officer holding the pistol demanded.

'Where are they?'

Dr. Jones replied slowly and calmly and in perfect German.

'Who exactly do you mean? I am a doctor, I am unarmed, I took an oath to do no harm, but I will protect my patients and my staff, if not myself.'

I looked around the tent. I could not see Doctor O'Connor. He had excused himself for a piss as he so politely put it. I had lowered my eyes from their scan of the room, not wishing to draw attention to myself. Then, the click of a pistol and a broad Irish voice. The German officer flinched as the voice spoke, this time in English.

'Captain, I too am a doctor, I am armed. I will have no hesitation in pulling the trigger if you do not remove your threat from my colleague and allow him to continue his work.'

The captain did not move but spoke again. 'Where are they, those deserters you harbour, the ones who murdered my men?'

In an aura, perhaps, just as, sometimes in a crowded place there is a moment of complete silence, he appeared from out of nowhere, a medieval archer dressed in leather and mail, bow slung over his shoulder and a long knife in his hand. The words followed, sternly but simply.

'Is it me you seek? For it was my men and I who killed your soldiers.' The Luger pistol switched quickly from the doctor to the towering figure of Gwyn ap Meredith. The shot caused chaos. It went straight through the body of the archer, killing the German rifleman behind him. The archer's knife took the German captain in the throat, through his windpipe and jugular veins. Deprived of speech, and rapidly losing consciousness he mouthed incomprehensible commands, falling towards the operating table, air bubbling with blood from the gaping wound in his neck.

Staggering, he grabbed at the huge paraffin lamp, one of two which lit the tent. As it fell over, setting alight Jo Delaney's theatre gown, flames licked up the walls of the tent and around the anaesthetic machine with its explosive mixture of ether and oxygen. Jo Delaney frantically tried to turn off the flow of volatile gas while the scrub nurse extinguished the flaming theatre gown in a wet drape. Pushing Jo away to safety, the scrub nurse took over the anaesthetic, skilfully manipulating the black rubber mask to secure the patient's airway. The tent was on fire.

Doctors Jones and O'Connor dragged the unconscious German officer off the operating table and dumped him unceremoniously on to the floor, gasping like a dying fish. They kicked the brakes off the wheels of the operating table and headed towards the fresh air, Jo Delaney and the scrub nurse somehow still in control of the anaesthesia. They burst into the night air. Crack! Another shot and Jo Delaney fell forward hit in the back of her head. She was dead before she hit the floor. Out of the darkness four men came creeping, silent, and unseen by most, faces blackened with mud, only one identifiable by his white, blonde hair. One by one the German attackers were dispatched, most frozen, their attention transfixed by the blazing inferno of canvas.

Several well aimed buckets of water doused the fire, but the damage was done, all but the most basic equipment destroyed. In the chaos of the attack no one had noticed the body of Josephine Delaney, face down in the mud beside the tent. As the smoke cleared, however, Sam O'Connor emerged from the smoke, his face stained with tears, carrying a body in his arms. He kept walking, a silent bereft figure, shoulders bowed, his burden cradled against his chest. As I watched I saw one huge hand open the tent flap of Hells Bell. He had taken her home. The place she had called home for the last three years at least.

Then there was calm, and Katie Brown took charge.

Walking through the triage area, issuing orders, 'I need two of you bloody malingerers who can walk, and I need you now, you two, come here.' Two spotty looking youths stepped reluctantly forward.

'But we're wounded miss.'

'Don't look wounded to me, what's wrong, shit yerselves have you?'

They looked at her insolently as she continued. 'Now drag those dead Germans out of the good doctor's tent, there's good boys.'

Outside the tent, the muddied smeared figure of a man I assumed to be Jack MacGregor was conducting an impromptu reunion with his wife. Alternately kissing her, hugging her, and talking nonsense, then berating her for being there at all.

Katie Brown was relentless. Within minutes she had the bodies cleared and the operating table back on its legs, the burned canvas sheets taken down and replaced with ones from another tent. Dr. Jones had successfully removed the bullet from Sergeant Munros thigh and the impromptu stretcher bearers had placed him in the Doctors own cot to start his recovery.

In the corner of the chaos, the field telephone rang. Katie answered it. 'Casualties en route!' were the two words she heard. All we heard was her answer.

'You'd better send more fucking medics then!'

Then she turned to me and smiled, a slightly manic smile. 'Come on then Red let's see what you are made of, let's get the show on the road.'

Tables were scrubbed, what instruments we could salvage from the dirt were cleaned and boiled in the cauldron someone found in the mess hall. Every scrap of clean linen was brought from Hells Bell where nurses had a tendency to hoard anything they considered suitable to make clothing from.

Amongst all this, whilst everyone was busy ripping bandages from sheets and tablecloths and righting upturned furniture, only three men patrolled our rickety barricade. Daniel Curry would live, but he would not fire a gun again, not in this war anyway, but arm in a sling, he made himself useful. Richard Flint was amongst the dead, so too was nurse Phyllis. The body of Josephine Delaney lay on her cot, curtains drawn around her, laid out in the manner of a medieval queen, all she needed was an orb in her hands and a small dog at her feet. No room at her feet though, for that space was occupied by a bereft Irishman.

I saw them coming along the road towards the destroyed gates, the first of the ambulances. Travelling faster than usual, it was rare for the exhausted animals who pulled them to go faster than a trot, but this one arrived like a Wild West mail coach. The driver was a girl, I recognised her instantly, it was Celine!

'I thought you were in London!'

'London! Pah!' she exclaimed in heavily accented English. ''Ow could I ever leave France, 'ow would she survive without me?'

She shrugged her shoulders and, tying the reins to the brake of the wagon, leapt off the driver's perch and summoned two stretcher bearers to the rear.

'Look after this one well, 'ee' ees verry important, n'est pas?'
Only one stretcher was on the ambulance and as the bearers lowered it down to waist height, I saw the blood smeared face of General Gerald Shipley.

'Where is he wounded?' I asked Celine.

''Ee 'as taken two bullets, one in 'ees left leg which is no matter, but the other is in 'ees gut, they think 'ee is bleeding inside.'

'Surgeon!' I shouted. But Robert had his eyes already in a patient.

'Sam, Sam O'Connor!' I screamed across the square, but Sam did not hear. Okay I thought, we can do this, I grabbed Rhianydd from the clutches of her husband.

'Scrub up!' She looked at me as though I had two heads. 'Mother, I can't.'

'Yes, you can, this man is the man who can save them, he holds the keys to all their lives, it is Shipley's brother!'

She rolled up her sleeves and poured hot water into an enamelled tin basin, with blue flowers painted on the outside. Another find from the nurse's quarters, no doubt. Then using the harsh carbolic soap, she washed her hands, scrubbing between her long agile fingers.

'Is he under?' she asked.

'No,' I replied, 'we have no anaesthetic kit. He's sedated with morphia but that'll be no good for an op on his belly.

'When you are quite ready,' Katie's voice cut through our thoughts.' I found this in Josephine's locker!' She held up a neat wooden box. Quickly unclipping the hinged lid she showed us the contents, a brown glass bottle of ether and a gauze mask. 'Don't worry, I've used this sort of kit before, lots of people still do!'

I scrubbed my own hands and, sleeves rolled up, Rhianydd and I approached the table. The General's slightly overweight frame lay exposed to the French night air. Katie applied her makeshift mask to his face, and gradually over about ten minutes, with a bit coughing and spluttering, he drifted off to sleep, his bushy moustache wiggling as he breathed in and out. 'You'd better be as quick as you can, I don't know how long this stuff is going to last and once the bottle's empty he'll begin to wake up again. It can't be that powerful, Sister Jo used it to help her sleep and she was never late for her shift, God rest her!'

The bullet in his lower thigh was easily removed. I did that myself while Rhianydd explored the track of the bullet into his abdomen.

I stood back from my work and dropped the remains of the bullet into the waiting dish with a satisfying 'ting.' Then I cleaned and stitched the wound. He would walk with a slight limp but nothing he couldn't make a great anecdote about, something to tell in his gentleman's club after the war was over. 'Indeed!' I thought. What was the silly bugger doing that close to the action in any case?

Rhianydd was just pressing a scalpel to the generals abdomen, her planned incision being a right paramedian, eight inches long, long enough to get a hand in. She had rolled him onto his back and wedged him in position with a rolled-up towel. His skin was swabbed with the acrid smelling carbolic disinfectant, then the area draped with boiled linen sheets. An Irish cough heralded the arrival of Sam. Rhianydd stepped back, deferring to the more experienced surgeon.

'Carry on, Lass.' came the reply. 'All good so far, and I'm no use to man nor beast at present.'

Rhianydd continued, giving a running commentary as she went. 'Through the skin and into the fat – retractor please – thank you - and then, gently lifting the peritoneum to free it from anything important beneath, make a nick and, we're in. Good, now what's what in here?'

Katie coughed politely to attract attention, adding, 'Just a mo, one of the orderlies just delivered these!' From the head of the table, she held up an x-ray image, a glass sheet, the image in negative. 'Apparently there is a machine on an ambulance at the first dressing station. Shame we don't have one here'

'As you can see, the bullet is here, somewhere up by the liver, quite a way from the entry wound.' She pointed to a black shape easily recognisable by its outline on the X-ray plate. 'The entry wound is here.,' said Rhianydd, pointing to the hole in the patient's lower abdomen, 'but the bullet has tumbled. Good job we decided to make a decent incision.' She was working as she spoke, gently dividing the delicate peritoneum allowing the rather bruised looking bowel to fall away, safe from her knife.

What the X-ray did not show was that the point of the projectile was lodged in the gut wall. To remove it now may cause a hole in the gut, a leak of its contents into the abdomen and a catastrophic infection, leading to a painful death.

'Think.' An Irish voice prompted her.

'Suture.' Came the response. I handed her a fine curved needle on a long holder, a length of cat-gut streaming from its eye and watched as she gently placed a purse string ring of the suture around an imaginary hole at the point of the bullet, so that, if there was a hole in the bowel, it could be immediately and effectively closed. She handed the needle holder back without taking her gaze off the bullet. 'One more, please.' I handed her another, which she tied off around the metal body of the projectile.

Rhianydd returned the needle holder into my waiting hand.

'Long toothed forceps, please.' They were already in my hand. She placed them gently around the blunt end of the bullet, then gently lifted the section of gut slightly, allowing it to fall away and the bullet to be safely removed, gripped by the forceps, and supported by the suture. She checked the site for damage, found a small rupture where the point had been, closed now by her stitching. She added one more neat stitch and tied off the suture.

'Like mending a bicycle tyre, while going fishing.' came the reassuring Irish voice over her shoulder.

'Anything else you'd like to do while you're in there?' Rhianydd looked at Katie over her face mask and raised an eyebrow, 'A formal laparotomy. I need to check that there's no other nonsense going on in here. How long do I have?'

'He's doing fine, girl, you take your time, I'll shout if anything changes.'

Rhianydd set off on a surgical 'Cook's Tour' of the abdomen, checking that there were no other holes in the bowel and that the liver and spleen were intact and no great bruises around the kidneys outside the peritoneal cavity. Some bruising to the bowel, but nothing that the omentum – that extraordinary piece of tissue known as the 'policeman of the abdomen' - couldn't take care of. 'Let's close the wound in layers,' she said, 'with interrupted sutures that'll let any pus out. He's a dead cert for a wound infection. Have we got enough string? Mother, would you be happy to close?' The team chuckled. Tension relieved.

'Very neat,' the voice again over her shoulder. As Rhianydd stepped away from the table, I saw Sam push his hip flask into her hand with a 'Well done lass, neat work, that.'

I took my own needle and thread and with 'witches stitches' I closed the wound, just a tiny bit better than my surgeon daughter would have done. He would have a nice, neat scar to go with the leg wound. I applied a smear of my own gentian salve and a light dressing and told Katie she could bring him round. They placed him in Sam O'Connor's cot, opposite Sergeant Munro, we were fast running out of bed space.

It was well past midnight. The guns were quiet. Charlie and Frankie came in from their patrol and were drinking a hot toddy and watching the ground towards the river. So intent were they on their watch, neither heard the two stretcher bearers behind them.

'Frankie Baker and Charlie Turner! You are Cowards.' were the first words Frankie heard. 'We have you now, where are the other two?' Both felt the business end of a gun in their back.

Fortunately, neither of Nurse Brown's reluctant recruits felt the invisible knife which opened their throat. Neither saw the bringer of death. Neither made a made a sound.

 I saw him, and I saw the look on the face of Jack MacGregor as he walked out of the darkness to speak for his men. Jack shouted into the darkness for Ralph Owen, Ralph was not there. But I saw him, disappearing like a wraith into the darkness.

Katie Brown spoke quickly. She had dragged the stretcher from the triage tent. 'Load them up. They came in with the wounded, they can go out with the dead, cowards the pair of them, fuck all wrong with those two when they arrived.'

'No, wait,' I interceded. 'no-one comes in wounded like that, find me a suture!'

Katie nodded and two lengths of silk and two needles appeared, a few minutes later, two throats were neatly stitched, surgery could not save them, witches sew stitches indeed. Charlie and Frankie were jolted into action. Walking as if it were the most natural thing in the world, they carried their loaded stretcher through the operating tent where Doctor Jones merely raised an eyebrow and carried on with his work. They placed the stretcher in the line of the dead and covered it with a sheet, returning to where Jack MacGregor had just finished throwing up on the grass, neatly mixing his stomach contents with the pool of arterial blood at his feet. The boys received the order, 'We make ourselves scarce.'

Jack embraced Rhianydd. 'I am alive, I will stay alive, go back to our daughter, you do not need to be here, she needs one of us at least.'

I watched just three of the four men leave. By the time Rhianydd had wiped the tears from her eyes, they were lost from sight, disappearing like bullets through the mist.

CHAPTER 51. I MUST GO HOME - Rhianydd

General Gerald Shipley recovered quickly. Within days he was sitting up and out of bed, issuing orders and trying to organise the staff. I visited him daily. He was not short of medical attention. He was, after all, sharing a tent with two doctors.

He demanded to see the surgeon who had saved his life, and the nurses who had helped. His face was a picture when he discovered that I was a woman. He did not know whether to be astonished, angry, or grateful. So, he resorted to being all in turn. It took him a full five minutes to recognise me as the red-haired harridan who had propositioned him in the foyer of his workplace. I was, he said, 'a most persistent woman, stubborn beyond belief and almost a complete nuisance.' I am sure that he would have said much worse things had I been a man, but he kept his language under control and bristled under his moustache, eventually declaring that he, hoped I was not embarked on some completely hair brained scheme, and that he didn't know if he should promote me or have me drummed out of the medical corps and struck off the medical register.

Once you got beyond the bluster, he was a plain speaking, down to earth man, essentially the second son of a wealthy farmer. He would not inherit the family estate or anything that went with it, in his case the crumbling pile of a house in the rolling Leicestershire countryside and the wealth and title which went with it. His mother had moved, more or less permanently, to London, leaving his older brother to run the estate while she enjoyed the benefits of city living without the benefit of a husband. Gerald and her younger sons had each been bought a commission in the army, commissions bought in peacetime without any thought of an oncoming war. He had found that he was an efficient soldier if not a remarkable one. He possessed a degree of common sense and a head for logistics and planning. He was a born organiser.

Never a man to take things at face value he had wanted to see for himself. Increasing reports of the dire conditions the men were forced to exist in had prompted him to visit the trenches. He had visited the very trench where his brother had been so terribly injured.

'My dear,' he said. 'My dear, I have never seen such a terrible place. I cannot imagine how terrible it must be to have to spend possibly your last days on earth there. We are foolish to think that morale is as good as the propaganda we spread, for it is not.'

He patted my hand in a proprietary manner, like a favourite uncle.

'Your husband, he is in the army?' He knew me as Rees not MacGregor and I did not intend to enlighten him. 'He is missing in action, sir. I do not know whether he is dead or alive.'

'My dear Rhianydd, I have the power to have you sent back home, either in disgrace, or as a hero. I did not become a General without having some modicum of intelligence, and without a smattering of perception of human nature. I also have eyes and ears.'

What was he inferring? I said nothing, just rose from my seat and busied myself checking his dressings and tidying his bedclothes.
He touched my arm again. 'Rhianydd, if you tell me the soldier you were embracing is not your husband, I will call you a liar – tent walls are thin you know. He is a brave man, that much I have worked out. Now tell me the truth, Rhianydd MacGregor, for it will out in the end.'

And so, I told him what I knew while he tutted and twirled his moustache, sucked on his teeth, and thought a great deal. I had not of course told him how I had arrived in France. Some things might push the boundaries of normal comprehension too far. Eventually he drew in his breath and pronounced.

'You will travel with me, to continue my care, and that is an order, Doctor MacGregor. You have a daughter at home, so at home you need to be.'

He was as good as his word and within a few days I was back in England, installed in the London mansion of Lady Arabella Shipley, the General's mother. I could, the General confided, also be tending one other patient and would have this patient's two nurses to assist me. The other patient was his younger brother, Montague.

I could, if I liked, arrange for Agnes to be brought up to London where Nanny O'Shea could assist in her care while I looked after the Shipley wounded. The phone call to Hengwm to broach that subject was met with point blank refusal, Uncle Edward taking great offense that his child rearing talents were being doubted and Agnes refusing to be parted from Zak. I took the path of least resistance and risked returning home eventually to a feral child who had been brought up on a diet of folklore and farming and a scattering of Faerie dust. I did not imagine that the three R's would be high on Uncle Edward's priority list.

As for Jack, as the General had said, 'He's a big boy now, Rhianydd, he's made it this far, he can look after himself.' Personally, I doubted this.

Mother would be my eyes and ears. She was staying, and where she went, HE would likely follow. For now, at least I must trust my parents to watch over my husband.

The journey home had been long, though the General's rank managed to propel us swiftly through most of the bureaucratic nightmare of wartime travel. My lack of any formal enlistment documents did not prove a problem. I was spirited through barriers under the guise of, 'The General's personal physician.' No questions asked. No answers required.

We arrived at Crosscommon House which was only a stone's throw from Mount Vernon, situated in Moor Park near the small town of Harefield in the early hours of a morning. We were greeted by a bleary-eyed housekeeper, Mrs Pitt, and a male servant, George, who seemed to perform the role of butler, footman, valet and also chauffeur. I was certain I had seen him behind the wheel of the huge Austin car the General travelled in.

A hasty supper was produced as George pushed the wheelchair into the formal dining room where we sat and ate at one end of a huge dining table, the sort with a candelabra at either end and no conversation in the middle. The General's bedroom was still on the first floor. He managed the stairs with assistance from my shoulder, his stout walking stick, and the banister rail. George would have carried him bodily up the stairs, but Gerald Shipley would not countenance such a thing. I assisted him to bed, careful of his stitches, both to his abdomen and his leg wound, and, with the assistance of Mrs Pitt, found my own small room in the attic.

That night as I lay in freshly laundered sheets for the first time in weeks and drifted off to a sleep not disturbed by scurrying rodents and gunfire, I dreamed of Jack. I could see him clearly, he was standing on some sort of cliff, looking out over treetops towards the sea. He was not alone. In the morning the images were still there, they had not faded like most dreams do. Maybe mother's gifts were rubbing off on me.

The following morning, the household awoke to the commotion caused by the arrival of Montague and his installation into the bedroom which had been made for him in the study. His bed had been moved downstairs and positioned so the occupant had a view through the tall French windows down the garden and out onto the park. Indeed, on the long summer evenings it was possible to wheel his chair out through the doors into the fresh air. He could wheel himself up to the big mahogany desk if he wished to write and could reach a selection of books from the tall bookshelves, all his favourite volumes having been moved to within arm's reach of him. Along with Montague came his two nurses, who would also assist me with his brother when needed. Gerald had come to an arrangement with the hospital that nurses Cameron and Munro would see to his brother between them in between their shifts at Mount Vernon. The family would pay any extra costs incurred.

I had heard a great deal about Fiona and Frances from Jack, and more lately from Charlie and Frankie but I had never actually met the girls affianced to these two brave men in person. All that was about to change.

CHAPTER 52. A MEETING OF MINDS – Rhianydd

London 1916

So here we were, the three of us, sitting round a small table with a battered scrubbed wood top and ornate wrought iron legs, nestled in the bay window of the Duke of Clarence, nursing our drinks, and conspiring like a coven of witches around a cauldron.

I had called at Mount Vernon on a spurious visit to Dr Bannerman who had been one of my tutors in training. 'Be sure not to lose touch,' he had said, 'especially if you have an interest in surgery, new techniques are always being tried and tested.' So, I had arranged to call and see him. We had talked over tea in his office, and he had mentioned, as I knew he would, his patient upstairs. It was he who had suggested I accompany him on a ward round and look in on Lieutenant Shipley who was still installed in his private room. Dr. Jones, Shipley's surgeon had returned to the army and was by now back in France. Shipley was due to go to his mother's home in the country to rehabilitate.

Until the ward round, Dr Bannerman had directed me upstairs to the nurses' common room. 'Look for Nurse Cameron and Nurse Munro,' he had said. 'Fiona and Frances. They are a font of knowledge when it comes to the care of these men.' It was there that we three had finally met. We had probably passed in hospital corridors before, but never spoken. There was an instant bond, a camaraderie between us as we spent the afternoon swapping stories of Jack and Frankie and Charlie. They had been doing their best to find out what Shipley had been up to and to find out if our men were still alive. That evening, all three of us caught the tram up to Town as we called London. Our menfolk had all talked to each of us about the others. They both knew I was Welsh, knew that I was a medic, as I knew that Fiona was a General's daughter, and that Frances was a Scot with two brothers, both in the Black Watch. Bound together by a common bond - our missing men, and their predicament - we now sat and discussed what we knew and what we should do next.

'Are they even alive?' Fiona asked. 'I suppose the must be, or Letty would have had a telegram by now.'

'Oh, they are alive!' I told her.

'How, can you be so sure?' Frances asked. 'Charlie's mother has heard nothing either.'

I told them of my mother, her gift of sight, and her search for Jack, that she had seen him alive and sensed he was with others. They were curious, of course, but Fiona was sceptical of such practices, mumbo jumbo she called it. I assured her that I had taken some convincing. But that my experiences at my mother's home had convinced me that she did indeed have a gift. I did not tell them that I had that gift too, or that my father was indeed alive and was nothing like the Pharmacist with a shop in a small market town that Jack had told Frankie and Charlie about.

Fiona and Frances had found out little from Shipley. He could not talk intelligibly and was reluctant to communicate anything other than pleasantries to them. His letters were never left unsealed, and they knew only that he wrote regularly to his younger brother Jeremy who worked in intelligence at the Admiralty building.

One thing Fiona did know, was that her father had worked from that same building and that Ethel Turner, Charlie's mum, used to clean the office for him. She thought, but she would need to check, that Jeremy Shipley was now occupying that very office. She needed to go through her father's things and find out which room he occupied in the Admiralty. Then we needed to meet with Ethel, and with Frankie's mother, Letty. Maybe they could help.

We had all been told that our men were on the deserters list. We had all seen the list. None of us believed the charges to be true and none of us had heard of Ralph Owen, though my mother had raised a suspicious eyebrow at the name. She had also found others on her journey through what she called the veil, others she obviously knew, but did not necessarily wish to renew acquaintance with.

We finished our drinks and walked together across the park to Fiona's family home, now a cold, dark, lifeless structure, uninhabited with no light at its windows and no fires in its hearths. All it contained now were the humps of furniture shrouded in dust sheets, the faint whiff of cigar and pipe smoke clinging to the heavy curtains, and memories. Fiona let us in through the tall elegant front door, which creaked wearily as it opened. Pulling an army issue flashlight from her carpet bag she guided us into the hall. At the far end, the study still held the tang of blood and gunpowder in its atmosphere. A person who believed in such things would say that the house and that room in particular had ghosts all of its own.

Then she led us through a baize covered door under the sweeping flight of stairs. The small room on the other side of the door was the gun room. Its racks now empty, the General's fine collection of shotguns had been sold off. The room smelled of gunpowder and cleaning oil. There was a baize covered table at its centre, a workbench with hidden cupboards beneath the green tabletop. Fiona reached under the surface of the table and, pressing a hidden switch, popped open the door hidden in the base to reveal shelves and a cupboard neatly filled with files of personal papers and a box full of keys, mostly spares for the locks to the house and the outbuildings.

With efficiency instilled in her by a succession of matrons and nursing sisters, Fiona had sorted her father's papers into boxes. His colleagues and his commanding officer had removed the contents of the safe and other army related documents when they had dealt with the shooting. Fiona still had nightmares about that night, the night she had shot her mother. She reached into the clutter of keys and after some shuffling around pulled out a steel ring holding three keys, examined them closely, then replaced them.

'Funny, they aren't the ones. Someone has been in here, I'm sure of it! Father's spare keys are missing!'

Then she pulled a file from the shelf and removed a piece of Admiralty headed vellum from it. Reading the neatly printed heading she spoke again.

'I thought so!' She smiled as she spoke. 'One and the same. Now we need to speak to Ethel.'

That night we made up a fire in the General's study and slept under what blankets and quilts we could find on the unaired beds upstairs, using instead the General's large, overstuffed chairs as cots. We were all too excited to sleep and I found myself awake and watching dawn arrive over the park and tried to find Jack with my mind.

There was nothing to eat in the kitchen, so without breakfast we made our way to Agar Grove early, hoping to find Ethel and maybe also Letty before they left for work.

As we arrived in front of the Turner house, we could hear that there was an argument in progress. The loud voice of Jesse Turner was berating his wife. 'How do ye think I feel woman? Half the bloody idiots in the Clarence have turned against them, it is all the fault of that boy Frankie! Cowards, all of the Bakers! Yellow down the back and soaked in cheap gin, the lot of them.'

'I will not have you say anything against my boy, or his pals! The truth will come out, Jesse Turner, It's not all about you!'

'How can I hold my head up with that notice stuck on the bloody wall in the bar?'

'Maybe don't go there quite so often. Without our Charlie's money we have little enough without you drinking it all!'

The door opened and Jesse Turner emerged onto the street, barrelling down the steps closely followed by his metal flask and sandwich tin, the tin hitting him square between the shoulder blades. Managing to catch the flask before it hit the ground and the insides smashed into a million pieces, he turned to face his front door, executed a very courtly bow to his very irate wife. 'Thank you, Ethel Turner, you are a diamond amongst women!'

The sound of the front door slamming could be heard at the end of the street.

Jesse Turner turned up the collar of his coat, shrugged his shoulders and strode off. On the doorstep of the house next door, Letty Baker could be heard clapping and from the upstairs windows of the Turner household came the sounds of a round of girlish laughter as they watched their father depart for his shift.

We three waited until the figure of Jesse Turner had disappeared down the road and around the corner out of sight, then we approached the battered front door of 4 Agar Grove. The young sentries posted in the upper window announced our arrival. I heard them shout in chorus just as Fiona was about to knock on the door, 'Mother, visitors!' Within a few seconds the door opened an inch. Assessing us as no threat to her safety, Ethel opened it further and recognising Fiona and Frances, bid them welcome. 'Come in girls, come in, do you have news, and who is this with you?'

I was hastily introduced as Jack's wife. Ethel shook me firmly by the hand with a grip which would break a docker's knuckles. 'Come in!' she gestured to her kitchen. 'Kettle's always on. Sit down the three of you. Now, tell me why you are here.'

Straight to the point, Fiona asked, 'Mrs Turner, Ethel, do you still clean Father's office?'

'Why would I? I only did it as a favour, your father trusted me. I cleaned his study amongst all those papers, so he paid me to clean the office as well. When he died, I lost both jobs.'

'Did the new captain not keep you on?'

Ethel became tight lipped. 'No, he did not.' A knock at the back door and a friendly shout announced the arrival of Letty Baker.

'Have you told them then, Ethel?' Letty was excited.

'Told them what? There's nothing to tell.' Ethel cut off her friends flow of words with a sharp look and a sharper retort.

Frances interrupted. 'What shouldn't you tell us, Letty? We need to know everything if we are to help our men.'

'Well……,' started Letty.

Ethel ploughed on. 'There is nothing she can tell you, there is nothing I can tell you. You must not meddle in what you know nothing about. Now, let sleeping dogs lie. It is nice to see you all and nice to meet you, Mrs MacGregor, but now you need to go, and I need to be on my way. If you please, ladies. And you, Letty.' Ethel ended the conversation and began to usher them to the door. Letty disappeared back to her own house, and we were ushered unceremoniously back into the street.

'She is hiding something.' I voiced my feelings.

'Tell us something we don't know!' added Fiona.

'Wait!' A voice called us back as far as the back lane of Letty Baker's house. Letty ducked out of the lane and grabbed the arm of my coat. 'Don't worry, they will be fine, trust me. Ethel can say nothing, she works for them you see. They pay her well and her girls depend on her.'

Then Letty Baker was gone.

We spent the rest of the day discussing what we knew, which was not much, and what we could do, which was not much. I needed to get back to Wales and to Agnes. They had to return to the hospital. Lieutenant Shipley was playing his cards close to his chest, and he appeared to be holding all the aces. I had told Fiona and Frances as much as I could about my mother, but both were sceptical, Fiona to the point of complete disbelief. My last avenue of attack, my last resort, was Gerald Shipley and, honourable man though he was, the lieutenant was still his brother. I boarded the train back to Cardiff, the start of my long journey back to Hengwm, no wiser than when I had left.

CHAPTER 53. THE ART OF DISAPPEARANCE – Red.

We were, after all, a hospital. Life and war went on. Tents were replaced and patched. Anyone who was able enough assisted in making the place functional again. We had lost friends and colleagues. One in particular would leave a large hole in the fabric of the unit, as it had left a large hole in the big Irish heart of Sam O'Connor. For years he had admired her from afar and unsuccessfully tried to court her affections. His unrequited love now followed her to the grave. He would endure, but a piece of him would always be missing.

It was a small gathering. It was raining. It rained all the more as the coffin of Josephine Delaney was lowered into her grave. There was a priest in attendance to perform the formalities and Sam O'Connor read from his book of poems, words he thought fitting to the occasion, and words that the eternal fighting Celt that was the spirit of Josephine Delaney, would like.

The Last Rose of Summer

'Tis the last rose of summer,
Left blooming alone;
All her lovely companions
Are faded and gone;
No flower of her kindred,
No rosebud is nigh,
To reflect back her blushes
Or give sigh for sigh!

I'll not leave thee, thou lone one.
To pine on the stem,
Since the lovely are sleeping,
Go, sleep thou with them;
Thus, kindly I scatter
Thy leaves o'er the bed,
Where thy mates of the garden
Lie scentless and dead.

So soon may I follow,
When friendships decay,
And from love's shining circle
The gems drop away!
When true hearts lie withered,
And fond ones are flown,
Oh! who would inhabit
This bleak world alone? [4.]

And a final prayer from the Scottish.

Thou angel of God who hast charge of me
From the dear Father of mercifulness,
The shepherding kind of the fold of the saints
To make round about me this night.

Drive from me every temptation and danger,
Surround me on the sea of unrighteousness,
And in the narrows, crooks, and straits,
Keep thou my coracle, keep it always.

Be thou a bright flame before me,
Be thou a guiding star above me,
Be thou a smooth path below me,
And be a kindly shepherd behind me,
To-day, to-night, and for ever.

I am tired and I a stranger,
Lead thou me to the land of angels;
For me it is time to go home
To the court of Christ, to the peace of heaven. [5.]

Amen.

The gathering echoed the Amen around the graveside, and as we all dropped a handful of French soil on the lid of the plain wood coffin hastily made by the last remaining carpenter in the town, we were all a little less whole.

The world would indeed be a bleaker place without her. Standing beside him at the graveside, the darkly determined figure of Katie Brown tried to buoy up his spirits.

Life went on, the war would go on, I had been absorbed into the fabric of the field hospital, and, in the endless round of wounded men, I had lost sight of why I was here at all.

Rhianydd had gone home, thank goodness. She at least was safe. Jack, well he was at least alive, but where? He had melted into the darkness along with his men, in the company of ghosts. I felt the pull of them, those invisible ties tightening on my gut, pulling me closer.

A small wake was held for Josephine, it was held in the big bell tent that she had made a home from home. For once there were no incoming wounded, the mourners trod the usual path to alcohol assisted oblivion, ending in tearful songs and reminiscences. Eventually Sam O'Connor drew proceedings to a close with a raised glass and a last toast to Sister Josephine.

That night I packed my essential belongings in my backpack and slipped away into the darkness, guided only by instinct and the stars. I was not alone.

To be at one with the night, to walk in its darkness, finding light where you can, using senses most humans have lost to navigate. I knew he was there with me, in spirit if not in person. I could feel him, they were his senses which guided me. Stumbling in the darkness, at first I made my way along the river bank and then towards the coast, following the flow of the water and the scent of the salt water. The path led into woodland, winding between banks of moss and grass, the rough stone cart tracks which once led to remote barns and cottages now riddled with treacherous potholes and fallen trees. As my eyes became accustomed to the lack of light, I found that I could see what was before me.

I had been walking for about an hour, I was dressed in the uniform of a British soldier, complete with boots a size too big, which had rubbed my feet nearly raw. Sitting on one of the moss banks, I removed the offending left boot and pulling up a clump of moist green sphagnum from its home I packed it into my boot, hoping it's healing properties and the padding it provided would give some relief to my blistered heel. I took a swig from the bottle of home brewed poteen I had liberated from Dr Sam's cupboard and looked around me for guidance. None came immediately. There was no moon visible. Dark clouds scudded across its face, giving an eerie creamy blue light. Closing my eyes, I rested my head on my knees and tried to conjure up someone, something to aim for in the darkness. Where the bloody hell was he, playing games no doubt, teasing me by his absence, or making me focus my mind?

I did not have to focus for long. I heard her, Lady Margaret, calling, reeling me in like a well-played fish on a hook. I might struggle briefly, but I was powerless to resist. I cleared my brain of thought and mentally screamed silently into the night.

'Get a grip, Red.' The voice was close beside me. 'See what is around you. Really see it.'

I looked and could see nothing. His voice was insistent.

'Don't just look, see, use your eyes and really see it.'

Breathing in through my nose, I resisted the temptation to snort loudly. These woods were still a dangerous place, silence was the order of the day.

'I am using my eyes!' I hissed at him.

'Well, use them better. You are the Red Maid remember. Be her, leave the rest behind!' came the reply.

When I looked again, I saw the outcrop of rock to my left, hidden in the dense foliage, had it even been there before? If it had, then it was truly invisible to most. Looking upwards I saw the grey wall rise in front of me, marked only by the darker void of the cave mouth. The climb up to the cave was difficult, hampered as I was by layers of wet serge and uncomfortable footwear. But, with some assistance from behind, I made it to the ledge, and the entrance to the cave. It was apparently deserted, the only sign that those I sought had been there was an abandoned flashlight. What good is a flashlight with no battery. I felt my way along the cold damp walls, the rocks rose upwards beneath my feet taking me upwards towards the summit of the rock. I twisted sideways through the narrow fissure and found myself in a large broad cave.

The view which stretched before me in the darkness rolled itself out like a great canvas, moonlight painted through dark clouds, its beams tinted yellow and orange by the dawn, the heads of the trees swaying beneath my feet, and in the distance a ship, no, a fleet of ships, ships with masts and sails, not puffing clouds of sooty smoke in their wake. 'Holy God, Eryr, what have you brought me to?' I muttered it under my breath.

I sensed a presence behind me, not one but two, and as I turned, I saw Eryr and Calon, father and son, both staring in rapt appreciation of the paintings on the cave wall, totally unconcerned with the view in front of them.

Both were attired the garb of the fifteenth century. What was it with leather and chain mail, both look slightly disturbing to my female senses.

'And Jack, where is Jack?' I enquired with as much dignity as I could muster. Without a by your leave, my clothing was now also of the period, the low-cut dress and apron of a serving wench. I smoothed down the front of the homespun dress and adjusted the decolletage in an attempt to preserve a little of my dignity.

'They are with the fleet, she has called them all, every man of them, we must follow or lose them to her completely.'

'And you, my son?' I addressed Calon, 'What is your part in all this?'

'I am just the messenger, mother!' He smiled a wide and heartbreaking smile. 'I go where my grandsire sends me.'

'Does he meddle in this as well?' I spat.

'Like all of us, mother, he has his part to play.'

'Doesn't he just! Is it he that pulls all the bloody strings, puppets, is that all we are?'

'Don't take on so, Red. He has helped you in the past and you may need him again. Now come, we must catch the fleet before it leaves.'

He gripped my waist in a vice like grip and with Calon at my other side, he launched himself out over the trees, launching us all into the troubles of another lifetime.

We landed unseen on the stern of the flagship, Poulian de Dieppe, under Captain Guillaume de Cazenove, Eryr in the guise of Ralph Owen. It was August 1485, and we were bound for Milford Haven.

CHAPTER 54. INVASION

1st August 1485.

It was a fleet of thirty ships, funded mainly by the Duke of Brittany and with money to pay for more soldiers and equipment. So, Henry could sail from France. The men comprised Lancastrian exiles who had rallied to Henry's cause during their time in Brittany, French mercenaries, nearly a thousand Scots and Welshmen, an army of 4,500 fighting men, crowded onto the ships which now anchored in the Haven just off the Welsh village of Dale.

The six-day voyage from France had been largely uneventful. The crossing had been calm with favourable winds and our band had been content to sit up on deck watching the seagulls playing on the breeze, imagining all manner of castles and monsters in the grey clouds which hung ominously in the sky, threatening but never quite producing the storm which had been predicted by Henry's advisors. We were on the same ship as Henry, who spent most of his time below deck writing letters and talking politics. His uncle Jasper spent time with us, leaning on the gunwales, talking, seeking our opinion on matters, some would say, appraising our loyalty to the cause, or was he just getting to know his men. I had met a leader of men such as this before.

Henry himself stayed below deck. Gwyn went below to talk with him, reporting to us that his pupil was now a man with an idea to end the wars between the great houses of York and Lancaster. He was a Lancastrian, but sworn to marry a daughter of York, though he had never met the girl, Elizabeth of York, the daughter of Edward IV and Elizabeth Woodville. She was a princess who had lived all her life in a time of war and knew well how to survive amongst the duplicitous courtiers and politicians of the day. Henry himself had been protected from this lion's den by his mother, who had sent him out of danger to live in France. Elizabeth of York was also the daughter of the Woodville Queen who, whilst a patron of many good causes was also thought by many to be a witch. The challenger for the crown of England who kept to himself below decks was an inexperienced twenty-nine-year-old indeed.

For now, we anchored in the sheltered bay, waiting for the tide to allow us to get to shore. Men played games of pitch penny on deck to while away the time, gambling away their meagre wages. Tempers became frayed. There was the occasional fight, a punch or two thrown and the aggressor restrained by his friends, order being restored with a drink or an apology.

Frankie had become bored with the waiting. He was never one to relish inactivity. I saw his blonde head leaning over the rail of the after deck by the ship's wheel, looking down onto the men gambling below. His face was lost in study, his eyebrow cocked in surprise and question at what he was seeing. I saw him whisper to one of Gwyn's archers, the whisper was passed along the line of men and fell on the ears of Edward Courtenay one of Henry's chief confidantes who was playing cards against Clarence de Bone and Taliesin Bowen. Clarence was cheating, Frankie had spotted it. The men were playing the French game, 'Glic.'

Edward Courtenay was losing and had been chasing his losses for several hours. With remarkable sleight of hand Clarence was concealing trump cards in the wide sleeves of his tunic. He was known to be a cheat, he had been called out for it before. There was tension and trouble in the air.

The men were playing standing around a water barrel, using its top as their card table. As I watched, I saw ap Thomas take half a step back, with his hand of cards in one hand, then he loosened his knife in his belt under the pretext of scratching his non-existent belly under the rough cloth of his shirt.

Clarence dealt the cards in lots of four, twelve to each player and, as he placed the remaining eight cards of the pack in the centre of the playing surface, he replaced the top card with one of his own choosing. Swift as a striking snake, the dagger was drawn and in a downward motion pinned Clarence's tunic sleeve to the barrel's lid, piercing the stack of cards as it did so. Inserting his hand into the offending sleeve, ap Thomas produced half a dozen cards, all high ranking potentially master cards. He proceeded to punch Clarence several times in the face, he still having his sleeve well pinned to the wooden surface. Nose broken and eyes blackened, and his purse of ill-gotten gains removed from his person, Rhys ap Thomas released Clarence to face his comrades who were now roundly mocking him. However, things were drawn to a sudden close by unexpected events.

The wind suddenly picked up from the west, the loose end of a sail flapped wildly in an attempt to break free of its bonds. Charlie who had been idly talking with Frankie was struck in the back by the heavy canvas, staggering forward at the same time as the ship lurched into the swell. When the heave of the ship steadied, Charlie was not there.

'Man, o'er board!' the cry went up. All hands looked over the side expecting to see Charlie's head bobbing in the now calm blue waters of the bay, but there was no sign of him, only the swift silver humps of a school of dolphins swimming by. We watched the water until the tide and the nervous French sailors forced us to disembark for the shore. There was nothing we could do. Charlie had gone, and we had orders to march. In shock we prayed for his soul. We continued our watch from the beach where we landed, hoping and praying we would see him washed up alive by the surf. We did not. Mustered into ranks, we began the march inland, leaving Charlie to his fate.

With his feet finally back on the soil of his birth, Henry knelt and kissed the ground, looking to the heavens and reciting from psalm forty-three, 'Judge me, oh Lord, and favour my cause.' He created eight of his men, including Edward Courtenay, knights on the beach as they disembarked. As he left the sands of the beach at Angle and led his men up the steep winding path towards Dale, his uncle Jasper, the man who had been father to him for so many of his twenty-nine years placed a great paw of a hand on his shoulder.

'It must be good to be home, Harri.'

'Uncle, Souscinio is more home to me than here. I have not felt the shores of Wales since I was a boy.'

'Harri, to these people you must be Y Mab Ddarogan, the leader who was prophesied. You must inspire them to follow you!'

'Uncle, I will do what I must. Whatever happens, there will be a battle at the end of our road, Richard will see to that!'

He pushed his long brown hair from his face, turning into the stiff sea breeze, steel blue eyes staring out to sea, watching the ships of his small French armada depart, for as soon as the last soldier had left his ship, the nervous French sailors could be seen lifting their anchors and making sail away from the shore. They feared the reception they might have if they ventured ashore. There was chance now of a change of plan, Henry was committed to his course of action, there was no going back.

The bards of Wales sang in prophecy that he would be the King born in Wales who would cross the sea to free them from the tyranny of the Saxons. The bards predicted a victory.

'When the bull comes from the far land to battle with his great ashen spear, to be an earl again in the land of Llewelyn,

*let the far-splitting spear shed the blood of the Saxon on the stubble . . .
When the long yellow summer comes and victory comes to us
and the spreading sails of Brittany,
and when the heat comes and when the fever is kindled,
there are portents that victory will be given to us.'*

In their strange bardic tongues this is what they had foreseen.

This army now committed to taking the throne of England, for now a Lancastrian King marched across Wales gathering men and arms as they went. Bolstered by men sworn by his mother's husband Lord Stanley, Henry and his uncle Jasper Tudor marched towards London.

The contingent of archers led by Gwyn Meredith numbered some two hundred. The ranks of marching men brought back memories of the march to Crécy all those years ago, those we had lost and those who had survived and returned to their homes, those men that Lady Margaret now mustered to fight for her son.

Henry had not been idle in the months before we left France. His messengers had been left busy with letters written to the loyal Welsh Lords, amongst them John ap Maredudd. In his own hand the future King requested help from his countryman.

'Right trusty and well beloved, we greet you well.

And where it is so that through the help of Almighty God, the assistance of our loving friends and true subjects, and the great confidence that we have to the nobles and commons of this our principality of Wales, we be entered into the same purposing by the help above rehearsed in all haste possible to descend into our realm of England not only for the adoption of the crown unto us of right appertaining, but also for the oppression of that odious tyrant Richard late duke of Gloucester, usurper of our said right.

And moreover, to reduce as well our said realm of England into his ancient estate, honour, and prosperity, as this our said principality of Wales, and the people of the same to their erst liberties, delivering them of such miserable servitudes as they have piteously long stood in.

We desire and pray you and upon your allegiance straitly charge and command you that immediately upon the sight hereof, with all such power as ye may make defensibly arrayed for the war, ye address you towards us without any tarrying upon the way, unto such time as ye be with us wheresoever we shall be to our aid for the effect above rehearsed, wherein ye shall cause us in time to come to be your singular good lord and that ye fail not hereof as ye will avoid our grievous displeasure and answer unto at your peril.

Given under our signet...H

Such a letter, were it to fall into the wrong hands, would indeed be advance warning of an attempt to take the Crown. Messengers are easily intercepted and by the time we landed at Milford Sound, word had been received that Richard had been busy assembling his own army. As we had sailed west along the coast towards Pembroke, we had seen the beacons being lit, Richard's advance notice that the attack on his Crown which he had anticipated was about to take place.

Messengers rode with great haste to the fortress at Nottingham where Richard had made his headquarters, a fortress in his northern homeland and central to the country to swiftly attack an invading army from whichever direction it came.

The north was also the homelands of the Stanleys, a vastly wealthy and influential family capable of arraying a large number of fighting men, which both Thomas and William Stanley had done on the order of their King. But the Stanleys also had connections to Henry. Thomas Stanley had married Henry's mother Lady Margaret Beaufort, a political move on her part. Richard was not ignorant of the danger which that posed. When Lord Stanley had travelled north, Richard had taken the precaution of detaining his eldest son Lord George Strange and holding him hostage against the loyalty of his father. The King of England was prepared for war.

Henry and his army had already taken the castle at Dale and were gathering men as they went. Y Mab Ddarogen was a powerful message, and the sign of the dragon a powerful symbol.

CHAPTER 55. MODERN WEAPONS - Ralph

Pembroke.
7th August 1485.

'Where are we?' muttered Jack, 'you've got a lot to answer for, Ralph Owen. It's all very well lying low from the British army in France but who the hell are this lot? We seem to have arrived in a different century! It's all very fine for you, you can walk through walls!'

'Looks a bit like West Wales,' replied Frankie. 'I came on holiday here once, Tenby, but one of those guys with the longbow says we're in 1485 and we've allegiance to Henry! Who the hell is Henry?'

I reassured them that we had nothing too much to worry about. We had marched the short distance inland from the coast and were camped in woodland a short distance from the Castle at Pembroke. Our reception had been mixed. The Welsh were a people whose loyalties were split between loyalty to Richard III as their King and whose spies were everywhere, and to Jasper Tudor who had been their Lord and who was of Welsh stock. As the campaign progressed, our number had grown by several hundred men. Weapons had been gathered. Those men who had their own brought them and there was a small cache of arms brought from the armoury of the Duke of Brittany. The army had settled down for the night around their various campfires. Frankie was exploring the possibilities held in one of the wooden chests of assorted weapons, pulling out a rough array of blades and blunt instruments, most of which had not seen the light of day for a great many years.

'What in the name of God is this?' Frankie examined a rudely constructed item made of iron and wood.

'That,' replied Jack, 'is a hand cannon. That, Frankie is the nearest thing our hosts have to a rifle.'

'It's too small to be a bloody musket, and it's too big to be a bloody pistol,' Frankie cursed roundly. 'I can hardly lift the damn thing.'

The item in question looked like a small iron cannon banded onto a wooden handle, roughly crafted to be held in the user's hand, the long handle to be pinioned under the user's arm. It came with a supply of black powder, a substance at least Gwyn and I were familiar with, and a small bag full of roughly spherical lead balls.

'I'd be better off hitting some bastard over the head with it!' Frankie grumbled on. 'It's more likely to kill me than anyone else, it's filthy, and it's rusty, it'll blow itself apart!'

'Well, that's what we have, unless you fancy a go at firing one of those.' Jack pointed to the huge cumbersome cannon being dragged on its rickety wheels by a team of ten men. 'And before you say, 'yes,' I have no intention of helpin' ye tae drag the damn thing, Frank Baker.'

'Is there nothing else?' Frankie cocked an eyebrow. 'Can Ralph not conjure up a few proper rifles, eh?'

'And get us all burned for witchcraft? They burn men as well, ye ken! I suppose you could try your hand with a longbow, or a sword.'

Jack sighed and paced slowly to the other side of our campfire where Gwyn was sharpening such a weapon. Its blade gleamed blue in the firelight, its edge sharpened many times, but the tracery in the folds of the steel still visible, random patterns made as a master craftsman had heated and folded the metal repeatedly, eliminating any flaws, and as the layers of metal welded together formed the appearance of creepers or maybe serpents in the surface of the steel. Its handle was bound in soft leather, once the purple of Scottish thistles but blackened with the palm sweat of ages, and the basket hilt was woven of metal formed into thistle stems, entwined to protect the hand which wielded the blade.

'A thing o' Scottish beauty, ay.' Jack commented to the huge Welshman who caressed the edge of the blade with an equally worn whetstone.

'That she is, and I'll not be parted from her. She was given to my father after Bannockburn, he said, by a Scottish noble for services rendered against the English. We've been together a long time. She's shared my bed in lieu of a woman for many a year now.' He seemed lost in the rhythmic scrape of stone on metal, mind far away, lost in another time.

Jack paced on, he was restless, another two silent circuits of the fire and he came and sat next to me on a large fallen log.

Eventually he spoke. 'I'd feel better if Red were with us. How long do you think they will keep her at Pembroke?'

'I fear she will be there until this whole matter is resolved the old witch Margaret needs her. Tell me, Jack, how much do ye know of yer wife's family?'

'Only what her sister has told me. Helena, you know Helena?' Jack replied. 'Annie,' he called her by her pet name 'is tight lipped about it. Until now she hadn't spoken to her mother for years, since their father died.'

'What, pray, has Helena told you?' I stretched out my legs before the fire, interested to know how Helena spoke of her mother.

'Helena will not speak of her mother, but she speaks highly of her father. She told me he was an apothecary of sorts who sold drugs and made perfumes from plants he grew in a big glass house, by all accounts a flamboyant character. She wants nothing more than to follow in his footsteps, but I gather that she and Annie did not have the same father.'

'No indeed they did not.' I stretched my back and scratched an itch between my shoulders through my leather jerkin, rubbing the spot on a hard knobbly lump of tree bark.

'Tell me more, man, ye must ken the family well.' Jack was curious. Was it time to tell him what he had married into, the danger it might cause for his wife and daughter who were at least safe now, in their own time.

'All I know, Jack, is that Rhianydd's mother Sibyl, or Red as we call her, is a great healer. She also has certain gifts which are of use to the Lady Beaufort. As long as that lady has a use for her, we will be treated well and allowed to live. Once that use is over, who knows. Be prepared to make an escape. You and Frankie. Do not worry about Gwyn, he will look after himself.'

'And you, Ralph, where do you fit in, you and Red, are ye sweet on my mother-in-law man, I see how ye look at her?' Jack was more observant than I thought, but it was not yet time to tell him all.

'Red and I have known each other many years. She has stitched many of my wounds and been the cause of many of my scars.' I thought this would end the conversation, but Jack continued.

'How is it that she can walk through time as she does, and I know it was her that found us in France, is she a seer?'

'Of sorts,' I chose my words carefully, 'but not one who will tell yer fortune or predict your future.' I took a breath in and looking Jack MacGregor straight in his very direct brown eyes I asked him, 'Jack, do ye believe in Faeries?'

There was silence for about five seconds, punctuated by the metallic whoosh of Gwyn now honing his knife.

Then the whole of our camp was sent into chaos by an explosion of thunderous proportions as Frankie plucked up the courage to fire his chosen weapon. In a cloud of black powder, and a stench of sulphur and burnt wadding he emerged into the clearing by the fire, his white, blonde hair blackened by smoke, his eyes red like a distressed ferret, shaking from head to foot. He threw the hand canon into the bushes announcing loudly,

'Fuck that for a game of soldiers! Gwyn, man, do you have a spare bow?'

I nearly fell off my log laughing, Jack could no longer swallow his mirth and we both descended into a fit of hardly suppressed giggles. Gwyn to his credit delved deep into his pack and from a rolled-up blanket pulled a hunting bow, made like a longbow but not so hard a pull, he said. 'It should do you well, Frankie, its last owner was a woman!'

We were further disturbed by the entrance of Jasper Tudor, accompanied by his nephew and, of all people, Sir Kenneth Fitzsimon. Sir Kenneth, ever curious, retrieved the hand cannon from the edge of the clearing. He examined it closely and then asked Frankie to pass him the powder and shot.

'I wouldn't risk it, sir,' Frankie advised as Sir Kenneth rammed the powder down the barrel and dropped the shot in after it. Finishing the job by ramming the wadding home, he walked off into the darkness with his companions, still carrying the offending object, disappearing down the track towards the castle to retrieve their horses and then no doubt to spend the night in comfort.

Gwyn was remembering another campfire in another land a lifetime ago. Shoulders still shaking he silently he gathered his weapons together rolled them in oil cloth, spread his bed roll by the fire and announced, 'I'm for sleep.' Before anyone could comment further had assumed a state of unconsciousness, laid out like a knight on a tomb, hands crossed on his chest, the rise and fall of which was the only sign that he was alive.

One by one they all settled for the night, curled up in gently snoring heaps. I pulled my cloak around my shoulders and went in search of my Red Maid. Captivity would not suit her, I hoped she would be wise and take the hospitality offered, rather than fight and be chained in a dungeon. I would do my best to keep her safe, and these men would not miss me until dawn.

I found her in the Tower Room, Margaret's private lair. I sensed she was uneasy. She paced the room, picking up books and turning a page here and there, reading the labels of the bottles and jars on the shelves. She had not touched the food that had been brought to her. Fresh bread and cooked meat and a jug of red wine from France stood undisturbed on the table. A warm fur cloak was laid on the dresser to keep a body warm against the night air. I could not spirit her away from this, or could I? Maybe there was a bargain to be made.

Henry her son was amongst the men, walking the campfires with his Uncle Jasper. What if some misfortune should befall him? He would need a healer. In an hour or so they would return to the castle for the night. The man who was about to steal the crown of England would not be safe sleeping in the forest, not when there were stone walls nearby to protect him.

I was still hidden in the shadow of the tower wall when the spark of horse's shoes galloping on the cobbles leading to the great gate jerked me from my thoughts. Three horses approached, ridden at breakneck speed three abreast, the middle horse controlled by the riders of the other two. I recognised that horse, and the rider. Sir Kenneth Fitzsimon. The rider was slumped forward over the saddle bow.

There was a commotion at the gatehouse as men struggled to open the gate to admit the party. I heard the words, 'wound, shot and mother' uttered in the same breath and recognised another of the riders as Henry himself. The third must be Jasper Tudor. The wounded man was important indeed, he was Lady Margaret's confidante, and some said her lover for many years.

Kenneth was pulled gently from his horse onto a hurdle and carried into the main building, headed no doubt for her ladyship's private rooms. Maybe providence had taken a hand. I was still hidden in the recess when a tug at my elbow pulled me further into the darkness.

'Father!' It was Calon's voice. 'I came through the woods. Sir Kenneth is shot. They fear him mortally wounded.'

'Where?' I asked.

'In the camp.' came the reply.

'No, fool, where on his body?' I was growing impatient.

'In his chest, the ball is lodged high in his shoulder, but has pierced his chest.' Calon elaborated. 'They were walking through the camp, back to the horses. They had just passed the time with our men and Sir Kenneth and Henry strayed off the path to take a piss. Then he bent and picked up something from the floor, there was a bang, and the thing exploded in his hand.'

'How the..... ', I began, then stopped. 'You must go back. I will remain here. You stay with the men, be mindful they do not get blamed for this.'

Sir Kenneth had been taken into an ante-room behind the great hall. The door was closed, but I crept in on the tail of a servant hurriedly carrying hot water and good brandy to the scene. Lady Margaret had taken charge of matters. Her orders were swift and brooked no argument.

Sir Kenneth's fine clothes were cut from his upper body to reveal a wound halfway up his rib cage on the right, a single wound which must run upwards through his chest for there just below his collar bone was a suspicious looking lump where the ball was lodged.

'Do not burn his clothing!' Margaret barked at the young page about the dispose of the offending items on the fire. 'Spread them out, over there!' She walked to the side table where the page was frantically doing her bidding. Calmly and quietly, she spoke to him. 'Do this thing slowly and carefully, lad, we need to find the hole.'

Sir Kenneth had been wearing a thick leather jerkin covered by an outer coat of fine cloth, and under it a linen shirt. The coat was worn open and was undamaged. There was a hole punched in the leather of the jerkin, but when examined, there proved to be no leather missing, the lead ball had pushed its way through. The shirt however was missing a roughly circular piece of the fine linen, the edges torn roughly where the projectile had burned through. Lady Margaret uttered a few curse words, then returned to the patient. He was still breathing. His breath could be heard sucking and gurgling in and out, shallow, and painful. His face was drawn and pale.

She leaned close to his face to listen, as he uttered two words.

'Fetch Red!'

Margaret stood back as if scalded. She turned her back to the table, conflicted. Would she put her prisoner in her debt forever, or would she allow the man she had loved since childhood to die a painful death? Decision made, she swept from the room in a swirl of robes, heading for the tower room. She returned minutes later dragging Red by a set of leather manacles. Red staggered into the room, struggling, and resisting all the way, then seeing who her patient was, she stopped and held her hands out towards her jailer.

'I can do nothing while I am tied like this.' she hissed at Margaret through clenched teeth. 'Will your spells not heal him, Witch?'

'You speak to the Lady Beaufort now, and you'd best remember that.'

So, the future king's mother was careful to keep her dark arts and her true self well-hidden for the present.

'We have little time. If we do not act, he will die,' Red interrupted her, thrusting the leather manacles towards Margaret's face.

A young man stepped across the room and pulling a knife from his belt, cut the leather binding Reds hands. Henry Tudor spoke. 'Madam what do you need to heal him. If it is in my power, I will find it.'

Red spoke quickly and quietly. 'Send a man to our camp, find a soldier of our party called Ralph Owen, ask him for the Red Maid's pack.'

A rider was dispatched, and I followed. I was, after all, the man they sought.

Red continued her assessment of the situation.

'I will need boiling water,' she demanded, 'not just hot, it must be boiling, and then cooled.' Two lads were dispatched to the kitchen, returning with a cauldron of hot water from the kitchen's water which they set to boil on the fire in the anteroom.

'Lady Margaret, have you any laudanum?' Red knew she had, she had seen it on her shelves along with other useful herbs and potions. 'And alcohol, rough alcohol, the stuff the soldiers brew themselves.'
Then Red set about examining the wound.

If Sir Kenneth was lucky the ball had travelled upwards inside his chest and had taken the lump of cloth with it. Removal of the ball was the easy bit, plugging the hole in Sir Kenneth's chest was the hard. In her haste, Margaret had made matters worse. The expensive leather of Sir Kenneth's jerkin had been tight against the entry wound. It had sucked into the hole forming a second skin. God bless the young page who had not removed it, not wishing to cause his master pain. Far above what any treatment I could give, the boy had probably unknowingly saved his life.

I returned with the encampment with the messenger and the requested pack, I watched on as Red threw her sharp knives and retractor into the boiling water. Lady Margaret poured a copious quantity of laudanum down Kenneth's throat, and they waited for it to take effect.

'Linen, I will need clean linen and a square of soft leather. I must let the air out of his chest so that the lung can come up, else it will remain collapsed, and he will die.' ordered Red, then walked across to the side table, and cut a good square of soft leather from the back of the jerkin, the least worn place with the cleanest leather. She would need a patch for the exit wound to work like a valve if he was still breathing when finished. Where had she learned this miraculous medicine? She was a healer indeed!

Margaret supervised the ripping of her bed sheets into wide strips. Several she left dry. The rest were boiled, clean though they were from the laundry.

The patient in an opium induced sleep, Red picked up the sharpest of her knives, and pressing the skin taught over the lump made by the lead shot, she made her cut. She felt the blade grate on the surface of the lead, then passed her slender fingers beneath the hard ball and squeezed. Slowly the hard black object emerged from the wound. There was no cloth attached.

She released the pressure on the wound and holding the mouth open with the retractor inserted the probe. She would use it to widen the passage. As Sir Kenneth breathed slowly under the influence of the laudanum she could hear air escaping through the wound from the inside of his chest.

'Light!' she demanded. A candle appeared. It would have to do. I focused all my mind to her eyes and there within reach, was that a few strands of thread? Red picked up the long-pointed forceps and took hold of what all watching prayed was thread, she pulled slowly and gently, and gradually a small blood-soaked ball of cloth appeared, blocking for a moment the rush of air outwards through the exit wound.

Red paused for a second, I was sure I heard Rhianydd's voice ghostly over her shoulder whisper, 'Think! Take time! Think!' Then, before she withdrew the plug from the wound, she had ready a patch of softened boiled leather. She placed it over the hole. 'Now,' she spoke, 'bring me the small roll of canvas from my pack. It contains stitching made from animal gut and curved needles of whalebone!' Red deftly passed a length of stitch through a tiny hole in the end of the whalebone needle and secured the leather patch to Sir Kenneth's skin allowing one edge to remain free. Then, as the knight breathed in the leather rested firmly on the flat skin. When he breathed out the flap gently rose allowing air to leak from his chest. By now the company looking on were dumbstruck. They appeared to have been watching a miracle.

Red handed the tiny ball of cloth to Margaret while she lightly dressed Sir Kenneth's wounds and watched as she uncurled the small mass and spread it out. 'Yes!,' she whispered. They had it all.

'Now we must pray,' Red whispered to her, 'to any god you like, for his fate lies with them now, I have done all I can. I will wait with him.'

'When he awakes,' Red continued, 'he will suffer with a fever for three days. If it subsides, he will recover, but it will take maybe a month. I will make a tincture of bark of cinchona, a tree from a far-off land. It will aid the pain and the fever.'

Cinchona bark, my mind flitted back to another flight, in another time, medication for another knight, maybe a prince struck down with fever.

I saw Red's lips twitch in half a smile, she too remembering.

'Thank you.' she replied, words I never thought to hear from a woman as corrupt as she. 'If he lives, I am truly in your dept.'

She left the room along with an entourage of attendants, leaving Red alone in a room with the two other men, Henry and his uncle Jasper and another who stood invisible to all but her. I stretched my legs by the fire, a glass of the good brandy in my hand and another on the mantel shelf. Red stepped across and took the glass. As I took my first sip, they seemed to ask in chorus, 'Will he live?'

It was a long night, Sir Kenneth roused from the laudanum after a few hours, then he lay on the huge oak table in the warmth of the fire, covered as much as possible in warm furs and his chest rising and falling in a worryingly shallow fashion.

His left lung was unaffected, but Red was fearful that his right lung would collapse, a sure thing if air intruded into the space around it. There was little or no bleeding from either wound. This was a good thing. He did not cough and Red encouraged him to breathe deeply. As the hours ticked by, all became more hopeful. Staving off a longstanding fever and purulence would be down to a small miracle. The ball Red had removed was a misshapen and dirty piece of lead. But the heat of its passage might, with luck, have cauterised some of the bleeding on its journey.

Sir Kenneth's incapacity could not be allowed to hinder Henry's campaign and at dawn the following day the army marched on. Henry and Jasper remained at Pembroke. Henry had awaited reply to letters written to his Welsh kin asking for their aid and assistance, and Jasper to accompany him and also bid his farewells to Sir Kenneth who he believed he may not see alive again.

I had heard Jasper tell his messenger, my son Calon, that he and Henry would re-join them at the fifth milestone. One day's march away.

CHAPTER 56. THE MARCH NORTH - Eryr

At Dale there was no sign of the men expected from the house of Rhys ap Thomas. Neither was there any sign of ap Thomas himself. Henry could not be sure if the man had received the dispatched commission of array asking for his support, and his fighting men. In the end we would not see ap Thomas for nigh on a week or know into which ring he had thrown his hat, for Richard had also sent similar letters, his bearing the seal of a King, not just the signet of one intent on taking the throne.

Unable to free Red from her bondage at Pembroke, I rejoined camp five miles outside Haverford West at the milestone. Jasper Tudor, Henry himself and their small entourage, apart from Sir Kenneth, joined us just before we marched out on the morning of August 8th.

I had heard the discussions between Jasper and his nephew. They were convinced that we needed to progress north as there was word that King Richard had already assembled a great army and, in a move to bolster the numbers of his men, had sent out further commissions of array.

Maybe Rhys ap Thomas and other of the Welsh Lords had opted to defer to the King's threats which commanded them to assemble their fighting men to fight for him on pain of forfeiture of their lands and their wealth. Many would comply with these orders for fear of the consequences, despite where their allegiances truly lay. They would fight with their heads and not with their hearts.

Henry sent out his own commissions of array, his having only the benefit of his signet, and promises of a better life for the Welsh under his governance and promises of rewards for the faithful - the carrot rather than the stick. Messengers including Calon had taken them, Calon dispatched to the far north, to the lands of John ap Maredudd, to deliver a reinforcement of the letter dispatched from Brittany some months earlier.

At the five-mile stone, we were joined by Gruffydd Rede of Carmarthen and his men, and also by John Morgan of Tredegar. They arrived at dead of night when the assembled men were camped around the picket fires. This caused much commotion amongst the guard, who stood all the available men to, fully armed and anticipating an attack, but finding only allies in the darkness. I found Jack and Frankie warming their hands at such a fire accompanied by Gwyn, Tally and Clarence - Jack and Frankie hastily becoming accustomed to a new way of life, for the present.

The progress of an ever-swelling number of fighting men and equipment through the often-difficult terrain of southwest Wales proved slow. The ground is rocky and hilly and devoid of any roads save for narrow farm tracks and footpaths.

Calon, the swiftest of messengers and an effective scout, would report back that King Richard had received news of our landing within four days of our ships being sighted. Richard, thinking that Henry would land on the south coast had posted lookouts and ordered beacons built. The message had soon travelled west, and the constable of Pembroke castle had himself ridden to Nottingham with the news, covering the two hundred miles in only four days. In those four days we had covered far less distance and were encamped at Llwyn Dafydd Hall just short of St Dogmaels, in a position to enter Cardigan on the following day. While Richard's messenger had covered the length of half the country, we had progressed less than half that distance.

Our company of men was at least, disciplined. Henry had been insistent. On previous campaigns the Lancastrian troops had developed a reputation for delinquent behaviour and drunkenness. He had sent word with all his commanders that his soldiers would be of good conduct. They would pay proper price for anything they obtained over and above that provided by Henry's harbinger, who was in charge of finding food and lodging for the men. So, in a mostly orderly fashion we made our slow progress north.

The decision to cross the Severn into England through a town in the north was made after long consideration. The crossings of the Severn further south were guarded by potentially hostile forces. Rather than face early resistance, at best a skirmish and at worst a fully-fledged battle, Henry sent word to his mother asking about the position and having received the reply he decided to cross into England near Shrewsbury.

At Haverford West we had been warmly welcomed and joined by Arnold Butler, a comrade from Brittany who had returned to Wales and who Henry had not seen in many years. Butler had gladly sent his fighting men to further the cause and swell the numbers of the army. If he were with Henry, surely ap Thomas would be as well. The loyalties of Rhys ap Thomas weighed heavy on Henry's mind. Scouts had been sent out and had sighted ap Thomas still on his own lands near Carmarthen, but no one seemed to know of his intentions. With known potential allies in the Stanleys to the north, who were after all his in laws, the decision to travel north over the Preseli hills was made.

Henry had also commanded that the French mercenaries march as a separate unit. As soon as they had disembarked from the ships, he, and his advisors, Philibert Chandee and the Earl of Oxford, John de Vere, could all see that the soldiers the noble Duke of Brittany had sent were inexperienced men, nervous of a strange land where the assembling men did not even speak English. They were badly armed and poorly trained and regarded the Welsh as barbarians. Chandee and de Vere did not want doubt of any form spreading amongst the men.

Our numbers grew daily, word spreading to even the most remote farms and cottages that Henry was for Wales, that he would be a fair ruler and relieve his people of the hardships imposed by English repression. Men and boys joined us at every crossroads.

Henry's army had no formal regiments, those men not attached to one of their Lordships fell in where they could. Armed with any weapon they could find, pitchforks, axes, pike staffs and the occasional sword, an inherited remnant from a grandfather, or an uncle too old to fight. There were longbowmen whose arms had not drawn a bowstring in anger for many years, but still practiced each Sunday out of habit, still more deadly than their English counterparts. At the end of every day's march, I watched with some satisfaction as Gwyn began to put the old soldiers, and Frankie, through their paces, though Frankie would never have the inherent strength in his arms to draw a longbow.

At night we made camp in the fields outside of a village or small town. Men hunted and foraged to pad out what the army provided, and we sat peaceably around our campfires entertaining ourselves with songs and stories, sleeping rough and waking early to face another day's march over ground more suited to goats than men. With spirits buoyed up by the rest at the five miles stone, on August 9th. 1485 Henry led us into the next part of the journey.

The Preseli hills are bleak and cold even in August, there is little cover or protection from the winds off the Irish Sea. The cold grey mist rolls in low over the hill tops and does not clear often until after noon. There were no roads, not even proper cart tracks. Those men fortunate enough to have horses or ponies were forced to dismount and walk. With each man carrying his own armour, provisions, and weapons and with few of the usual army camp followers and women to service the marching troops, the progress was hard and slow.

Marching up to thirty miles a day we passed through Bwlch y Gwynt, the windy pass, and south of Cilgerran where Henry and his lieutenants found shelter in a large farmhouse where the occupants were hospitable. For the rest of us, it was a bed on the mountain turf staring at the kestrels and kites which wheeled in the skies above us while we tried to shelter from the grey all penetrating damp of the mist off the Irish Sea.

The second day's march over and the Preseli Hills behind us, we camped by the river Nevern not far from the walled town of Cardigan. On the morning of the following day, we covered fourteen miles to Ffynonddewi where we rested and drank from the well of fresh water, water straight from the rocks beneath the hills over which we marched. Thirsts slaked, we marched on, covering a further twenty miles to Llandysiliogogo. Henry now seemed in great haste to leave Wales behind him.

Our next day's march took us to Aberystwyth, a stronghold of loyal supporters of King Richard. This was the first real resistance the army had encountered. Other garrisoned castles in the area had either surrendered without much fight or were loyal to the Tudor cause.

Messengers and Scouts had by now sighted Rhys ap Thomas, also making his way north, up the spine of the Welsh mountains, still not committed to Henry's cause, but not obviously declared for King Richard. Of King Richard's main loyal supporter in Wales, Walter Herbert, there was no sign.

Just outside Aberystwyth, I was summoned to Henry's presence.

'Take your men, and what arms you need, I have been told they are well trained and can keep themselves out of sight. I need word on the strength of the garrison at the castle at Aberystwyth.'

I gathered Jack, Frankie, and Gwyn, along with Taliesin Bowen, Clarence de Bone, and several of our archers. Before we could move out, Calon was at my elbow.

'Father, I have been to the castle. The garrison is weak, mostly old men. Lord Ferrers is fiercely loyal to his King, but he is absent, and his men will not fight without his command. The castle is weak, they have not affected repairs since the days of Glyndwr, it is an easy and a soft target.'

We moved on the fortress under cover of darkness. We saw not a soul. The great door opened at a push, creaking on its hinges to announce our arrival. No guard challenged us, no pikeman asked who came. We found six old soldiers of the garrison sleeping in their cups in their refectory. Roused to wakefulness by several buckets of icy water, they informed us that they had no loyalty to a king who left them in poverty and to, 'Come in and be welcome.' I bid Tally tie them up and gag them for shame's sake. Then I sent Calon with word to Henry.

'Tell my Lord that the castle is easily taken!' I jested, not thinking that Calon would relay the message exactly as it had been said. No matter, a little self-publicity would not do our party any harm.

On 13th August, Henry left Aberystwyth, marching the twenty-three miles across the Dyfi river to Machynlleth, still wary of rumours that Rhys ap Thomas still sided with the King and watchful for attack.

That night, together with Henry and his lieutenants, I spent the night at the house of Dafydd Llwyd. Llwyd was known as a poet, a mystic, and a man of prophecy. I raised an eyebrow at this, for he was not of my blood, but Henry listened to his poetry and was well entertained for the evening. Engrossed in his words, he asked the man to prophecy for him.

Dafydd Llwyd was no fool. He wisely told the Tudor Earl that he would need to sleep on his thoughts and would speak on the morrow. In the dead of night while all slept by the poet's fire, I heard him in his kitchen in conversation with his wife. The good lady gave good advice and told him, in words only he might hear,

'The man may one day be King. Tell him this is so, and he may reward us. If he does not become King then he will surely die, and then it will not matter.' Welsh women have a reputation for their shrewd minds, the wife of Dafydd Llwyd was no exception.

Over breakfast, the poet confidently predicted victory for the Tudor cause. Henry went on his way, lighter of heart and a happier man, his usually dour countenance for once smiling on all around him, and his steely blue eyes sparkling like the sun on the water of Carmarthen Bay, with the dolphins laughing behind them.

On this heartwarming day, as we marched cross country and away from the roads, Calon brought news from Rhys ap Thomas. He had accepted Henry's offer of the title of the Lieutenant of Wales for life in return for his support. Rhys ap Thomas and his men had committed, albeit at a price. It was a day when all had come right. The gods were indeed smiling on Henry Tudor.

It was two day's hard march into the mountains. We marched on through Newtown, not stopping for rest, through Bwlch y Fedwen and on to Castle Caereinion. Only the pitch darkness of the night prevented Henry from forging on eastwards towards England. It had been a cripplingly exhausting thirty-mile march through relentless mountains. Men were bone tired and hungry when, the following day, we arrived above Welshpool and the English border on the huge undulating mountain top of Cefn Digoll. The Long Mountain.

This border crossing from Wales into England was where, centuries before, the rulers of Gwynedd had fought the battle of Long Mynd and lost control of the stronghold of Gwynedd to the Northumbrian King Edwin. The Welsh, allied with the Mercians, would have their revenge at the Battle of Hatfield Chase some three years later, when Edwin met his death in a boggy field just outside Doncaster.

Such were the tales told that night, tales of battles won and lost hundreds of years earlier, but still remembered, the finer details often elaborated over time and told with enthusiasm as is the Welsh way.

We were joined by the men of Rhys ap Thomas, wearier and more footsore even than us. They had marched hard through the mountains of mid Wales, via Llandovery and Brecon. Their leader now decided to fight with the Tudor cause, against the King.

To make Henry's joy complete, more and more well-equipped men joined his cause, men from the local land holders, the farmers themselves bringing provisions of cattle and sheep to feed the army now assembled on the mountaintop overlooking England. As a reward for our action at Aberystwyth, Jasper Tudor informed me that we had been selected to form part of Henry's personal bodyguard.

That required me to requisition horses. Frankie would not be best pleased. Jack was a fair horseman, and Gwyn would rather walk. I bargained amongst the men and camp followers of Rhys ap Thomas for what we needed, for he had brought with him over two thousand fighting men all well mounted and armed, along with enough camp followers to form a rear guard. Indeed, he went so far as to send many of the women and children home.

My negotiations produced two spirited and stocky Welsh cobs for myself and Jack and an older, safer four-legged conveyance for Frankie, though he chose to lead the beast rather than ride it until we arrived at Shrewsbury.

Henry found the great gates of Shrewsbury closed to him. Thomas Mitton the town bailiff had been well paid for his loyalty to King Richard. He had been rewarded both with gold and a manorial title. Thomas Mitton had given good service to his King during the recent rebellion of the Duke of Buckingham and was not to be easily manoeuvred into allowing the Earl of Richmond and his army to pass through.

Rather than risk a confrontation, Henry decided that we should fall back as far as the village of Forton. That night, nearly ten thousand men with horses and equipment made camp on the heathland surrounding the village. Henry found lodgings at the house of Hugh Fortune.

On the morrow, the good Bailiff of Shrewsbury appeared to have had a change of heart. A messenger reported that the gates would be open and on assurances of their orderly behaviour, the army of the Earl of Richmond would be allowed to pass through. Evidently the Stanleys, who controlled much of the land in the surrounding area, had come into play. The arrival of Richard Corbett who was Thomas Stanley's son-in-law with another one thousand men to swell Henry's army may have influenced the decision to open the gates.

Rumour had it, though I did not see it myself, that Mitton, who had sworn to defend Shrewsbury to the death and to yield to Henry, 'over his dead body,' was last seen lying under the great portcullis allowing Henry's great horse to step over his prostrate form.

Suffice to say the townsfolk made us more than welcome and the bailiff was more than generous in his provisions for Henry's entourage, and also provided wages and expenses for a number of soldiers from the town who marched away with Henry's army.

Further information of the position of the King was provided by Henry's spies and messengers who had been sent out into the country to assess support and gather information on the deployment of Richard's troops. Jasper Tudor was no fool when it came to warfare and considered intelligence a necessary commodity, both the obtaining of accurate intelligence regarding the enemy and the spreading of false intelligence in regard of our own strength - or the lack of it.

Calon, being the best and most ethereal of agents, soon reported that while we were gaining access to the bridge at Shrewsbury, Richard had spent time at his hunting lodge just a few miles from Nottingham. On his return to Nottingham, he had received the news that Henry had been allowed to cross the Severn.

'Father, I have never seen a man in such a rage. He was white and shaking, his anger could be heard throughout the great castle. Truly father it was not safe to stay there and hear more!' Calon had laughed.

'What manner of man is King Richard then?' I had asked him. 'Is he a great warrior that he shouts so loudly. Is he as loud as your grandsire, my son?'

'Father, he is a man with a twisted spine, but he is a fine swordsman. He rides a horse as if he were born in the saddle and he is ruthless both in in battle and in his life. He is not a man to cross. You would not know that he is so deformed until you see him walk, for he shuffles slightly and has a pronounced limp. We should not take him lightly.'

'How many men has he, to fight his cause?' I asked my son.

'The streets of Nottingham are filled with his soldiers as are the taverns and whorehouses of the city. He has men sworn to him from all over the country. Some say he has command of at least fifteen thousand men if not more. I fear that despite all those gathered here we will be outnumbered, should it come to a pitched battle.'

'And it will Calon, it will.' The thought lay heavy with me all that night.

Calon disappeared as is his habit, invisible in the night and the day alike, passing unseen amongst the crowds and disturbing no one.

'I will find out more and I will return, were his parting words.'

We progressed towards Lichfield, now supposedly in country loyal to the King, yet we gathered more men. The five hundred well trained and fully armed soldiers of Lord Talbot swore to Henry's cause, but there was still no word on the intentions of William or Thomas Stanley. They would not pledge any more than friendship to The Earl of Richmond and seemed reluctant to commit themselves to either cause.

It was not hard for Richard's spies to report on our progress, or on the welcome which the Tudor Earl received from the clergy and dignitaries of the town. Lichfield, it seemed, was loyal at least to the Stanleys and Henry was welcomed, some said, as though he were the king himself. Could this be an indication that Lord Stanley, always the politician and always mindful of his best interests, was not yet decided on which camp he was in. He must, despite his apparent lack of concern for his son, have been mindful of the fact that George, Lord Strange, was held hostage pending his father's next moves.

Before dawn, Calon was back. He staggered exhausted and very drunk into our tent.

'Richard's army gathers to leave Nottingham, but he does not have the numbers of men he expected. The southern Lords have not had time to assemble men, they have brought only a fraction of the numbers they were commanded to array. Richard is not happy. But fifteen thousand is no small number. They march out this morning.'

I dressed in haste and rushed to pass the news to Jasper Tudor who in turn would inform Henry.

It is not easy to hide a great army, and Richard's men swept out of Nottingham with banners flying, Richard at their head, mounted on a great white charger. Behind him his nobles similarly mounted, then column after column of marching men, the more wealthy and the professional soldiers equipped with armour, the arrayed men with what they could gather together at short notice and armed with rudimentary weapons, some only adapted from the tools of their trade. Some of the wealthy were mounted, but they would not fight on horseback. The fighting would take place on foot.

Other spies and scurries reported that Richard's army had joined with that of the Earl of Norfolk at Leicester and that now we were outnumbered by two to one.

With Richard's army thus assembled on 20th August 1485 we made camp close to the castle at Tamworth, but Henry Tudor, Earl of Richmond was not with us. At some point during the days march he had gone missing.

CHAPTER 57. A KING IS MADE – Gwyn

John de Vere was beside himself. Jasper Tudor was incandescent with rage and worry. The main body of the Tudor army was encamped outside the walls of the castle at Tamworth. Henry's tents and those of his nobles were set up. A council of war was expected, a chance to talk tactics, decide on the disposition of men.

King Richard's army was on the move. Reports from the messengers, spies and scurriers told of an army of over twelve thousand men. However, there were several notable defectors from the Kings cause, of note: Brian Sandford, Simon Digby, and John Savage, known warriors who brought with them seasoned fighting men, men who expected to be welcomed to our cause by the Earl of Richmond himself.

Jasper and de Vere had searched the camp from the laundresses to the lords, from the pot washers to the privy and could not find Henry. His absence was indeed a matter for some concern, for he had told no one what he was about and was last seen riding alongside the men towards the rear of the column, passing the time of day and making himself known to the men. By mid-afternoon he was riding alongside the body of Welsh archers, one of whom was a familiar face.

'Gwyn ap Meredith, ride with me.' Henry Tudor reined his horse up alongside me as I marched in the main column with the archers.

'I have no horse, my lord, I will only hinder your progress.'

'I will find you a mount, I would speak with you, alone.' He turned and rode further down the column, returning with the stolid old conveyance Ralph had acquired for Frankie.

'Here, he's not much to look at, but he's sound, and he'll take your weight, man.'

I dropped out of line and mounted.

'What troubles you, my lord? I asked him. I could see the frown line of concern between his brows and the look of worry which haunted him.

'Come, let us ride alone for a while, I need to breathe, and I need space from all of this.' He gestured helplessly towards the lines of marching men. We rode away from the column and into the countryside, towards a small hamlet, a group of tiny cottages in the distance. Once out of hearing of the men, Henry answered.

'Gwyn, my friend, you have been with me since we fled to France. It was you who trained me in arms, and you along with my uncle who has taught me what little I know of command.' He paused. 'Gwyn, I am afraid. My uncle Jasper is set on a course. He is blinkered like a dray horse. He cannot see my fear. He thinks me as brave and as fine a soldier as he is, but he is mistaken.'

'Harri.' I called him by the name his uncle used. 'Harri, all men are afraid on the eve of battle, that is normal. If you were not, you would not be a man.'

'No, Gwyn, I am afraid I will not be man enough to be king. I am not afraid to die, I am afraid that I shall win, and then having won I will fail.'

We dismounted and walked, leading the horses further towards what proved to be a small roadside inn.

'Refreshment, Harri, something to damp the dust,' I suggested.

For once he was dressed in clothing more fitting to a soldier than nobility. I sat with this unremarkable looking young man that no-one recognised. Two lone soldiers, on their way to join an army. We sat outside in the sunshine and drank good ale brought by a serving girl who openly praised the army of Henry Tudor, who told how the people mistrusted Richard, who feared his rule, resented his ever-increasing taxes and who had heard that Henry Tudor was a good and fair man.

'You see, Harri, the people are for you, more and more of them side with you, have faith in yourself.'

I placed my hand on his arm where it rested on the table, stopping him from raising it and revealing his identity.

'Sit a while. Let us watch and listen, talk as we used to in Brittany, man to man, not soldier to his lord and future king.'

We sat. We drank several more mugs of ale. I paid from my own purse for Henry carried no coin with him. We watched. We saw men in ones and twos shouldering bundles of their weapons and asking the innkeeper, 'Which way to the Tudor cause?' making their way slowly towards the rear of the column of men we had just left.

'I fear I am unfit for command. I have never led men. I have not spilled a man's blood before. I have trained with a sword, but I am not the fighter that Richard is. Tell me Gwyn, what should I do?' Henry rested his head on his arms.

'It is true that Richard of York is a fine soldier. He is experienced in battle, but when the day of the battle comes, I will be there, Ralph will be there, and our men, we are there to protect you. Your uncle and the Lord de Vere and your other Generals, they will order the fighting. They will give the orders. And you will be victorious, as it was prophesied.' I reassured him.

'Gwyn ap Meredith, did you of all people believe that old fool's prophecy?'

Henry's blue eyes cleared, and he threw his head back and laughed. He laughed as if his sides would burst.

'Harri,' I said. 'Oh, Harri, no I did not believe in that prophecy, that was a platitude made up by an old man, to please a king. I believe the words of one who has knowledge of what will come. She is a prophetess who sees through time itself. She has seen your triumphal entrance through the gates of London!' I offered my own platitude, given with the benefit of Red's history.

'Is that so, is it she my mother holds captive at Pembroke? The healer you brought from France, she should be with us, but no matter, I know my mother values her beyond all else, and the Lord Stanley?' He changed the subject, moving away from his mother and her politics.

'The Lord Stanley will do what serves him best, as he has always done. He will hold off and wait until the last.' I assured him.

Darkness was falling. I was running out of silver, the horses were grazing still in their harness, hobbled in the field behind the inn. I counted what coin I had left.

'I have enough to get us some bread and meat, and another ale, and a rough sleep by the fire in the bar. Harri it is too late now to ride back to camp.'

'Then that is what we shall do. I need to clear my mind of thoughts, steel myself for what is to come, that is best done without the company of those who only seek to please me.'

We both rose from our bench and, while Henry made provision for the horses, I made arrangements for our accommodation.

Sitting by the fire inside the inn was a hooded figure clad in black, a spy, ears and eyes tuned to take note of every nuance of conversation around him. I pulled the hood from his head and lifted him bodily off his seat. I knew full well who I would find inside that black garb.

'Calon, my friend, go fetch your father, bring him here and swiftly, tell no one else, but I have need of him.'

Henry and I ate in silence. The chatter of the inn gradually became quieter. Wedged in corners, men settled down for the night, those who had wealth adjourning upstairs, maybe with one of the serving maids. As the great fire in the hearth popped and spat to itself, Henry gazed into its embers. I wondered what he could see. It was gone midnight when we were joined by Ralph. He came unseen and remained that way, though I knew that he was there, a majestic presence standing guard over the future king of England while the doubting boy who had sat down to drink ale with a soldier made peace with himself and slept under his cloak, legs curled up like a child on a hard bench, to wake up slightly hung over but with the mind of a man.

We left the inn before dawn on 20th August and before the cock crowed the day, we were within sight of Tamworth castle, and a very angry Jasper Tudor.

Anger soon turned to relief. Henry was fed breakfast, his welfare assured, and he was ushered away to be bathed and dressed in clean clothing and made presentable to welcome the defectors from King Richard's camp.

He resisted these attentions insisting that he could dress and feed himself, that they had no need to cosset him so. Even Uncle Jasper noticed the change in him. Overnight a steel had arrived in his manner, a determination in his face and the look of a King in his light blue eyes. Overnight, the boy had truly been left in a small little-known inn alongside the road just outside Tamworth.

Not before time, for the two armies were drawing ever closer to each other. And still there was no decision from Lord Stanley, or his brother.

CHAPTER 58. A SLEEPLESS NIGHT - Red

I was still held in the Castle at Pembroke. My work as a healer done, I was now confined to my rooms which were more like a dungeon. The Lady Margaret would keep me for her own purposes, so I thought.

Sir Kenneth Fitzsimon was making a slow recovery, his wound healing well, his great age the only thing hampering his return to fitness. He could no longer shake off the aches and pains caused by many old scars and war wounds, the stiffness in his joints no longer cleared with exercise. He walked supported by a stout staff. The distinguished old knight had become an old man.

I still medicated his aches and pains, but increasingly he brushed aside my attentions with a peremptory,

'You mean well, my dear, but it does no good. Not even you can cure old age, and I have been old for too long.'

Then he would walk another circuit of the courtyard nursing his back and his knees and sit on his bench in the sun until it set behind the west tower

I had been locked away for nearly two weeks when I was summoned by the witch. I was taken to her tower, taken there in manacles by my two female guards. They pushed me in through the door and shut it behind me, not daring to venture across the threshold lest they be transformed into some form of vermin, a good idea, in my mind, if not beneficial to them. Rats, the pair of them.

'I need your help.' Margaret began. 'I need to see how my son fares.' She removed the manacles.

'Do you not have messengers to bring you such news?' I enquired icily, not holding the sarcasm from my voice. She did not rise to my bait, she was calm, cool, all business.

'Oh, indeed. They tell me he is well and that his army grows by the day, and that Richard is close by. The battle is to be soon. But I need to see how he is, in himself, and I need to help him if I can.'

'He is in good hands, my Lady Beaufort. Is not his uncle with him, and you have the men you called from France to fight alongside him?' I countered. I did not know what she wanted of me.

'I feel that he dithers, he is not certain, and he must not doubt himself. He must be sure that his cause is just, and right.' She was all concern, like a mother hen, strange for one of her ilk. 'You will help me, Red. You will help me to look for him, and we will look for king Richard also, see into his mind, read what schemes he makes to defeat my boy.'

There it was, hidden in her words. It was Richard she wanted to see. Not Henry. The cat was stalking the king rat. But what would she try and do? As she talked, she was busy, her gazing pool and mirror were filled with water which she had had her servant bring from the spring in the mountains, the Dragon's spring, the spring which flowed from the rocks above the Meredith lands at Hengwm, water sulphurous and warmed with the breath of y Ddraig.

'Clear your mind, Red. If you help me all this will be ended sooner. I will release you once my work is completed.'

The words were sweet, almost kindly, bidding me help her cause, but my mind was filled with doubt. I had been warned I should not believe a word she uttered for she had more faces than the devil himself. I had little choice other than to obey her. My life was in her hands for the present. I stood beside her, my hand on her shoulder and hers on mine, a connection dead for centuries forming between us. I attuned my thoughts to hers, then I allowed myself to think with her, to see what she saw. Then I realised that she only saw shadows, her power was dim, and it was my mind which provided her with clarity. I was the colour and the detail of her seeing. All her energy and mine was focussed on Richard, it was Richard she called, Richard of York she sought to enchant.

I saw a great tent, hung with velvet drapery, a twisted man being undressed by his manservant, being made ready for bed. A goblet of wine was served on a salver, the goblet made of gold encrusted with jewels. The twisted man drank deeply, then he slid his arms into a long velvet coat over his night shirt. He crossed the tent to where a bright suit of armour was laid out. A sword gleamed sharp in the moonlight which pierced the gap in the tent flap. This twisted man picked up the sword and, holding it up to the moonlight, he swung it deftly in long sweeping strokes, then short ones moving easily for one so deformed, his arm strong and his actions smooth. Drills completed, he held the blade up to the moonlight knelt and whispered a prayer to a god other than his own. A prayer to a Norse god to strengthen his arm, to guide his blade.

'Great Odin, Allfather and wise ruler, I call upon your ancient might. Grant me strength and wisdom. Guide me through the battle to come.'

Then he turned and knelt at the altar to his one God and recited his Catholic prayers for the forgiveness of sin.

'O, my God, I am heartily sorry for having offended Thee, and I detest all my sins because of thy just punishments, but most of all because they offend Thee, my God, who art all good and deserving of all my love. I firmly resolve with the help of Thy grace to sin no more and to avoid the near occasion of sin. Amen.'

'Hypocrite!' she muttered beside me. 'He prays to his gods that he may triumph in battle and to his one God that he sleep well this night. Well, I shall give him dreams he shall not forget!'

Lady Margaret reached two jars from a nearby shelf, and a pestle and mortar, and adding a large pinch from the contents of each jar she ground them together. 'Valerian and Mug wort.' she advised me. 'He shall get no sleep tonight!' She sprinkled the powder into the gazing pool and stirred, watching the powder disappear down the vortex made by the sulphurous waters and into the ether. She spread her hands over the swirling liquid and began to chant. Her voice thin as a reed, hoarse with age but still with the power to cast her will across the ether.

> *'Dogs of war, snap at his heels.*
> *Bite and break the sleep he feels.*
> *Fill his mind with thoughts of dread,*
> *Dreams of death should fill his head.*
> *Hound of wrath, chase down his calm,*
> *let his swords weight tire his arm.*
> *In blood of York then let him drown.*
> *Then will there be a Tudor Crown'*

She recited her words calmly, carefully, all the while stirring the waters into which we gazed. Then as her voice dropped into silence, the waters stilled. The reflection in the rippled surface showed the twisted form of Richard pulling the bedclothes up over his humped shoulder and the crown of England placed on the table alongside his bed. He tossed and turned once, trying to settle. Happy with her work, Margaret emptied the silver vessel, rinsed it carefully and refilled it.

'Now I will visit my son, and you must leave me, you will go back to your cell.'

She clapped her hands and from outside the door my two jailers appeared. Roughly, they reapplied the manacles to my wrists and needlessly dragged me down the tower steps and into the dungeons beneath. Richard of York was not the only one who would not sleep tonight.

I wrapped the thin blanket around my shoulders and curled up on the straw mattress in the least damp corner of my prison, the corner furthest from the stench slop bucket. I closed my eyes and called HIM, but tonight, he did not come. I tried to bring him to mind, but my mind was exhausted, all I could sense was the howling of dogs and the muttered cursing of the anointed King of England.

CHAPTER 59. REDEMORE

22nd August 1485

Richard of York, King of England, woke early. He had not slept. His night's rest had been beset by dreams, dreams where he was chased by a great hound. It had hunted him, its teeth stained with the blood of its victims, its breath rank and hot on his neck. He had tossed and turned in a sweat, throwing off his covers and waking to stare around his tent, reaching for his knife or his sword to dispatch the creature.

He summoned his body servant well before dawn. If he could not sleep, then he could at least pray. He would say a private mass before he addressed his army. He would make confession and meet this day with a clear conscience. His servant rushed to bring water for the king to wash and fresh clothes to replace the sweat-soaked night shirt.

'Where is the priest? Find the priest, why does he lie abed when he is needed?'

The servant knew better than to answer. He bowed and nodded and tugged at his forelock then ducked back out through the tent flap in search of missing cleric.

'Why is there no bread? Is there no food for your King? Bring me food, I would break my fast after I pray, and before I address the men.' Richard's voice was raised in anger as he found no preparations had been made for the day.

'Sire, it is still before dawn, the fires are not yet warm, the cook is still abed!' one timorous flunky interjected!

'Well, wake him, is there no one to serve me, will no one find bread and wine, how shall we fight the Tudor imposter on an empty belly?'

Richard pushed back the tent flap and strode off on his own search for the priest. This was not a good omen for the rest of the day. Usually a man who had few nerves before battle, a feeling of trepidation began to grow in his gut, a little gnawing knot which grew as the dawn broke. His back ached from his poor night's sleep, and this made his whole misshapen body feel as if it had been trampled by his charger. He must make his peace with his Lord and give ease to his thoughts. He must know that God at least was with him, if not several of his best lieutenants. If God granted him victory, which he had faith he would, then he would deal with the traitors later, speaking of which, there was still no commitment from Lord Thomas Stanley and his brother William, but he still had the Earl's son, Lord Strange, captive, a valuable pawn, was he not?

Without the benefit of a private mass, Richard donned his armour, polished to a brightness which glinted in the morning sunshine and also, without breakfast and not in the best of tempers, he called his Generals for a final council and then mounted his great white charger and went out to address his assembled army.

His address however was not couched in words of encouragement. It was not a rallying cry to his men. It was a threat of what would come should they fail.

'Should we lose, and Henry Tudor become your King, he will destroy the homes and the families of all who stand against him. Fight well and win! To fight well is a sign of manliness! Win or fear the loss of all you know and hold dear!'

Despite the men who had deserted completely or changed sides to support the Tudors, Richard commanded over 15000 men, split into three fighting groups called 'battles'. He himself would lead the centre. It was only fitting for a warrior king such as he.

His address to the massed men rang out across the fields around Ambion Hill, near Sutton Cheney, the place he had chosen to make his stand, claiming the higher ground, and putting the morning sun in his enemy's eyes. Richard the master of tactics had laid claim to the best lie of the land, a downward slope to where the Tudors must assemble, easier for a charge on foot or on horseback.

Still having no word from the Stanleys, they, having command of six thousand men between them, Richard sent a written message. It was short and to the point.

'Be loyal to your King or lose your son, and if we are victorious, your heads.'

Thomas Stanley's reply was equally as short.

'I have other sons.'

This response incensed the monarch so greatly that he held off executing the hapless Lord strange before the battle. He would, he decided, execute all the Stanley's together. Their heads would grace the gates of York as a family. He smiled to himself at the thought.

Richard was ready for battle.

Henry Tudor rose that morning to find that still more of Richard's men had defected to his side. However, the Tudor army was still vastly outnumbered, and they could see the masses of Richard's men in the distance. Richard had cannon and ordnance drawn from the Tower of London and three battles of five thousand men where Henry's whole army numbered only seven thousand.

Henry had delegated the disposition of his troops to The Earl of Oxford and to his Uncle Jasper Tudor. They had discussed their tactics at length. He had even met in relative secrecy with Lord Stanley, whose men resolutely stood off, some distance from the field. Stanley would still not commit but had sent a detachment of men commanded by his brother Humphrey, to bolster Henry's troops, to even out the numbers. But the main body of the Stanley's many thousand men stayed firmly positioned where they could judge what was to come and take sides accordingly. The Stanleys were practiced at walking between the fires, and sitting on the fence, however precarious that position proved to be.

Henry's address to his troops was more hopeful and encouraging. He made reference to, 'doubtful friends,' a wry jibe at the Stanleys. God was on their side and there would be rewards for the victors and those loyal to his cause. With luck and God's blessing they would vanquish their proud and arrogant enemies and adversaries.

With his troops martialled into one tight formation by The Earl of Oxford, with the right flank under the command of Rhys ap Thomas and Gilbert Talbot, the left under John Savage, Henry Tudor's army took to the field.

Oxford was a shrewd man. Not wanting to demoralise his men with time spent staring across the battlefield at the vast numbers of the king's army, he moved forward quickly. Keeping the marshland on his right and using the boggy land as protection, he skirted the Duke of Norfolk's cannon. There was exchange of fire between the lines of archers, with negligible effect. Then the battle fell to hand-to-hand combat.

Many of Richard's soldiers were arrayed men. They took the first opportunity to run from the field. Wealthy professional soldiers in full armour fought with swords and war hammers against working men in leather jerkin and chain mail, fighting with a halberd and rondel, the small sharp knife ideal for piercing the armour of fallen knights. Men battered each other ruthlessly, regardless of their own safety, with axes, blades, and clubs, spurred on by the Lancastrian hatred of York and also by the deep personal hatred the Earl of Oxford held for the Duke of Norfolk, to whom he had forfeited lands under the York King. The ferocity of Oxford's attack took Norfolk by surprise. A pause to regroup, and Oxford saw an opportunity to split Norfolk's men. A swift messenger was sent with orders to call in the right flank under Rhys ap Thomas and Gilbert Talbot to drive a wedge through the side of the York army.

The move was a success and caused many of the York foot soldiers to turn and run. Richard called on his rear guard led by the Duke of Northumberland, men held in reserve. Whether by prior arrangement with supporters of Henry Tudor or by miscommunication, the Northumberland men did not arrive. The men of the York flank were surrounded. Turned to face the elements, they no longer had the benefit of the slope and were themselves blinded by the low sun. Norfolk was killed and his men routed.

Richard himself in command of the centre, realised that Norfolk was beaten, and he also saw a chance. On a low hill just outside of the melee, but with the advance of the Tudor army, was Henry Tudor himself, protected only by his close bodyguard and standard bearer.

Whether in a fit of rage or frustration, Richard had declared that God forbid that he should retreat by so much as one step, and that he would leave the field as a king or he would die as one. With a number of the few mounted knights still in the fray, he signalled the charge, round the perimeter of the marshland heading straight for Henry, intent on only one thing: The death of Henry Tudor.

CHAPTER 60. CHECK MATE - Gwyn

We rode out together, all of us mounted, me on Jasper Tudor's spare horse. Henry would not have me walk. The four of us and Jasper Tudor, riding at a walk behind the main body of men, Henry dressed in full armour, flying the Tudor colours as his standard alongside the Dragon colours of Glyndwr, colours I carried as standard bearer. It brought to mind another prince and another battle. Jasper rode on one side of Henry and Ralph on the other, all of us dressed in full armour, armed with sword and shield and battle hammer. Jack and Frankie rode behind.

We took up a position on a low hill to the left of the Earl of Oxford, from where Henry could see the whole field in front of him: the vast array of the York army, his own hugely outnumbered troops and to the right the inactive troops of Lord Thomas Stanley, and to the left the equally inactive men of Sir William Stanley.

Henry watched intently as John de Vere, Earl of Oxford, skilfully conducted his part in the battle, engineering a rout of the men led by the Duke of Norfolk, using his Welsh archers to maximum effect, and avoiding the Duke's great serpentine cannon. As Oxford advanced, we followed, always keeping to the higher ground and in sight of the fighting where we could hear the crash of the cannon and the screams and cries of men fighting and dying for either cause.

The battle was nearly two hours old. Miraculously, the Tudor army was winning. Many of the Yorkists had fled.

Out of the melee came a small party of mounted knights at the gallop, the leader mounted on a white horse and wearing the colours of the White Boar together with a crown atop his helmet, Richard himself, headed full tilt for our position.

We closed ranks forming a protective ring around Henry. Horses and riders crashed into us, knocking Frankie from his horse. He rolled a short distance away, lying like a stranded beetle in his armour. The attacking party paid him no heed, they were focussed on Henry. One helpless knight stranded under foot. He was not important.

Richard's standard bearer was hacked down, bravely holding high the Kings standard, both his legs crippled by the great sword wielded by Ralph who fought to my front and to my right. The clash of steel on steel was deafening as he fought off Richard's party one after another.

Jack, to my left and behind me, protected Henry's back valiantly, striking blow after blow with his war club. James Harrington and Richard Ratcliffe were slain and lay bleeding amongst the dead and Richard was left, unhorsed, and alone still fighting, the circlet crown dislodged from his helmet and hanging loose from his visor, the chin strap of his helmet undone, cut through by some close call with a blade. His sword arm tiring, he fought to within a sword's length of his goal. I drew my father's sword and fought as I have not fought before, the old blade seemed to have life and power of its own. I felt its blade strike the shoulder of the king's armour. I heard him grunt in pain.

Richard fell to his knees, blows from a club or a halberd breaking his armour, smashing his helmet and his head. In the noise and chaos that followed I heard the cries of the men of Thomas and William Stanley joining the fray, then the fading screams of the soldiers of York as they fled the same treatment as that which had killed their king.

The body of Richard of York lay at our feet. A small, twisted and insignificant looking man, but one with the heart of a lion, a brave man who did indeed die like a king. Henry too was blood smeared and weak legged from exertion. His uncle Japer leaned on his sword, gasping for breath, and surrounded by the dead. Frankie rose to his feet, shaking with fear and frustration, but alive.

As calm descended, Lord William Stanley emerged from the copse of woodland to my right, untouched by battle and smiling. Wily old fox, he had sat on his fence watching the flock of sheep for two hours, then when the sheep had fled and only the fattest of the lambs were left, he had struck. His own men had been saved by his inactivity, yet now, he and his brother showed their hand for Henry Tudor.

In his gauntlet clad fist, he held the dented crown of York. He knelt before Henry, the circlet raised in front of him, then rose and handed it to his older brother Thomas who placed it on the young man's head, uttering the words,

'Henry Tudor, I crown you King of all England!'

Word spread fast and after just over two hours, news of Richard's death and Henry's claiming the Crown spread like wildfire. Fighting ceased, York troops fled, and cries of victory rose from the Welsh and the English Lancastrians alike. Then there was a quiet, the quiet of death, broken only by the plaintive whiny of an injured horse, or a cry for help from a wounded man.

Now came the great task of burying the dead and making order from chaos. The broken body of Richard of York was stripped naked, and in a final humiliation tied to his horse and taken to the city of Leicester where it would be displayed, lest anyone doubt that he was indeed dead.

The bodies of nobles and men of rank would be taken to their estates for burial. The bodies of the rank and file were collected at the church and buried nearby in mass graves. Dead horses were first butchered for meat and then burned. Artillery and armoury which could be salvaged was dragged away, and, despite Henry's orders, the French mercenaries and many of the arrayed men roamed the field looting the dead of valuables. They would have no need of coin or a weapon in the hell they were destined for, but then what man in his right mind would want a silver badge bearing the sign of the Boar of York in times when the king was not of that house. In general, the looting was kept to a minimum. Oxford had a firm grip on his men and Henry's wishes were carried out, while the villagers from the nearby cottages watched on in the safety of the church tower.

Henry was in good spirits, well who wouldn't be, he had just taken the throne of England, now all he had to do was keep it. His destiny was fulfilled. Did this mean we could go home?

For the moment, the witch who lived in the body of his mother controlled all our destinies. Jack and Frankie did not find this way of life easy. They needed to go back to their own time. We believed Charlie had drowned. Ralph, well he was restless as always, he needed Red. I had never seen him worried before, but he seemed preoccupied with her safety. For myself, I just needed peace. I did not trust the witch. I held out faint hope of ever finding my family again, they were indeed lost for good.

In the aftermath of Redemore, we marched to Leicester where we were greeted as heroes. Henry was welcomed and feted as King. We took rooms at the hastily renamed Blue Boar inn, its sign repainted a gaudy shade of turquoise lest the innkeeper be mistaken for a supporter of Richard of York. We feasted and drank. After three days, the publicly displayed, naked body of the deposed king was removed and given to the church for proper burial, and King Henry Tudor began his royal progress down the cobbles of Watling Street to London.

Through Coventry and Northampton and many other small towns we were greeted in the same manner. Town officials who had entertained Richard on his progress north and declared their loyalty to York now hastily changed their views and welcomed Henry Tudor as the king they had been praying for. Henry had matured sufficiently in the weeks since our arrival in Wales and the march across country. He had discovered the fickle nature of men. Since childhood he had learned not to place trust in many. His newfound popularity did not change this view.

He began his kingship straight away, writing letters to the local officers and to the local lordships. He would not tolerate any form of looting whether it be from the dead lying on the ground or from salutary evictions of Yorkists from their homes and lands. He would have no resurrection of the old quarrels, for he would marry a York bride. Elizabeth had been released from the Tower of London to await his pleasure at the home of her mother. This would merge York and Lancaster in the house of Tudor, there would be no more fighting over the crown.

Prisoners were taken, the York nobility were to be kept captive and impotent until Henry's government was established and his seat secure.

On the journey south we pondered all of this and what it meant for us. For now, we were the King's bodyguard, we rode at his side, we dined in his company, and we ensured his safety.

On 15th September 1485 Henry Tudor was welcomed into the city of London. He took up residence at Greenwich and made the long-awaited reunion with his mother, recently arrived from Wales. His mother, it seemed, had other plans for us.

'They are rough soldiers.' she declared. 'Mercenaries, not fit to guard the kings person.'

She demanded we be housed elsewhere than at Greenwich, yet she would not let us go. Like a cat playing with mice, she kept us alive with enough hope that we did not die of despair. Ralph was sure of her intentions, sitting in our newly allocated barracks at the Tower of London, trying to warm the chill from our bones and dry our clothing from the incessant London rain.

Head in his hands he spoke.

'It is the Red Maid she wants, not us. We are collateral damage to her. She has had her use from us, and we are now expendable.'

'You,' he addressed Jack and Frankie, 'you cannot get back without my help. Red will not leave without you, Jack, for it is you she came to aid. She will see you back with your wife, or she will die. Frankie, she sees you as part of that, you are to her part of Jack's men. She will not leave without you either.'

'And you?' said Jack. 'You could leave any time, you don't need us. You could save her and leave us to rot in this miserable dump.'

'The witch is dying.' Ralph replied. 'Slowly, her power leaves her. That which she drew from Y Ddraig of Wales is gone. The great Dragon has turned away from her evil. She sees great power in Red, Merch Goch. She holds her prisoner, seeking to use her now as she used Margaret Beaufort. As a host, I can prevent that. So, I must stay and bide my time, do her bidding. For the present.'

'She has us all neatly tied then.' Frankie whispered. 'We cannot leave without you, you will not leave without Red. Red will not leave without us, and she is the witch's prisoner.'

'Correct.' I concluded. 'The king will have a fine coronation, then he will attend to his marriage. I suspect he will delay the marriage until his bride is with child. But his mother will see to that. Once he has the crown firmly on his head and a child in his queen's belly, then he will feel safe, then she may allow us to leave.'

'And until then?' asked Jack.

'Until then, we do what we are commanded to do, we make the best of it, we keep our own counsel, and we trust no one.'

Ralph's words dripped like ice into the already frosty atmosphere.

'Come, it's not so bad, we have food and clothes and a roof over our heads, and the whole of London to enjoy. I will feel it when she makes her move, but for now SHE is content to be My Lady the Kings Mother. That she has earned and for that she needs none of her sorcery. Besides, she also has Elizabeth Woodville to contend with.'

He chuckled. 'If the devil would only cast his net in that direction, the pyre he could build would be sulphurous indeed!'

And so, we occupied ourselves with endlessly practicing our archery. Even Frankie developed muscles in his arms that he did not know he had. Jack became a very accomplished swordsman. He was naturally a man of discipline and had an aptitude for weapons.

Occasionally we were called upon to ride alongside the king, on procession through the city, to guard against the occasional Yorkist throwing rotten fruit and vegetables at his majesty. Despite the insistence from his mother that these poor fools should be arrested and suffer the full wrath of the king, Henry was disposed to mercy towards the common man, if not so much so towards the York nobility.

On Sunday 30th October 1485, there was a massive and ostentatious Coronation. Jasper Tudor carried the crown. Thomas Stanley carried the great sword of state, and the Earl of Oxford guided the train of the king's robes. The public lined the streets to see the new king in all his glory. We took up positions amongst the crowd, ever watchful for dissenters amongst the crowd. Nothing could be allowed to mar the king's great day.

Parliament met for the first time in the following week. Sir Rhys ap Thomas as a fellow Welshman had told us of the rewards that the new king had bestowed. For sir Rhys, the promised position as Chamberlain of South Wales. For his uncle Jasper, the restoration of everything he had lost under the Yorks. The Earl of Oxford was also to have his lands restored and was also made Keeper of the Tower of London including the animals in the Tower Zoo.

Jack raised an eyebrow at this snippet of information. 'Does that make the man our keeper as well?' he commented dryly. 'Maybe that gives him the power tae set us free.'

'No,' came the response from Ralph, who was stretching his great frame, leaning against the door frame of our rooms, 'that means there is another person who has a call on us, another who can keep us here. Oxford will see to himself, he knows our worth as fighting men and we are now his, if he needs us.'

The greatest gifts were however given to Henry's mother on who he now depended for advice in most things. She was installed in apartments close to his at court, apartments which she retained even after his marriage. All her lands and titles were reinstated, as was appropriate for My Lady the Kings Mother, the mother of the King of England.

It was not until January that the King married Elizabeth of York who soon announced that she was with child.

It was shortly after this that we were called to the royal presence once more.

CHAPTER 61. DIRTY WORK - Gwyn

London,
January 1486.

    Life in the service of Henry VII for a small group of mercenary soldiers, not attached to any of the great lords of the land and with no known alliances was best described as precarious. We kept out of people's way as much as we could, avoiding the taverns and the ale houses where most of the other foot soldiers congregated.
    The King himself, if he even knew of our existence, had no use for us. The Queen certainly did not know of our existence, we were a tool to be used solely by Milady the Kings Mother. We were fed and we were clothed, and we were paid a small retainer. We occupied our time with endless sword and archery practice to while away the days, while Milady decided what she should do with us.
    This in itself caused a stir. Ralph on occasion advised me to,
    'Just miss occasionally can't you, there are those about who are taking bets on our accuracy, my friend.'
    Our barracks were within the Tower of London, and we had found a quiet grassy courtyard on which to set up our practice area. Jack and Frankie were still unused to the living in a time other than their own. Whilst both could fight with a knife and fire a rifle, and Frankie had a natural eye and was not a bad shot with a bow, neither was proficient with a sword. This was then an ideal time for Ralph to put both of them through their paces.
    Our courtyard was also the playground for two young boys. We were told nothing about them, save that they were there for their own safety and that we should not speak to them, if they were at play, we should go elsewhere. They lived in rooms on the upper floor of the Tower. They were well dressed and happy lads and, if they were not outside on the grass, would watch us from their window high up in the wall. They thought they were unseen, but I could sense them there, two sets of eyes which would bore holes I my back as they watched each arrow I fired, hitting the target set at the far end of the green.

At the bottom of the stairs to their rooms was a small alcove which was inhabited by two men in the uniform of gaolers, though they professed not to be. It was they who took lots on my performance, sometimes with other men who came to share a jug of ale with them to pass the time. One of the gaolers let slip in his cups that the lads upstairs were indeed important and valuable and, in some ways, dangerous to the King. They were the two young sons of Edward IV, the king whose death had led to the escalation of the feud between Lancaster and York. Edward and Richard were kept confined, but not prisoners. York heirs to the Tudor throne, these were dangerous boys indeed.

On some days we drew quite a crowd, gathered at the foot of the tower, men lounging on the grass drinking ale and watching Ralph and I fire arrows at the Butts. We could hear the clink of coin as they bet on which of us would get closest to the centre of the target. On occasion they would watch Frankie and Jack practicing and bet on which would miss the target completely most often. I do not like to admit to it, but it was not unknown for Frankie to place his own bets with the Gaolers to subsidise out meagre soldiers' wages. They were usually too drunk or stupid to realise that he and Ralph were more or less joined at the hip, and that Ralph and I had been playing this game for a long, long time.

Then, one day the two lads stopped coming down to play in the autumn sun on the grass outside their Tower. I could still feel that they watched us, but they no longer played in the sunshine or felt the rain on their faces.

Not long after that, I was given one last job.

One last job, she had said. I had been summoned to her presence and ordered to take only two good men with me, those whose lips could be sealed forever, ones who I could trust not to betray her at this, the final act. The task was one I did not relish. It was a step more than she had gone before. I would take Ralph. He could be ruthless when he chose, and he could be relied upon, but I took Frankie to keep watch. He could be relied upon not leave his post and to blend like a grey man into his surroundings. No-one ever noticed Frankie until it was too late.

High up in their stone walled rooms, deprived of all the comforts to which they were used, removed from their family by their uncle, they were destined to be prisoners for the rest of their lives, if they only knew it. Two tousled blonde heads lay peacefully asleep in the one bed their keepers had thought to provide. Brothers sleeping close to each other for both comfort and warmth, the company of others denied them, living now in the blind faith that the elder was one day to be crowned King of England.

I had been given strict instructions how to enter the Tower, which postern door to use, which rooms the guards slept in. She had assured me the guards would be drunk, she herself had sent an extra hogshead of her best 'strong ale' for them. They would drink it. All the guards were sots if the truth be known. Who else would do such a job? The old witch knew that both Ralph and I could go undetected, the choice of any other man was my own. Charlie was missing, that left Frankie, or Jack. Jack was far too honest and honourable for this job. I did not even know if I was up to this particular task myself. At least I knew that Frankie would do as he was ordered.

Frankie kept watch at the postern door, hidden in the shadows. Ralph and I climbed the steep stone stairs which wound up to the room on the top floor, a room with a view only of the private garden, a garden they could see, but no longer visit. For they had now changed from being guests in the care of their uncle, to being prisoners, viewed as a danger to the throne although the king himself knew nothing of this night's plan.

As the air in the room was disturbed by the door opening and our entrance, the younger lad stirred, pulling the quilt over his shoulder, and rolling towards his brother. He moaned slightly and turned onto his side shrugging further into the covers and wriggling closer to his sibling. I was sure I heard the word, 'mother,' in the breath that hung white on the chilly night air. Watching them sleep, I saw the sleeping heads of my own children. What could they have been had they lived?

For Edward was not my Edward, my boy was dead, and my daughter too. I pictured them as they had been the last time I saw them as children.

'I cannot do this, Ralph. This is a step too far. I will not do it,' I whispered to him as we stood invisible in the alcove by the door.

'We have no choice. If we fail, she will chase us through the years. She will not give up. For me that is nothing, nor for you. It is everything for the others and she will hunt all of us until we are dust under her feet.'

'Can we not free them, get them to safety?'

'Shhhh, they stir, we do not have long, dawn will be upon us.'

'Take them, you can take them to the coast, find a ship, a passage to the Low Countries, they have support there.'

'And risk our new king's safety?'

'Give him proof then, that they are dead, something that also shows him complicit in this deed.'

Ralph looked at me in desperation.

'Take the younger one, make sure he stays silent, wrap him in your cloak, and follow me.'

So that is what we did. We took them, invisible to all, the boys sleeping forms wrapped in the cloaks Ralph had given me, doors unlocked before him, and behind him, gaolers stayed sleeping in their cubbyholes, snoring over their cups, oblivious. We left from the water gate straight onto the river, the two lads rendered magically unconscious and silent, huddled in the bottom of the small boat. We rowed back up the great river Thames to the dock at The Steelyard, where the Flemish merchants did business on the north bank at Dow gate.

The place stank of sewers and the night-time silence was punctuated by the squeal of the rats as they scurried along the wooden dock out onto the foreshore. Moonlight lit our way, casting a white shadow like a turnpike along the water. The trade ships of the Flemish merchants bobbed in the channel waiting for the rise of the tide to give them enough draught to reach the jetty. One small flat bottomed rowing boat lay tied up at the edge of the mud.

'Stay with the boat.' I ordered Frankie, as Ralph and I disappeared into one of the warehouses. We carried the charmed and sleeping children in our arms, made invisible by the cloaks we wore.

The part opened doorway was lit only by a storm lantern, the candle flickering in the draft. The door closed gently behind Ralph and, as the lantern moved, two shadows appeared above me, and I passed our cargo out of its resting place and into the care of strangers. I was not party to his transaction, and I did not see the faces of the men who took them. I prayed they were friends. Ralph returned in minutes carrying a bloodstained rag which he hastily stuffed into his pouch. I raised an eyebrow at him in question. Frankie sat open mouthed at the horror of what he thought he had just witnessed. We rowed with all haste back to the palace, then on foot back to our quarters. We would be called for an audience with milady in the morning.

At cock's crow, she sent for us. We had barely made it to our beds before her lady's maid rapped on our door. We were taken into the inner sanctum, rooms hung with rich tapestries from France given as gifts by the house of Burgundy, the furniture made of good wood, ornately carved mainly with religious figures but some betraying a more pagan heritage. All glowed with a deep patina in light from the candles and scented rush tapers.

My Lady the King's Mother was stick thin, her frame bowed prematurely from pious starvation. Nonetheless, she carried herself like a Queen, with an aura of power about her wasted shoulders.

'Is it done?' she demanded.

'They are gone, ma'am.' replied Ralph, truthfully enough. 'I bring you proof.'

Ralph unwrapped the blood-stained cloth and dropped the tips of two fingers on the table before her. The fingers of children, severed at the second joint. 'They will not trouble our king further.'

'You have done well tonight, and I am good to my word. You may take your men and have your freedom. You will take what horses you need from the king's stables. There will be a ship for you to France from Pembroke. Provision there and go with God.'

We wasted no time. We left the following day, Gwyn's archers fading into nothing as was their way, their fighting souls returned to rest, but always eager for the call to arms should it be heard again. Mounted on good riding horses and with a wagon pulled by two sturdy cobs, we made good time along our route through the English countryside, heading for the wilds of Wales.

'We must be gone before she finds out,' Ralph warned, 'for she will find out.'

'Where are they gone to?' I asked.

'I left them with friends, a Flemish merchant, and his family. They are half-way to the Low Country by now. Should they return, they will be named imposters. They are the young queen's brothers after all, she will not endanger them. The witch believes them disfigured, each lacking the same finger from their right hand, and the old witch cannot own that knowledge without admitting to doing them harm. It will not serve the king well to kill them again. They are safe. We are not. She will hunt us for this, be assured of that.'

We packed our belongings in haste, such belongings as we had, for whilst we had been guests of the court we had been billeted in soldiers' accommodations. With provisions for two days' travel we left London for Pembroke, me, Ralph, Frankie, and Jack.

CHAPTER 62. SOWING THE SEEDS – Gerald Shipley

London 1916.

Gerald Shipley arranged the papers before him on the huge oak desk. His brother had been thorough in his collection of evidence and, when viewed in isolation, the case against Sergeant MacGregor was damning indeed. The men who had gone with him could be said to be only following orders, though from what the General knew of MacGregor, he would have been honest with his men. They would all have known the risks they took. There were reports from other officers, reports from others of the rank-and-file soldiers, notably none from the officers of the Black Watch.

The General also knew his brother, his indecisive, well-meaning but incompetent brother, the brother with a vindictive unforgiving streak who carried a feeling of inferiority with him wherever he went. Gerald racked his brains for a solution. He had read and re-read all the documents. The Court Martial would be blinkered in its view, it was simple enough in their eyes. MacGregor had acted without orders, had not been present at his post when the order to advance was given - Q.E.D. Jack MacGregor, if he were ever found alive, would no doubt be found guilty of cowardice on those facts alone. As for his men, well Gerald Shipley had no doubt that they would follow their sergeant to his grave. They would not lie to save themselves. They would take the consequences.

A knock at the office door along with a rattling of the doorknob disturbed his train of thought. This was not his office, it was that of his other brother Jeremy, a Captain in intelligence. Lord knew who may knock the door next, he had already dealt with several rough looking customers both in and out of uniform, all looking for the Captain.

'Come.' He invited the visitor in, brusquely.

The woman who entered was not in uniform, she looked more like a char woman. A huge grey overcoat covered an ample frame, her greying hair was scraped to the back of her head in an untidy bun.

'Oh!' she exclaimed, slightly taken aback to see him. 'Where's Captain Jeremy, Sir?' The intruder thought on her feet.

'You are?' The General enquired of the visitor.

'Mrs Turner, sir, Ethel Turner. I clean the office, I used to 'do' for General Cameron when he worked here, the Captain kept me on sir.' She lied convincingly.

'I fetched up these from the post room.' She dropped the pile of folders onto the desk, their loose contents spreading over the General's neat arrangement of papers causing an avalanche of correspondence to fall to the floor.

He blustered and swore under his breath, char woman or not, he would not curse at a lady, no matter what frustration and inconvenience she had just caused him. Ethel bent to retrieve the paperwork and caught sight of the names at the top of the paper. MacGregor, Turner, Baker, and Owen. Her blood ran cold, she spoke before she thought, her words running away with her.

'Them boys is innocent sir, brave and loyal men they are, wherever they are, load of tosh them being deserters, you'll see!'

'Turner, you said, Mrs Turner, so one is your....'

'My eldest son sir, him, and his pal, Frankie Baker, been missing for months, is there word of them? You've a lot of papers there, is there any news?'

'I am afraid not Ethel, may I call you Ethel? Frankly, it's all a bit of a mess.'

He sat back in the leather desk chair, pushing its casters back across the polished wood floor. He let his inner thoughts out in words he had been afraid to say before.

Ethel thought frantically, searching for the right words, how to put the dog on the right scent, she picked up a few more sheets from the floor. Most were neatly typed, some were written in a flowing copperplate hand, black ink neatly covering flat white paper. Then she saw it! It had not fallen from the desk. It was not part of what Montague Shipley had assembled for his brother to read. It was a crumpled sheet of dispatch paper, clipped to a handwritten note. It was protruding from under a cabinet, as if it had been thrown at the nearby waste basket and missed its target.

Ethel picked it up with the rest of the papers. The General was busy putting his papers back into neat piles and rows, all paginated and in order. He did not pay much attention to Ethel as she smoothed out the creases and nosily read what she had found.

'Have you read this sir?' she gasped. 'The sergeant what came for them with that list said they went without orders, so he did, but these are orders, sir.'

General Shipley snatched the paper from her hand. 'Where was this?'

'On the floor sir. Why? Is it important?

Gerald Shipley read the letter written by Mrs Ferris. He flattened it out with his huge hand and then read the crumpled sheet which was clipped to it. There at the bottom he saw his brother's signature, in pencil and feint, but then it had been written under fire and in a hurry. This put a whole new perspective on the case. He needed to speak with his brother, and soon.

'Thank you, Mrs Turner, you may leave, you have done enough for today. I'm sure the captain will call you when you are needed.'

Ethel left, closing the door firmly behind her, raising her eyes heavenward and thanking the Lord and providence for their assistance. General Shipley was a good man, she could tell that from his eyes. He had eyes like General Cameron, the trustworthy eyes of an honourable man. She prayed that Letty's work would bear scrutiny. Someone had obviously read that note and decided it must disappear. Things in the intelligence world were fluid that way. Facts were moulded like putty to fit in whatever hole they needed to fill. The truth was an expendable pawn in the great game of war. Ethel was halfway down the stairs as Gerald Shipley was gathering his papers under his arm and calling for his driver to take him to speak with his brother.

Gerald Shipley climbed into the back of the big Austin car. It was pointless, he knew, to try and persuade his brother to withdraw his allegations, but there may be another way. What was it that Red headed woman had said to him? Ah, yes, **'the country needs its heroes**.' He rested his head back against the leather of the seats and considered his options. She may have a point. The country wanted heroes, oh, yes. There was too much bad news. The battle for the Somme had gone on for months, the losses had been horrific, millions of men dead, there were few families not touched by grief. Morale was low. The men did not need more executions, for that was what his brother demanded.

From what he had read, MacGregor had been frustrated, a man with troops trained to do a job yet denied an opportunity. From what little he knew of MacGregor's character, he was an inspiring soldier, respected and loved by his men. Gerald placed himself in MacGregor's shoes. What would he have done?

Then there was what had followed. Had his brother not been so badly wounded? Had the advance not been such a disaster, things might have been different. Montague would have been hailed a hero and would have bathed in the glory. Then there was the defence of the hospital, such bizarre memories. He himself had been there wounded, and treated there, his life saved by, of all things, a woman surgeon, almost unheard of. Then, the strange sightings of ancient archers, the unit of men who had defended the wounded and those who looked after them and then vanished into the night, now they were indeed heroes. A plan was forming, but he did not yet know how the pieces would fit. First, he needed to tackle his brother.

Montague Shipley was in the garden of their mother's country home. He had had his valet wheel his chair into the arbour which had a view down the grassy slope towards the lake. He was sketching, a talent he had recently discovered, his drawing pad balanced on his blanket covered knees, supported on an embroidered tapestry cushion. His current work was a remarkable sketch of a heron spying for fish, beady eyes searching the water for carp, totally still until the moment it would strike. His charcoal had captured every feather, the sleek wings, the soft breast feathers, the long sharp beak, and the dark light of its eye. He would colour it later with watercolours in his small studio.

'That's impressive, Monty, very good, I can almost hear it thinking.' Gerald stepped into his brother's line of sight.

His brother looked up, putting down his charcoal and pad. Still unable to speak, he signed back to the General, 'Shall I frame it for you, brother, you can have it as my gift?'

'That would be grand. You should exhibit them, even locally, you have talent.'

Montague Shipley smiled, praise from his oldest brother was rare, a little lump of pride swelled in his damaged throat and generated a tear in his eye. He coughed, noisily, and wiped his face with a large handkerchief, anxious for his brother not to see his emotion. 'Warm day today,' he signed. 'let's go into the shade.'

Gerald took the handles of the lightweight wheelchair his brother spent his days in and pushed it gently up the slope and into the nearby summerhouse where Montague had his studio. He admired the sketches of the landscape and of the birds and then his eye fell on the small oil painting hanging above his brother's worktable. It was a miniature of a woman. He knew that face, but when had his brother ever seen her. It was the face of the woman who had saved his life, Rhianydd Rees, Dr. Rhianydd Rees. As far as Gerald knew she had never worked at Mount Vernon Hospital and had only recently been posted to the front.

'Gorgeous, is she not?' his brother wrote on the note pad he sometimes used to write his words on.

'Who, who is she?' Gerald was cautious with his question. He knew the lady in the painting, he knew her well.

Montague wrote swiftly. 'A visitor I had when I was in hospital, wife of a coward.'

'Tell me more.' Gerald raised an intrigued eyebrow.

'Her name is Rhianydd MacGregor. Her husband is a wanted man. She visited me. My nurse was her friend.'

'You saw her often, then?'

'No, just once, but I could never forget that face. I feel she will have need of me once her husband is gone.' Montague wrote, his writing becoming less legible with the frustration and anger in every word.

Gerald swallowed. 'That is what I have come to discuss, brother. Sergeant MacGregor.' Gerald pulled the file from under his great coat. He extracted Mrs Ferris' letter and the paper attached to it.

'Have you seen this before?' He pointed to the signature, jabbing it with a thick finger.

'No.' Montague shook his head vehemently.

'Is that your signature?' His brother badgered him.

'It seems to be, but I did not sign that.' He signed the response and then shook his head again.

'If it looks like your signature, how can you be sure you did not?' Gerald questioned. 'In the confusion of the day and after your injuries, can you really be sure you did not?'

Monty breathed in, took a clean piece of paper, then started to write.

'I would not have allowed MacGregor his crack brained mission. It was suicide for him and his men. And in any case, I needed him, the men would follow him anywhere, even into the pit of hell we were about to send them to. He was the best of my men. Even if I had allowed it, there were orders from above, no man was to leave, for any reason. Every man we had would go over the top.'

He stopped. Then began again. 'The bastard defied me. He should have been there, on that ladder, it should have been him!'

Montague Shipley sobbed for the first time since he was wounded, his body shook with emotion and tears spilled down his face, running over the still red scars of his wounds. There was the crux of it! He blamed MacGregor for his situation. He blamed MacGregor for everything.

Gerald sat down beside him, hugged his brother to him. Maybe now was not the time for his plan. He let his brother compose himself.

As if soothing a child, Gerald spoke again, 'Shall I go and ask what's for tea? I could smell baking in the kitchen.'

They would have tea, then Gerald would try again. High Tea was served in the drawing room with its chintz furnishings, polished mahogany tables and long windows with views stretching down the lawns to the ornamental lake where Montague had sketched the Heron.

Lady Elspeth fussed around Monty, arranging his tartan monogrammed rug over his knees and seeing to it that his plate was kept filled. Monty did not have much appetite for food since his return. His jaw still ached and he was self-conscious of dribbling like a baby when he chewed. His over attentive mother did not help matters. He brushed her away impatiently.

Lady Elspeth ignored his dismissal of her attentions she filled his plate and handed him a linen napkin to dab away the crumbs from around his mouth.

Conversation was stilted, largely confined to banal pleasantries about London society, which Elspeth missed desperately, and local gossip in which neither of the men had much interest. It was late afternoon when Gerald took hold of his brother's chair and suggested,

'A tour of the gardens before supper?'

Monty did not have much choice in the matter but was pleased for some relief from his mother's cloying attentions.

'She means well.' Gerald pacified him.

'She's an interfering old besom.' was signed back. There was no sign for the word besom, but Gerald understood perfectly well what his brother meant to communicate.

'You'd be lost without her.'

'I need a nurse, brother, a full-time nurse. Mrs MacGregor will do splendidly!'

Gerald realised at that point that his brother was, indeed, slightly deluded. There was little if no chance that the Dr. MacGregor he had met would ever consider such a post, not under any circumstances.

'Montague, we need to talk about this case of yours.' he began.

'Nothing to discuss, it's cut and dried.' Montague signed his replies, gesturing eloquently with his hands, his meaning conveyed perfectly.

'I can see a way, a way which might serve you better.' Gerald was thinking on his feet, feeding his brother maybe what he wanted to hear.

'Could they not be heroes? The country needs a boost. You heroically led your men over the top, brother. Did you not send an advance party first, to deal with the Bosch snipers?' He let his brother digest his words and after a moment continued.

'I've heard that that same unit acquitted themselves with valour at Abbéville. I, myself, was witness to some of their bravery. It's there in black and white. Maybe you did sign those orders. Memory does play tricks under stress, Monty.' He paused again and continued to push the chair towards the silver expanse of the lake which stretched in front of them.

'And after all, they are all still missing. MacGregor the hero will leave a far more amenable widow.'

Gerald sowed the seed. Then, he turned the chair back towards the glittering chandeliers of the house.

'Think on it, brother.' He said no more on the subject. 'I must get back to town, I will leave you in mother's capable care.'

Gerald said his goodbyes and summoning his driver from his cosy seat by the kitchen fire, he climbed into his motorcar and was gone.

Montague Shipley looked at his mother with a mixture of feelings, none of them particularly friendly, surely his life was worth more than this. The face from the portrait he had painted from memory danced in his mind. Maybe his brother had a point. MacGregor and his men had been missing for months, it was likely they would never return. He was aware of what people in the regiment thought of him, aware that he was talked of with scorn in high, and lower places. Maybe it was time to try and smooth the record.

That night Montague Shipley tossed and turned in his sleep, his mind took him back to that summer's morning, the last time his body had been whole, and he had stood on his own two feet.

The field telephone had rung, and Shipley had answered it. The order was short and to the point as orders should be. The voice on the end of the crackly line was clipped and decisive.

'We advance at dawn tomorrow. Prepare your men to go over the top.'

Shipley was not a brave man. He had blustered his way through training on a wave of what could only be described as bullshit. He could not equate training with real life. The bullets were not real. The strategies and scenarios were not real. In training he could play at soldiers, and no one died. In war it was so, so different.

Nothing had prepared him for the reality of trench warfare, the mud, the stench, the cold, the lack of everything. He had not slept for weeks. From the safety of his cubby hole dug into the wall of the trench, he had heard the sniper fire ricocheting off the helmets the men sacrificed, as they tried to pinpoint the exact locations of their tormentors. He had seen the body of the trooper of the Black Watch, the man who had braved the crossfire and survived to bring them badly needed supplies of food and ammunition, the man whose only mistake had been to be a very tall man sitting in the wrong place at the wrong time. It had been after that terrible shooting that MacGregor had begged to be allowed to take his men out. Macgregor had a plan. Shipley had not.

Shipley had known then that he should have let the man go. It was the right thing to do, it was a decisive move, it would cut out some of the danger to the morning's advance. Instead, he had wavered, he had blustered, he had been weak. The bullets were real, and he had been terrified. He knew that MacGregor would go before him up that ladder and he knew that the men would follow MacGregor without question. To save his own face he had condemned those men. His brother was right.

The images of that day swam through his mind and his broken body, and he began to twitch and to sweat, he cried out in his sleep, and no one came. In the hospital there had always been a nurse to comfort him, Nurse Munro or Nurse Cameron, but provision of physical comfort was a step too far for his mother and his dreams terrified the servants. Strange, but in the convulsions of this dream he was sure he had felt a tingling in his toes.

Maybe even heard some words through the screams which struggled through his torn voice box.

In the morning, he woke, his pyjamas soaked in sweat and the contents of the bags which held his waste spilled over the bed. He rang for his valet. He was bathed and dressed and then ate a small breakfast in his room away from the attentions of his mother. Then he made his way under his own steam pushing the big wheels of his chair out to his studio. Holding the portrait of Rhianydd in his hand he made his decision.

CHAPTER 63. TURN AGAIN – Arthur Cole

Wales 1916.

Arthur Cole did not stop walking until dusk on the day that he had paid his visit to Nant Ddu Farm. The tears stopped streaming down his face by lunchtime. Later he considered whether they had dried because he had run out of tears or because the fresh wind had dried them on his face.

As dusk fell, he found himself on the coast near Southerndown. He had spent the night sitting atop the cliff staring across the Bristol channel thinking. His plan was to make his way to Cardiff and seek work there as a journalist. He knew he could write, and he had seen an advertisement in the local paper, the Gazette, for such a position. With the lack of men not called up to the army and having a fair education, he had been successful and had rapidly impressed the editor with both his enthusiasm and his obvious talent with words. The paper in Cardiff had connections with a national newspaper in London and Arthur was soon commissioned to write pieces for a larger publication. Eventually he was called to their head office in London where he was asked whether, with his experience, he could write a series of articles on the heroes of the war and eventually return to the war, this time as a correspondent. Walking back to his lodgings with a spring in his step for the first time in ages, he decided that it was time to write to Angharad.

My Dearest Angharad,

I feel slightly awkward to call you Harri, I write to let you know that I am alive, and I am well. Do not worry for me.

War will change a man. The sights and sounds and even the smells remain with you. It seems my ghosts are set to stay with me for the rest of my days. The first thing I find I must do is release you from any vows you made to me, we were young and impulsive and maybe it was a decision made in haste, with a war coming. You seem happy with your lot in life, you have made a good life for yourself and for our boy, a better life than I could ever imagine.

All I ask is that you tell him about me, for I am after all his father. He may have the gift they say I have for words. He may wonder where that came from.

After I left you, I wandered for a while. That wandering took me far into those hills we call home, and then to the coast where I found a peace within myself. I found I slept easier in the fresh air than in a bed and that my mind rested better. After several days of wandering, I found myself in Cardiff.

A man needs employment. I took a job with a local newspaper, but now I am writing to you from London. I hope soon to become a war correspondent for there is a move to boost public morale with stories of heroic events from 'the front.' I hope to be there. I hope to be the one writing the men's stories.

I fear our marriage must remain in place at least until we can both make some sense of the situation, but you may show this to a lawyer if you will, it may help you should you choose this course.

I will never forget you, Angharad, and part of me will always love you, and of course little Myrddin.

You may tell Cefin Thorne that I do not hate him, but warn him that, should he do wrong by you or my son, I will haunt him from wherever my grave may be. I fear I may never return to Wales, though it will always be my true home.

I must sign off now, my editor asks for an article about a medal presentation, it is to a crippled officer who I know of, he being in hospital at the same time as I. It is a strange turn of events, but I am not to reason why the man is declared a hero, when many of his men thought him otherwise.

My best regards to your family and all in the valley.

Arthur.

CHAPTER 64. HEADLINE NEWS

London 1916.

The article appeared in the newspapers, not on the front page but half a column on the third page, along with a photograph of a smart looking officer in uniform and another of that same officer, seated in his wheelchair, a tartan rug over his knees, his cap at a slightly jaunty angle, his smile slightly lopsided, and beside him stood General Haig himself. He was one of the first whose story would be published in this way.

The Germans lauded their heroes and made them household names. Every German boy wanted to fly like Von Richthofen, 'The Red Baron,' and knew exactly how many of the Royal Flying Corps planes had been shot down by their flying aces. The British army did not like their heroes named. They feared that loss of a man the public could grow to know and love would demoralise the people, not spur them on in support of their country. Thus, the exploits of many of the brave men fighting abroad were never heard of as they happened or afterwards. Reports from the war were dry lists of casualties, actions, and bad news in general. Gerald Shipley had suggested in a few high places that a different tack could be tried. He had then suggested that his brother's story could be used as a guinea pig. The powers in charge of such propaganda were open to the power of suggestion, they had taken the bait, a few strings had been pulled. A journalist from The Mail had been briefed. Not front-page news, but it was there.

The writer was a slightly self-effacing Welshman, new to the paper, recently travelled to London from Cardiff and hoping to report on more stories of action from the front line. He had been briefed by his editor from a neatly typed file supplied to him by an office at the Admiralty. He had read its contents and from them had compiled his column, to appear in the morning's paper and to be sent to the regional press.

A Hero is recognised

Today, at a low-key ceremony held at the country home of Lady Elspeth Shipley, a presentation was made to her son, Lieutenant Montague Simon Shipley of the Sussex regiment attached to the Queens own rifles.

Lieutenant Shipley, who was wounded on the first day of the battle of the Somme, was today awarded the Military Cross for his bravery and his meritorious action which saved the lives of many of his men.

In preparation for an assault the following morning, Lieutenant Shipley realised that his men, should they try and advance, would be easy prey to sniper fire from two enemy positions embedded in nearby woodland. Lieutenant Shipley had the forethought to order a detachment of four highly trained riflemen under cover of darkness, out into the adjacent woodland to eliminate the enemy snipers. This mission was successful and as a result no further men were lost to sniper fire when the order to advance was given.

Lieutenant Shipley himself then led his men into action, sustaining severe injuries from which he is still recovering.

The brave men who undertook the mission to eliminate the enemy snipers subsequently found themselves isolated from their unit and have now been listed as missing in action. However, sources from the front have reported that a similar unit acting independently was responsible for the defence of the military hospital at Abbéville where many lives were saved during two raids by the enemy. The men concerned, Sergeant Jack MacGregor, and Privates Charles Turner, Frank Baker and Ralph Owen were believed to be making their way back to their unit, but they are still unaccounted for. All four soldiers have been mentioned in dispatches and awarded the military medal, to be awarded posthumously should they never return.

The article went on to describe the defence by a few brave men of the field hospital under attack by a ruthless German foe. The journalist had been thorough in his work. There was an eyewitness account of the action from Gerald Shipley, though he was not named, and an account from one of the other medics, Doctor Sam O'Connor. It was a fine piece of writing, praising the heroes of the day and denigrating the actions of the Germans.

Gerald Shipley never met the journalist, but the man wrote with emotion as though he had been at the front and had heard the guns and experienced the terror. The article was written by A. Cole.

Montague's medal was presented by General Haig himself. The action concerned being on 1st July 1916 and Lieutenant Shipley too seriously injured to receive his award until this time.

Gerald Shipley slapped his brother on the shoulder. 'News like that does the whole country the power of good, boosts morale, gives you a good feeling doesn't it, Monty!'

'I suppose it does, Gerald, but it's still me in this chair,'

'Did I hear you say you could feel your toes a few weeks ago?'

'The local Doc says it's just phantom pains in my mind, never come to anything. He says my feet are like the lamps on a chandelier and someone has cut the cable, no hope of it mending, but I'm sure I felt something. I'm sure those nurses from the hospital wouldn't give up on me as quickly, or Doc Bannerman. Do you think he'd see me again?'

Monty smiled at his brother, 'Could you ask him Gerald, please?'

Gerald was seeing his brother through new eyes. Families were strange beasts, he thought. This one was run on tradition. His father had been a military man, now long dead, his body buried in some hot and dusty graveyard in a far-off foreign land, a memorial plaque decorating the wall of the local church and bearing his name, Major General Harold Montague Shipley. He was a man who had barely known the four sons he left behind, and the wife who had kept the 'Ship' afloat in his absence.

His oldest brother, young Harold, would inherit the estate and all that went with it. The three younger brothers had been steered into the army, commissions bought for them, officer training school and the hope of a peacetime career. He, Gerald, had made a good career of it, rising through the ranks higher than his father. Jeremy had thrived in the grey world of military intelligence, but Montague had always been different. He had always been more like their mother, gentle, artistic, a bit flighty and indecisive, hot tempered and stubborn to go with it. Monty had been spoiled as a child, he was used to having his own way, but his talents had never been nurtured, until now, now when he was half a man and confined to a chair, now he seemed to be finding himself.

Montague was an artist. He should never have joined the army, but it was a sad fact that in these times, the army would have taken him anyway. Gerald saw new hope and a new light in his brother's eyes. He would speak to Dr Bannerman, privately. He would not fan a false hope, but if there was a hope, an outside chance, then surely his brother deserved it.

At 3 The Parade, Cardiff, Moses Morgan was pouring his second cup of tea. 'Most decadent,' he thought to himself. Tea was in short supply, wasn't it, but if it was in the pot and made, why not? His wife wouldn't surface until lunchtime, his niece had taken off to Scotland to visit her brother-in-law. Helena had grown up so quickly, she was independent like her mother, she had done well in school, determined to get to Scotland as a reward for her studies. Was it Scotland or the brother-in-law she saw as the reward. Moses mused to himself and smiled. Was there room for another MacGregor in the family. Most certainly.

Yesterday's paper was still on the sideboard, unread. Yesterday had been so busy he had had no time to catch up on the news. His office at the docks had been chaotic, the miners of the South Wales Coalfield threatening to strike despite the war, their union lobbying for more miners. They were working around the clock to produce coal for the war and the workforce could not sustain the effort. Moses had ships waiting to sail, but no coal to fill them. He could see another fruitless trip to Westminster on the horizon.

The local newspaper he bought every morning would contain nothing to brighten the day, so he had left it under the big tea pot on the sideboard for the housekeeper to read. There it was, undisturbed.

Moses finished pouring his tea, added milk, and dropped in two lumps of sugar, carried the strong brew to his seat at the long table and then reached for the newspaper and began to read. Bad news from the front, more massive casualties, more men needed, more fodder for the war machine. The miners were considering strike action, yes, he knew that all too well. General Haig was back in London in talks with the PM.

He turned the page and scanned the headlines. His eye caught the larger print, 'A Hero is recognised.' 'Poor sod,' he thought on seeing the figure in the wheelchair. He read on, good story he thought, familiar, where had he heard it before? Then he saw the names of the men. He spluttered into his tea. Jack MacGregor, Rhianydd's husband! He dabbed his chin with his napkin, knocking the tea over with the heavy square of linen. He stood. The chair pushed backwards across the polished parquet flooring. He strode into the room next door, his study, lifted the receiver of the telephone, tapping the connecting bar three times. The operator answered with one word 'EXCHANGE' and Moses demanded they put him through to St Harmon 3. There was no exchange at St Harmon, but the operator knew what he meant. He listened as the connections were made from one switchboard to another. In his mind he visualised the operators making the connections with their plugs and sockets and switches in the polished Bakelite boards in front of them. Then silence, followed eventually by a man's voice.

'Who is it?' The voice was gruff, and the question blunt.

'Edward? Is that you, Edward Meredith? I need Sibyl, put her on.'

'Yes, this is Edward, who the devil are you?'

'Just put her on, can't you?' The voice was brusque and impatient. Then he heard noises in the background and Edward surrendered the receiver.

'Uncle Moses? Is that you?' The voice sounded young, younger, and brighter than he expected.

'It is, have you read the paper, do you get the Western Mail down there, page three, read it?'

'Uncle, we haven't had a paper in days. Dickie the paper boy has been called up, his father runs the shop and has to do everything now himself. He can't get into town to pick them up more than once a week.'

'I shall read it to you then – you must tell Rhianydd.'

'Uncle, this is Rhianydd, mother is called away.'

'Oh! Then my dear, I must read it to you, it gives hope, it is a great turn up for the books!' Rhianydd heard the gruff voice clearing its throat and the pages of the newspaper rustling themselves into order. Then he began to read. Rhianydd listened, heart lifting with every sentence.

'Uncle, send me the page, by mail, which will get here faster than we can get Tom the shop to go to Newtown. Our men may be alive, not maybe, they are, I can feel it. Thank you, Uncle, thank you so much!'

Rhianydd replaced the receiver, ending the call before she was asked awkward questions about her mother's absence. With a spring in her step, she called Agnes down for breakfast. Today would be a day for Agnes to spend with Edward. Rhianydd needed to compose herself, then she needed to contact her mother.

After her return from France, Rhianydd had spent several weeks in the employ of Gerald Shipley. She had personally supervised his recovery from both his wounds and his surgery. He was a fit man and an uncomplaining patient, determined to get back on his feet and back to his duties as soon as he could. He had been a breath of fresh air. She had had little to do with his brother Montague, though they were under the same roof.

Once Gerald was no longer in need of her services, Rhianydd had returned to Hengwm and her daughter. In time she would have to return to her duties, but Gerald had promised to pull a few strings and get her a posting which suited her needs, all she had to do was call him when she was ready. Rhianydd saw Gerald's hand all over the newspaper article. Only he could have talked his brother round, made Montague a decorated war hero and massaged his ego enough to make him believe it was true. Rhianydd raised her eyes to the heavens.

'Thank you, Lord, for Gerald Shipley. Now please help me find mother or if not mother, HIM!'

Pulling her old coat off the kitchen door and pulling on her boots, she clattered down the stone stairs to the cave they called the cellar, opened the huge chest which occupied the whole of one wall. As the ancient hinges creaked, she shivered and looked away, each time she had opened this lid she had expected to find a body. Sense told her that there was no such thing contained there, but she still got the feeling of it. Reaching in she pulled out the lumpy cloth bag which contained the stone charm her mother had left for her, and the pewter dish polished to a mirror finish by the hands of time. She slung it over her shoulder. Back up the narrow stone steps to the kitchen she saw Edward and Agnes crossing the yard, Edward holding Agnes by the hand and Agnes with a rope halter slung over her shoulder and a small trug of feed in her other hand, off to find her beloved Zak. She would be happy for the day then. It crossed Rhianydd's mind that before long she would need to instil some formal education into her daughter. Edward Meredith would teach her many things, how to lay a hedge and carve a thumb stick, what not to feed the sheep, how to whistle to the sheepdog and how to use a hammer. Mathematics and grammar were not included in the syllabus.

Rhianydd crossed the yard calling out to them on her way, 'I'll be back by teatime, you pair behave yourselves. I want no broken bones when I get back!' She heard Edward chuckling to himself as they disappeared up the back field. An old, old man kept young by two forces of nature, one of them her daughter.

CHAPTER 65. CROSSING THE VEIL – Rhianydd & Red

Wales 1916.

I strode up the mountain to the Druid's cave, the sun was nearly high enough, I knew I could do nothing until its rays fell on the altar stone. I unpacked the bag and waited. This was the first time I had tried this alone. Before, I had always had my mother beside me, as a sort of guide, and HE had been there too, but those were in days when I had doubted my powers. Now I knew the strength of them. Now, I knew I had to be ready, for Jack and for the others.

At midday the sun hit its highest point, the hint of light penetrated the gloom of the cave, but not quite there yet, another hour should do it. As the sun dropped lower its glow lit the huge flat rock. I poured the water I had carried from the spring nearby into the pewter dish, lowered the smooth purple veined stone into its centre, bowed my head, covered myself with the pungent smelling cloak of the forest, no one must see me here. Placing my hands over the stone, I focussed my mind. One word was all I needed,

'Mother,' but the waters stayed calm, undisturbed. 'Mother, where are you?' Again, nothing.

I racked my brain, what was I doing wrong, there was more to this, then, than making a subterranean phone call. My mother was still in our time, she had been in France staying with the men, her job to keep them safe, what could have happened?

The light was moving, the sun dropping too low, I did not have much time. Time, yes that was the key, the others were not of this time, what had they called her?

I tried again, focussed all my energy, both hands on the cool surface of the stone as it lay in the water. 'Merch Goch, Red Maid where are you?'

The water moved, its surface rippled above the shining surface of the bowl that held it, it swirled around my hands on the stone. As the swirling stopped, an image formed. Clearly it was my mother, I would recognise that mop of greying red curls anywhere, but the woman I was looking at was dressed in the garb of a medieval servant and was wearing chains. My mother was manacled and was that some sort of dungeon? I instinctively withdrew my hands and the image disappeared. My mind screamed, 'Mother!' but the word came out 'Eryr!' The light passed over the huge stone altar and the cave became dark.

I must go home, I was expected there, yet I could not move, the cave was closing around me wrapping me in its walls, what must I do? Instinct guided me to the fissure in the wall, my hand slid through it, then my shoulder, then my whole body. I was standing in a stone passage outside a heavy wooden door. It was dark, the walls ran with damp and the only light was from pine torches hung in brackets from the walls. I heard movement, heavy footsteps, someone was coming. I ducked into an alcove. Two figures rounded the corner of the passage.

'The old witch has her way then.' a man's voice. The answer was from a woman,

'We've to prepare her, without this woman the witch will die. Her power fades daily, maybe it would be better if...,'

'We do as we are told, Mary. She's to wash and dress herself and we are to see she is fed, then take her up to the tower room.'

'But her ladyship is still in London, who is to know if we do her bidding or not?'

'Mary, we do as we are told, she sees everything, she hears everything, we cannot disobey her.'

I listened in the darkness, knowing that they could not see me. I pulled the cloak tighter round me, seeking its security. I must follow them.

'Come in then, Eli, let's get this over with then we can go on our way.'

The two shambling figures, passed within inches of me and I fell in behind them. At the end of the passage, they produced a huge set of keys. The man looked in through the small, barred window at head height.

'Stand back, hag!' he commanded.

I heard the clank of manacles and bare feet shuffling on the stone floor. The couple stepped into the cell. I followed unseen behind them.

The woman threw a bundle of clothes at the ragged figure which stood before them. 'Dress in these, Milady calls you.'

The ragged figure stood up straight, towering over Eli and Mary. I watched as my mother threw the bundle back at them, shouting,

'Fuck Milady and fuck you!' She sprang across the cell to the extent of the leg chain which was fastened to a staple in the floor. Eli dodged the attack which had sent Mary tumbling into the overfull slops bucket. He grabbed mother by the throat, pinning her against the wall.

'Listen, bitch, you dress, do you hear me,' He pinched her cheeks together with one hand around her face. 'or you will go there naked. I'm not to harm you, or I'd find out what a red cunt feels like. Mary is dried like a prune, but you look juicy enough!'

The slap that followed echoed round the walls. The response was swift. Mother's unchained leg hit Eli between his own and he doubled over clutching his balls. This could not end well. Mary was already coming to her husband's aid, brandishing a lump of wood from the extinguished brazier, the only source of heat for the prisoner. Dripping with liquid excrement, the woman closed on her target.

I dropped the cloak from my shoulders. Red jerked back in surprise. I picked up the empty slops bucket and hit Mary on the head with it with all my strength, the remains of its contents dripping down her face as she fell unconscious.

'Keys, he has the keys!' Red screamed. Eli was crawling towards the door. We could not allow him to leave.

I leapt on him from behind. Raking him in the eyes, I fought him like a cat. Eventually relieving him of the knife he carried at his waist, with a surgeon's skill I ran its rusty jagged blade across his throat, holding his head firm against my chest. I felt the skin break and with a little more pressure just below his ear, a fountain of blood spurted out. Eli Jones fell like a stone, dead nearly as he reached the floor.

Throwing the keys to mother I dragged both bodies to the back of the cell. I cared little whether Mary was still alive, Hippocrates could go hang for today. Surely, he was due a day of rest. Locking the cell door behind them, mother wearing Mary's good boots, provided no doubt by her mistress, we fled.

'Which way out?' I gasped.
Stopping to catch their breath, Red composed herself. She breathed in deeply.

'Smell that, it's the sea, we must be at Pembroke, head for the sea, there is a postern door somewhere leading to the loading dock!'

The dock was devoid of boats, the only vessel being one of the tiny coracles the local men used to fish the river. Round and shallow, made from tar cloth stretched over a willow frame, it barely supported the two of us, and having only one paddle we made slow progress. Reaching a small beach on the first turn of the river, Red spoke.

'We must hide, she will hunt us, she will not stop!'

'So, we are at Pembroke, but when is this, what year is this, where are the men? I have news!' My words fell on deaf ears for several minutes but eventually my mother answered.

'Welcome to 1486 daughter. The men are in London, I believe, but it is not safe for us there. You have my things?'

'I have the stone.' I replied, feeling it's comforting weight in her pocket.

'That will have to do, the rest we can improvise, first we find somewhere safe to rest.'

We hid the tiny coracle out of sight of the river, then began to walk inland. At first, the path followed the coast, winding its way along tall cliffs, then it climbed through lush green fields and then upwards onto springy mountain turf.

'Where are we headed?' I asked.

'Where she may not be able to see me,' my mother replied, 'to the circle at Waun Mawn, it is a powerful place, its stones were used to build the Henge on Salisbury plain. The auld ones moved a whole henge there because it suited their needs, but the earth has more power here in the Preseli hills. The site of the big stones remains and some of the smaller ones still remain in place. Eryr's father lives here, though it is best not to disturb him, but his very presence around us may afford some protection.'

We walked on. Mother demanded,

'Now, what is this news you bring, why have you come here, though I can't say your arrival wasn't in the nick of time?'

I explained, breathless,

'The officer who sought to have them shot, well he has relented, he himself has been decorated as a hero. Haig himself presented his medal. Jack and his men have been mentioned in dispatches and their defence of Abbéville is now known, they too have been put forward for medals. Surely this means they can come home.' I sighed.

'Tread carefully, Rhianydd, do not trust them fully, be cautious, make sure it is not a ruse to entice them out of hiding.' her mother advised.

'And where are they now, mother, why are they in London?' she asked.

'They were taken on business for the king, for Henry VII, but they were pulled here by Milady Margaret de Audley, witch that she is. She now lives in the body of the king's mother. It is she who pulls the strings. Though she grows weak, her evil knows no bounds. The Dragon of Wales has deserted her, she no longer has his power, so she seeks to use mine. Once she was my mentor and I trusted her and respected her, for she did only good with her power. Now she has changed. One of us must die. She set the traps and we walked into them. Her prophecy is fulfilled. There is a Welsh born king on the throne, but it will take much to keep him there. So, she still plots. She has promised the men's release after the Coronation. I was her hostage. If she was true to her word, that ceremony was days ago. The men should have left for Wales by now, that is why she wanted me brought to her, moved to her tower to await her arrival. Then she would harness my will as her own, even take my body as she took that of Lady Beaufort. She lives on false promises, there is no truth left in her and I do not recognise what she has become.'

'So, we find the London Road and wait for them?'

'No, Rhianydd, we cannot. She looks through the same veil as you did. She will find me. The stones of Waun Mawn may protect me, and we will need your father's help. Tonight, I will call him, he will hear me. He does not know I was imprisoned. It will anger him. Once he is here, the tables will turn, and she will not be safe. Then you must go home. I will tell you how.'

It took two days of hard walking to reach the bleak hillside of Waun Mawn. This must have been an impressive place before the great stones were removed, taken to the more hospitable site where they now stood, on the Great Plain at Salisbury. Aegir had wept when the auld druids had taken them away, leaving only the holes they had stood in and some of the smaller monoliths to say that there had ever been a great circle above his subterranean home.

Hundreds of men had used wooden rollers to move them, then taken them on great barges around the coast, dragged them again to their final resting place. Had the druids and the prophets but asked and given him good reason, he could have moved them with the flick of his finger. But they had not, so he had not been disposed to help them in anyway. In fact, he had beset them with trials, making sure that those in the future would eventually know exactly where the great structure they so revered had come from. The blue stone was only found here, it grew in Welsh soil, it was quarried from a Welsh mountain, his mountain.

Aegir was old now, he had become more solitary with the years, he no longer relished the company of others, he was bound by blood to help his kinfolk, but if he did not acknowledge their presence, how could he consider their requests.

In these times he kept his own counsel, he would neither help nor hinder any being unless he was obliged to. He heard them above him now, rare visitors to his rooftop. Few pilgrims darkened his doorstep since the Saesneg druids had stolen his stones. What were they about, two women, and alone, but not alone? Aegir sensed this. The older one, she was in great danger, and she was kin, she was one of his kind, yet she seemed not to know how close she was to her nemesis. And the younger, she would be taken too.

The great red beast y Ddraig slept in his lair, no longer wakened by the call of his mistress. He had turned on her, he no longer obeyed her. His breath now warmed Aegir in his halls at night. The dragon again waited for his time. Maybe Aegir would have use for him soon.

There was little shelter on the hillside, the rain was already soaking the two women to the skin. They had made a makeshift tent between two of the hardy gorse bushes which thrived in the holes where the blue stones had once stood. The younger one seemed distracted and the older one unaware of what awaited her.

Unseen and deep below their feet, Aegir picked up his old wooden staff, a great knobbly blackthorn root weathered with age and with the patina of handling. Muttering to himself he called upon his own powers, unused for centuries. The sky grew black overhead, the clouds collided, and torrential rain began to fall. Thunder bounced off the mountain tops and lightening flashed all around the two women sheltering on his roof. The older woman stood and stared in amazement.

Red pulled Rhianydd out into the centre of where the stone circle had been.

'See, it is there.'

'What is where?' came the reply.

'The circle, it protects us, the storm is all around but not here, here it is calm.'

Rhianydd stepped beside her mother and as she wiped the remains of the rain from her face, she saw that all around her was a ring of standing stones, huge, blue tinged monoliths, planted in the ground, the lightening a force between them and over them.

Through the silver light of the circle a dark form appeared, a warrior dressed in leather and in furs, armed with sword and longbow and leading two horses. Before she could greet him, the figure spoke.

'Mother, Sister, how are you?'

'Calon!' Red threw herself at her son.

'Brother! How are you here?' Rhianydd stumbled over her words.

'We have little time. Father and the others are captive, the witch does not keep her word, she has held them prisoner these last months in her castle at Pembroke.'

'But we have just come from there, they cannot be....., we would have heard them!'

'They were taken just before they reached the harbour. They were promised release before they took ship, then her servants took them. They are held in a different part of the castle. She will leave them there to die for there is plague there, many have already died from it!' He drew breath and spoke again.

'I am followed, and I am known to her, I cannot help them alone!'

Red spoke. 'You must take your sister back to safety. You know the way through, then return to me, please Calon. Much depends on you, but Rhianydd has her own daughter to think of.'

'There is more.' Calon spoke quietly, 'The witch has taken everyone in her anger, but she does not have little Agnes. I have taken her to safety. She is with her father's kin in Scotland. It was the only place I could think of to put that blessed pony of hers for she would not leave without him. They will keep her close. They were most understanding. But Edward, she has taken Edward and Hengwm is in ruins!'

Rhianydd had overheard everything. 'Then I must go now,' she insisted, her maternal instinct coming to the fore, 'now Calon, I must go now, and mother, you must come with me!'

'Calon, you must take Rhianydd back. I will wait here for you. I am protected here.'

The voice that spoke to them then was deeper than thunder and smoother than chocolate. Aegir spoke from deep beneath their feet. 'There is another way. I will take your daughter home Red. It is but a trifle for me. I will get her to where she needs to be. I will reunite her with her daughter.'

With that, amongst the clashes of thunder and the silver sheets of rain a tree appeared. 'Come, Rhianydd, daughter of Eryr, child of the mountain, you have only to touch the mother Oak, she will take you there. Trust me, for you must!'

'Trust him sister, he is, after all, your grandsire.' Calon drew her towards the gnarled bark of the trunk and taking her by the shoulder, lifted her arm towards it.

As her skin touched the bark Rhianydd vanished.

'Mount up, mother, we have no time to lose!'

Red took the proffered reins and mounted the spare horse. The rain stopped as suddenly as it had started, and the sky became a magical shade of blue. Calon spurred his mount to a gallop, urging Red to do the same. Unused to riding and bouncing around in a most undignified manner on her mount's saddle, she followed.

In the distance, above the clouds and over the mountains to the north Red was sure she saw the tail of the great Ddraig Goch disappear over the horizon.

They had ridden south all day when Red insisted that they stop to give the horses a break and for her to think. She left her horse with Calon, drinking from a small dew pool on the mountain top and grazing quietly on the scorched mountain turf.

'Where are you?' she called under her breath. 'All the signals are confused, I can neither hear you nor see you.'

As the thought left her mind, an eagle dipped low over the landscape. Calling out in its haunting shriek, it swooped to within feet of the grass beneath her before soaring upwards and disappearing to the west.

'We must follow it, Calon, I sense that is the way we must go.'

They mounted up and headed off, following the flight of the bird which became a pin prick on the horizon.

Slowing to a sedate trot and finally to a walk, Calon and Red left the mountain and joined the parish road. After a few miles, Red saw movement in the distance. 'Stop, wait, there are men up ahead.'

The travellers ahead had seen them, and they too had stopped and were attempting to take cover in the brush alongside the road. They were not making a bad job of it and given more time may have been undetectable by the time Red and Calon came upon them. As they passed the largest of the gorse bushes a figure leaped out into the road waving its arms and shouting

'Red, it is you, thank goodness, we were starting to despair. Ralph left us. The bastard looked after himself. He said he would return but he did not, he left us to our fate!'

'He will return, he will not be far away. Come, off the road all three of you, it is not long until dark and we must rest.'

They turned into a nearby field and hobbled the horses, then Calon unpacked the food he had brought with him and helped Frankie and Charlie to make a small fire. Uncle Edward scratched his old head and tutted at me, muttering apologies, 'I could not stop her.' over and over again.

'Charlie,' thought Red, 'where had they found Charlie?' He had been thought dead. That would be another tale to tell at another time, she thought.

She wrapped her old cloak around her and found some tussocky springy grass on which to curl up for the night. She was well used to sleeping under the stars. Looking up she could see that the sky was clear and black, and the buckle of Orion's belt was as shiny as it should be. Too tired to sleep, she began to count the stars, pondering her life as it was, unconsciously deciding what she would do with the rest of her life if she ever made it home again.

'Spend it with me.' The voice was quiet in her ear the breath disturbed her hair and tickled her neck.

'Why would I ever want to do that, Adain Eryr, son of Aegir. Where the hell have you been hiding?'

'I float on eagles wings, I hide amongst the clouds, you could be there too.'

'At this moment I'd rather have warm bed and a soft mattress.' I replied.

'Hold tight, my lady!' He gathered me up with one arm and leaving only a humped shape of my cloak on the mound of grass where we had lain, he swept me away.

'Eryr, where are we going?'

'We are going to set you free!'

CHAPTER 66. RESURGAM - Red

We seemed to fall through the mountain like water from a geyser, a wild and uncontrolled exit from the land and time which had held us. As if the earth no longer wanted us in her midst we were spat out, vomited, like some form of poison. I held tight to him. He was the only thing that held my consciousness. If I let go, I would be lost for good. My bones shuddered in my body, my muscles burned, and my mind seemed to shatter like the crystal glass I had once thrown into the back of the fireplace in temper, millions of rainbow-reflecting shards burning in the fire of hell. Had the devil finally caught us then, was now the time for us to face our nemesis and pay for our sins? But what sins were they? We had only followed a path which time and history dictated. We were the servants, not the masters. I closed what I thought were my eyes and felt the last breath I could muster form into a word, a name,

'Margaret.' It echoed through my brain lengthened in its syllables Mar.... gar...et... like a mother calling an errant child in from play. Then there was blackness, my arms fell slack and then nothing.

'Red, Sibyl, Red, oh, god no........,' the voice was frantic, my mind tried to answer yet no voice came. I felt his long-fingered hand feel for a pulse at my wrist, then under my jaw, 'Diolch I dduw,' I felt my pulse beat on his fingers, I focused on the rhythm, 'dub, dub, dub......Come back to me, Red, hold on!'

His voice was desperation, panic even. Then I sensed others around me, hovering above, faces swirling in mist, some I knew were lost forever, others merely wandering in time. Rhianydd and Jack, Calon and Celine, Gwyn, Frank and Fiona, Charlie, and Frances, even Uncle Edward. Above them all a greater being pulling me down, Margaret de Audley...., she who had once been a force for good, now tainted by the dark arts which had ensnared her, corrupted by power, acting only for her own good. Now in the guise of Margaret Beaufort.

I could not fight her, she had me in her grip, yet I was held by another. The fight was with them now, my life a bone between two demons.

'She shall not take you, Red!' Hands ripped at my clothing, I felt him pressing on my chest, listening for a breath, then his mouth over mine, breathing. One breath was all it took, the pressure of air woke my dormant lungs and like a drowning woman breaking the surface I coughed and spluttered, then I threw up, vomit spraying all over him. Then darkness, and through the darkness I could see her, not the regal, elegant woman she had once been, long dark hair flying around her face, silver eyes gleaming in the firelight. She was now a thin old crone, her face haggard, her body wasted away, hair white and thinning, her dull grey eyes fixed on me. Her reflection rippled and for a second broke, then formed again, I was seeing her as she was seeing me, through water, the old witch was gazing me, gazing me from her precious silver dish! I could not let the whole image form. Margaret.

'Water!' I gasped.

I felt my head tipped forward and a flask placed to my lips.

'Not drink!' I shook my head fiercely. 'She is using the water!'

The waves took me again, waves of nausea. My head spun. The world rotated around my head, spinning every way it could. She tried to wring the life force from me and drag it through her own vortex and into her grasp. I felt that she was dying, that she needed my life force to continue her existence. I thought it seconds before he acted. I felt his grip tighten around me and then felt all his muscles tense as he leapt.

Back into the water, and down, down into the black depths, further down than before, carried down life's spiral, away from her, but to who knew where. I was drowning, Eryr was drowning me, water filled my lungs, and there was peace. Gentle floating peace, the songs of water filled my ears, a swooshing washing lullaby, but I must not sleep, maybe just for a moment. Would I have Peace, never ending peace?

At the eye of the storm there is a calm, and her grip was like a hurricane's grip on the soil, fierce and taking all in its path.

I heard him then, commanding me, 'Hold fast, Red, I will never let you go!'

I felt the water leave my lungs, as though I had coughed and spewed an ocean. He breathed life back into me, and for a second I saw him, but this was not my Eryr. His face was that of a gargoyle, carved from stone, an expression of anger, a concentration of evil like you could not imagine, a picture conjured from the works of Dante. Was this his true self? I banished the image from my brain, was he not a being of many parts, I had only seen what he chose to show me, in all these years I had only scratched the surface.

Water engulfed us again, down, down, and further down, his mouth over mine, his breath in my lungs, his heart beating for me, no thoughts in my head but his. I felt him fight her, her hooks snagged at my skin but did not impale me, her nets did not imprison me, for every lure she threw out, he countered with flame, boiling the waters distorting the surface so that she could no longer see me. With the maelstrom raging behind us we hit the bottom.

Rocks opened beneath us and again we fell through time's doorway. The air was warm, slightly sulphurous with a whiff of stale dead flesh, it carried us up wards. Then I realised we were flying, but it was not Eryr who carried us, we were lifted by Y Ddraig, his huge red wings beating their rhythm up from the pull of the witch and home, home to Wales.

We landed on mountain turf, springy and green under our bodies, deposited like items of prey dropped from his huge claws. We lay on the grass entwined together, breathing as one until we both became fully conscious.

I was first to speak. 'Is she dead?'

'She is as dead as time can make her, Red.' came the reply.

'But did you see her dead?'

'Her path to you is broken, to her, you are now dead, she cannot feed on you anymore.'

'But is she fucking dead Eryr,' I paused, all manner of images, sounds and thoughts replaying in my mind, 'or am I?'

'How do you feel cariad, do you feel alive?'

I made a mental inventory of body parts, from the bottom up. Everything moved, all my senses seemed to be active, I could smell the freshness of the air, I could feel the muscles of his chest under my head and the tickle of his hair as it fell over my face, the warmth of the sun on my skin. I could talk, and when I opened my eyes I could see the endless blue sky above us. 'I do.' I answered him.

'Then you are alive, and by the grace of all our gods and with a little help from below I am also alive.'

He rolled towards me. 'Red, you have no clothes.'

I ran a hand down my body feeling for cloth, for skirts or shift or anything which passed for a garment. I found none. Feeling sideways I felt his skin under my hand, warmed by the sun, smooth and lightly hairy to the touch, hard flat stomach muscles quivered slightly as my hand strayed lower, and I turned towards him

'Neither have you.'

He silenced my laughter with his mouth, kissing me this time, lightly, each kiss a little further down my body, mouth, eyes, forehead, chin, neck. I squirmed as his mouth found each breast then plotted a course to my navel and lower, pinning my hips with his hands. I offered myself to him, poised to receive his lips and tongue where I craved them most. I felt him kiss my feet, and pulled away, but he held fast,

'They are clean as a baby's, Red.' His suppressed laughter rippled up the inside of my left leg, to be joined in seconds by the right.

He was very much alive, more alive than I feared I could cope with, and his intentions were very plain.

I closed my eyes and abandoned myself to another death, a 'petit mort,' as the French would say. I came round on my stomach, his hands beneath me raised me to my knees and I felt him, he took me then like an animal, his chest wrapped over my back, his teeth grazing my neck and his left hand massaging that place where we joined. His own small death came with a howling cry which seemed to echo through the hills. Our breathing calmed and gradually we both regained consciousness. He spoke first.

'Are you alive then, Red?'

'I am, damn you!'

'So am I, and glad of it.'

He took my hand and placed it on his balls. 'Hold those for me for a minute, Red.'

I felt the attached cock swelling under my wrist, 'Let me know when you're ready to go again.'

I answered him with my mouth. His response came in unintelligible gasps, ending in ae eerie scream.

Several hours later, as we watched the sun drop out of the sky and into the sea behind Ireland, he took my face between his hands. 'I love you Red, please come home to me.'

In the last forty-eight hours I had been through four hundred years of time, been sucked down through hells drain hole, drowned and been reborn. Did I even have another home to go to?

'You are my home, Eryr, no matter where we are, where I am. Home is not a place for me. You live in my soul, the rest is just things.'

It was growing chilly. Goosebumps were appearing on arms and legs and nipples were standing erect in protest.

I turned my thoughts to clothing, and my subconscious closet attired me in leather breeches, linen shirt and a warm cloak in dark velvet lined with the furs of the forest.

'Merch Goch,' he growled behind me, 'your arse looks fine in leather.'

I turned and looked him up and down.

'Not so bad yourself, for an old Faerie.'

'Less of the old, please, we Faeries have feelings.'

'That,' I said, 'is what I am most afraid of.'

CHAPTER 67. THE HUNTED - Margaret

January 1486.

Her job was done, her life was fulfilled, the boy Margaret Beaufort had given birth to was finally fulfilling the destiny she had made for him, and she was living her life through him. She believed herself all powerful, the woman behind the throne. The King deferred to her, and even the Queen treated her with the utmost respect. She was, 'My lady the Kings mother.' She had put him there, hadn't she? Now only she could keep him there or remove him.

Lady Margaret de Audley was old now, older than time itself, withered with the years, her energy and power sapped by the constant quest for more. She felt the conflict between her present and her past grow inside her and realised she could not keep up the façade for much longer.

Installed in the sumptuous apartments usually reserved for the Queen herself, her power was waning. Her stick thin body was worn out with praying, praying to the Auld Gods, and to her Catholic god. The black wooden cross and rosary beads which hung round her now scrawny neck could once have been jet, but no longer, for jet would burn such as she.

She gazed into the pool of water in the ornate silver vessel in front of her, drapes and tapestries drawn over the high arched windows, the darkened room lit only by candles, all entry forbidden to others, her private guard outside the door. She had called the Red Maid, Merch Goch as she was known, searched for her through the veils of time, drawn her out of her peaceful existence. The woman was still blind to her own power, or if not blind, still unwilling to be all that she could be. Lady Margaret's once pure soul, corrupted by witchcraft, had descended into blackness. She coveted the power she felt in this other woman's blood. In the Red Maid was the strength that would keep her own wretched form alive.

She must keep them all, that was the only way. She had promised them release from their bonds, but no matter, they would all dance to her tune for a little longer for she was not ready to surrender. She knew it was only flames that awaited her on the other side from life, she had felt their heat once before, she did not relish that death.

All her plans were falling apart. She had demanded too much of them. Had her power been strong enough, they would have obeyed without question, but they had defied her at the last and now they were gone.

She had watched them leave, the last four of her private army. She had provided them with horses and a wagon and with food and promised them passage on a ship from Milford. Then her duplicitous mind had swung on its axis, and she had sent other instructions by messenger bird to the great castle. None were to leave, the men should be welcomed into the fortress and made comfortable and then lured into captivity in the north dungeon, the one which had housed the plague prisoners. Let them rot, rot how her boy's father had rotted when she had been a young wife and expectant mother.

She could no longer see them to hunt them down. Her anger threatened to consume her. She turned from the gazing pool and walked to the window, looked out over the grey water of the Thames and inhaled slowly, gathering herself and calming her temper. She needed to be calm to see.

What if those she held in her castle were already gone? She could not feel their presence in her grasp, they had been there, like a team of well-trained horses, guided to their fate by the reins she held in her hands, but the reins were snapped, and the horses had bolted. She would hunt them down. They had deceived her.

Her fury engulfed her and using charms she had not uttered for centuries she sent the wind of her wrath, sent it to destroy, sent it to transport. She felt the very roots of the mountains shake and she felt her harpies leave with only one soul, one she could hold to ransom if she must. She calmed herself, steadying her hands and breathing deeply, focusing again on the pool of water in the vessel before her.

The boys, those boys, they lived, she was sure of it, she felt their life force still with her. They were supposed to die, the last hopes of the house of York were supposed to die, then she could rest, rebuild her strength, using that of Merch Goch.

The waters rippled before her as she blew over the surface, sending wind to clear the fog from her mind, a slight circular movement of her hand and the water spun, and Margaret could see plainly down the vortex. She sensed her target was there but protected by another, who or what was he? This was a being she could not control. Did they think they could hide from her beneath the hills, did they not know she would find them, then she would have the strength to find a new life for herself? Y Ddraig would again warm her cold old bones and heal her. The sibyl's aura would make her rise again, stronger than ever. The dark waters started to clear and her fading silver-grey eyes under wrinkled lids found their mark.

> 'From earth and water, power divine,
> surrender all, your soul be mine.
> Life or death are yours to choose,
> tis journeys end, and one must lose.'

The surface of the water boiled under the weight of the spell, swirling and bubbling, controlled only by the force of her mind.

The eyes that met hers through the vortex were not the deep blue of Sibyl named for a prophetess, but the piercing green pinpointed with red of her defender. It was he who answered the call, the words unspoken in sound but heard plainly in her mind.

> 'Sweet water is the source of life,
> I call you false, the devil's wife.
> Your time is come to leave this earth,
> for you there will be no re-birth.'

Then he was gone and Sibyl the Red Maid with him, the water seeming to swallow them. Her bony hand swirled over what had been her liquid mirror, yet the water would not clear, she could no longer conjure the images she sought. The shallow pool pulled her down to its surface, the once purified water stank of sulphur and brimstone, the breath of y Ddraig blew through the vortex, the waves in the veil parted and the dragon took back the life that he had given her all those years ago.

Engulfed in his eternal flames she fell screaming through the centre of the storm, downwards ever downwards. She had betrayed the trust of her creator. Y Ddraig Goch would not suffer such duplicity. Margaret de Audley was gone.

In the apartments of the queen, My Lady the King's mother, Margaret Beaufort knelt before the altar in her private chapel, tucked the jet crucifix into her bodice next to her skin and then turned to her private priest to make confession. She felt a lightness of being that she had not felt for years, in fact it was the first time she had felt truly alive since the birth of her son.

She shut the chapel door behind her and glided soundlessly along the flagstones of the cloistered passage. It was getting late, her old bones felt the cold these days, but she eschewed wearing the sumptuous fur cloaks she found in her closet, far too rich for her tastes. Whatever had possessed her lady in waiting to commission such vanities? She pulled the plain woollen wrap around her shoulders and went to seek audience with her son, the King. No doubt he would chide her for her sartorial inadequacies if he deigned to speak to her at all. He had been distant, distracted of late.

Today she felt as though her prayers had been heard, felt that something had changed. Why had she chosen this time to wear Jet, the jewellery given to her by Henry's father on their wedding day? She had not worn it since her confinement. Why now? For the first time in years, Margaret Beaufort felt whole.

'Mother, how are you this evening, you look refreshed.'

'Thank you, my son. I feel as though the Lord has heard my prayers at last. How is the Queen, is all well with her?'

'If you spent a little more time in the land of the living and a little less time on your knees you would know that she is with child.

'Do you not wish me well, lady mother?' the younger voice of Elizabeth of York, the king's wife entered the room.

'I am pleased for you, my dear. Pray God it will be a boy.' The voice for once was not dripping with sarcasm. The young queen was taken aback.

Did the King's mother not resent the Queen's growing closeness to her son. A marriage purely of convenience, but this girl from the York line knew how to conduct herself, knew the ways of political life. It was a life she had been born into, had lived amongst since she was a child, whereas Henry had lived in protected exile and was unsure of his way.

Daily she grew closer to him, undermining Margaret's hold. Margaret's grip was slipping. Now things were happening which she had no knowledge of. There were men bound to her by some strange oath she did not understand. They were mercenaries, but she did not clearly remember why they had not been released from service, they were little use locked up in the dungeons of Pembroke. Yet, a messenger bird had brought a message only yesterday that they were still there. She must make enquiry after them. If they were still loyal to her son maybe they could be of use to him, or if they were at least no threat, maybe they should be released from his service. She would send a messenger.

Sometimes she felt as though she had lost part of her mind, ordered things that her usual self would never have dreamed of. The only constants left seemed to be Henry, and prayer.

The Castle at Pembroke was an imposing structure. It had guarded its position on the coast of Wales for several hundred years. It had withstood raids from sea and land and from both raiding English barons and Welsh rebel tribes. It was implacable, it shrugged all attacks from its great stone shoulders like a great giant shedding his cloak after the winter. The dungeons were cold, the walls thick and the sea wind whistled through the slit windows, a wind straight from Ireland with no break in its path since the great ocean. There was little light, what there was carried in the narrow dust filled ray that came in with the wind at daybreak or came in through the opening in the roof with the incessant rain.

Gwyn was used to this rain, not so his comrades in arms. Even Ralph had complained of the cold. Gwyn pulled Frankie close to him under his cloak, felt him shivering as he burrowed closer to him to absorb some of the heat from his body. Frankie was quiet. Without Charlie it was as if half of him was missing. Jack urged Frank and Ralph move to keep warm, refused to let either of them sleep for too long, kept the feeble peat fire alight and tried to keep everyone's spirits raised. Frankie had not been himself since they had lost Charlie. Charlie was dead. They had seen him fall overboard, seen the waves swallow him before they had even reached the shore before the march north.

Why had the old witch kept them here? They had done what was asked of them, they had fought for her, they had ensured her son's rise to the throne of England. Two of their number had even disposed of the two inconvenient children who were kept in the Tower of London. That had not been right, they were not soldiers in battle, they were two political pawns and only children. Yet the witch commanded murder, so murder was done, but never in the name of the King.

The night before they had left London, they had been promised a return to their own place and time. Gwyn had made the men draw lots for the task no one wanted. He had seen the tears running down Ralph's cheek when he returned. It had been Frankie who had gone with him, and Frankie was a gentle soul at heart.

Gwyn did not ask how the deed had been done. All he knew was that this was the final act the lady required, then they could go home, wherever home might be.

For Ralph it was only a few miles away over the mountain, back to the farm and a fresh start. For the others it would be a return to whatever awaited them in France in another time.

Gwyn felt Frankie move. His shoulders were bony against his ribs, his own clothes hung from him, his breeches in danger of descending to his knees if he stood up too fast. He was reaching the end of his great strength. The four of them, Frankie, Ralph, Gwyn, and Jack, had been here for nearly a month. At first, their jailers had been attentive, food was regular, and they had a good supply of fresh water. One of their number was allowed to empty the slops bucket and then go to the well for fresh drinking water. Now they had not eaten for over a week and their last pail of water would last only another day. The slops bucket was overflowing creating a stench which was wafted away by the biting wind which blew through the tower. It was the only good thing about that wind. If they did not get out of this place soon, they would die. Gwyn suspected they had been left to exactly that fate.

It was Ralph who spoke first.

'We have no food, and water for only one day, have you heard the guards lately? No! Well neither have I. We have been left to rot!'

Gwyn confirmed his fears. 'I was thinking the same, there has been no movement in the courtyard for days.'

He walked to the heavy studded wooden door and kicked it. It did not move. Then he looked upwards, he could see daylight but there was no way to climb the sheer walls inside the tower. 'We must decide what to do.'

Frankie stirred. 'We cannot go upwards, and the door is secure. There is a sheer drop from the window to the river below, it must be forty feet. You have been here before, Gwyn, and you too Ralph. Is there anything beneath, can you remember?'

It was Gwyn who answered. 'We are on the river. It wraps around the castle walls in a kind of lake. When I was a boy my father brought me here, but only once. There is a cave underneath. Small boats brought supplies in from the ships anchored in the main river. We came by boat from Aberystwyth and were brought in through the sea gate. I saw the cave, there was a staircase to it from the great hall, and a passage leading to the kitchens. That is all I recall. I was just a lad then. I don't know where the hall or the kitchens are from here.'

'When we first came to the castle, before they put us in here, I saw the cooks going back and fore, close by. We are not far from the kitchens, you can smell them when the wind is right.' Ralph added his knowledge.

Frankie spoke, 'The floor beneath us is flagstone. Why would they lay flags on top of rock in a dungeon, maybe the flags are hiding a weakness?'

They swept back the thin layer of dirty straw from the floor, most of what was revealed was stone, worn smooth by the feet of many previous occupants, but there in one corner were four large flat stones, laid with their edges flush together.

'Pass that stew pot.' muttered Gwyn, reaching for the iron pot which had held their last ration of thin soup. Taking it in both hands, he examined it intently, then taking hold of the handle swung it with all the strength he possessed. The pot hit the stone wall and fractured across its width, and the handle detached from its mountings, the brittle cast iron now in four sharp edged pieces. 'Now dig!' Gwyn started to scratch at the lines where stone met stone, gouging out years of moss and dirt which sealed them in place.

After an hour or so of hard scraping, 'I can feel a draft.' Ralph looked at Gwyn in hope. 'There must be a void beneath.'

A few more hours of scraping and digging with the rough pieces of cast iron and one of the stones became loose. Sliding his strong fingers into the gap between it and its neighbour Gwyn started to lift it. 'Help me, Ralph. Hold that corner, Frankie, lever that end with the pot handle.'

Little by little they lifted one stone to reveal a set of stone steps descending into darkness. Feeling their way, for they had no torch for light, they inched down the flight of stone steps, groping along the wall. At the bottom of the steps was a passage, with doorways on one side facing out onto a sheer rock wall, no windows, no light, narrow wooden doors. Frankie found an unlit pine torch and managed to raise a spark from the two flints he carried in his underwear, hidden from the guards. Cells, this was a passage of cells. Cobwebs draped the doors, no one had been here for years. He pushed open the first cell door, empty, though manacles hung from the walls. There was nothing save the scurry of a rat amongst the ragged pile of a blanket in the corner, the disturbed animal making a hasty exit, expecting death which normally came with the approach of humans. Then, three more empty cells whose doors hung open, hinges broken, unlocked. The next door was locked shut, though the wood was showing signs of rot at the bottom, signs that the occupant may have thrown the contents of his bucket at the door. The whole place stank. A few well-placed kicks dislodged enough wood for Frankie, the smallest of their number, to crawl through. A nondescript mound of cloth piled against the far wall moved slightly.

'He's alive! There is someone in here, alive!'

In the dim amber light of the pine torch, Frankie could see a figure lying on the floor, face towards the stone wall, curled up, legs to his chest, arms wrapped protectively round his knees, hardly breathing. The man, for it was a man, had thick bushy white hair and whiskers sprouting from a gaunt starved face, his hands gnarled and calloused by hard work, their nails now permanently stained by the dirt of ages. The man's clothes were not of this time, neither were they any with which Ralph or Frankie were familiar.

'Leave me be.' the figure groaned. 'Let me die, please, if there is a god, let this end.'

'We have you, my friend, all will be well. Are you injured?' Frankie enquired. 'Water, pass through some water.' A flask of water was passed, and Frankie offered the last of their precious supply to the man. He made him sip. Slowly and gradually the prisoner came back to full consciousness. 'We have no food to give you.'

'I couldn't eat if I wanted to, my belly is shrunk with hunger.'

There was a loud crack behind them as the wood of the door gave way.

'We must go. Now!' hissed Gwyn. 'We cannot be found here.'

Without pause for breath, Gwyn swept the figure on the floor up and over his shoulder. With Frankie ahead with the torch, they reached the end of the passage where it opened up into a huge cave. The vaulted ceiling was coloured red and good with mineral deposits, the start of stalactites clinging to the surface. Frankie looked upwards in awe. The cave was closed off from the outside by a set of iron railings but outside the railings was a narrow jetty and then the manmade lake which formed the small harbour and surrounded the castle walls, making it impregnable from the sea and with only one access by land. The inside of the cave was filled with supplies, barrels of wine and ale, bales of cloth, dried goods, and grain. And there bobbing in the harbour just outside the cave, a small boat.

'Shhhh!' Ralph heard footsteps. They ducked behind a stack of barrels, Gwyn with his hand over his passenger's mouth to silence him. The old man was fractious and recalcitrant, he did not want to be carried but was too weak to walk. As they hid, they saw two fully armed soldiers, swords at their waists, daggers in their belts, saunter into the cave. They sat down on a bale of wool, and one took a leather flask from where it hung on his shoulder.

They were within three feet of the barrels. If anyone twitched so much as a hair, they would be discovered. Gwyn quietly rendered the old man unconscious with one hand, a knack he had acquired. They all froze and for a few minutes listened to the men talk. Their voices slurred with drink, it was William Williams and his brother Albert, the last of the castle's constables

'They've all gone then, Albert?' William spoke first.

'Seems so. His lordship is away to the north to keep the king's peace, her ladyship is at court. While the cat's away, Will.'

'Tis not like her ladyship to leave things so slack, my friend. No one was paid this last quarter, so everyone is gone, walked out down to the last kitchen maid.'

'Then where should we put this one?' He poked a toe into a bundle of rags at his feet.

'Damned if I know. Leave him here shall we, he isn't long for this world.'

'But the bounty. There's a guinea on his head, we'd be set up for life.'

'No use to us if there's no one to pay it, Bert, and they'll not thank us for another dead body to bury.'

Albert kicked the bundle of rags again and it made a slight groaning noise, the twitched and uncurled slightly revealing the sticklike legs protruding from its folds.

They passed the wine flask from one to the other until Will up ended it and declared it empty. 'Plenty more here, though. Fill them up before we leave, ay, and leave the gates open, the townsfolk had just as well feel the benefit of his lordship's wealth.'

Will went to tap one of the small casks sitting atop the huge hogsheads of beer which concealed Gwyn and his men. While he was busy with hammer and spile gaining access to the wine, Albert wandered to the jetty edge and adjusting the fly of his breeches launched a stream of piss out into the river. Seizing the moment Gwyn nodded to Ralph to deal with Albert and then in one swift action grasped Will by the throat and twisted, Will's neck snapped like a twig. At the water's edge, Albert struggled briefly before his head was held under the water and he lost his fight for life. Gwyn turned to the bemused figure propped against the barrels, white whiskers bristling in umbrage.

'Now, your face looks familiar, my friend. Who the bloody hell are you?'

'Edward Meredith of Hengwm.'

'Iesu Mawr, Dada…. You must be'

'Very, very old…. Yes, I am… too bloody old for this shit.' he added, pithily.

'How did you get here, man?'

'She took me, too. She has all of us, but I was bound to survive, wasn't I. Can you get us out of here?'

'If that boat has no holes, then I think we can manage that.'

The bundle of rags on the floor began to turn over and a faint voice called out in desperation, 'Frankie?'

Frankie leaped as though scalded.

'It's Charlie! Dear god what has happened to you?'

As he spoke, Ralph was dragging the boat towards the water. It was a sailing boat with one canvas sail and a set of oars. Crowded with eight occupants, Gwyn and Ralph dipped the oars and they rowed away from the castle and out towards the main channel.

'Keep an eye out, Ralph, we are going to need a bigger boat. This will not last five minutes in open water.'

Keeping close to the shoreline, they hoisted the sail and made their way towards the sea. With their small cache of supplies and a barrel of ale in this small boat they would not survive for long in the massive swells of the Irish Sea in winter. Hugging the coast, they inched their way, beating against the wind until the weather forced them into the tiny valley which led to the even smaller church of St Isfael. Bedraggled and exhausted they made their way inland, crawling up the rocks from the inlet, finding shelter in the minute sanctuary nestled in the armpit of the earth. The church was of habit left open for passing pilgrims to give devotion, its simple interior of lime washed walls and polished oak benches giving shelter to all travellers.

Frankie crossed himself before the altar in the Catholic manner and knelt to mumble a prayer to the gods who had freed them. His eyes searched the building for the confessional and for a priest. He had much lying heavy on his soul for which to ask forgiveness.

Charlie was not much into prayer. He found a quiet corner and settled down to rest as much as he could and broke open the supplies. Edward Meredith quietly borrowed one of the communion vessels from behind the altar, in larger buildings, the chancel, but here only a narrow space in which the priest did his blessing of his tools. He filled it with ale from the small barrel and wondered how much longer he could continue. He knew the answer, had known it for years, but he didn't much like it. He drained the vessel and curled up on his side on one of the narrow benches. If death were not an option, then at least sleep would do for the present. If they were headed to Hengwm, they had several days journey ahead.

They had been awoken by the priest of St Isfaels early the following morning. Cadwen the Younger had opened the small side door, which was the nearest to his cottage, his priestly nose instantly assailed by the smell of unwashed bodies, ale, and wet woollen clothing. He had coughed loudly, not to rouse who or whatever was seeking sanctuary in his church, but to clear his throat of an odour so strong he could taste it. It smelled like the Abbot's pet wolfhound on a rainy day. That was it, exactly, the smell of wet dog.

As he coughed, heads rose from their sleeping places on the floor or the benches. Eyes were rubbed and opened. The men broke wind softly in respect for their accommodation, then excused themselves and went outside to piss against the gravestones lining the path.

'Have some respect.' murmured the priest as he surveyed the small section of humanity crowding his church. It was his largest congregation for months. Sickness had decimated the villages nearby and St Isfaels was too remote for the townsfolk, they preferred the bigger establishments closer to the castle and its safety. He lifted his communion vessel to his nose and smelled the ale within and snorted in disgust, then placed the pewter chalice behind the altar. It would need several blessings and commendations before he used it again.

Whilst the majority of his visitors tidied and rearranged their clothing, one, a blonde headed young man with feral blue eyes the colour of forget me nots, but red ringed and over bright with exhaustion, approached him.

'Father, will you hear confession?' The question took Cadwen by surprise. Had the youth demanded the collection money or the church silver he would not have been at all perturbed, but confession, that was unexpected.

'Certainly, my son, let me don my robes and make my peace with the Lord before we start. Is there much that troubles you?'

Suitably attired, Cadwen guided Frankie behind a curtain in a small alcove adjacent to the door.

Frankie coughed and then began the stilted hesitant words, 'Forgive me father…..'

Frankie had not been to confession for years. He did not have the sort of conscience which troubled him in the normal round of things, but since they had left London he had been unable to sleep and Jack heard him crying softly to himself, praying for forgiveness for something awful.

They were all waiting patiently in the frosty air of the churchyard when he emerged, shaking the priest's hand, and thanking him. Cadwen bid them farewell. They thanked him for the use of the church, and he disappeared back into its shelter and puzzled at what he had just heard. Bound by the seal of confession, he could tell no one, but he had been a Yorkist once, a loyal follower of Richard of York. What he had just been party to was information which could dethrone a false king if used in the right circles. But he was a priest, a man of the cloth and he was sworn to keep his counsel.

And so, they began the long trek across the green fields of Pembroke until they found the long sweeping stretch of St Brides Bay. Then they would follow the coast north to Aberystwyth and from there make their way across the mountain to St Harmon, Hengwm, and eventually home. Whenever that would be, Ralph seemed unconcerned. When they made camp in a field alongside the road on the second night of walking, Ralph had spoken to Jack.

'Do not worry Jack, all will be well, but I need to leave you at the next crossroads. Continue straight on the same road until you come to the village of St Harmon, and an ale house called The Sun. Wait there and someone will find you.'

Early on the third day of walking they came to the crossroads and parted company. Jack doubted he would ever see the man again.

CHAPTER 68. THE CLOCK STRIKES THIRTEEN - Red

Wales 1486.

Our destination was another two days walk through the rough terrain of the hills, but eventually I began to find the paths more familiar and well-trodden, strewn with tufts of wool where a fleece had caught in brambles and littered here and there with rabbit droppings, narrow tracks only as wide as a person's feet, better suited to sheep than humans. As I had done as a child, I began to imagine friendly faces in the patterns worn into the huge rocks which formed the only breaks from the weather. These rolling hills with their vast expanses of tough brown grass are bleak in winter, but still alive with fowl and small animals living amongst the reeds of the marshy areas and gorse bushes.

On the first night since leaving the meeting point of the crossroads we made camp in the shadow of such stones. It was not a stone circle but a small horseshoe shaped bluff. Sheltered from the wind and facing the afternoon sun, it was on the far western edge of the Meredith lands. I remembered that the spring flowers always bloomed first in this hollow, and the grass was always greener. There was a small spring which dripped trough the rock at eye level into a stone bowl, eroded over hundreds of years. The bowl overflowed onto the soil beneath. Water from this spring was always slightly sulphurous in its taste, but not unpleasant, and it was never truly cold until the depths of winter. It was here that we settled for the night. Jack and Charlie made a fire while Frankie, Gwyn and Eryr went in search of what food they could hunt or forage. Uncle Edward sat down and rested his old bones.

'I am sorry I let you down, Red.' the old man began.

'You did not, there was nothing you could have done.' I replied.

'But you left me with little Agnes. When her mother did not return, I was worried, I went looking for her. I took the child with me to the cave, for I knew that is where Rhianydd had gone.' he sighed. 'When she manifested herself, the child ran. I have not seen her since, how can she be safe out here, alone.'

'Do not worry, Edward, she is safe, and the Lady Margaret is gone, she cannot trouble us further.' I hesitated to use the word dead. I did not believe that she could truly die.

'What do we do next then, girl?' He blew out through his teeth and prodded the end of his knife into the soil, digging a small hole between his feet, from which he pulled a small stone. He threw the stone into the fire. He was not digging for anything in particular, just occupying his hands while he composed his thoughts.

One by one, everyone returned to our small encampment, and we shared out our meagre supplies of food, supplemented by several rabbits and washed down with the remains of the Pembroke beer, its quantity padded out with spring water. Edward stared into the flames, still prodding the ground with his knife, as if the earth would tell him what he should do next if he poked it hard enough. Then he began to speak.

'I have lived on this mountain for many years.' he began. It was given to the Merediths as their own, in the time of the Black Prince, but Merediths have been here for many hundreds of years before that. In the time of King Uther Pendragon...' He drifted off into a trance like state and began the tale of Bran ap Meredith who had gone in search of his flock of sheep. The sheep were lost in a blizzard so harsh that the snow filled the valleys and hollows in the mountains in drifts many feet deep. Reaching the furthest point of his grazing, Bran had heard a cry, but not the bleating of his ewes. What he heard was the cry of a newborn baby. Edward went on to tell of how Bran had taken the child home and raised him as a twin to his own newborn son. The child had survived because the hollow he was found in, the very hollow they now sat in, was warm, warmer than any other place on the hill. The child was a royal child, a twin who should have been left to die on the hillside, but his nurse would not have it so. The soil of the hollow is warmed from beneath. Edward continued. 'For beneath this mountain are the great caves where Y Ddraig lives and breathes. It is his breath that gives the spring its taste and his breath which warms the soil. It was his warmth which saved the child who would become the great King Arthur.'

Eryr stretched his legs before him and, looking up from under his eyebrows, elaborated on Uncle Edward's tale. 'Bran ap Meredith and his wife Beda raised the boy alongside their own son, Taran, until they were teenagers. Bran taught both to fight with bow and sword and knife until one day a wandering knight, seeing them practicing in the fields, offered to take both boys to train. This was no knight, this was Arawn, the ruler of the world beneath, a place called Annwn. Annwn is a place of eternal life and youth, a land of plenty, but also a land of danger. It is a land of mystical beasts where not all is as it seems. The people of Annwn have powers to see through the veil of time, to walk through the time passages beneath the earth. Arawn took Arthur and Taran into his world and taught them to use their inner selves, to use their powers, for both boys were possessed of the blood of Annwn, Faerie blood as mortals would call it, Arthur through his true father and Taran through his mother, Beda.'

Eryr continued to tell the story of Arthur and the less well-known tale of Taran until the fire began to die. Without adding more logs, he stared hard at the embers and roused the glowing logs back to a blaze.

Jack added a log to the fire and cast a sidelong glance at Eryr. 'And you, you are one of them, aren't you?'

'Arawn was my great grandfather. My father, Aegir, still dwells in the Halls below, though he is old now, for even in Annwn, age does come eventually, though he will never completely die, He will change form. He will live forever in the flora and the fauna of the earth.'

I spoke now, roused from the gentle doze I had fallen into. 'It was Aegir who guided Rhianydd home. He created the great storm which shielded us from the witch. He is old now, but he still commands great power. I am grateful for his kinship.'

I could see Jack turning things in his mind, the cogs eventually aligned. 'So, Rhianydd....'

Eryr answered him. 'She is my daughter, and Red's daughter, yes. She is one of 'us,' but she is also your wife, and the mother of your daughter, and, yes, young Agnes is also of our blood. It is no bad thing, believe me.'

The stories continued into the night. One after another, each told a tale. Jack recounted tales of Scotland. Frankie told tales of his life in the slums of London, stealing from the wealthy, and the tale of his being found by Letty Baker and taken by them as a baby.

'Come then, Charlie,' Eryr urged. 'finish the night for us, tell us what happened when you were washed overboard.'

Charlie replenished his cup and cleared his throat. 'The tale I tell is a strange one, but I think that all of us around this fire are now used to things being strange. I trust that you will believe me.' Then he began.

In the light from the flames of the fire, Charlie sat with his arms around his knees and began to relate what had happened to him since he had disappeared over the side of the Breton nearly four months ago. He pushed his floppy hair away from his face and scratched his sparse unshaven beard with one hand.

'To start with, I was pushed.' he said. 'I have no idea who by, or why, but I was definitely pushed. I thought I would be okay. We were inside the Haven. The sea was calm. I am a strong swimmer. If no one thought to throw me a line, I could at least swim ashore.'

Charlie went on. As he hit the water, he felt the sea had become rougher, the swell was huge, and the undertow had dragged him down.

'But the weather was fair, the sea was flat calm where we landed, there were no waves.' Frankie observed.

'Ay,' said Jack, 'ye could ha grabbed the anchor chain, ye could ha' climbed back aboard.'

'I couldn't move.' said Charlie. 'After the big wave, the water began to spin. It pulled me down, right down into the depths of the sea, to the bottom, then it seemed to spit me out, as if it didn't like the taste of me, or had the wrong person. I bobbed right back up to the surface and I floated around for a while. I could see the cliffs, and the beach, but I couldn't seem to swim any closer. The ships had gone. You had gone.'

'So, what did you do, Charlie?' Gwyn asked,

'I floated, and I prayed, and then I tried again, but the coast got no nearer. Then I felt something nudging at my leg. It was a dolphin. It nudged me in the leg and pulled at my clothes, so I grabbed hold of its fin and it started to pull me. It was as if it had been sent! It towed me right into a cave beneath the cliffs. I managed to climb out of the water inside the cave, onto a wide ledge. The cave went back a long way, but I could see that, at the back, there was light shining down through a cleft in the roof. The walls of the cave sparkled with crystals, part of the rock, and there were iron rings in the walls as if small ships had tied up there, and there were barrels and boxes of goods there, guns and explosives, Jack, and there was gold! I was still there looking at it in amazement when they caught me.'

He went on to tell of the gang of Irish pirates who had taken him prisoner and made him a slave. They had pressganged him into service on their ship, making him work for them as a deck hand. The captain's name was O'Malley. 'Strange thing was,' said Charlie, 'he was from our proper time, he was not a pirate like you'd think. He was running guns stolen from our army to Ireland, loads of them, all in wooden crates, marked with the army stamp. For 'the rebellion,' he said. It wasn't me that he wanted, it was you, Frankie! He said you'd done for his brother, said he wanted revenge for his brother's death, and he wanted your skill with a rifle. He was most put out to find he had me, and not you, Frankie! There was a woman with him, I'd seen her before, I'm sure it was Fionas mother. She had terrible scars on her chest and her arm, there was no way that she should be alive, Frankie, nearly all her face was missing. She was really angry when she saw it was me, swore like a trooper, said that I was the wrong man and that she had been played false.'

Red spoke up. 'I see the devil's hand in this. Philomena Cameron has been dabbling in the dark arts, I sense it. The bay has a 'blue pool.' It is a whirlpool, said to have mystic properties. People have often disappeared there. It must be a portal, like the druid's cave.'

'And she pushed you in, thinking you were Frankie.' added Gwyn. 'How did you get back?'

'O'Malley was a busy man. He was running guns and explosives to Wexford and bringing tin and gold from Wexford to St Ismaels. They put me to work as a sailor until we got to shore in Ireland, then they had me check all the weapons in the safety of the sand dunes. We made several trips, until the excise men were alerted, and it became too dangerous. On the last trip, we landed the rowboat on the beach with a load of guns. We were met by British soldiers. O'Malley and I managed to get off the beach and back to the ship then back to the cave.

'They kept me until they had finished their work, until the cave was empty. Then they tied me, in the water, with water up to my nose. I was supposed to drown on the next tide. That's the thing, the miracle, the dolphin, she came back, with others. They freed me from my ropes, they took me back to the pool, they took me back down to the seabed, then they pushed me into the vortex and left me!

When I surfaced, I was ashore, on the beach. People from the village of Dale took me in. They treated me well. Then a messenger came from King Richard. They had news of an army coming ashore. Any strangers were to be questioned and kept prisoner.

They managed to hide me for weeks, they were a family loyal to Henry Tudor. They hid me in a space in their house, a small room between the walls, out of sight from all. Eventually the constable threatened to torture them if they were found to be hiding anything or anybody. It became too dangerous for them, and I surrendered myself to Will and Albert. Folk said they would like as not be too drunk to hand me in, I would find it easy to escape them. They marched me all the way to Pembroke Castle, the rest you know.

From what I heard O'Malley say, there will be great unrest in Ireland, unrest which will last for many years. I am just glad I have escaped it. I will be glad to get home to good old London.'

One by one our company curled themselves up by the fire, cloaks pulled over their heads and wrapped tight around their shoulders. All, save Eryr and I, fell into a restless sleep. We were still awake as dawn broke over the hills to the east. As the others began to stir, he kissed me softly on the top of my hair, breathing in the smell of it.

'You smell of the hills, Red, and the sky - and the damned evil smelling water from the spring! Maybe it's time we all went home.'

The path down through the hills was well worn, the bracken on either side less abundant than usual. There were no brambles catching in clothing or hair, no sprouting gorse prickles to be pushed out of the way. In fact, all the usual vegetation seemed to be leaning away from us, sulking, in retreat, not its usual intrusive self. We rounded the corner, and I pulled up sharp! Eryr stood on my heels, Jack fell into my back, Charlie into Jack, and Frankie into Charlie. The sight that greeted us was no ordinary form of homecoming, it was a scene from an Armageddon. This was destruction of biblical proportions.

Hengwm was in ruins – the little stone cottage which nestled into the crook of the hill's shoulder was decimated. Margaret had created a storm which had destroyed the very fibre of the cottage. It been reduced to a shell, the roof had fallen in, its rafters exposed like the ribs of some long dead animal, slates like the scales of a gutted fish covering the yard and the pathway, their fragments glistening in the light. The windows through which we had watched for arriving visitors, and which had once been shining like a child's eyes at Christmas, were smashed, the glass lying in shards on the flagstone path. Uncle Edward's floral bedroom curtains flapped like Monday's washing in the breeze. The little blue front door hung from its hinges. Only the house was touched, the outbuildings still stood, the stable and the barn and the cow shed were still intact.

The other place unaffected by Margaret's great wrath was the cellar. The door to the cellar remained as it had been. Closed. Uncle Edward shook his head in amazement, his big white whiskers oscillating around his wrinkled face. Then, hoisting up his trousers by the belt, he disappeared into the yard, his gait rolling, and his shoulders set, like a prize fighter returning to the fray. Eryr rested his hand on my shoulder and I leaned into him for comfort. I felt him exhale deeply, saying nothing, his arm tightened around me.

I felt tears well in my eyes. I should not be crying, it was only a house after all. I walked in front of him to the broken front door and with one finger dislodged it from its remaining hinge. Stepping over the broken wood of the banister spindles I progressed up the hallway. Always narrow, it was now partly blocked by the floorboards which had fallen through from above. I heard Eryr wince as he banged his head on what proved to be the legs of Uncle Edward's old bed which were hanging through the ceiling.

The door to the 'best room' at the front of the house was swinging open, the chintz curtains flapping out through the smashed glass and broken sash of the window. The blue and white China which inhabited the dresser was in a million pieces, the top of the huge dresser fallen like a giant tree and lying across the room. Of the lustre jugs which had hung from its shelves, one had survived. I smiled a little, it was the one I kept oddments in, those bits and pieces you collect, they stay in your coat pocket for a week, then you examine them and if they could be useful, you put them in the jug. If you ever need a 'thing to do something with,' no matter what it may be, try looking in the jug. Should I look in there now for a means to rebuild our home? For this was home.

The silence was broken by a whirring sound and then the comforting sound of the big old clock chiming. **Bonnngggg!** he called from the corner of the room, then ***bonnnnngggg*** again. He was still here then, marking time as always. What time was it, even? The sun in the sky above declared it to be about midday, as did the shadow on the old sundial in the tiny front garden. Pushing past the remains of my good furniture, I pulled the remains of one of the curtains from his face, the glass which covered his dials was unbroken, his hands were still on his face, and yes, pointing straight upwards towards the XII. He continued to bong in a comforting manner, and I thanked him for it, mentally of course, who would ever think of talking to a grandfather clock. A voice from behind me thought differently.

'That's thirteen, you old fool, you can stop now! And you've fifteen minutes rest before the quarters!' Eryr chided the clock. Eryr had no need of clocks, he was as always perfectly attuned with the seasons. He saw no earthly use for a device which he could not easily move, and which made what were, in his view, unnecessary noises every fifteen minutes. By the tone of his voice, I suspected he wished my beloved clock had been found missing in action. We would find out in time that following the maelstrom which had marched through Hengwm, he would always strike thirteen at midday and at midnight. No amount of fixing would ever make him strike twelve again, though his pendulous heart still ticked and tocked, marking the heartbeat of the house that had fallen around him. We had been through a lot, that clock and me.

This was a fine mess. Indeed, I began to pick up random items and return them to order. It was a futile effort, what was the point of tidying a room with no window and no ceiling? Leaving the 'best room' in the care of the old clock we progressed to the kitchen.

What kitchen? Lady Margaret's wrath appeared to have entered by the kitchen chimney, the contents of the hearth, the pot racks, the heavy cast iron range, the hearthstone itself were moved. The old, scrubbed table was upended and thrown against the pantry wall, the chairs were smashed to matchwood. The stone sink was cracked into two large pieces, the pantry door was missing completely, the only recognisable surviving thing was the huge stone slab where we cooled the milk and the cheese. There was not a stick of furniture left whole, except for the big Windsor chair which had become wedged in the remains of the fireplace, still draped in its covering of shawls and with its tapestry cushion wedged in the seat as a guard against the draft which sometimes whistled under the back door. As I picked things up and helplessly put them back down trying to restore order, it dawned on me that my clock should not be here at all, we were still in her time, my clock would not be invented for at least another hundred years. The witch had indeed caused chaos in the firmament. But there was no one present who had not seen him before, and visitors to Hengwm were rare. A shout from the rear yard. Uncle Edward appeared.

'The barn is sound, and the cow sheds and the stable, I have walked up the field and the cows are still here, the sheep seem to have run up onto the hillside.'

In his left-hand, Edward held a rope halter and over his arm was hanging a trug of oats. 'Zak,' the old man said with a catch in his voice. 'I must find him< He was in the stable when she came. He is missing, but the door is closed. I will search the mountain. If he is missing, Agnes will be heartbroken.'

Off he stumped, across the fields heading for the hill, calling as he went, that long lilting call with which farmers call their animals. I hoped that his mission would be successful, but I had a feeling it would not. Had not Calon taken Agnes to safety? If he had taken Agnes, then small or not, she would not have left without Zak.

In his own inimitable way Calon had vanished. He was like an outbreak of firedamp or a smouldering firework, there one minute, exploded and gone the next, he did not like to be confined. More of a wanderer even than his father, but at least he had had the presence of mind to remove his niece from harm's way. Both she and Rhianydd were safe somewhere, I hoped, but where I could not be certain. Calon had mentioned Scotland, but in his transient world nothing was guaranteed.

I turned the big kitchen table back onto its legs, one was a bit loose, but nothing a four-inch nail in the right spot wouldn't fix. Straightening my shoulders, I dumped my belongings such as they were onto the table's battered surface.

'Where on earth do we start?' I wondered.

'Forget the house, Red, let's get all we can salvage out into the yard, and if all else fails we have the cellar.' Eryr's voiced my thoughts, reading my mind.

'Don't even think about it!' I jested. 'Those stairs have a habit of getting walled up. Spend the rest of time with Uncle Edward and his habits? Never!'

CHAPTER 69. SEEING THE LIGHT – Jack MacGregor

I was perplexed. The events of the last few days, and the last few hours in particular, had made me doubt my sanity. What strange cult had I married into? Not that my wife or my mother-in-law overtly demonstrated their heritage, but what should I call her? Was Rhianydd human or not? Did it really matter? I loved her whatever she was. And what should I call HIM? Father-in-law seemed hardly adequate. I had followed them this far, could I trust them to get us home, back to my wife, HIS daughter, and Agnes, HIS grandchild?

With what I now knew of our predicament in our own time, I knew that we must return, if that was possible. I also knew that my body was feeling more and more exhausted with every journey they made, that my bones and muscles felt that they had been torn apart like a disjointed chicken being prepared for the pot.

If Rhianydd was to be believed, and what her uncle Moses said was correct, then return we must, and sooner rather than later. We must go back to our own war, to the fighting.

We were all pitching in to make some form of order of the ruins of Sibyl's precious home. The rest were clearing out the kitchen of broken furniture. I pulled Eryr aside.

'You must get us back to France. We cannot just appear in London. It must be as if we had not left the fighting.'

Eryr nodded. 'You need to rest. To travel through the veil and through the belly of the earth will require great strength. You may think it easy, my friend. To travel through one time to another in the same place is hard on the body and on the mind. To move through time and through distance is testing even for me.'

'How long then? Charlie told us that his Irish captors believed that the war would end. They planned their rebellion around it. We cannot wait until it is all over.' I stressed the importance of this to him.

'We must wait until winter, but you will be home before Christmas, believe me.' He had dragged me down into the cave which formed a cellar behind and beneath the house. 'Maybe you should know a little more about our kind, Jack. Sit.' He gestured towards a huge wooden coffer and the small box bed, the only items which seemed untouched by the storm.

I sat and I listened as he told me of the history of the Merediths and the mountain, and of the deals which had been done between his folk, the Faeries of Annwn, and Kings, and between his folk and the Witch, and the truth of Uncle Edward. He would never leave Hengwm unless he was released from the charm which held him. After about half an hour he rose.

'The stories which are told around the fire are our history, they are not just tales to pass the time, stories for your amusement. In this part of the world, the Faeries of Annwn and humans live lives which are intertwined. It has taken half a lifetime for Sibyl to learn. Rhianydd is just starting her journey. Agnes, more than either of them, will want to learn. You must let them have their heads. They are strong women. They must be allowed to go before they come back of their own accord. Now we must make sense of the storm, there is work to do before we can think of leaving.'

In the end we stayed at Hengwm for nearly three months, the leaves had fallen from the trees, and it was growing colder. Between the six of us we had nearly rebuilt the cottage. We were gathered in the kitchen warming ourselves by the fire when Calon burst in through the kitchen door.

'The tide of your war is turning.' he said. 'The German army is in retreat.'

'Then it is time.' Eryr spoke. 'I must make ready. Jack, Charlie, Frank, rest well, we will leave soon. You must be strong and clear of mind for what we are about to do. Few mortals have walked through the seams of the earth, but that is what you must do.'

It was early November when we made our way down into the cellar of Hengwm. Eryr pulled the great coffer away from the wall to reveal the opening to yet another tunnel. The opening was just large enough to admit a man's shoulders. Eryr seemed to melt through the very rock itself, disappearing from sight to reappear seconds later.

'Come, do not show fear, you will be safe, fear is in the mind. Clear your minds all doubt, think of where you would go.'

I must have looked at him as if he were the devil, which indeed he appeared to be. His unusual green eyes seemed to glow in the darkness of the tunnel as I crawled into the darkness behind him. Frank and Charlie followed reluctantly.

The tunnel was cramped and narrow, but the floor was smooth with wear, there was no chance to deviate from the path. After a few minutes of crawling, I emerged into a cave. The roof of the cave sparkled with a dark eerie light which filtered through fissures in the rock and reflected on the myriad of tiny crystals embedded in the bluestone rock walls. The ceiling was high enough to stand up, but Eryr sat like a Satyr on a ledge in the rock.

I took a seat beside him, and we waited for Frankie and Charlie to emerge from the tunnel behind us. It was only as Frankie's blonde head poked into the space of the cave that I realised that Eryr was naked.

'We must go now.' Eryr's voice was urgent. 'Follow me. Hold this and do not let go.' Eryr stood and handed me a length of rope. Moving swiftly forward he disappeared through a narrow fissure in the rock wall. I followed, turning myself sideways to accommodate my shoulders, feeling the cool of the rock against my chest and smooth floor under my bare feet. It was pitch dark, but again there was no room to deviate from our path. The floor sloped downwards gradually descending through the earth. We edged through the gap in the rock slowly until it opened into another chamber, similar to the last.

'Leave your clothing,' we were instructed, 'and trust me. Here you must trust me with your lives.'

I felt the length of rope in my hand. I looked back along the dark of the tunnel as my eyes got used to the black. I saw Frankie crouched against the wall, the whites of his eyes the only things visible in the pitch blackness. I gripped the rope for all I was worth with my left hand and followed. The floor of the tunnel was marked with hoof marks, and we tripped over the remains of iron rails. I motioned for Frankie to follow. There were tools, pick axes with shortened handles, hammers, and spikes for driving into the rock face. We were in a mine. There was fallen rock strewn in the tunnel. When we turned our faces upwards, we saw that roughly hewn wooden supports braced the ceiling against the weight of the earth above, supports carefully placed but bowing under the massive strain. Frankie looked terrified, almost in a trance. He was not certain how they had arrived in this subterranean void. In some bad dream he heard the noise of war, but not his war. I could not see Charlie, though I knew that he was there, somewhere.

I remembered the crone who had stolen us away from France. We had thought it a rescue and it had been a rescue of sorts. We had done her bidding, helped her fulfil her wishes in a time I had only read of in history books, but history could not be allowed to find any trace of us there.

She had wanted more, demanded a price that I was not willing to pay, and neither was Frankie. It was time they went home. Was this really the way home. I must place my trust in this being, Eryr, so must Frankie and Charlie.

I felt a tug on the rope.

'Come, but the roof is low, you must crawl, keep your arms in front of you, do not get stuck.'

I lowered myself to my belly in the darkness and inched forward, hands stretched out before me. Before me, the blackness changed subtly and I sensed a gap in the rock wall, a mere two feet in height, barely enough to fit my shoulders, then I saw two hands in front of me, and a pair of intense green eyes, their centres an unearthly red. Surely a man, or a being so large, could not function in this confined space. I felt rope bracelets placed over my wrists. The deep voice hissed at me.

'Do not be like a worm, think like a serpent, use your mind to guide you.'

The rope went taught and my arms stretched out before me. I could not move. The only thing I saw in my mind was death, my breath was starting to come in short, panting, panicky gasps.

The voice came again. 'You are a serpent, not a worm. The worm will be buried, the serpent has guile, it has strength, use it. Think like a snake or you will die, and we will all die with you.'

I closed my eyes. I pictured myself as a child on a highland hill. I had found a grass snake. In my memory I felt its dry scales moving over my hands, trying to escape my grasp, its sinuous body weaving itself out of my clutches and back to the ground where it belonged. My body started to move, how I do not know, imitating the passage of that snake through the shady grass, following the line and the slight pull of the rope bracelets. I felt myself inching forward. Inches became feet, feet became yards, then I emerged into yet another cave. Eryr was sitting, his huge frame pixie like on one of the rocks. 'Well done, Jack, you are learning.'

Then he took in a deep breath and removing the ropes from Jack's wrists, snaked himself back into the darkness headfirst, some minutes later, emerging feet first, followed by the coal covered, bemused and terrified Frankie. Then he repeated the process with Charlie. All was well so far.

All I could see in this cave was the gleam of the damp on the walls. I reached out with one hand and felt along the wall. There was the rope, held by iron pegs, pegs which had been there for many years. I shuffled myself into a more comfortable position, my hands searched about me on the ground. Leather, hard, dirt encrusted leather, a boot, yes definitely a boot. Oh, Christ, no! The boot had an occupant. Only the bones remained of the foot, and the ankle, the remains of a miner lost forever to the bowels of the earth, but where, and more importantly, when.

No time for thought, Eryr brought us back to the present. 'You can swim?' It was not a question. It was an assumption and a statement.

'No, I cannot.' murmured Frankie. 'I never learned.'

I knew that Frankie was terrified of deep water, he swam like a cat expecting a bath.

'I think you must, Frankie. We will help you. We will get out of here together.' Charlie encouraged his friend.

Eryr's stern gaze hit us. 'From here there is water, some of it is very deep, some we can crawl through easily. I have not been here for many years, but it has changed little since my father destroyed the mine. Stand up now, in this tunnel we can walk, then prepare yourselves to think like fish.'

'Where does this go, if ye din'nae mind me askin'?' I enquired.

'Safety, for you, at least for a time. I have not travelled this way for many years, yet I am certain there is a way through.' Eryr seemed to read Jack's thoughts. 'Yes, it was once a mine. The coal is rich here, but the seam is dangerous. It is here that it dips to the ocean floor to rise again in America, it is the same great fold in the earth. And yes, men have died here, many of them, my father in his own way tried to warn them.'

'Your father?' I raised an eyebrow.

'Yes, Jack, I have a father. His name is Aegir. He is powerful indeed. He does not often intervene in matters in the human world, but when humans intrude into his existence, he will stamp his old feet until the very ground shakes.'

'Tell me more, what did these men do, that offended him?'

'They did not offend him, but they offended mother earth herself, they were greedy, they still are. They would pile the spoil from their mines above ground creating new mountains of black, mountains which have no roots below the surface of the earth. Aegir can see what is to come, so he sent a warning. He collapsed a few tunnels, but he killed no-one. The mine owner was old, he gave charge of the mine to his son. It was the son whose greed killed him, trying to re-open the deep seam.'

'How?'

'My father just shook the earth a little, enough to collapse the tunnels. The boy sought to blast his way back through when the roof fell. He was a fool, driven by greed, he was also a drunk and a gambler. Because of him, many souls were lost, that was many years ago, he was no loss to society.'

'And we can get through, where he could not?' I asked.

'I am my father's son, Jack. Trust me that I know where to go. Trust also that Aegir can hear you, these walls have ears. All we say and do will be heard in my father's halls, do not insult him, we would not want the earth to shake for us, would we?'

'And Sibyl, I mean Red, where does she fit in?'

'Ah, your wife's mother, she has more of our blood than she knows. I feel she will need to use it, but she chooses to live as a human for it suits her needs, for the present.'

It was Frankie who spoke next. 'You love her greatly, don't you.'

'Frankie, I die a little for every day she is away from me, I would have her with me always. She will come home one day, but that is her choice, and I cannot make her choose.'

'Like my Fiona, she will not choose either.'

'Hold her in your mind, Frankie, we must go. Red can only hold out for a short while and you must be through the water at least before I leave you.'

Eryr and I stood, facing each other. I could still only see the unearthly glow of green eyes in the dark and the huge shadow of his shoulders.

'If it's any help,' Eryr spoke, 'you are a brave man, Jack MacGregor. The world needs brave men. My daughter is as lucky to have found you as you are to have found her. But always remember, she is her mother's daughter.'

Jack felt Frankie rise to his feet slowly behind him, a tottering step forward, bumping into the back of Jack's clothing. He took Frankie's right hand and placed it on his shoulder. 'Grab the rope as well, man. Now walk.' I waited for Eryr to move forward. It was an easy journey for an hour or more. They picked their way through small rock falls, the only hazard being the darkness.

'Where is Charlie?' I whispered.

'I am right behind you. Keep going, for heaven's sake do not stop.' Charlie's voice trembled with fear.

Eryr stopped suddenly. Jack cannoned into his back and Frankie into Jack.

'Listen!'

I stilled my breathing, closed my eyes, and listened.

'Do you hear it?'

I could hear nothing, but Frankie spoke. 'I can hear singing, Jack, I can hear men singing.'

'Block it from your mind, my friend, it is the song of the dead. Banish it, think only of life. Hold on to the living, Frankie.'

'I hear nothing.' added Charlie.

When I opened MY eyes, I saw the glimmer of water, black deep water. There was a huge pool before us. Steam rose from the surface, rippling upwards in the little light which penetrated through the roof of a great cavern. Eryr's nose picked up the whiff of sulphur, the smell of slightly over cooked eggs and rotten meat.

'Ddraig is home then,' remarked Eryr, 'but he is no danger to us. His breath warms the stones and the waters. There will be an early spring this year.'

'Dragon!' The word fell incredulously from my lips.

'You have learned some Welsh, then? I hope Rhianydd will teach you more. Now come, we must go through there.'

He pointed to a small opening in the far wall of the pool, a notch in the rock not much bigger than a man's head, and only just above the level of the water. They followed the rocky ledge which bordered what smelled like the Dragon's soup kitchen until it became too narrow for feet.

Frankie was shaking like a terrified puppy. He was clearly missing his clothes, abandoned at Eryr's command several caves and tunnels ago. The chain mail, loose shirt and leggings and leather jacket and boots from the escape from Henry's London, all left behind. I had done the same. Eryr's attire had vanished, too. He stood there gloriously naked, glowing like a well-polished statue of some ancient god, dark patina glowing in the dimness.

'I will take you through, one at a time. Frankie, my friend, think only of life. Picture someone you treasure in your mind and hold them there. Now, into the water and hold on to me. Do not let go, I am your breath, I am your heartbeat, breathe with me.'

He wrapped himself around the terrified, shaking body of Frankie Baker and as Jack watched, they disappeared below the surface.

As they descended into the darkness Frankie tried to think of the living, but the only faces he could see were those of the dead, their hands reaching, clawing out trying to pull him toward them. He struggled desperately for the surface. He tried to picture Fiona but could not assemble the pieces of her pretty face in his mind. Then suddenly all he could see was Charlie.

He felt rock walls graze his naked back and shoulders as he was fed like so much thread through the eye of a rocky needle. Sometimes close to the glistening rocks which formed the ceiling, sometimes driven downwards deeper into the labyrinth of water filled tunnels, his picture of his friend held in his mind's eye.

Frankie's head broke the surface in a large cavern. The walls sparkled with flecks of quartz. Light drifted in through a long narrow fissure. The rock was still warm to touch, and, as he emerged from the water, he realised that he was still alive.

Eryr looked at him, one eyebrow raised in appraisal. The eyebrow lowered and Frankie found himself clad in the uniform of a 1916 rifleman.

Good as his word, Eryr saw us all safe through that maze of water-filled tunnels. How long we travelled I do not know, time seemed not to matter, but we found ourselves together, back in the uniform of our own time.

'Where are we, my friend?' I asked him.

'You are in Mons, Belgium, Jack, and it is November 1918. I am on this journey with you, for Ralph Owen needs to be taken home.'

CHAPTER 70. BACK-TO-BACK

November 1918.

Eryr had equipped us with uniform and weapons. We looked quite as though we had been roaming the battlefields of Northern France for eighteen months, unshaven, and our uniforms and ourselves in need of a good wash. Ralph had disappeared as usual, our envoy between the living and the dead. Surely it could not be only I who had worked out that Eryr and Ralph were never in the same place together.

Dawn would see us back in our own time, in the Belgian town of Mons, we would rejoin the fighting there. The troops seeking to liberate the town were mostly Canadian, but as long as we were fighting alongside them, we should fit in just fine.

The Germans had been driven from the nearby town of Valenciennes. The fighting there had been vicious, the Germans unwilling to accept defeat, defending every yard of their territory with gun and mortar fire. But retreat they had. The Canadians now fixed their sights on Mons. The city so bitterly lost to German occupation at the start of this great conflict, the citizens of Mons had been subjected to German rule for four long years. The Canadians were now set to restore it to the Belgians.

As the sun rose, we three emerged from the under croft of an ancient building onto the war-ravaged streets of an ancient city. It was quiet, ominously so.

Frankie needed space. He had not coped well with the journey back, forced to travel through what seemed like miles of underground tunnels, on times having to entrust himself completely to another and submit to being unceremoniously dragged beneath the water. He took his rifle and shouldered his pack and went out into the street. Eryr, or was it Ralph, had kindly thought to provide him with a ration of cigarettes. Narrow and cobbled, with tall buildings on either side, it was not unlike the place we had left five hundred years ago. Frankie stood, stretching himself in the alleyway, cigarette dangling from his lips, a small plume of smoke rising from its glowing tip. On his left, the broken glass and overturned furniture of a small café was a sign that all was not well.

A voice called out from inside the shattered building. 'Monsieur! Fait attention!'

Frankie looked about him, he could not see the source of the voice, he seemed disorientated, confused even.

The voice called again. 'Monsieur Tommy! Fait attention!'

High in the steeple of the great church on the very far side of the great square the German sniper stretched his aching muscles and looked out from his hide. The rest of the German army was retreating, running like mice before a Canadian cat. Well, he would not run, he would have at least one more squeak before he gave himself up.

He could survive in his chosen nest for several days He took a draught from his flask and then, ferreting in his pack, he pulled out another clip of five bullets. He had plenty of ammunition left for his Mauser rifle. He knew he only had one round left in his side arm, but that was for him, for his personal use. He would not surrender. By the time he descended from his roost high above the rooftops, his comrades would have marched out. Tired and without supplies, they would flee as far as they could, then, if they had not found safety, they would surrender themselves. He would not. He had fought too long and too hard to surrender. He would never see his motherland again.

There was movement in the alleys below. The people of the town knew of his presence, they kept themselves well under cover. He could sense a different movement, someone who was not afraid. The sniper wiped the barrel of the rifle and the stock with the chamois cloth he kept for only that purpose. He liked to keep 'Mausi,' as he called her, clean, dry, and well oiled. He slid a clip into the rifle and looked over the top of the ancient stone parapet. He had little food and water but a pack full of ammunition.

Frankie ran his hand through his spiky blonde hair, he scratched his head and then his arse, the latter through his trousers. He felt the short hairs on his neck stand up, his sense of danger alerted. Then he saw the movement above and in front of him.

As the bullet struck the stone wall just to the left of his head, sending splinters of stone into the air and through the smashed glass of the window, he ducked, a door opened, and he was pulled in amongst the broken furniture. Jack and Charlie ducked back into the safety of the darkness.

Mons, it seemed, was well stocked with churches. Jack could see the towering spire from which the shot was fired in the distance. Whoever was up there would have the streets well covered. It would be like shooting rats in a barrel. He looked up and around, there was no place higher, and they had no idea how well supplied this man was. He was obviously well trained and a marksman, but he was complacent. Jack saw that he believed his position unassailable. He showed himself above the gargoyles of the steeple, not much, but enough. Looking up, he saw that the building above him also had a tower, not as grand or as tall, but it had a clock tower. He could shorten the odds. Now where was Frankie?

The door of one of the shattered shopfronts twitched and a hand beckoned. Frankie had found company.

Antoine was a swarthy looking man, dressed in old blue work trousers made of a fabric of Nimes, dyed dark blue with indigo but faded with wear, belted with a thick leather belt, an old, faded linen shirt hanging loose at the waist and a jaunty red neck scarf at his collar. He was at least fifty years old, his dark brown face tanned from working in the sun. His remaining teeth were white, but they were few. He had the look of a sailor, but he was far from the sea.

Jack and Charlie ducked low and crept into the building. Antoine greeted them with a gap-toothed grin. 'Les Anglais, oui?'

'Mais, oui!' Jack responded, praying that the man spoke English. 'Parlez-vous Anglais?'

'I do.' responded Antoine. 'French is not even my first language. We Belgians speak Walloon, but no one else understands it, so we adapt. I speak French, German, English and a little Dutch, we get by. Pastis?'

The last word was a question accompanied by four glasses and a bottle. It was a little early in the morning, but the bullets were already flying. In the surrounding streets, Charlie could hear the sharp rapport of pistol and small arms fire.

Antoine continued in heavily accented English. 'That sniper, he has been up there for days. He has kept us all indoors, and he has kept the Canadians busy.'

'Canadians?' Jack was puzzled.

'Yes Canadians, we have suffered the Germans for nearly four years, now they are being pushed out. Most have gone but there are still a few hard-core units who resist. They are holding the rear while the rest of their army runs away, n'est pas?' He dropped into French.

'And you, the people, where are you?'

'We are here, and there, living amongst our ruins, avoiding the trouble and keeping our heads down.'

'Where are the Canadians?'

'They are in the next district, a few streets away, but him, up there, he keeps them from clearing the streets of the rest of the rats. Antoine refilled his glass and spat viciously on the floor. 'We cannot bury our dead, we cannot pray in our holy mother church, we cannot even put our heads out of the door, as your comrade found out.'

'The building we were in, how do you get into the clock tower?'

'That will not be easy, Jacques. The Germans stole the bells to use the metal, as they have stolen everything else. They did not take care in getting it out. I fear there are no stairs, only the remains.'

'Will you show us? Now?'

'Come then, follow me. You need not use the street.'

They followed Antoine through to the back of his shop, down into the cellar, then through a ragged handmade hole in the thick stone walls into the vaulted underground chambers beneath what he said was the Town Hall.

'This is the base of the tower.' He pointed to a small arched door in a wall. The door was not locked, or even secure. It fell off its hinges. Jack stuck his head into the void and looked up. Above him he could see the splintered wooden ends of the narrow stairs, and at the top the space where a great bell had once hung.

'Frankie,' he beckoned to Frankie to come and look, 'can you get up there?'

'I have not climbed for a while, but it looks easy enough, did our friend leave rope?'

Jack instinctively looked into the corners of the cellar. There in the corner was a coil of rope and alongside it a metal case which Frankie recognised as containing .303 ammunition.

'Point me to it, then.' Frankie began to lay out the rope for climbing. 'Are you up for it, Charlie?'

'Just let the dog see the rabbit. Will you be alright down here by yourself Serg?' Charlie winked at Jack.

'Don't worry yourselves, lads, I have Antoine.' He turned to see Antoine emerging from the darkness, two belts of cartridges slung over his shoulders and an ancient shotgun held in a very belligerent fashion over his arm. Jack also noted the huge knife worn in a sheath strapped firmly between the cartridge belts hanging between Antoine's shoulder blades.

'Done this before, have ye, Antoine?' Jack winked at the Belgian.

'In another war, another time my friend.' came the reply.

Ropes in place, Frankie and Charlie climbed the tower to the great beam where the bell had once hung. It was a fine position, not quite as elevated as the Cathedral tower but nearly so. In fact, they had a view of the German sniper through the spaces between the cathedral's great gothic gargoyles. It was not a clear view, but it would do.

They pulled up their packs, stuffed with ammunition and enough food and water for the day. Satisfied that the only access to the door was through Antoine's shop, the other entrance was blocked by rubble, Jack set about organising provisions. Who knew how long his men could be up in their eerie?

Frankie and Charlie started to make themselves comfortable. Looking down through the binoculars they each carried, they could see the Canadian troops, hidden in cover, out of the line of fire, but unable to move. They could see evidence of other snipers, hidden on rooftops, the telltale signs of an abandoned helmet here, a piece of discarded uniform there, the disjointed body of a dead soldier lying bent and broken over a roof parapet. They could also see the terrible destruction the shelling had caused when the Germans had taken over the city, the roofless houses where families still tried to exist amongst the remains of their possessions.

As they watched, they could see the main body of the German army moving away, retreating, in a long slowly moving snake, their only protection from the advancing forces the carefully positioned snipers and a few random pockets of resistance. The boys could also hear the occasional sharp 'snap' of a rifle as a Canadian head dared to raise itself.

The sniper settled down for a long day. He sat with his back against the wall and waited to hear sounds of movement below. He could hear the sounds of an engine starting easily. He could even hear the tread of boots in the quiet streets where a population in hiding were afraid to venture.

It was mid-afternoon before his next target presented itself. He heard a motorcycle coming towards the square in front of the great church, a motorcycle, and a motor vehicle. He looked through the holes of the gargoyle's eyes. A red and white flag flew from its bonnet. A khaki clad officer sat in the passenger seat. He lifted his faithful 'Mausi' from her resting place, took aim through the eye of the gargoyle and fired. He must be tired, or his sights dirty for he missed. The bullet ricocheted off the cobbles. He swiftly chambered a second round and fired. He saw the motorcycle escort slump over his handlebars. The driver of the car frantically tried to accelerate away, but in his panic stalled the engine leaving the vehicle stranded. No time to turn a starting handle. That would be certain death.

Charlie unslung his rifle and, without any particular aim, he fired, the shot designed to distract the sniper, to give his target time to escape, to get to cover. It worked. The Canadian Officer and his driver scurried from the vehicle and across the square and took shelter in the cathedral itself, right in the building below the German sharpshooter. It had, however, given their position away.

The German saw the flash of white, blonde hair in the clock tower 'It is him.' he thought to himself. 'I owe him a bullet for Hans. It was him, the blonde one, he killed my brother, Hans.'

Jack and Antoine, drawn to the action on the square, ducked and dived their way to the abandoned car. The escort was dead. The sniper in the tower did not see them. Antoine whistled, a sharp high whistle. From a nearby building a small boy appeared, in a doorway, then quick as a flash crossed to the cathedral steps and disappeared in through its great front doors. 'My son.' he muttered to Jack. 'He will tell them help is coming.'

Frankie and Charlie watched their sergeant and his new comrade work their way towards the steps. Occasional fire from the side streets pinned them down, the last remnants of the German army fighting a rear-guard action, firing shots from cover. They fired covering rounds into the shadows, unable to see their enemy, not knowing if they hit their mark.

As if the small action in the square had been some form of catalyst, all around the city, there were flashes of gunfire, from shops and houses. It was unclear to Frankie and Charlie who was friend and who was foe, so they held their fire. The sniper in the steeple held his fire too. He watched and waited. He had his orders, but he had only one target. Antoine and Jack had disappeared into the maze of alleys and walkways which are only found in a medieval city, taking with them the Canadian General and his driver.

'I'm going down mate.' Charlie informed Frankie. 'You stay here, but see that roof over there,' he pointed to a roof overlooking the trapped

Canadians, 'I think I can get there unseen. If I can then I can give them covering fire.'

'Take care my friend, I will cover you from this bastard.'

Charlie lowered himself down from the tower and, making his way back through Antoines bar, Frankie saw his friend climb agilely onto Antoine's roof. Ducking behind the chimneys, Frankie heard a round ping off the stonework of the parapet. Aiming at the gargoyles of the cathedral, Frankie shot back. He saw the Germans head jerk as stone dust flew from the damaged gargoyle. The head of the gargoyle dropped the three hundred feet or so feet to the floor.

Frankie saw Charlie disappear over several rooftops and then signal that he was in position.

Darkness fell. Frankie fell deep into thought. If he ever got home, what would await him? He thought of Fiona. He knew that she loved him, but he was also a realist. She was a General's daughter with a fine house, even if it was in use by the War Office. He was a foundling from the slums, a criminal. He had no doubt that if he ever got home, he would never find a legitimate job in civvy street. Before the darkness fell, he reached in the side pocket of his pack and found pencil and paper. Half an hour later, he curled up round his bag of supplies and drifted into an uneasy sleep.

Dawn broke in a shower of feathers and mess from the pigeons roosting in the eaves above his head. They had not been disturbed by the gunfire. He drank from his water bottle and checked his rifle. Hardly necessary, she had only been fired three times yesterday, but it was his routine and routine mattered to Frankie Baker.

In the streets to his left, where the Canadians were holed up, he heard movement, then gunfire, the sound of the movement of men, a large number of men. He saw fire returned and saw Charlie repeatedly loading and firing. He looked towards the cathedral. No sign of the sniper. Maybe he was still asleep. No such luck. As Frankie risked a look over the parapet a Mauser round embedded itself in the great beam which had once held the bell. Splinters of wood and stone flew. Too bloody close for comfort.

Shouldering his Enfield, he took his aim. It was a nearly impossible shot, but he could see the sniper's head straight down his sights and through the hole left by the missing head of the stone model of the devil which had once channelled the water from the cathedral roof. He breathed in then slowly out and squeezed the trigger. He saw the sniper twitch and the rifle fall from his hands and the spread of blood as it mixed with the water in the lead guttering. Time to move. Frankie tied his pack onto the long rope which hung from the beam above him and lowered it down into the void of the tower Then he began to lower himself. He did not see the damage that first bullet had done and when the final strand of rope unravelled and snapped, Frankie fell back first, his fall broken by the remains of the ancient staircase. His final view of the morning was the clear blue sky above the clock tower of Mons.

In the thick of the fighting, Charlie did not notice his friend's absence. The Canadians made short shrift of the remaining German stragglers. The General ordered the remains of the occupying army who surrendered from their hideouts be treated well as prisoners. Charlie climbed down from his rooftop to a hero's welcome by the troops below. Without him they would, they said, have been pinned down for a week.

Jack and Antoine returned from the narrow streets, dirty and bloodstained. They too were welcomed into the Canadian fold.

It was just after breakfast time on the 11th November 1918, when the Canadian General received the order that hostilities would cease at 11am that day. 11am, with its celebrations that the war was over.

Jack, and Charlie went in search of Frankie.

When they reached the base of the clock tower, they found only Frankie's pack lying alongside a long length of frayed rope but there was no sign of Frankie.

Antoine wiped his red neckerchief across his dusty face and propped his shotgun in the corner of his bar. As he began to pour his best brandy into glasses, they heard the footsteps of many coming down the alley. The city was coming back to life. They drank to Frankie, wherever he was. Then they drank to him again. It was late that night when Jack took a very drunken Charlie by the arm. 'We'd better go and find the Canadians. They are our ticket home.'

CHAPTER 71. FINAL RESOLUTION - Sibyl

December 1918.

St Pancras Station in winter is a bleak place indeed. Muffled in cloaks and hats, we stamped out feet and waited. In a cloud of steam and smoke and a blast of its whistle, the second train of the day pulled in to the platform and the doors began to open, spilling men into the arms of the waiting, all eager for home.

'I knew it, I knew it in my heart, I felt him go.' Fiona looked at me with tears in her eyes as three men walked down the platform towards us, emerging from the smoke and steam of the engine, shrouded in its mist, three men still dressed in the khaki uniform of soldiers.

'He never thought he was good enough.' she continued. 'He doubted himself, and I could never change that.' She turned the ring he had given her around on her finger, feeling the rough crowns of the stones against her clenched palm.

The man standing beside her placed a proprietary arm around her shoulder as if keeping her warm against the chill of the wind which blew the leaves and the litter along the platform.

General Gerald Shipley spoke. 'He was a brave man, Fiona, none braver, and you loved him because of it.' He squeezed her shoulder, the squeeze of a friend, but hoping for something more.

'I let him down, I should have said, 'yes.' I should have married before he left, he would have had something to come home to.' Fiona turned her face into the broad chest of the General's uniform. She felt him draw his breath in under her cheek as she hid her tears from the others.

Like a greyhound from the traps, Rhianydd thrust Agnes' chubby little hand into mine. 'Stay with Gannie.' The instruction was one not to be disobeyed.

She sprinted down the damp flagstones, dodging embracing couples and small groups of families savouring reunions, hair and skirts flying behind her.

'Jack! Oh, Jack!' She flung her arms around his neck. Dropping his pack and Frankie's on the floor he gathered her into his arms. Feeling the warmth of her through his great coat, they seemed to weld together into one person in front of me, then in a moment of realisation, Rhianydd called to her daughter.

'Aggie, come to mummy, say hello to your daddy, he's home, home for good!' They swallowed the child between them wrapped in their love for her and for each other.

Charlie and Frances were walking hand in hand towards the station gates, heads together, talking in earnest, so much to say, and now plenty of time to say it. I could smell wedding bells a mile away.

Fiona still stared at the emptying carriages, waiting, in the forlorn hope that a skinny blonde boy with a lopsided grin and a cigarette would be the last to get off the train, waiting for space, waiting for the crowd to clear. But the guard was slamming the carriage doors and blowing his whistle to signal its departure, back to Dover to be filled once more with those who had returned.

As the train pulled away from the station, a sheet of paper dislodged from the Frankie's abandoned pack. It drifted on the breeze, floating towards destruction on the rail tracks. On instinct Fiona ran after it, chasing it, her outstretched hand swatting it to the floor and her foot holding it there.

'Dearest Fiona,' she started to read, then her legs gave way under her, and she collapsed into an undignified sobbing heap. 'But Frankie, we could have been happy, couldn't we?'

As I watched the rear of the train disappear from sight, I was sure I saw him, his rifle on his shoulder, his white, blonde hair, spiky with damp, and his cap in the back of his head. His clothing did not move in the breeze, no smoke rose from the glowing end of the habitual cigarette. He was smiling.

As I watched, he threw up a mock salute and waved, then turned smartly on his heels and in the blink of an eye, vanished.

Fiona lifted her head, and I heard her whisper, 'Goodbye soldier, be happy my love, wherever you are.' Then she waved, seemingly to the rear of a departing train. Gerald Shipley lifted her easily from the floor where she sat and carried her in his arms towards the exit and his waiting car. In her hand she still clutched the letter, but at least she was smiling.
With all the commotion around me, I quite forgot Eryr. He stood, like a khaki monolith, several feet away from me.

'Well, Red,' I stepped into the circle of his arms, and he wrapped his great coat around me, I felt its fur lining warm against my body, not usual, I suspected, army issue, lined with the skins of rabbits and squirrels from a long dead past. If I wished myself invisible just for a minute, would it still work. As if reading my mind, he whispered, 'Not yet, we must wait.' but his lips on mine made my body sing with anticipation.

The General's car had plenty of room for all of us, and we were driven in some style to his home at Cross Common House. 'Formalities,' he mumbled into his moustache. 'Sorry and all that, no time to waste.' He chivvied us along through the great front doors. A neatly uniformed maid servant showed us to well-appointed rooms. Tall windows gave a view down the long garden to the lake. Crisply made-up beds looked inviting to weary travellers more used to the comfort of an army cot or the hard ground beneath a hedge. The rugs were Aubusson and the furniture well-polished oak and mahogany.

Baths were poured and, when we were all clean and presentable in what clothing we possessed, we meandered down the sweeping stairs to be ushered into Gerald Shipley's study. In the black and white tiled hall was a man in a wicker wheelchair. Dressed, now in tweed with a brightly coloured waistcoat and cravat, Montague Shipley was a changed man.

The occupant of the wheelchair had an aura of assurance and calm about him. No longer in uniform, he was now Montague Shipley, war hero and artist. His work was proudly displayed on the walls of the long galleried landing. There was a pride about him which had always been absent before. His first words were to Jack.

'MacGregor,' he reached out a hand. 'Sergeant MacGregor, it is good to see you alive.' Jack did not understand the sign language, which was hastily translated by the General.

Jack was taken aback, but he took the proffered hand. 'Sir,' he muttered as he pressed his own over it in greeting.

The rapid hand movements of sign language continued, then abruptly stopped in a shrug of frustration. Montague reached into the canvas saddlebag which hung from his chair and produced a rather dog-eared notebook and a pencil. He began to write.

'MacGregor, may I call you Jack?' Jack nodded assent and the man continued. 'I am sorry. Many mistakes are made in the heat of a war, and I made many. I did you and your men a great wrong. I hope you can forgive me. Let us all move forward. It is not good to live in the past.'

Jack stifled a laugh. In my mind I heard Eryr's whisper unheard to the others, 'But the past is always with us, is it not.'

Montague bid Jack push him out to his studio, from where a delighted Jack returned, holding a small portrait of his wife, in oils, done from memory, the artist had told him. 'Look after her, Jack, she is a rare being. I saw her only once you know, she was quite unforgettable.'

The newspaper reporter was a self-effacing Welshman. Fiona and Frances said he had once been a patient of theirs, a talented writer, a bit of a dreamer, and a poet. Medals were presented, photographs taken, the men told of their war, where their journey had taken them, well nearly all of it. The journalist left them, his notebook overflowing, destined, he said, to file his copy with his editor and then be away back to France.

That evening Monty and Gerald presided over a grand dinner. The men adjourned to the billiard room for Brandy and cigars and more war stories, Gerald becoming increasingly curious about the last year of their absence. Jack, Charlie, Ralph, and Gerald talked long into the night. Rhianydd, having settled an over excited Agnes into the nursery, joined Fiona, Frances, and I in the drawing room.

'He fancies you; you know!' Frances joked with Fiona.

'Who, Gerald? Don't be silly!' Fiona blushed.

'You could do a lot worse,' Rhianydd added. 'He's quite a catch, he still has his own teeth, and he comes with all this.' She gestured around the room.

Fiona dissolved into laughter. 'I have one of my own, house, I mean. I don't need another, and all the trappings, well, I really have no time for 'all of this.' She gazed about her at the fine furnishings.

'He has lovely twinkly eyes, and he's quite dishy in a military sort of way.' Frances chipped in. 'If I didn't have Charlie, I'd be tempted!'

'Jennifer Frances Munro, for shame on you, and you, nearly a married woman.' Fiona blushed, remembering the solid comforting warmth of Gerald Shipley, so different from the free spirit that had been Frankie Baker. Gerald was growing on her. He did make her laugh and he was unflappable in a crisis. So, he was sixteen years her senior, but did that really matter?

The maid poured the sherry in generous amounts and left the decanter on a small white doily on the lid of the baby grand piano. The warm, amber liquid warmed the vocal cords and loosened tongues and they fell to telling nursing tales, the scandal over Dr. Robert and his lady friend, the tragic death of Jo Delaney and the grief of Sam O'Connor. Where was Vera Battle? She had moved to Wales and stayed there. Since her good friend Marion had so tragically died, she had not been back to London.

Pleading tiredness from the day's events, I excused myself from the gathered company and made my way up the stairs. I heard the billiard room door click shut, closing the fug of cigar smoke inside. I could sense the footsteps on the stair behind me. They smelled of brandy and cigars and something indescribably male.

The morning would find a well disturbed but empty bed, but there would be no sign of its occupants. We had gone home. Wherever home was.

EPILOGUE. VIVE LA FRANCE

April 1919.
Just Outside Abbéville,
France.

Arthur still had the occasional day when he missed the hills of Wales, but he would never go back. Today he sat on another lush green hillside, his ever-present notebook and pen lying in the grass alongside him, and looked out across a now peaceful land. The river meandered like a wandering drunk wanders towards an ale house, its progress slow but steady and always sure of its destination. He could see the gentle spiral of smoke rising from the chimney of the farmhouse in the distance. He could hear the occasional lowing of one of the milking cows in the field alongside the farm. But he could no longer hear the guns, and he no longer smelled garlic in everything. These days it was only in his supper. The stench of death had long since left his nostrils.

He lay back in the grass, and turned onto his stomach, stretching his back and his belly. He snapped the stem of a long frond of grass from a tussock which was in front of his nose and, sitting up slowly, ran its fluffy pollen laden end lightly down the spine of the naked body which lay beside him.

The body convulsed into life in a cloud of French expletives, half of which Arthur still did not quite understand. Pulling her towards him, he silenced her tirade with his mouth, and turning her onto her back, began his quest for words of endearment and noises of a more submissive kind. His lips progressed from hers, down her body, feeling her squirm beneath him and her body arch away from the grass beneath, hips tilted towards him, in an unspoken insistence.

'Now, Cheri! Now!'

His nose parted the fluff of her hair and his teeth and tongue grazed gently as she laid herself open for him. He felt her wetness on his lips and moving up her body, now slightly plump from regular food, he kissed her mouth, she tasted herself on his lips and wrapping her legs around his back, guided him home. Feeling her flesh close around his, he lost all control and with two thrusts of his hips he spent himself into her, groaning, teeth clenched, stars exploding before his eyes. They rested now with her lying along his length, chin resting on his chest, one finger making patterns in his chest hair, the sunshine warming her bare back and her body warming his.

On days like this, Arthur did not miss Wales at all. Her sharp ears heard the 'click' of the latch of the field gate and she raised her head.

« Alors, vite, mon amour ! Papa, il est en-route. »

Arthur quickly made a grab for his clothing which was with hers an arm's length away where it had fallen half an hour earlier. Wriggling back into a state of decency, he laughed, watching Celine frantically wrestling with her underwear which had become hopelessly tangled in their haste.

The sound of tuneless whistling assailed their ears as Monsieur Dubois, papa, drew closer, giving them discrete warning of his approach. In a few minutes more they saw the top of his cloth cap and his white hair emerge into view, holding by one hand a toddler no more than two years old.

'Has he walked the whole way, papa?' called Celine.

'Non, ma petite, he was on my shoulders until the gate, then he wanted to walk, like a big boy, didn't you Albert?'

The child, out of breath from walking, did not reply.

'We were just coming down, back to the house, papa.'

'I'm sure you were, you lovebirds, you need your privacy, n'est pas!

Your son, he was missing you, so we thought we would bring you some lunch.'

Papa produced a small basket covered with a cloth, and from inside his brightly coloured waistcoat, a bottle of red wine.

'If we may join you for some food, then I will take the young man home for his nap and leave you to yourselves.'

The old man's eyes twinkled blue in his dark weathered face, made bluer and darker by the snowy white of his hair.

'You may like to check on Nuage in the top field, perhaps walk back through the woods, it is a pretty walk, especially when the flowers are in bloom.'

Celine spread the cloth and the contents of the basket on the ground, and they ate, bread and pate and creamy cheese, rich sweet fruit jam, and drank the smooth, fruity red wine made by M. Dubois from his few fields of vines at the farm. Arthur played with his son, tossing him up in the air and delighting in hearing him squeal, 'Papa, Papa!' laughing every time he was thrown in the air. Arthur never forgot that he had another son, but that seemed a lifetime ago.
He had written to his wife Harri and had forgiven her long ago. His life was now with Celine.

Lying back again in the sunshine he listened to Celine chattering away in French and admonishing her father and little Francois for some minor misdemeanour. He was getting the hang of the language, slowly, and understood most of what she said until she talked too quickly. Then he would look at her confused and shrug his shoulders in a very Gallic manner and ask her to repeat, 'un peu plus lentamente, ou en Anglais s'il te plait.' – a bit slower, or in English, please. Thoroughly content he closed his eyes and recalled how he had come to be here.

Employed as a wartime correspondent for a London Newspaper he had cut his teeth writing pieces about the soldiers arriving back from the front. He was required to paint a certain picture of the war as it progressed and was fed a line in propaganda by his editor, though the men he interviewed had a different story, and the editor frequently forgot that Arthur Cole had been there at the start. Unless much had changed, the propaganda was not to be believed. After writing several, 'Pen portraits of our Heroes' for the War Office, he had begged to be allowed to do something meatier.

He had been dispatched to Abbéville. His editor had given him his brief,

'You are to write a piece about the medical corps. Go to the hospital, interview who you wish to, but keep it factual, I want none of your Welsh romanticism, keep it factual, you hear me?'

Arthur had been halfway out of the door when he replied, 'Loud and clear boss, loud and clear.' He was halfway across the channel on a troop ferry when it dawned on him that he had been to Abbéville before as a casualty.

He had interviewed the doctors, one of whom had treated him, who remembered the poetic Welshman who had hallucinated about archers in the fog. He had been shown, but had not mentioned in his writing, an arrow the doctor kept as a souvenir. He found that what they told him had driven out most of his demons. He was not deranged. He was not the only one to have seen them.

His suitably sanitised work, no mention of ghosts or arrows, was hailed a masterpiece. It was published on the front page, and he was told to stay, keep the people at home abreast of what their men were facing. He had been leaning on the sandbag parapet looking out across the valley towards the river smoking a rare cigarette. He did not often smoke, but sometimes when he was missing home and his old life the nicotine calmed him. His mug of tea was steaming quietly to a drinkable temperature alongside him.

A hand had tapped his shoulder and a French voice had asked in heavily accented English,

' 'Ave you got a light, pleez?' He had turned to find a petite woman with a mass of curly black hair and blue eyes holding up a Gitane cigarette towards his lit match. Frozen for a moment, the match burned down to his fingers, and he dropped it to the floor, shaking his hand as he did so.

'Mademoiselle.' He struck a new match and lit her cigarette.

'Je m'apelle Celine, I am Celine.' She introduced herself.

'Arthur,' he replied, leaning on his elbows which were atop the sandbag wall.

'I was 'ere you know, I saw it all, my papa, he has a farm, out there.' She pointed to a stone house in the distance. 'He stayed. He hid from the Germans. They wrecked our home, but they did not find him. After they retreat, he was still there, stubborn old fool, him, and his old horse. That is his smoke rising up the chimney, so I know he is still alive.'

'Why are you here now?' Arthur asked. 'Should you not be with your father?'

'He sent me to England, but I came back. I drive the ambulances. I fetch the injured from the fields where they fall. I fight for France and my freedom. And you, Arthur, you are no longer a soldier, what do you fight for?'

'My freedom and my sanity.' he replied.

'Ah, a dreamer, a poet.,' she joked.

'No,' he replied. 'just a journalist, a newspaper man.'

'Maybe you should ride with me, on the ambulance, then you would see everything for yourself.'

The dreamer and poet seized the moment. 'Celine, I would love to.' He had left word that he had gone and when Celine's ambulance headed back to the frontline, he was there. He had no uniform, he was no longer a soldier, but if needed he could handle a rifle, and he was there, where he felt he needed to be. He had sent his copy back to his editor from the hospital, and on a regular basis. His pieces regularly made the headlines, sometimes gritty factual pieces, sometimes morale boosting articles. He was always careful to disguise his location and keep a balance of what pleased his masters and what he actually saw.

He wrote about soldiers, about the air corps, about the ambulance drivers and the horses and their handlers. At his shoulder, all the while, was Celine.

Arthur still had still had the occasional 'bad night,' when he lay trembling under their wagon, curled up like a woodlouse with his imaginary armour surrounding him. Over the months, though, they had become less and less frequent. With Celine there was no history and no expectation, she lived for the day. He found this calming. He was for once just, 'Arthur.'

They had become colleagues, then friends and then lovers. Arthur remembered a drunken evening in a small French village further south. They had been drinking with the villagers, toasting the retreat of the German army, and singing rude songs about the Kaiser in bawdy French and English. Their refuge for this impromptu celebration was the blacksmith's shop, it was the only building in the village left with a roof not destroyed by shelling. It had of necessity a stout chimney which had held everything else more or less together. The blacksmith's tools lay scattered around the long dead forge, the merry band sitting on boxes and piles of sacks, using any available surface as a table. Bottles of wine and a small barrel of cider which had been well hidden appeared, along with any remaining food. Their only light was the candle each person brought with them. Into the midst of their gathering a lone and wounded German soldier had staggered waving a pistol. Battle worn and bleeding from his leg, he had held the pistol to Celine's head, demanding help. Arthur had felt such a pang of protective rage he still could not imagine how he had reacted. He had seized a knife from the nearby anvil where it rested alongside his mug and thrown it. Had someone guided his hand that night, for the knife had impaled itself in the young soldier's neck. And, as the boy fell to the floor, he had heard the redundant 'click' of the trigger on an empty chamber. The boy was out of life, out of luck, and out of ammunition. Arthur was not to know, and he felt no remorse. No one would ever take Celine from him. That night as they slept in the ambulance, they had made love to each other, slowly and patiently. Celine had taken the lead for, as Arthur told her, he had not made love to a woman since he left home, he was a little shy and very out of practice.

He was just sinking further into his reverie when the piping high pitched voice of his son broke through his thoughts, 'Papa! Papa! I go see Papi now!' Daddy, I'd like to go and see Grandpa, now! Two small chubby arms wrapped around his neck and his cheek was anointed with a kiss laden with butter and apricot jam.

Arthur tickled the child in the ribs, making him laugh fit to burst and kissed him firmly on the forehead, lifting him up with straight arms so that little Francois felt that he was flying, flying on the love of a father for his son.

Grandpa took over, taking the child by the seat of his small trousers and placing him firmly, feet on the floor.

'Allez, Albert, your mama and your papa will be home in time for supper!'

He winked at Arthur and took the child by the hand, then swung him upwards onto his old French shoulders, sitting atop the brightly coloured waistcoat, his little hands immediately removing the old man's cap to reveal his bald crown, usually well hidden under his headwear. 'Grandpa no hair!' The child waved the cap around and threw it to his mother.

Placing it back on her father's head to protect the old man's vanity, Celine did not admonish the child, it had been far to pleasant an afternoon to end in tears.

Linking her arm through Arthur's, they watched grandfather and grandson disappear over the crown of the slope waving all the way, then turned and headed up the hill to check on old Nuage in his pasture, and to stroll back to the house through the woods.

French woodland is a remarkable mix of trees and undergrowth, the gaps in the trees filled in with low growing berry bushes and moss.

Ivy creeps along the ground so thickly it traps the feet. They are old woods, and this one not shredded to pieces by shell and gunfire, though it had seen its share of action. Even here there was evidence of war, a German helmet buried in the undergrowth, a tobacco tin fallen from a soldier's pocket. Celine had found her fair share of these artefacts on her daily walks to check on the old horse who lived in the top field.

As the couple made their way down the stony track which ran along the edge of the wood, Arthur felt a chill run down his back, as if he were being watched.

'Do you feel it Cherie?' he remarked. 'That chill?'

'It is just the dusk falling, the sun going to her bed.' came the reply.

'No, I can feel them, they are here with me, I am sure if it.'

'Arthur, mon cher, you 'ave ad too much wine and too much sun this afternoon!' She bounced upwards and kissed the cheek which was several inches above her shoulder. 'We must 'urry, it will be dark soon.'

'No, stay, sit here just for a few minutes, you will see, please Celine, then you will know for sure, you will know.'

'But, Arthur, I already know, I always believed you, now come, away, allons-y!' She tugged on the sleeve of his shirt.

Thud! It embedded itself in the bank between them, its stem vibrating as the iron point buried itself in the earth, an arrow, fletched with woodpecker feathers, red, black, and white.

Between the trees they both saw him, a giant of a man, dressed in medieval garb of an archer, longbow in his hand, the colours of the Black Prince worn over his leather jerkin. Celines's hand went to her mouth in complete surprise. She breathed in a breath she thought she would never let out. Standing with the man was a woman, the woman was dressed from the same age, and holding the hand of a small child.

Only Arthur heard him as he waved to them from another time, 'Hwyl fawr fi ffrind, goodbye my friend.'

Arthur echoed the words, 'Hwyl fawr, Gwyn ap Meredith, pob lwc!' Then he watched them walk into the night, a family once more.

In the dusk he was sure he saw the white, blonde head of a British soldier dressed in khaki and carrying an Enfield rifle. The rifleman fell in behind the archer and both disappeared into the half light of the woodland.

Celine let out the breath, tears ran down her cheeks as she sobbed into Arthur's chest.

'He is home, then.'

'As am I Celine, as am I.' He bent and kissed the tears from her face.

'Will you ever see him again do you think?' she asked.

'When the world is restless again, he will be there, he and the rest of them. War may bury their bodies, but it doesn't bury their souls.'

'Spoken like a true poet, Arthur. Will you be writing home about them, then?' she quipped.

'Best not.' he answered. 'The editor might think me deranged!'

He turned to pull the arrow from the banking where they had sat, but all that was there was a pile of earth and moss.

The End

APPENDICES AND USEFUL TRANSLATIONS

[1.] Chapter 19 page 99 Translated (French to English)

"Ah, good morning, sir! I'm sorry, but I don't speak French well. We need help please.
So, you can understand, we are British soldiers. We warn you that the German army is coming to take the town of Abbéville. They have artillery and men just behind the trees.
We need your horses and your wagon to get the wounded out of the hospital. »

"I only have one draft horse and a saddle horse that will shoot a trap. If you take my daughter with you to a place of safety, you can have the horses and the wagon."

"Thank you, sir, please.", Charlie continued as Frankie looked on, clearly impressed.
"Send your daughter with us, we will make sure she is safe."

[2.] Chapter 22 page 124
Dafydd y Garreg Wen Translated (Welsh to English)
David of the White Rock

Bring me, said David, the harp I adore;
I long, ere death calls me, to play it once more.
Help me to reach my belov'd strings again;
On widow and children, God's blessing remain.

Last night I heard a kind angel thus say,
"David fly home on the wings of thy lay".
Harp of my youth, and thy music, adieu;
Widow and children, God's blessing on you.

Traditional

[3.] Chapter 36 page 224 Oes Gafr Eto (Welsh to English)
The Goat Song translated

Is there a goat left? Is there one not milked yet?
On the rugged rocks the old nanny's wandering.
One that's white, white, white,
yes white-lipped, white-lipped, white-lipped
bare and white-tailed, bare, and white-tailed
white of flank and tail
White, white, white.

Is there a goat left? Is there one not milked yet?
On the rugged rocks the old nanny's wandering.
One that's black, black, black,
yes black-lipped, black-lipped, black-lipped
bare and black-tailed, bare, and black-tailed
black of flank and tail
Black, black, black.

Is there a goat left? Is there one not milked yet?
On the rugged rocks the old nanny's wandering.
One that's red, red, red,
yes red-lipped, red-lipped, red-lipped
bare and red-tailed, bare, and red-tailed
red of flank and tail
Red, red, red.

Is there a goat left? Is there one not milked yet?
On the rugged rocks the old nanny's wandering.
One that's blue, blue, blue,
yes blue-lipped, blue-lipped, blue-lipped
bare and blue-tailed, bare, and blue-tailed
blue of flank and tail
Blue, blue, blue.

Is there a goat left? Is there one not milked yet?
On the rugged rocks the old nanny's wandering.

One that's pink, pink, pink,
yes pink-lipped, pink-lipped, pink-lipped
bare and pink-tailed, bare, and pink-tailed
pink of flank and tail
Pink, pink, pink

Traditional

[4.] Chapter 53
Page 320 The Last Rose of Summer by Thomas Moore

[5.] Chapter 53
Page 321 Prayer for the dead From Carmina Gaedelica

ACKNOWLEDGEMENTS

Firstly, this is a work of fiction and not an historical reference work. All the characters in this book are fictitious and while some circumstances may be based historical events, they in no way relate to history itself or those involved in the making of it. While events in these chapters may be loosely hung on real events, they are in no way to be treated as factual. I state again that this is a work of fantasy fiction.

Where references have been made to surgical procedures, research has been carried out using numerous sources, including the Royal College of Surgeons archives and library. My grandfather had his face reconstructed in 1917 having been invalided home from WW1. Details of his surgery and the surgical implant used are held in our family archive. On other medical matters I have deferred to my brother and the editor. Dr Giles Morgan. He has also proven useful in advice on the practicalities of navigation and the English Channel in winter

A very great thanks to my good friend former colleague and fellow writer Arthur Cole for donating one of his poems, originally entitled 'The Archers of Mons,' also for allowing his name to be used as one of my characters. The character of Arthur Cole as he appears in this book bears no resemblance to the aforementioned individual.

Also, to Kevin Thorne for allowing me to model the character of Cefin Thorne on him. The result is nothing like the real person. Farming being probably the only thing they have in common.

Writing a book is a team effort. I need to thank my husband for putting up with me writing at odd times of the day and night. Being distracted when researching and insisting on watching endless documentaries on certain subjects. I also need to thank my daughter for endless patience and certain of my friends for their honest opinions on my work. You know who you are. These are also the people who have encouraged me when I have considered throwing in the towel.

I would like to acknowledge the trojan effort of my brother Giles Morgan for his editing skills. It is he who has to deal with my complete disregard at times for spelling and grammar and especially punctuation.

I would also like to thank the uber talented Lyn Fuller for her rendering of two old photographs into pastel drawings, those which have been used as part of the cover artwork. They are in fact copies of old photographs of my Great Grandmother Sibyl Helena Rees and my Grandfather Jack Morgan.

COPYRIGHT

The right of Maggie Jenkins to be identified as the author of this work has been asserted by her in accordance with the Copyright, Designs and Patents Act 1988. All characters and events in this publication are fictitious and any resemblance to real persons, living or dead, is purely coincidental

Bullets through the mist by Maggie Jenkins 2024

All rights reserved. No part of this publication may be reproduced, stored in a retrieval system, or transmitted in any form or by any means without the prior permission in writing of the publisher, nor be otherwise circulated in any form of binding or cover other than that in which it is published without a similar condition, including this condition, being imposed on the subsequent purchaser. A CIP catalogue record for this book is available from the British Library. ISBN 9798880342884 INDEPENDENTLY PUBLISHED.

OTHER BOOKS BY THE AUTHOR

This book is a sequel to:

An Arrow Through Time: The Adventure starts on the hillsides of West Wales and in the hilltop town of Llantrisant.

The authors first book

Ginger Like Biscuits – The adventures of a mountain pony: A short book written for my riders in Riding for the Disabled

A series of books of poems inspired by the Outlander Television Series and the work of Diana Gabaldon

Unofficial Droughtlander Relief.

The Droughtlander's Progress.

Totally Obsessed.

Fireside Stories.

Je Suis Prest.

Après Le Deluge

Dragonflies of Summer

Semper in Aeternum

Sia air Ochd

Intervallaqua

Facing the Storm

Reading Between the Lines

The Blue Vase - illustrated by Lyn Fuller

Mille Basia Volume 1

Mille Basia Vol 2

Mille Basia 3 Part 1

■■ ■ ı

The author is currently working on:

Cassandra's Web:

A police-based crime drama based in South Wales, Bristol and Glasgow and embroiled in the criminal underworld and the corruption of the judicial system. A murder is committed, and Cassandra Weaver loses her family, everything she loves and nearly her sanity. Will she ever regain what she has lost.

All books are available in both paperback and Kindle through Amazon or through the author direct.

The author can be contacted by email: authormaggiej@gmail.com

Printed in Great Britain
by Amazon